Illuminations

ALSO BY MARY SHARRATT

Summit Avenue

The Real Minerva

The Vanishing Point

Bitch Lit (coeditor)

Daughters of the Witching Hill

Illuminations

A Novel of Hildegard von Bingen

Mary Sharratt

Houghton Mifflin Harcourt

BOSTON · NEW YORK

2012

For information about permission to reproduce selections from this book,
write to Permissions, Houghton Mifflin Harcourt Publishing Company,
215 Park Avenue South, New York, New York 10003.

www.hmhbooks.com

Library of Congress Cataloging-in-Publication Data
Sharratt, Mary, date.
Illuminations : a novel of Hildegard von Bingen / Mary Sharratt.
p. cm.
ISBN 978-0-547-56784-6
1. Hildegard, Saint, 1098–1179—Fiction. I. Title.
PS3569.H3449I44 2012
813'.54—dc23
2012014252

Printed in the United States of America
DOC 10 9 8 7 6 5 4 3 2 1

*Dedicated to women of spirit everywhere —
many blessings on the quest*

She is so bright and glorious that you cannot look at her face or her garments for the splendor with which she shines. For she is terrible with the terror of the avenging lightning, and gentle with the goodness of the bright sun; and both her terror and her gentleness are incomprehensible to humans. . . . But she is with everyone and in everyone, and so beautiful is her secret that no person can know the sweetness with which she sustains people, and spares them in inscrutable mercy.

— Hildegard von Bingen's vision of the Feminine Divine, from *Scivias*, III, 4.15, translated by Mother Columba Hart, O.S.B., and Jane Bishop

Hours of the Divine Office

Hour	Time celebrated	Clock time for 21 March
Matins	the eighth hour of the night	2:00 A.M.
Lauds	dawn	about 5:30 A.M.
Prime	the first hour of the day	6:00 A.M.
Terce	the third hour of the day	9:00 A.M.
(Daily Mass follows Terce)		
Sext	the sixth hour of the day	12:00 noon
None	the ninth hour of the day	3:00 P.M.
Vespers	before dark	about 5:30 P.M.
Compline	before going to bed	about 7:00 P.M.

—From "Charting the Divine Office," Lila Collamore, in *The Divine Office in the Latin Middle Ages,* Margot E. Fassler and Rebecca Baltzer, eds.

Prologue: Apostate

Rupertsberg, 1177

THE MOST ANCIENT and enduring power of women is prophecy, my gift and my curse. Once, centuries before my existence, there lived in these Rhineland forests a woman named Weleda, she who sees. She took no husband but lived in a tower. In those heathen times, her people revered her as a goddess, for she foretold their victory against the Romans. But the seeress's might is not just a relic of pagan times. Female prophets crowd the books of the Old Testament—Deborah and Sarah, Miriam and Abigail, Hannah and Esther.

And so, in my own age, when learned men, quoting Saint Peter, call woman the weaker vessel, even they have to concede that a woman can be a font of truth, filled with vision, her voice moving like a feather on the breath of God.

Mother, what is this vision you show me? With my waking eyes, I saw it coming. The storm approaching our abbey. Soon I would meet my nemesis face-to-face.

My blistered hands loosened their grip on the shovel, letting it fall into the churned up earth. At seventy-nine years of age, I am no longer strong enough for such labors, yet force of necessity had moved me to toil for half a day, my every muscle shrieking. Following my lead, my daughters set down their tools. With somber eyes, we Sisters of Rupertsberg surveyed our handiwork. We had tilled every inch of our churchyard. Though the tombstones still stood, jutting like teeth from the rent soil, we had chiseled off every last inscription. My daughters' faces were etched in both exhaustion and silent shock. Our graveyard was a sanctuary as holy as the high altar of our church. Now it resembled a wasteland.

Tears caught in my eyes as Sister Cordula passed me the crook that marked my office of abbess. Whispering pleas for forgiveness to the deceased, I picked my way over the bare soil until I came to the last resting place of Maximus, the runaway monk whose plight had driven our desperate act. The boy fled to us for asylum after his brothers committed unspeakable sins against him. Despite our every effort to heal his broken body and soul, the young man died in our hospice, and so we gave him a Christian burial.

But the prelates of the Archbishop of Mainz, the very men who had ignored the cruelty unfolding in the boy's monastery, had declared Maximus an apostate. Tomorrow or the following day, the prelates would come to wrest the dead boy from his grave and dump him in unhallowed ground as if he were a dead mongrel. So we razed our burial ground, making it impossible for any outsider to locate his grave. Had the prelates ever imagined that mere nuns would take such measures to foil them, the men we were bound to obey?

Raising my abbess's crook, I spoke the words of blessing. "In the name of the Living Light, may this holy resting place be protected. May it remain invisible to all who would desecrate it."

My heart throbbed like a wound when I remembered the boy who died in my arms, the one I had sworn before God to protect. He had committed no crime, had only been a handsome youth in a nest of vipers. Maximus had only an aged abbess and her nuns to stand between him and the full might of the Church fathers.

The November wind crested our walls, tossing up grave dust that stung our eyes. My daughters flinched, ashen-faced in the dread we shared. What would happen to us now that we had committed such an outrageous act of sedition? The prelates' retribution would be merciless.

Foreboding flared again, the fate awaiting us as terrifying as the devil's giant black claw rearing from the hell mouth. Somehow I must summon the warrior strength to battle this evil. Seize the sword to vanquish the dragon. Maximus's ordeal proved only too well what damage these men could wreak. In a true vision, Ecclesia, the Mother Church, had appeared to me as a ravished woman, her thighs bruised and bloody, for her own clergy had defiled her. The prelates preached chastity while allowing young men to be abused. In defending the boy, my daughters and I risked sharing his fate—being cast out and condemned. The prelates would crush my dissent at all costs. Everything I had worked for in my long life might be lost in one blow, leaving me and my daughters pariahs and excommunicants. How could I protect my community now that I was so old, a relic from another time, my once-powerful allies dead?

To think that seven years ago I had preached upon the steps of Cologne Cathedral and castigated those same men for their fornication and hypocrisy, their simony and greed. *O you priests. You have neglected your duties. Let us drive these adulterers and thieves from the Church, for they fester with every iniquity.* In those days I spoke with a mighty voice, believing I had nothing to lose, that the prelates would not trouble themselves over one old nun.

The men I'd railed against gathered like carrion crows to wreak their revenge and put me in my place once and for all. It was not my own fate that worried me, for I have endured much in my life. This year or the next, I would join the departed in the cold sod and await judgment like any other soul. But what would become of my daughters? How could I die and leave them to this turmoil—what if this very abbey was dissolved, these women left homeless? A stabbing pain filled me to see them so lost, their faces stark with fear. Our world was about to turn upside down. How could I save these women who had placed their trust in me?

"Daughters, our work here is done," I said, as tenderly as I could, giving them leave to depart and seek solace in their duties in the infirmary and scriptorium, the library and workroom.

Leaving the graveyard to its desolation, I pressed forward to the rampart wall overlooking the Rhine, the blue-green thread connecting everything in my universe. Nestled in the vineyards downriver and just out of view lay Eibingen, our daughter house. Our sisters there, too, would face the coming storm. Then, as I gazed at the river below, an icy hand gripped my innards. A barge approached our landing. The prelates had wasted no time.

I was striding down the corridor when Ancilla, a postulant lay sister, came charging toward me, her skirts flapping.

"Mother Abbess! We have a visitor."

The girl's face was alight with an excitement that seemed at odds with our predicament. She was a newcomer to our house and, as such, I'd spared her the grim work of digging up the graveyard.

"A foreigner! He doesn't speak a word of German."

My heart drummed in panic. Had the prelates sent someone from Rome? Oblivious to my trepidation, Ancilla seemed as thrilled as though the Empress of Byzantium had come to call.

"The cellarer will bring up the very best wines, won't she, Mother? And there will be cakes!"

The girl was so giddy that I had to smile at her innocence even as my stomach folded in fear. I told her I would receive our guest in my study.

After washing and changing, I girded myself to confront the messenger who would deliver our doom. But when I entered my study, I saw no papal envoy, only a young Benedictine monk who sprang from his chair before diving to his knees to kiss my hand.

"Exalted abbess!" he exclaimed in Latin, speaking in the soft accent of those who hail from the Frankish lands. "The holy Hildegard."

Our visitor appeared no older than twenty, his face glowing as pink as sunrise.

"What a splendid honor," he said, "to finally meet you in the flesh."

"Brother," I said, at a loss. "I don't know your name."

"Did you not receive my letter?" His soft white hands fluttered like doves. "I am Guibert of Gembloux Abbey in the Ardennes. I have come to write your Vita, most reverend lady."

Lowering myself into my chair, I nearly laughed in relief. So I still had allies and well-wishers after all, though this young man could hardly shield us from the prelates of Mainz.

"My brother in Christ, you flatter me too much," I told him. "Hagiographies are for saints. I'm only a woman."

He shook his head. "Your visions have made you the most farfamed woman in the Holy Roman Empire."

Guibert's face shone in a blissful naïveté that matched that of young Ancilla, who attended us, pouring him warm honeyed wine spiced with cloves and white pepper, but he ignored the fragrant cup. His flashing dark eyes were riveted on mine.

"Tell me, Mother Hildegard, does God speak to you in Latin or in German? And is it true that you bade your nuns to wear *tiaras?*"

Before I could even attempt an answer, he blustered on.

"Your writings are *most* extraordinary! I have never read their like! Did I correctly understand that God appears to you as a *woman?*"

Brother Guibert was not the first to ask this question. I told the young monk what I'd told the others before him.

"In the Scriptures, God appears as Father, and yet the Holy Spirit chose to reveal God's face to me as Mother."

I never dreamt of calling myself holy, never presumed. Yet God, whom I called Mother, chose to grace even one as flawed as I am with the ecstasy of the Holy Spirit moving through me. And so I became the Mother's mouthpiece, a feather on Her breath. How was I to describe such a mystery to Guibert? I never sought the visions, and yet they came. All I wanted was to know the ways of wisdom and grace, and walk them as best I could. But had I succeeded? My many sins and failings weighed on me. My superiors had only tolerated me for as long as they had because of the prophecies.

I was torn. Honestly, I should warn Guibert away, send him back to Gembloux. The good man was wasting his time here. What use was there in writing the Vita of a woman soon to be condemned?

Then something niggled at the back of my head. What if the key to saving my daughters from the coming tempest lay in my past, in examining my life from its genesis? Past and future were connected in an eternal ring, like the circle of holy flame I'd seen in my visions, that ring of fire enclosing all creation. If I allowed myself to go back in time, to become that graceless girl again, perhaps I might find a way to preserve us.

PART I

The Tithe

1

GREEN LEAVES DANCED in the gardens of Bermersheim, my parents' stone-built burg. Five years old, I sat on the grass with my wooden doll. Beyond the hedge, my older sisters played with our brother Rorich, still too young to join our father and older brothers in the Crusades. How my siblings' shrieks and laughter pierced the air, and how my loneliness stabbed me. My wheezing lungs, still clogged after a long bout of grippe, stood in the way of my joining their games. When Rorich or my sisters, Clementia, Hiltrud, Odilia, Bertha, Roswithia, and Irmengard, so much as squeezed my hand, I bruised as though I were an overripe pear.

Cradling my doll, I wondered if my longing would be enough to turn the dull wood into living flesh. A shadow passing overhead made me glance up to see an orb come floating out of the sunlight. A ball of spun gold, yet as clear as glass. Inside grew a tree adorned with fruits as dazzling as rubies. The tree breathed in and out, as a living creature would. My doll tumbled from my arms as I reached out to clasp the heavenly orb when, like a bubble, it burst.

"Where did it go?" I demanded, turning first to Walburga, my nurse, and then to Mother. "Where did the ball with the pretty tree go?"

Mother and Walburga whispered behind their hands. *What could be wrong with the child? Is she mad, or simply bad?*

After I told my mother about the floating tree, a crippling head-ache struck her down. She staggered to her bed, commanding Walburga to draw the draperies fast around her, and there she lay, moaning in darkness, until the following afternoon. The stony looks my sisters threw me sent me cowering behind the sacks of oats in the undercroft. How horrible I was, bringing down this illness on Mother. Deep inside I must be wicked. Good children did not see the invisible. Walburga accused me of telling false stories to vex the poor woman.

Afterward I tried my best to earn my mother's favor so that she might love me as she loved my sisters. I learned to pretend that the floating golden orbs weren't there. If I had succeeded in forever banishing that otherwhere, I might have grown up to lead the life Mother wished for me — to marry some high-ranking knight and to bear his sons.

Every night, huddled in Walburga's arms, I prayed to be spared the visions. Yet there was no escaping the orbs. By night, they lit up the darkness. In the clear light of day, they whizzed close by my head, echoing with music that sounded like the harps of angels. I kept it secret, not breathing a word. My happiness lay in pretending to be a girl as uncomplicated as my sister Clementia, beautiful and always smiling, our mother's darling.

When I was seven, I was content, walking hand in hand with Walburga through greening April fields past the village left half-deserted with every able-bodied man, and a number of women, off with the Crusades. Only the children, the elderly, and the lame remained behind.

"Did the girls really go off to fight?" I asked my nurse, never tiring of the story of how some young women, caught up in the same fervor as their menfolk, had disguised themselves as warriors and marched away under the banner of the cross.

"Disgraceful," Walburga huffed. "Women dressing up like men, sleeping in the same camps as the soldiers. May God forgive them."

I dared to smile at her slyly. "You're jealous! They got to go off and see the Holy Lands while you're stuck here."

"War isn't a pretty ballad, child. Have you ever seen a razed village? Crops set to fire?"

"But, Walburga! Whoever fights will be saved from hell."

Even I had heard how Pope Urban II had promised instant salvation to all who joined the Crusades. Ignoring Walburga's mutterings, I allowed myself to sink into a daydream of Rorich and me in armor, riding forth with Father and our two eldest brothers, Drutwin and Hugo. I pictured us arriving victorious before the gates of Jerusalem, that city covered in gold where seraphim sang beneath the sun.

Meanwhile, a cow, escaped from her pasture, ambled across our path. White with brown spots, she feasted on the rich new grass. As I stepped close, the animal lifted her head, her huge moist eyes locking on to mine.

"I'll have a word with the bailiff," Walburga said. "Those dunderheads from the village should know better than to let a cow run loose."

"She's not *running* anywhere," I pointed out.

She had merely broken through the flimsy fence of her overgrazed enclosure to reach the better grass. I patted her soft flank and giggled when she swung her head around to nuzzle my hair. Her breath was as sweet as the milk she must give.

"What a splendid calf!" I blurted out, forgetting myself, forgetting that my safety lay in silence.

"What calf?" Walburga shook her head.

"A bull calf." I saw it as clearly as I saw Walburga's face. "With brown and black spots, and four white legs."

Our shadows disappeared as a cloud veiled the sun. With one last snuffle through my hair, the cow strolled on, the bell tied to her neck singing and ringing. Walburga grabbed my shoulders.

"You're making up stories again."

Spinning around, I bolted for home as fast as my shaking legs would allow, but Walburga soon caught up, seizing my arm, leaving a bruise as big as her fist.

"Don't tell your mother."

Jagged sobs racked my body as I made my vow not to say a word.

A month later, Mother learned from Walburga what I, her tenth child, had foretold. The cow had borne her bull calf, his markings exactly as I had described them.

"The girl sees true," my nurse told my mother, while I peeked around the edge of the drapery I was hiding behind.

Mother's face was white and pinched, as though someone had just delivered the news that Father, Hugo, and Drutwin had been slain by the Saracens and left to rot in unhallowed graves.

But Walburga went on beaming like a simpleton. "My lady, you should give the calf to Hildegard. She's blessed by God, that child."

Walburga's thunderstruck proclamations soon spread as swiftly as the pox. Much to my mother's mortification, my prophecy regarding the calf was all anyone in Bermersheim and the surrounding villages could talk about.

I shrank from Mother's gaze and sought refuge in Walburga's lap, in her engulfing embrace. Walburga hugged me close, her heart beating against my ear. My nurse loved me more than my own mother did—this I knew to be a fact. Yet Walburga had sealed my doom. Mechthild von Bermersheim's youngest daughter saw true—what would people say about our family? Either I was touched by God or possessed by Satan. How was Mother to know which?

That evening after Compline in our family chapel, Mother made me stay behind with her after my siblings, the servants, and even the chaplain had quit the place. Mother drew me into the chilliest corner, near the shriving bench where we knelt to confess our sins. Unsteady candlelight sent Mother's shadow rearing against the painted walls. Walburga had told me that Mother was thirty-five, an ancient age, and indeed my parent looked like an old woman—toothless, a few wisps of sparse gray hair poking out from where her wimple slid back, her spine buckled from bearing so many babies. *At least with your father away in the Holy Lands,* Walburga had confided, *your poor mother can take comfort in the hope that there'll be no more.*

"Hildegard." Mother stared down at me. Even with her stoop, she was a tall woman. "You are the tenth child. You know that."

An awful tightness clutched my throat. Unable to look at Mother, my eyes slipped to the fresco of Eve with the apple cupped in her palm. Naked and glowing, the first sinner lingered beneath a tree that was nearly as exquisite as the one that had appeared in the golden sphere. Her softly rounded belly, almost like that of a pregnant woman, revealed the lust and corruption lurking inside her beautiful flesh—this was what our chaplain had told us. Eve lifted her face to the serpent, whose sinuous body boasted a woman's head and breasts—the creature was none other than Lilith, Adam's first wife, whispering wicked knowledge in Eve's ear while Adam just stood there like a dullard.

"Do you know what a tithe is?" Mother asked me.

I nodded, fighting tears.

"Tell me," she commanded, her voice as cool as her fingers gripping my shoulders.

"Every good Christian"—I gulped and swallowed—"must give a tenth of all he owns to the Church."

Mother knelt before me so that our faces were level. Her hazel eyes seemed as huge as the orbs that swam across my vision.

"You are the tenth child," Mother said again.

I was the tithe.

"It's not a bad place, Disibodenberg," Mother told me the following morning, as if to soften the blow.

She allowed me to perch in her lap as she worked the bone teeth of her comb through my flaxen hair while Walburga held up the mirror of polished silver to reflect my face. Though my eyes were swollen from crying, I gazed greedily into the mirror for as long as I was allowed because this might be my last chance. Mirrors were forbidden to those in holy orders. *Mother wants to be rid of me.* What would happen if I threw my arms around her neck and begged her to let me stay? I twisted in Mother's lap, but she told me to sit still.

"You won't be alone, child." Her voice was gentle and soothing. "You are to accompany Jutta, the Count of Sponheim's daughter, as her chosen handmaiden. Think of the prestige!"

My family swore fealty to the Sponheim dynasty. On feast days in their hall, I had seen Jutta dancing in a circle with the other girls. At fourteen, Jutta was ripe for marriage, the most beautiful young noblewoman in the Rhineland, so everyone swore, with her auburn hair and cornflower eyes, her slender grace, the necklace of seed pearls and garnets adorning her white throat. But there were rumors—even I had heard the gossip. *Jutta von Sponheim is as mad as a box of frogs.* According to my sister Odilia, this was why Jutta's family could find her no husband, despite her stunning looks and huge dowry. To make matters worse, Jutta fancied herself a holy woman. Nothing but the religious life would do for her.

"But why Disibodenberg?" Walburga dared to ask Mother, forgetting her place. "Two young girls given to the monks—it doesn't seem proper. Surely they'd be better off with the nuns at Schönau."

Mother's reply was icy enough to make me shiver. "Don't offer your opinions on things you know nothing about."

She snatched her prized mirror from Walburga's hand and set it down on the table.

"Sweetheart," she said, turning me in her lap so that we faced each other. "It *is* a great honor to be chosen as Jutta's companion. You will bring glory to us all. Your father will be so proud when he hears."

I ached to tell her that I had no wish to spend the rest of my life with a mad girl no one wanted to marry, but my tongue turned into a plank and I said nothing.

"You and Jutta von Sponheim." The smile on Mother's face allowed me to glimpse the ghost of the lovely woman she had been ages ago, before she had all the babies who had left her as swaybacked as an old plow horse. "The pair of you will be holy virgins who take no husband but Christ Himself. You are lucky, my girl. The chosen one. You know, I wanted a religious life. I begged my parents to let me join holy orders, but instead I was given to your father when I was only thirteen."

My eyes prickled in confusion. Was Mother doing me a kindness, then, by banishing me to the monastery? Was this truly a better fate than being married off like other girls?

"But I don't want *any* husband," I told her. "Not even Jesus."

"Every girl must take a husband, either mortal or divine," Mother replied, as though she were stating the plain truth to an idiot.

"Walburga didn't!"

"Walburga is a peasant," Mother said, with Walburga only a few feet away. "Does a noble falcon share the same destiny as that of a barnyard goose? You were born to grander things than she was."

Catching my eye before turning her back on Mother, Walburga's contempt for my parent filled the room like a bad smell, as though my nurse had let out a fart. I wondered if Mother was terribly wrong, if she was making a mistake so enormous that even the servants saw through her.

The following day Mother rode off to the court of Sponheim to discuss my future with Jutta's mother, the countess. Blessing of blessings, she whisked away my six beautiful sisters, still unbetrothed owing to their paltry dowries, and left me alone with Rorich and Walburga. The first thing Rorich and I did after solemnly waving goodbye was to sneak out the gate and through the vineyards where the grapevines grew tall enough to hide us. When we reached the forest, we tore around like heathens, beating down nettles with hazel sticks.

"They'll be gone for weeks!" I shouted, delirious with happiness.

What joy could be greater than spending the summer days with Rorich, just the two of us? Rorich was my most beloved sibling. Ten years old, he was close enough in age to be my friend. He hadn't changed like my sisters had, turning to women before my eyes, abandoning our childhood games as they set their sights on marriage.

"They'll be feasting on roasted swan every night in Sponheim," Rorich said, leading the way to the brook, where he slipped off his shoes, leaving them to lie on the mossy bank.

"And they'll dance!" I kicked off my deerskin slippers.

My brother and I joined hands and threw our noses in the air to mimic the counts and countesses, margraves and margravines. Humming courtly dance tunes, we reeled through the shallow stream, our feet splashing and prancing, until my skirt and my brother's tunic were soaked.

"Dancing is forbidden in the monastery."

I shrugged to prove to Rorich that I'd never much cared for such fripperies anyway.

"They won't really send you away." My brother flung himself on the bank to laze in the sun. "Not for a long while yet. That girl in Alzey who went to the nuns in Schönau—they wouldn't take her until she was twelve. That gives you five years, Hildegard."

Gratitude tingled inside me as I waded in the brook, savoring the gentle click of water-washed agates between my toes. Five years! It seemed a whole lifetime. Anything could happen in that stretch of time.

"Mother will change her mind," Rorich said. "She always does. Remember how Father wanted Roswithia to marry that fat widower with the gouty leg?"

This had transpired before I was even born, but it was Walburga's favorite story and Mother's finest hour and bravest deed. Father was about to give our Roswithia to someone old and hideous, but Mother had overruled him just as he was about to set off for the Holy Lands.

The minute he was gone, Roswithia had thrown herself at Mother's feet and wept in relief.

"At least you don't need to worry about who they'll make *you* marry." I snapped a wand off a willow. "You're the youngest son — you'll have to be a priest."

Rorich kicked in the water, splashing me in the face. "I'll run away first."

"I'll come with you. We'll be bandits."

"We'll be poachers and hunt the Count of Sponheim's deer. We'll feast on venison and hide in the trees." Rorich eyed me critically. "But you wouldn't be sturdy enough to survive that kind of life, Hildegard."

"I've been well," I insisted. In this warm and dry tide of summer, my lungs were clear, my breathing easy. "Not sickly at all."

"Prove it." He pointed to the weeping willow. "Show me how high you can climb."

First I hitched up my skirts, knotting them over my knees to free my legs before I launched myself onto the first low bough. Grabbing the trunk, I worked my way up, placing one bare foot and then the other on the next highest limb till I ascended to the upper branches. There I swayed, clinging white-knuckled lest I fall, while Rorich howled with laughter. A dizziness filled my head as the orbs spun around me. Gulping for air, I slithered to the ground with as much bravado as I could muster.

"I did it." I looked my brother in the eye.

He only lifted my arm to study the yellow bruises, the fruit of my grappling with the tree.

"Walburga will murder me," he said. "Let's go back before she skins us."

"We'll be bandits." Grasping his hands, I clung to our daydream. "We'll live on berries and wild mushrooms. We'll find the white hart that lives in the deepest forest! Except we won't kill him. We'll build a pavilion for him, and I'll weave my hair into a collar for him."

Rorich wrapped his arm around me. "Maybe Jutta will take Clementia instead of you. Jutta's so crazy she probably can't tell one girl from another."

Filthy and bedraggled, Rorich and I crept through the kitchen garden then darted through the low door leading into the cavernous undercroft beneath the burg. Here we parted ways, hoping to escape the servants' detection. Hiding behind sacks of barley, I watched my brother melt into the darkness like some renegade Saracen. After counting to twelve, I tiptoed between the barrels of beer and wine, my plan being to steal up the stairs to my chamber and put on a clean shift and kirtle before Walburga pounced on me. But echoes of sobbing made me freeze.

Wishing Rorich was still there, I inched forward, deerskin slippers padding the dust until I came upon Walburga behind stacked crocks of cheeses and honey, her hands clutching her face.

"What is it?" I asked, petrified, for I'd never seen Walburga weep, never even thought it possible that so stalwart a woman could break down and bawl as though she were a child no older than I.

Blinking through her tears, Walburga hugged me so hard, as if she'd never let me go. As if she were my true parent and I her beloved daughter.

"Your mother is cruel. How can she do this?"

My heart swelled at Walburga's devotion. At what my nurse risked by standing up to Mother and taking my side. Mother could cast her out, send her back to her village to grub in the fields like the lowest serf. Still, it was my duty to defend my blood kin.

"There are other oblates. That girl from Alzey," I said, remembering what Rorich had told me. "She went to the nuns at Schönau, but she had to wait till she was twelve. Besides, Mother says it isn't so bad. You learn to read and write, and to play the psaltery, and you sit and stitch silk like the ladies at court, except the nuns have to wear plain clothes."

"If they were only sending you to live with ordinary nuns, love, I wouldn't be crying my eyes out." Walburga's tears drenched my hair. "That Jutta wants to be an anchorite and she's dragging you down with her."

My mind was a blank. "A what?"

"An anchorite." Seeing the confusion on my face, Walburga rocked me in her arms and keened as though an unspeakable wrong had been done to me. "Poor child, you don't even know."

During that long, happy summer, Walburga turned a blind eye as Rorich and I ventured out in the forest day after day, tumbling through the undergrowth, coming home grubby, with spider silk in our hair. I caught toads and salamanders, cupping their wriggling bodies in my hands before freeing them. Rorich snared rabbits. With his bow and quiver of arrows, he stalked deer while I shadowed him and watched, my heart in my throat as the arrow went singing through the air only to miss the hind as she dashed away. What would it be like to escape so easily, to just vanish into the green?

He was never much of a marksman, my brother. That was why Mother was content to let him stay home with the women instead of sending him away to join Father and our elder brothers in the Holy Lands and learn the arts of war. Besides, everyone but Rorich himself saw his future chiseled in stone — the boy was not destined to be a knight but a cleric, as bound to the Church as I would be if Mother had her way.

In September the anniversary of my birth came and went. I turned eight and still Mother did not return from Sponheim. She and our sisters stayed away so long that Rorich decided they had forgotten about sending me to the monastery.

"They'll spend the rest of their days at court," he said. "Preening before the countess and fighting to dance with her son."

I discovered a cave in the forest, its opening just wide enough for us to squeeze through. It opened into a dry cavern big enough for us to light a fire.

"This is where we'll live," I told Rorich. "This is our hideaway. They'll never find us."

The moon waxed and waned. The vines covering the keep wall turned blood red. One evening at twilight, Rorich and I straggled back from the forest to find Mother awaiting us in her chamber.

"Rorich, leave us," she said. "I must speak with your sister in private."

Cold and trembling, I dragged myself forward to take my mother's hand and kiss her knuckles.

"Welcome home, Mother." I gazed into her eyes and wondered where my sisters were, why they were so quiet. I expected the silent rooms to explode with their gossip.

Mother smiled, running her hands through my snarled hair. "My wild child. You have elf locks."

I tried to speak, but my throat silted up, the unhappy knowledge rising in my gorge.

"Irmengard and Odilia are to be married next spring. The countess is paying their dowries." Mother's eyes gleamed with the joy of answered prayers, burdens lifted. "Walburga must pack your things at once, my dear. Tomorrow at first light we leave for Disibodenberg."

2

MY DAMP CLOAK STANK like a wet dog as I shivered on the barge. A death shroud of fog clung to the Nahe River's wooded banks — anything could be lurking out there, just waiting to strike. Guards, both on the barge and marching along the shore, scanned the glowering hills for brigands. *Let them come.* I willed bandits to burst from the trees and pelt us with arrows, slaying everyone aboard, until the river ran red with blood. Only Rorich and I would be spared. My brother and I would then flee home to Bermersheim and live in our secret cave. What would happen if I spoke this unholy fantasy aloud? With any luck it would convince everyone that I was unfit for the religious life.

"May God send the Saracen hordes to slaughter us," I said, my voice strained and pinched. The wind carried away my words and no one paid me any mind.

Rorich traded jokes with the countess's seventeen-year-old son, Meginhard von Sponheim. How my brother's eyes shone as he basked in the attention of his new hero. Rorich acted as though this journey were the greatest adventure of his life. He was far too busy enjoying himself to plot our escape. *Traitor.*

I narrowed my eyes at Mother, who seemed flushed with happiness, sitting only inches away from the countess. She cozened so close that anyone would think they were sisters or bosom friends.

"You've seen for yourself how delightful our Clementia is." Mother practically purred. "My most beautiful daughter. Would you not consider taking her on as your handmaiden, countess? Clementia is our jewel."

I wanted to stop my ears. If *I* was beautiful, Mother would not be shunting me off to a bunch of moldy old monks in the hinterland. Too wretched and lost to even cry, I decided that I despised everyone except Walburga, but Mother hadn't allowed Walburga to come along, probably because Mother knew that if she had, my nurse would have put a stop to this. She would have upended the barge and drowned everyone to save me.

"Why so glum, little one?"

Jutta von Sponheim swept down beside me. Pearls of moisture beaded her long, loose hair where it flowed free from her cap of white marten fur. The cold wind stinging her cheeks only made her lovelier. She petted me until I wriggled away. *I'm not your lapdog.*

"Have I told you the story of holy Ursula? A princess from Britain." Jutta spoke of the distant kingdom as though it were as wondrous and unreachable as fairyland. "A heathen prince asked for her hand in marriage, but she spurned him."

Jutta's brother Meginhard burst out laughing. He was telling my brother some bawdy joke not meant for female ears. I perked up, hoping to eavesdrop, but Jutta enveloped me in her cloak, trimmed with white marten fur and lined with sheepskin. Her voice was insistent in my ear.

"Ursula chose ten companions, all of them virgins of noble birth, and then Ursula and her ten maidens each chose one thousand virgins to join them. Eleven thousand virgins, Hildegard! They boarded eleven ships and sailed over the sea and down the Rhine. They crossed the Alps and rode to Rome to visit the graves of the apostles.

"*I* desired to go to Rome," she added. "*And* Jerusalem. Why should I not, now that it's in Christian hands? I longed to visit the holy sepulcher, but Meginhard said it was too perilous a journey for a girl."

She seemed to spit venom when she spoke her brother's name. With their father and his knights, my father among them, still in the Holy

Lands, Meginhard acted as head of the family and Jutta had no choice but to obey him as she would her father. I wondered what I would do if Rorich started bossing me around. Tickle his feet and taunt him until he turned red in the face was what I'd do.

Jutta bit down on her lip till I feared it might bleed. The girl's huge blue eyes threatened to spill tears and her nails were bitten down to the quick. Jutta was so pretty and rich, yet she seemed fragile, as helpless as a baby bird cast out of its nest. She reminded me of the blackbird chick with the broken wing I'd once held in my skirt, coaxing it to feed out of my palm. Taking Jutta's hand, I hoped to give her some comfort. She rewarded me with a blinding smile before continuing her story.

"Ursula and her virgins were returning from Rome. They sailed up the Rhine. When they reached Cologne, the Huns descended on them. The king of the Huns demanded that the holy Ursula marry him. Naturally she refused, for he was heathen. Then the Huns murdered her and all her eleven thousand maidens." Jutta recited the mystical number as though it were a charm that carried great power. "Not one survived. Clematius discovered their skeletons in a field near Cologne."

Jutta stared straight ahead as though she saw that field of hacked-up virgins, as though that corpse stink filled her nose.

"I can hardly wait," she said, "till we reach our holy enclosure."

At that, she knelt and began to pray, her eyes squeezed shut as if to block out this sinful earthly realm. Only heaven seemed to interest her. Leaving Jutta to her prayers, I joined the others who spoke of the worldly things that gave me courage, or at least distracted me from what lay ahead.

"My husband sent home bolts and bolts of damask silk," the countess told my mother. "I would have used it for Jutta's wedding dress had she not chosen this life."

"Save it for the girl Meginhard marries," Mother said. "He's such a fine young man."

Meginhard was tall and curly-haired, muscled and sturdy looking.

He was betrothed to some highborn girl, yet he acted as carefree as Rorich. The two of them were casting fishing lines into the churning green water.

"Even the holy Jutta is allowed to eat fish," Meginhard said.

His booming voice sent a quiver through his sister's body, seeming to shatter her prayers, but only for an instant. She lifted her palms in the *orans* position, as if willing us all to vanish. Meginhard made a face, handed his fishing line to Rorich, and strode over to his sister, his heavy footfalls causing the barge to lurch and sway. Jutta raised her voice, praying as though she were halfway to heaven already, but he forced a kiss on her. *He's just teasing her, the way brothers do.* I couldn't understand why his attentions made her cry and shake. She screamed her psalms at him as if warding herself from Satan. The fuss only ended when the countess stepped between them and took the heaving girl in her arms.

"Hush, don't be a fool. That's only your brother."

Meginhard shrugged and was about to saunter away when he caught me staring. I ducked my head, but it was too late. He closed in, wrapping his bear arms around me. *His sister won't laugh at his jokes, so he'll amuse himself with me instead.* I decided I didn't mind—it was better than being completely ignored.

"Do you know anything about Saint Disibod?" he asked, his beery breath fanning my cheek. "He who gave his name to your monastery?"

"He was from Ireland," I said, proud to show off my knowledge. Of course, Jutta had already told me the saint's story. "He came here five hundred years ago. He was a missionary."

"Clever girl," Meginhard said, his fingers strumming through my hair. "You want to know something else?"

Ignoring Jutta who sobbed in her mother's arms, I nodded.

"If it wasn't for the Irish missionaries, we'd still be heathen," he said, his voice so fiery that I felt its flames licking me. "Just imagine."

That he would say something so sacrilegious! I grinned at the forbidden thrill.

"Gutting stallions for Old One-Eye and sacrificing goats to his son, the Thunderer," Meginhard went on.

He was saying this just to test me, to see if I would burst into tears as Jutta would do, but I wouldn't give him the satisfaction. I'd prove then and there I wasn't some weepy wet rag like his sister.

"He'll pollute Hildegard!" Jutta wailed to her mother.

"Stop filling that child's head with nonsense!" the countess told Meginhard.

Mother only smiled her blandest smile. I felt ashamed of her then — she wouldn't dare reprove the likes of Meginhard von Sponheim, no matter what he said or did. He could set the barge on fire and boil his sister in oil, and still my mother would stand there and do nothing.

"And if the Irish missionaries had never come to this country, *you*," Meginhard said, pinching my cheek, "wouldn't be sent off to a monastery to be walled in and left to rot."

Walled in. Those two words struck me with a greater horror than any yarn he could have spun of heathen gods. But then I burst out laughing, shaking till the tears sprang from my eyes. Meginhard, that joker! To think that for a moment I had nearly believed him. Still giggling, I looked to my mother, but she dipped her head and turned away.

At the place where the Nahe and Glan rivers meet, a tall forested hill arose from the mist — Mount Disibod, where the saint once lived. Stout walls and a squat church tower capped the promontory like a crude crown.

At the landing, the Abbot of Disibodenberg stood alongside Archbishop Ruthard of Mainz to welcome the countess and her holy daughter. As joyous as a bride on her wedding day, Jutta glided off that barge, her palms raised heavenward. Behind Jutta came her brother, now forgotten, outshone by the eighty monks who formed a ring behind their abbot. A parade of servants bore the trunks containing her dowry.

Mother took my hand, tugging me in the wake of Jutta's entourage. Like a sapling in a storm, I swayed, my heart hammering in such panic that I thought it might stop. I was afraid to even look at those monks who now controlled my destiny. Could Mother not see that I wasn't the least bit pious, that I was just a grimy girl balking like a mule?

"Take me home to Walburga," I pleaded.

If Mother could not endure the shame of my refusal to take holy orders, I'd go off and live with my nurse. I'd wear the rough, undyed wool of the lowest peasants and toil in the fields if that was what it took to break free of that monastery looming in the mist.

"You're giddy with excitement," Mother said, her arm around my shoulder. "Come along, darling. Jutta will look after you. Her mother has been so generous, paying your sisters' dowries. We remain in her debt."

Rorich pulled a face, trying to coax a smile from me. I could have scratched out his eyes. Behind him, a servant heaved my single dowry chest off the barge.

The path, snaking steeply uphill, took us through a tunnel of trees, bare autumn branches knit overhead to block out the sky. *Walled in.* Meginhard's words pricked me. What if he had been telling the truth? Those two words fell like boulders crushing my lungs. Already I felt as though I were trapped inside some tight, close place. The trees fell away, the path curving through a sheep meadow and then a garden flanked by orchards. Fog enclosed everything, obscuring any view of the surrounding countryside. I knew without anyone telling me that this was a remote place, chosen for its very seclusion—no villages or farmsteads for miles. Tomorrow, when it was over, Mother, Rorich, and Jutta's kin would board the barge and sail back into the land of the living. But I would never be allowed to leave.

When those gates closed behind me with the clang of iron and the thud of oak, my heart plummeted, a bird pierced by an arrow. The monastery was in shambles, half-ruined, its stone walls pocked and cracking, as though foreign armies had sacked it. The crumbling church with its eight-sided tower, chapel, refectory, kitchen, and ramshackle dormitories jostled together within the confines of those walls clinging to the hilltop. Eighty monks made this place their home. How could they squeeze another two bodies inside this place?

Even Mother looked as though she were having second thoughts about abandoning me here. I clung to her hand, silently imploring, *Change your mind!* But before I could put my terror into speech, Abbot Adilhum appeared, his head bowed as if he were offering himself as Mother's bondsman.

"My lady, as I was telling the countess, this monastery, once the hermitage of holy Disibod, has been in decline for many years. We hope to restore it to give honor to our saint. I offer my thanks to you, noble Mechthild, who have come with God's blessing to allow us to accomplish this task and make it a home worthy of your daughter."

I gaped at Rorich, who stared back and shook his head in disgust. Like me, he could see right through the abbot. The man was eager to welcome Jutta and me because our dowries would fill his empty coffers.

When we gathered for supper in the guesthouse, my mother seemed so astounded at the glory of sharing a table with the archbishop that I feared she might swoon. Likewise, Jutta seemed enraptured, as though she had just arrived in the holy city of Jerusalem. The archbishop praised her as if she were covered in gold.

"Blessed are the anchorites who live beneath the church eaves," said Ruthard of Mainz, "for they uphold the entire structure of the church with their blessed prayers and holy lives. For this reason you are called anchorites—you are like an anchor under the Church, which is the ship of faith, and you hold it steady so that all Satan's huffing and blowing can't pitch it over."

Our meal was spare: the river fish Rorich and Meginhard had caught; millet, beans, and carrots from the gardens; the monks' cheese, made from the milk of their sheep; and cloudy apple wine from their orchards.

Rorich, famished from the journey, wolfed down his portion with a greed that made the prior stare. While she would have indulged him at home, Mother cringed to see Rorich gorging in the presence of the archbishop.

"Son, mind yourself. Gluttony is the mother of all other sins."

I wished I could offer him the food on my trencher, which I could not bring myself to eat. My stomach was a cauldron of seething bile. If I took one bite, I feared I would spew.

Jutta did not eat a morsel, only sipped well water from an earthenware cup. Such peace shone on her face. She looked as though she were some angelic being who didn't need food to sustain herself the way ordinary mortals did.

Before me, I saw the floating orbs, which left me faint and fuzzy headed. There they came again, my cursed visions that had left me unmarriageable, cast out, only fit to offer companionship to a mad girl.

After reproving Rorich for his appetite, Mother turned to me, begging me to eat, her eyes moist as though she were fighting tears.

"Please, darling, just a few bites. You'll need your strength for the ceremony."

At dusk on the Eve of All Souls, the rite began.

In our guesthouse chamber, I froze, bare feet on the cold stone floor, as Jutta tugged my earthly garments over my head and let them tumble to the ground.

"You don't need these anymore," she told me.

She wore nothing but a death shroud of sackcloth woven from the coarsest, scratchiest goat hair. As goose pimples rose on my naked flesh, Jutta made me raise my arms so that she could fit an identical shroud over my body. The goat hair dug into me, making me want to claw my skin to relieve the itch.

Jutta then bowed her head as low as it could hang and shuffled out of the room, leaving me to shuffle after her. We processed to the abbatial church, alight with tapers as though a funeral were underway.

At the west end of the church lay a bed of black earth strewn with bare branches and dead leaves. Jutta flung herself belly down in the dirt. *Dust to dust.* I bridled, my stomach lurching. I remembered the story of Saint Ursula, the murdered virgins, the rotting flesh, and then it struck me like a blow, the full weight of what it meant to be an anchorite. The funeral tapers, the bed of earth—this night I was to *die.* To be buried with Christ.

Seeking out Mother, who watched with the rest of the congregation, I mouthed the words *Save me.* Weeping in earnest, she stepped toward me while my heart pounded in hope. But her gaze left me mute. It was as though she had taken a silken thread and sewed my lips shut so I could only mewl, as weak as a kitten, not sob or wail or rage. Taking my hands, Mother guided me downward into that dirt.

"It's God's will," she whispered. "We must *all* obey those who stand above us."

With trembling hands, she arranged my prone body until at last I lay corpse-still beside Jutta.

Holy water fell on my back like rain, wetting me through the prickly hair shirt. Incense and the stink of dank earth filled my nose. Finally the archbishop commanded Jutta and me to stand. Numb, my head ringing, I staggered to my feet and chanted the words they told me to chant.

Abbot Adilhum gave Jutta and me burning candles to hold in each hand.

"One for your love of God," he said, as the hot wax dripped down to sear my fingers. "One for your love of your neighbors."

I felt no love at all, only shuddering emptiness.

The monks sang *Veni creator.* At the abbot's prompting, I mumbled, "*Suspice me, Domine.*" *Receive me, Lord.* I placed my candles on the altar before hurling myself back into the grave dirt beside Jutta. My ears burned as the monks chanted what even I recognized as the Office of the Dead.

"Rise, my daughters," said the archbishop, leading us out of the church and into our tomb, our sepulcher, the narrow cell built onto the edge of the church.

My eyes flooded as he swung his incense thurible round and round.

There was only the low doorway and no windows, save for the screen that faced into the church and the revolving hatch where the monks could pass in food to Jutta and me without our even seeing who stood outside. Mother and Rorich were already lost to me in the courtyard, chanting along with the monks. *I'll never see their faces again.*

"Here I will stay forever," Jutta sang. "This is the home I have chosen."

I choked and coughed as the archbishop sprinkled ash on us. Every part of my body shriveled as he spoke the Rite of Extreme Unction, reserved for those on their deathbed.

"Obey God," he told us before leaving our cell.

Tears slid from my eyes as I watched the lay brothers brick up the doorway that Jutta and I had passed through but would never be allowed to exit. *Walled in.* Only Meginhard had been honest about what was to become of me, and I'd just laughed in his face. This was what Walburga couldn't bring herself to tell me, why she had howled in protest and sobbed over me. As Jutta murmured her prayers, I lay rigid on that cold stone floor as though I were truly a corpse in my crypt.

When the last brick was laid in its place, blocking every hope of escape, Jutta took my hands and pulled me to my feet. In the light of the single taper the monks had left us, I saw her smile.

"My dearest dream has been made real," she said.

At that, she blew out the taper. Coffin-darkness enclosed us.

3

MY FIRST NIGHT in the anchorage seemed to last forever. At some point I must have fallen asleep, for I awakened with a swallowed scream to disembodied chanting. A faint glow came from the screen looking into the church and that square of light framed a black shape that might have been Jutta, or even a demon straight from the depths of the damned. I quaked, too frightened to move, as the chanting went on and on.

When night finally waned, a fragile glimmering beckoned around the edges of a drapery. Scraping the crust of sleep from my eyes, I scrambled to my feet before casting a look at Jutta who slept on, slumped on her knees before the screen looking into the church. When I turned away from her and pushed the curtain aside, the gray half-light seemed strong enough to blind me.

The drapery had concealed a doorway leading into another small chamber graced with a high window, its panes made of polished horn. Glory of glories, beneath that window was a low door. My heart exploded. Had I discovered my escape? Could I flee into the forest, follow the river to find my way back to Rorich and Walburga? A band of robbers might adopt me, teach me how to steal through the woodland, my feet falling as silently as a deer's. They would teach me to shoot arrows straight into the heart.

With one backward glance at sleeping Jutta, I let the curtain fall back into place and crept to that door. Palms sweating, I undid the wooden latch, tugged it open, and rushed through. Scabby stone walls reared around me, as high as a tall man standing on another man's shoulders. This was no passage to freedom, only a narrow courtyard with a smelly drain and broken cobblestones. But when I arched my neck as far back as it would go, I saw the pale morning sky, as blue as Walburga's eyes. As blue as hope.

My tears wet the ash still coating my face, making it run down my cheeks until I tasted the grave dust on my lips. If I stood perfectly still and pricked my ears, I could hear the two rushing rivers far below, the Glan flowing into the Nahe. Tree branches whispered secrets while the wind stirred my hair. Then, oh wonder, a rust-colored beech leaf swirled down on the breeze to nestle in my cupped palms, the most beautiful thing I would touch that day. The wild forest rustled and murmured, just out of reach.

I broke down, wailing for my mother, pleading and sobbing until I thought my yearning would summon her out of the cold air. Mother would change her mind, bully the monks until they hacked open the anchorage entrance, allowing me to burst free into her arms. But the chilly place in my heart told me that Mother would leave this very morning, boarding the barge that would take her home. Her hand on Rorich's shoulder, she would tell him it was for the best. *Hildegard is in God's hands now.*

What if Mechthild von Bermersheim wasn't my real mother, I began to wonder. Perhaps she was just an imposter, or a wicked stepmother out of Walburga's fairy tales. A good mother wouldn't leave me to molder here. No, my true mother would have fought for me with the ferocity of a she-bear. She would have stood by me.

As if in answer to my desolation, a golden orb came floating down and I saw her in the midst of that pulsing sphere. A face like Walburga's but not Walburga's. A face bathed in tenderness, the Mother of my deepest longing, she who gave me all the love I craved and more. *Beloved, don't give up hope. When the time is ripe, I will set you free.*

"Hildegard!"

You are the seed. The anchorage is the husk. Here you will grow and grow until you grow too large for this place and then it will burst and you will step forth.

"Hildegard, did God strike you deaf?"

Whirling in a panic, I crushed the leaf in my hand. There stood Jutta, her face corpse gray from ashes and earth.

A peal of bells burst through the quiet of dawn.

Her voice raised to scold, Jutta snatched my wrist and dragged me back into the dank inner room. "I let you sleep through Matins, you lazy slug, but now it's time for Lauds."

"Matins?" I remembered the chanting in the black cavern of night.

Jutta knelt before the screen that faced the candlelit church where the monks assembled. Falling to her knees, her palms outstretched, Jutta joined her voice to theirs. Her song soared, high and ethereal, above the monks' deep drone. A boy hurrying through the nave to join his brothers in the choir turned around to glance toward the screen, his eyes widening as though in wonder to hear Jutta's singing, so beautiful and pure. Deep inside my heart, I offered up my secret prayer: *Please, God, you who can work miracles, let me see Rorich again. And the forest.*

If Rorich was trapped inside this place, he would launch himself over that wall, falling down the cliff and landing in the river where he would swim to safety. But I was just a girl with weak arms and legs. My thoughts wandered to my days in the forest with Rorich when he chased me through the trees, making me squeal with laughter till we tumbled on the grass and gazed up at the sunlight sifting through the leaves.

When at last the monks filed out of church, Jutta slammed the shutters, blocking my only view out of the anchorage.

"You weren't singing along," she accused. "You hardly paid attention."

"I don't know the words."

"Your family never gathered in the chapel for Lauds?" Jutta seemed scandalized.

"Mother's headaches," I stammered. "We never saw her face until Terce. She wanted no noise before then. I'm hungry," I added, thinking that if we were to be awake to pray at every hour, the monks must surely feed us in return. Last night I'd eaten so little. My throat burned with thirst and my hunger left me fuzzy headed.

Jutta regarded me in scorn, as though I were a spoiled child demanding honeycake after I'd just stuffed myself with roast venison. "Our meal comes after None."

That wasn't till afternoon. My hollow stomach rumbling up a storm, I sank to the floor, my head drooping between my legs.

"The spirit comes before the flesh, child. We have left worldly things behind."

Ignoring her, I tried to conjure up the orbs of light, anything to ease my misery. My hair shirt scratched every inch of my skin. How I longed to tear the cursed thing off.

Jutta rummaged through a trunk in the corner and returned with a pair of glinting blades. Before I could even gasp, Jutta seized a lock of my hair and sliced it off, as close to the scalp as she could manage without cutting my skin. Ignoring my shrieks and sobs, Jutta hacked away until I was as shorn as a male serf, the flaxen curls that had been my only beauty lying in a heap on the floor. Deftly, Jutta gathered up the tresses and braided them into a blond rope, binding each end with a silk ribbon.

"Keep that safe. One day, if you succeed in living a holy life, it will become a relic."

As I stared dumbstruck at my own severed hair, Jutta began to slice off her own shining auburn mane. Dropping my braid, I fled to the courtyard where, pretending I was as sturdy as Rorich, I stuck my fingers and toes into any little dent in the stone. Back home I'd climbed a willow tree, just to show him. Perhaps I could scale this wall. But it was useless—I only broke a fingernail.

Jutta appeared again, her face still smeared in ash, but now she was as bald as a woman being shamed for adultery. Her auburn plait coiled like a snake in her arms.

28

"Earthly vanity must be left behind," she said. "The monks have their tonsures. Holy women must have their heads shorn four times a year—the Rule of Saint Benedict demands it. No one will see us here anyway."

Disconsolate, I explored the two small rooms, my entire world. The innermost room, with its screen facing into the church and the revolving hatch, was furnished with a brazier, two narrow beds, and Jutta's trunk. The outer room, with its window and door onto the courtyard, had a table and two chairs. Each room I could cross from one end to the other in five long paces. Mother wouldn't even keep her horses in so narrow a space. Had Jutta chosen me because only a small child could fit inside these tiny chambers with her?

"Do you want to see something exquisite, poppet?"

Jutta opened her trunk to reveal ells of silk in fantastical hues that seemed to glow in the murky cell. Sapphire, saffron, vermillion, deepest violet shot with silvery threads, and emerald adorned with golden threads. I fevered to touch the sumptuous fabric, yearning to yank off my hair shirt and wrap my itching body in the smoothness.

"My father sent these back from the Holy Lands," she said. "Silk and brocade from the city of Damascus."

Using the same shears she had employed to slice off our hair, Jutta cut the damask that might have made her wedding gown and a dozen other gowns besides.

"Will we be allowed to wear it?" I asked, hoping against hope.

"No, silly. We'll fashion altar cloths and banners. And vestments for the Archbishop of Mainz."

Jutta set down her shears and turned to me. Her teeth as white as seed pearls, she smiled as though inviting me to trust her, share her friendship.

"Are you thirsty, my little one?"

When I nodded, Jutta fetched me a cup of water from the jug the monks had passed through our hatch.

"I promised your mother I'd give you a noblewoman's education. I shall teach you to play the psaltery and to read and write the psalms in Latin. I'll teach you to embroider as well as my own mother can."

So I was emboldened to draw close to her while we worked, stitching the splendid silk.

"Do you miss life back at court?" I asked, imagining Jutta swirling in a gown made of the selfsame garnet damask she sewed. "The music and dancing? My sister Clementia said your mother once brought in a tame bear and one of the servants saw it and ran screaming from the hall." I giggled to picture the scene.

Jutta regarded me with a face like stone. "Silence, child. Gossip and empty prattle are forbidden here."

"We can't even *talk?* But we were talking just a moment ago."

Her cornflower eyes were huge. "Did no one ever tell you that when two females engage in idle chatter, the demon Tutivillus appears and pushes their heads together so they jabber all the more? Then he copies their every vain word on his scroll and reads it back to them on Judgment Day."

If such a thing was true, I worried that the demon must have an endless scroll with Walburga's name on it, for she always had the most scandalizing gossip rolling off her tongue.

Jutta composed herself once more, her serene face bent to her sewing, and so we worked on without another word, as though we were two mutes, but from outside the anchorage we could hear a tumult of sawing, hammering, and stone-breaking. The monks had wasted no time in putting Jutta's fortune to use rebuilding the abbey. The racket grew louder and louder, making a mockery of our silence until Jutta seemed to grow bored. Then she returned, as she always did, to the virgin martyrs. Dreamy-eyed, she spoke of Catherine of Alexandria who matched wits with a thousand philosophers and won each debate.

"Noble virgins, consecrated to God, can achieve things no commonplace girl can dream of," she told me.

Ursula and her eleven thousand maidens traveled, free and joyous, through the Holy Roman Empire, not bound by their parents or anyone. The pope himself followed in their train. Ursula and her virgins had their own navy of girls just like Jutta and me. *At least they had a merry time of it*, I thought, *before they were hacked to pieces*. And Catherine! I tried to imagine myself arguing with the abbot and archbishop, the words flowing from my tongue until the men bowed to my wisdom and didn't know what to say anymore. I'd dazzle them with my wit until they knocked down the anchorage walls and let me walk free. To make Jutta happy, I'd take her on a pilgrimage to the Holy Lands. Rorich would come along and, somewhere on the journey home, he and I would run away and live in the forests of a faraway land. We'd find an abandoned castle and feast on wild boar every night.

As my needle passed through the silk, my fingers guided by Jutta's, I allowed myself to dream of happy things.

The one daily meal the Benedictine Rule allowed us in the winter months came through the revolving hatch. Famished, I fell upon my trencher of millet and beans, cheese, onions, and wrinkled cellar apples, and gulped down every last drop of the sour apple wine in my beaker.

But Jutta left her own food and drink untouched, fleeing the room in disgust, as though the sight of me stuffing myself sickened her. Too ravenous to bother about Jutta, I devoured every last morsel, even the doughy trencher that, at home in Bermersheim, we would have thrown to the hounds or given to hungry beggars. When my own food was finished, I looked around the empty room with the curtain drawn shut over the doorway before I launched myself at Jutta's portion, eating as much as I could cram inside myself. If this was going to be my only meal of the day, I wanted my belly good and full. At last, I hid the leftover apples, cheese and the trencher bread beneath the blanket the monks had given me. Placing the empty wine beakers back into the revolving hatch, I turned it so they faced the outside again, thereby concealing my crime.

I found her in the courtyard, pacing in the shadows, her hands rubbing each other as though she were trying to wash away some invisible stain. Her bare feet were blue against the stone. From the tang in the air, I guessed it would freeze that night.

"Come back inside." I tried to take her hand, but she shrugged me off.

"Leave me, child." Her eyes were worlds away.

Jutta only came in at Vespers, when it was too dark to sew or do any useful work. Her veil covering her shorn head, her hands knit over her stomach, she huddled on her pallet until Compline, the last devotions of the day.

Afterward we lay on our pallets to sleep.

"Don't undress," Jutta said, as I prepared to pull the hair shirt over my head. "The Rule of Saint Benedict says we must sleep clothed."

Crawling under my blanket, I waited until Jutta blew out the taper. Then I silently wriggled out of the sackcloth and shoved the thing to the foot of my bed. My hands rubbed my naked skin, now covered in an angry rash. I wanted to scratch myself until I bled. But most of all, I was still hungry, hungrier than I ever imagined I could be.

Biding my time until I thought Jutta must surely be asleep, I found the food in its hiding place and nibbled the cheese and trencher dough as quietly as I could, but when I bit into the apple, I gave myself away.

Jutta whipped the blanket off me and snatched the fruit from my hand. She had drawn back the curtain so that the shivery moonlight revealed everything—my gluttony and my nakedness.

"Horrible child! Do you think you can hide your wickedness from me? I could smell that cheese a league away."

Jutta crammed the bitten apple into her own maw, then spat it out, sobbing, and began to beat herself, falling to her knees with such a crack that I thought she had smashed her bones against the stone floor.

Clutching the blanket to my chest, I could only stare in terror, my tears stinging my face. So passed my first day of monastic life.

• • •

We are sealed in a tomb. We are no longer alive. Yet somehow life went on, though the two of us remained hidden away like the women in the glittering harems of the East that Rorich had told me about, except the only things that glittered here were Jutta's tears as she flailed her soft white flesh with her knotted rope with its seven spiked tails for the Seven Deadly Sins. She whipped herself until the blood ran.

The Hours of the Divine Office ruled our days and nights. In the pitch black, the bells summoned us to the screen for the Night Vigil of Matins, during which we sang the psalms for what seemed an eternity. The words of Psalm 129, sung every Wednesday at Vespers, burned themselves into my soul: *De profundis clamavi ad te, Domine. Out of the depths I cry out to you, O Lord. I've been cast down a pit and will never rise again.*

Though Jutta didn't expect me to flagellate myself as she did, my hair shirt did it for me, nettling my back and chest until my skin bled and wept of its own accord. I thought I would never again know what it was not to hurt or ache or suffer cold and hunger. *God, take me. Just let me die.* Real death had to be better than this never-ending pretend death.

Jutta said the flesh was a thing to be abhorred. Suffering, she told me, purified the soul and purged it of sin. Indeed, our cell seemed arranged so that our bodies could be mortified every day and hour. Though we had a brazier to heat our inner chamber, I was always chilled, having to go barefoot even when snow dusted our courtyard. The Rule of Saint Benedict made us sleep in our separate pallets and forbade us to huddle together for warmth as I would have done at home, snuggling up to Walburga or my sisters on freezing nights. Hunger bit into me even more than the cold, leaving me to sob in my sleep and dream of plump pheasants crackling on the spit, of the warm honeyed wine that Walburga used to spoon into my mouth when I was ill.

"Hunger is your weakness," Jutta said. "You are but a slave to the desires of the flesh."

True saints, she insisted, could live on water and air alone. Fasting cured every disease. It dried up the bodily humors, put demons to flight, banished impure thoughts, cleared the mind, sanctified the body, and raised a person to the throne of God. Yet for all her lofty talk, there were bitter winter days when even she devoured every last crumb the monks gave her.

I never knew which side of herself Jutta would show me next. She could be merciless, upbraiding me for the sin of being unable to sit still through the hours of prayer. When Jutta told me I would burn in hell for fidgeting, I let out a shriek and tore through the tiny rooms and courtyard, banging around like a trapped bat until I winded myself. Yet even when I was a proper hellion, ripping in half a piece of the precious damask silk I was meant to be stitching, Jutta never raised a hand to strike me. Sometimes Jutta acted as though I weren't even there. There were days when Jutta prayed herself into a swoon and lay like the dead for hours. Other times Jutta could act like the kindest soul I had ever met, teaching me to play her ten-string psaltery, patiently correcting my mistakes, and teaching me to sing in harmony with her so that our devotions became a thing of beauty that fed my soul even when I thought I was about to faint from hunger. Missing home in spite of herself, Jutta whispered about her life back in Sponheim—her dapple gray mare and merlin falcon—while we sewed altar cloths or mended the monks' coarse wool habits. On the best days Jutta reached for her wax tablet and stylus, and taught me to read and write in Latin and in our native tongue, hour by hour and week by week, until at last the letters carved in wax came alive and sang inside my head.

One dark winter morning, near the beginning of the fast of Advent, when cheese was denied us and we lived on turnips, millet, and scraps of fish, Jutta refused to arise for Matins. Lauds came, and still she did not stir from her bed. I shook her shoulders, slapped her cheeks as hard as I dared, even sprinkled water on her, but Jutta only lay there, her eyes glazed and unseeing, lost in some stupor.

Panicking, I wondered if I should scream for help. What good would that do—the monks couldn't enter the anchorage to help unless they tore down the wall. What if Jutta died and I was trapped here forever with her cold, rotting corpse?

Shrinking into the corner farthest away from Jutta's motionless body, I made up stories in my head to keep myself from crying. Once there was an orphan. Her evil stepmother cast her out into the winter forest where the hapless child fell under the enchantment of a sorceress — a maiden of high birth who was as mad as she was beautiful. But now the witch lay bound by her own spells and if only the girl had the courage, she might escape. She must flee the enchantress's shadowy hut and run into the farthest reaches of the forest. Deep in my heart, the path opened before me. I saw each ice-tipped branch, felt the snow crunching under my bare feet, the cold biting into my soles as I careened headlong, my arms outstretched, beseeching the angels and saints to come to my aid. *Save me. Save me.*

Now came the Office of Prime and still Jutta didn't move. She breathed, but her skin was clammy to the touch, her eyes fixed on the ceiling. I tore open the shutters and knelt at the screen to perform my devotions, the prayers tumbling dull and wooden off my tongue. My every muscle trembling, I clung to the screen and dared myself to break one of Jutta's innumerable rules. After the office ended, instead of closing the shutters, I kept them wide open and gawked at the men as they shuffled out of the church. One novice monk remained behind to trim the candlewicks, moving on sandaled feet to each side altar. For a long while he lingered at the Lady Altar before going to that of our patron, Saint Disibod. He looked about Jutta's age. My loneliness and desolation rising in a pure white flame, I stared fiercely, my eyes burning a hole in his back until he turned and made his way toward the screen. With a start, I recognized him as the same boy who had glanced back at the screen our first morning at Lauds when Jutta's lovely voice rang out to join the monks' song.

Every part of my brain screamed at me to slam those shutters, yet I gaped at the boy in unholy curiosity. His face was mild but inquisitive. He was tall and slight, with light brown hair and gray eyes. He stood so close that I could smell the wool of his habit.

"Little girl, why are you crying?" he asked. "Where's your magistra?"

"My what?"

"Your magistra. Your mistress. The holy Jutta."

"She's in bed. She won't get up."

"Is she ill? I can send for medicine from the infirmary. Special rations, too. A tureen of turtle soup. Never fear. Brother Otto is the best of physicians. For every ailment under heaven, an herb grows to cure it."

My mouth watered at the thought of soup.

"She's sick from melancholy," I whispered, choking on my fear that Jutta would suddenly come to and berate me for betraying her.

"That's the hardest thing to cure." The boy looked crestfallen. "Brother Otto might even say there's no cure but prayer."

"She prays all the time and it only makes her *worse*," I hissed.

At home, Mother would have slapped me for such irreverence, but the boy regarded me with thoughtful gray eyes.

"How old are you, child?"

"Eight."

"You sound melancholy yourself."

I couldn't stifle my sobs. "I'm hungry and cold. This hair shirt is so scratchy it makes my skin bleed. I want to go home. It's awful here. Jutta says we can't even talk because the demon Tutivillus will write down every word we say."

For a moment the novice monk was silent, as though searching for words.

"My parents sent me here when I was five," he said. "There were too many of us to feed. They thought me girlish and my father knew I would never make a good warrior. The first year I missed my mother so much that I thought I would die. I was sick in body, sick in my soul, practically living in the infirmary under Brother Otto's care. Then they discovered I was clever, and Brother Ulrich taught me to read and write in a good hand. When I was as old as you, they put me to work cutting quills. From my very first day in the scriptorium,

I learned that I could be happy here. When they were satisfied that my handwriting was good enough, they let me copy my first manuscript. As for Tutivillus, the demon you mentioned, he's the patron of scribes. If our attention wanders, he causes us to smudge our ink and misspell our words, even miscopy the Scriptures."

"What's the scriptorium like?" I asked, anxious to keep him there, talking to me.

"It's a wide and airy room, with a ceiling nearly as high as the church's. It has windows on three walls. New windows made of glass," he added, "thanks to the endowment we received from your magistra and her family. The place is flooded with light, even in winter. There are long tables and benches where we copy texts.

"Our library is huge, Hildegard, with every sort of book, not just writings of the Church, but the wisdom of the pagans," he said, dropping his voice a notch, "of ancient Rome and Greece, whose knowledge has never been surpassed. And we have the books of the Saracens, Persians, and Arabs, whose physicians and mathematicians are far more advanced than any in Christendom."

So the infidels that Father and my two eldest brothers had gone to kill were civilized people. The damask silk, woven by Saracen hands, that Jutta and I sewed into priestly vestments, might have clothed some great scholar of the East if Jutta's father hadn't seized it in the spoils of war.

"I don't know if your melancholy can be cured, but it might be eased," the boy said, "if you could only find your place here. Your way will be harder than mine because you're an anchorite and so restricted. But you're very clever, I think. You must find your skills, the vocation within your vocation. What do you love to do?"

"I miss the forest. Do they ever let you out of the abbey gates?"

"On long summer days, when Brother Ulrich can spare me in the scriptorium, Brother Otto sends me out to gather wild herbs. In autumn I pick mushrooms. Because I'm a scribe and have read all the herbal and botanical texts, they trust me to pick the right ones so I don't poison the whole monastery."

I smiled at the first joke I'd heard since entering Disibodenberg, but I managed not to laugh since it was forbidden here.

"Listen, little sister, I must go to the scriptorium before Brother Ulrich comes looking for me. But if you hear something being placed in your hatch, know that it's from me. And think about what you love, Hildegard. Trust it. That's where your talents lie and that's where you'll find happiness, even here."

I pressed my hand to the screen. The boy briefly lifted his hand to mine before departing. Through the wooden slats, I felt his warmth, his strength. *Little sister,* he'd called me. He believed in happiness, believed that I could somehow be happy, too. I didn't even know his name.

Closing the shutters, I crept to Jutta's pallet, stared into her blank eyes, and squeezed her hand, calling to her until she blinked and hugged me, her tears soaking into my sackcloth.

"Forgive me," she whispered. "Poor child, what have I done?"

She sounded so lost. I didn't understand if she regretted what she had done to me—convincing Mother to let her drag me into this cage—or what she had done to herself.

When we sat down to sew, I heard the sound of something being placed in our hatch. Before Jutta could stop me, I sprang up, twirling it around to reveal a tureen of soup and a loaf of wheaten bread. Ladling the soup into the two wooden bowls provided, I passed one to Jutta, then broke off a chunk of bread.

With trembling hands, Jutta pushed her veil back from her face and stared as the fragrant steam wafted up.

"Turtle soup," she said. "That's what they feed invalids."

"They thought you were ill," I said between mouthfuls of the piping hot liquid. "They didn't hear you sing at Matins, Lauds, or Prime."

Though I ate and ate till my soul felt anchored in my body once more and my belly filled with warmth, Jutta only gazed, as frozen as a statue, at the soup until I thought it would go cold. It was up to me to act, to be Jutta's nursemaid, as kind and resourceful as Walburga.

What do you love? Did I love Jutta, the one who held me prisoner? Who else was there to love? I lifted the spoon to her mouth. Obedient as a tot, Jutta let me feed her. *Is this my talent? Can I cure Jutta of her sadness?*

After Prime the next morning, the novice monk, this time accompanied by an older man, made his swift way toward the screen. Jutta was about to slam the shutters when I grabbed her hands.

"They want to speak to you," I whispered.

The older man, who introduced himself as Brother Otto, the physician, asked if Jutta was feeling quite well.

"Yes," she said, sounding stiff and shy. "Thank you for the soup, but it was unnecessary. I can keep the Advent fast as well as any in this abbey."

My heart sank. I wanted to twist away from Jutta, hide myself in the courtyard, and wail. No more soup, just long dark days of hunger until Christmas.

"No one doubts your resolve, magistra," Brother Otto said, addressing her with all the deference due to the Count of Sponheim's daughter. "But my young friend, Brother Volmar, thought that the fast might perhaps be too arduous for your companion, a child still growing. Hildegard will be provided with extra rations. If we have your permission, magistra, Brother Volmar would like to bring texts from the library so that you and Hildegard might continue your studies."

"You are very generous," Jutta murmured, eyes cast down to her folded hands.

As long as it was food for the mind rather than the body, Jutta would not deny herself. *Or me.* I smiled at Volmar through the screen. Now I knew his name.

Later that day, while Jutta was out pacing the courtyard, I heard footsteps approach the hatch. Quick as a rabbit, I swung it around to find an illustrated herbal, filled with pictures of every plant that grew in the forest. Accompanying the book was a branch, freshly cut, the severed wood still moist.

"Hildegard," Volmar called from the other side of the hatch. "Can you hear me?"

"Yes!"

"Do you know what day it is?"

"Tuesday?"

"December fourth. The Feast of Saint Barbara. Do you know her story?"

"Of course! Her father locked her in a tower and chopped off her head because she wouldn't marry the heathen king! But God struck her father with lightning and he died horribly."

It was always the same with virgin martyrs. Their willfulness made them disobey their fathers and older brothers—but because God had inspired their willfulness, their disobedience was made holy. Perhaps this was why Jutta, when she spoke at all, would never stop talking about them.

"That's what we call Barbara's Branch," said Volmar. "It's cut from an apple tree. Now you can barely see the buds that are waiting for spring. But if you place it in a beaker of water, Hildegard, it will bloom by Christmas Eve."

"Nothing blooms in the middle of winter!"

"Keep it in a warm place. Wait and see."

"Who are you talking to?" Jutta came in, shivering and rubbing her arms.

"Volmar. He's gone now." I listened to his sandals slapping against stone as he hurried off, probably to his sanctuary, the scriptorium, which, trapped in this place, I would never see.

"He gave us a stick?" Jutta picked it up, examining it from all sides.

"It's for Saint Barbara, the holy virgin martyr!" I cried, afraid that she might snap it in half and burn it in the brazier.

Instead she found a beaker of water. We kept the branch in the warmest and brightest corner of the anchorage.

"Now we must pray to holy Barbara," my magistra instructed, "on this, her feast day."

Barbara, the patron saint of prisoners.

In the pool of sunlight pouring through our window of polished horn, Jutta and I curled up side by side. Open in Jutta's lap lay Volmar's herbal. Breathless, I leafed through the illuminations he had painted himself.

"Patience," Jutta said, speaking more like an older sister than my magistra. "Don't tear through it all at once. Let us read it page by page."

In her voice, which was as beautiful in speech as it was in song, she read aloud, beginning with the admonition on the very first page, penned in bold black letters.

> *If anyone steal this book, let him die the death. Let him be*
> *fried in the pan. Let the falling sickness and fever seize him.*
> *Let him be broken on the wheel and hanged. Amen.*

We burst into smothered laughter as we imagined gentle Volmar penning such wrath. I pictured him cracking a grin while he wrote it, following some older and less sweet-tempered monk's dictation.

The herbal was written not in Latin but in German, and it described the worts and weeds that grew in the woodland and meadows around the abbey. Jutta read out Volmar's words as I followed along, my finger on the page.

Vervain promoted felicity. Marjoram was good for treating bruises. Saint-John's-wort, which bloomed at Midsummer Day on the Feast of Saint John the Baptist, was ruled by the sun. The monks used it to treat pain and infection. Wormwood cleansed the gut of parasites. Iris root healed dog bites. Blessed thistle, which grew in every monastery garden in the Holy Roman Empire, guarded against plague. Cowbane, though poisonous to cattle, banished lust in men and women.

"Do they grow all these things here?" Closing my eyes, I tried to envision having the freedom to walk through the snowy plots, if only to see the dormant stalks. Beside us in the fragile midwinter light, the Barbara Branch seemed to come alive, touched by an invisible hand, its flat, hard buds swelling.

Although the Twelve Holy Nights of Christmas were still three weeks off, Volmar's gifts kept appearing in our hatch day after day.

One morning a pair of sandals and a child-size linen shift and woolen habit appeared to replace the sackcloth that turned my skin into a mass of sores. He had only been able to find a boy's habit, but Jutta helped me alter it into something suitable for a girl. Jutta, however, would not be parted from her own hair-shirt shroud.

The herbal had only been in our anchorage a week when we finished it. Volmar brought another book, even more wondrous—a bestiary with illuminations and descriptions of every known beast, from the common to the exotic and rare.

The manticore, we learned, boasted a man's face, a lion's body, and a scorpion's stinging tale. Swordfish, with their great pointed beaks, could sink ships. Most terrifying of all was the basilisk, whose smell, voice, and glance could slay. Some creatures brought joy. Whenever the halcyon bird laid her eggs, the weather was fine and clear. The swan sang most exquisitely before he died. The lynx's urine hardened into precious amber. Some animals were tender. The pelican, like Christ, fed her brood from her own flesh. Bear cubs were born unformed, but their mothers devotedly licked them into shape.

Next Volmar lent us a lapidary, which revealed the miraculous properties of gemstones. Once these jewels had adorned Lucifer, in the days when he was the brightest of angels. But when he was cast into hell, the precious and semiprecious stones rained down upon the earth. Since they had their origin in heaven, they could only be used for good, for healing.

"If a diamond is brought into a house," Jutta read aloud, "then no demon may enter that dwelling." Her brow furrowed. "A pity my mother never possessed a diamond, although Father gifted her with rubies and jasper."

"The monks don't possess one either," I suggested.

"What makes you so sure?"

"Volmar talked about Tutivillus interfering with the scribes. He makes them spill their ink and copy things wrong!"

"There are scores of demons, Hildegard. Not just Tutivillus." Jutta juddered, as though a specter had laid its icy hands on her spine. "And they are strongest at this time of year when there's so little light."

Volmar's gifts, as enchanting as they were, only made me long even more for the outside world. After Vespers, I went to see if our Barbara Branch still had enough water. Though the buds had once seemed to swell, the branch now felt like a dead twig I could snap between my fingers. The forest would not stop haunting me. How the wild places called out to me in the face of Jutta's direst warnings. Again and again she told me that I must dread everything dark and untamed.

Demons ruled the nocturnal hours, she insisted. On stormy nights, outside our anchorage walls, trees writhed, tossing their branches against the moon-drenched sky. As I lay in my narrow bed, my ears rang with the shrieking wind, the cries of owls and wolves in search of prey.

Little did it matter that Christmas was fast approaching. For centuries before the Irish missionaries brought the faith of Christ to this land, before Carolus Magnus toppled the Irminsul, the idolatrous pillar of the heathens, my ancestors had held the Rauhnächte, the Twelve Nights of Yuletide, in awe—time out of time when fate hung suspended, when secrets were revealed and fortunes could be reversed. This I knew from Walburga's tales. The servants and peasant folk back home had muttered stories of the Old Ones roaring across the midwinter skies: the Wild Hunter of a thousand names in pursuit of his White Lady with her streaming hair and starry distaff, the whirlwind before the storm.

Leaving the dreaming Jutta to choke in her sleep and sob her brother's name, I crept out of bed and stole into the courtyard where

I pranced barefoot in the swirling snowflakes like the mummers who came to Bermersheim every Yuletide in their fearsome wooden masks to frighten away harmful spirits.

A gale howled overhead, and the cold stung my soles, sending me spinning as the Wild Hunt of Walburga's nursery stories raged overhead, that endless stream of unbanished gods and the souls of the unchristened dead. Anyone who dared venture out on a night such as this risked being swept along in that unearthly train.

But did I cross myself and flee inside to safety? No, I raised my face to the clouds racing across the full moon and I begged those invisible riders to take me with them.

Clouds shrouded the moon. Everything went black. I plummeted, down and down, as if there would be no end to my falling. *De profundis clamavi ad te.* Gazing up from the depths, I saw a circle of sky, now emptied of moon and stars. Had I been cast into hell for my sin? From out of that murk came a white cloud bursting with a light that was alive, pulsing and growing until it blazed like a thousand suns.

In that gleaming I saw a maiden shine in such splendor that I could hardly look at her, only catching glances like fragments from a dream. Her mantle, whiter than snow, glittered like a heaven full of stars. In her right hand she cradled the sun and moon. On her breast, covering her heart, was an ivory tablet and upon that tablet I saw a man the color of sapphire. A chorus rose like birdsong on an April dawn — all of creation calling this maiden "Lady." The maiden's own voice rose above it, as achingly beautiful as Jutta's singing.

I bore you from the womb before the morning star.

I didn't know whether the maiden was speaking to me, lost and wretched, or to the sapphire man in her breast. My vision of the Lady was lost, but her voice lingered. *You are here for a purpose, though you don't understand it yet.*

Barefoot and mother-naked, I found myself within a greening

garden so beautiful that it made me cry out. Each blade of grass and newly unfurled spring leaf shimmered in the sun. Every bush and tree was frothy with blossoms and heavy with fruit at the same time. In the midst of that glory, the Tree of Life and its jeweled apples winked at me, and yet I saw no serpent. The Lady's voice whispered: *See the eternal paradise that has never fallen.*

I saw a great wheel with the all-embracing arms of God at its circumference, the Lady at its heart. Everything she touched greened and bloomed.

Pealing bells wrenched me back into this world. The monks were ringing in Christmas morning. I lay on my pallet, the blankets piled over me, my legs swaddled in damp cloth. Above me hovered a maiden with glowing blue eyes. Her veil had slipped and the sun shone through her halo of cropped auburn curls. Whispering my name, she held out a blossoming apple branch, each pink and white flower redolent with the scent of the Eden I had glimpsed.

Jutta kissed my brow.

"At last you're awake! You lay in a fever for three days and nights. I found you half-frozen in the courtyard. Were you sleepwalking, child? I must bolt that door firmly so it never happens again. What if I'd lost you?"

Sweat trickled down my face. I was too weak to lift my head from the pillow. All seemed unreal: Jutta, dazzling even in her sackcloth, held the Barbara Branch that flowered at Christmas just as Volmar had promised.

Beside my bed was a tureen of soup that had gone cold, but Jutta warmed it over the brazier and then she fed me, spoonful by spoonful.

"The fast is over, child. Tonight, if you're well enough, there will be a feast delivered to us. Brother Volmar said there will be river carp and quail. And apple cake with nuts and currants."

"Volmar." This was the first word to pass through my lips after emerging from that otherworld where I had lain for three days and nights. "You talk to him through the screen?"

"Of course! You were ill. I had to ask him to bring food that would help the sick. Volmar ran to the infirmary and came back with damp cloths for me to wrap around your legs to lower the fever."

Jutta flushed when she said his name.

So Volmar isn't just my secret friend. He whispered through the screen to Jutta. Could he see her beautiful face through the slatted wood, see how her long eyelashes beat like butterfly wings against her creamy skin? What if his kindness to me had only been a ploy to woo her, the holy and aristocratic anchorite? Weren't they the same age, Volmar and Jutta? Jutta's nightmares of her brother made her writhe and shudder, yet Volmar was as different from Meginhard von Sponheim as a boy could be. And I, Hildegard, was destined to come in a poor second, to live forever in Jutta's shadow.

"You were dreaming three days long," Jutta said. "And such dreams they must have been—you were *raving*, my child."

She kept calling me that. *Child.* But in those three days and nights, I felt I had grown impossibly old. My childhood had been lost forever, stolen from me the moment they bricked me in here.

Jutta bent close, her face prickling with concern. "If you're having . . . visitations of any sort, you might be prey to demons, Hildegard. You must confess everything to Prior Cuno and be shriven of your sins."

Were my visions evil, then? Did Jutta, the girl who starved and beat herself, who thought that demons lurked in every shadow, think that I was the crazy one? My heart raced in terror that she might be right.

"Don't cry, little sister," she said, calling me by the special name Volmar had given me. "I have a surprise."

She bustled to the other side of the chamber and returned with a bundle that looked like an infant tucked in a lambswool blanket.

"This is my gift to you." Jutta placed it in my arms as carefully as though it were a baby of flesh and blood.

Staring down at the doll's wooden face, I wished I had the strength to hurl it across the room. Who did Jutta think she was, imprisoning me here, stealing away my only friend, leaving me with nothing but the visions that kept exploding inside my head? The final insult was trying to win my affection with some stupid toy.

"I'm too old for dolls," I told her, not hiding my contempt.

She flinched as though I had slapped her. "It's not a plaything, child. It's meant to represent the baby Jesus. Volmar said it's customary to give young female oblates dolls for this purpose."

"I don't need a *doll*." Sinking back into my bed, I closed my eyes, allowing the ghost of my vision to envelop me—the maiden holding within her beating heart the sapphire man with his arms outstretched. *I bore you from the womb before the morning star.* Was it truly Mary and Jesus I had seen, or some demonic illusion?

"We must pray to him, our heavenly Bridegroom," Jutta said. "Let his image fill your heart."

The sapphire man regarded me with Volmar's gentle eyes. He held out his ink-stained scribe's hands. *You are here for a purpose.* If only I knew what that was.

Later that day came Volmar's gift—an illuminated volume of the lives of the virgin martyrs. Jutta took it from the hatch, her face alight, and, sitting by my bedside, read to me in a voice as smooth as damask. I wanted to hate her, stop my ears, and tell her to go boil herself, but the stories and pictures were so beguiling that they soon caught me in their thrall.

"Let me have the book," I begged, anxious to pore over every illumination.

When Jutta retired to the outer room to lose herself in contemplation, I threw the blankets off my body, tore the damp rags from my calves, and tottered around on shaky legs. I was bored with being an invalid.

Muffled footsteps on the other side of the screen made me rip open the shutters and glare into Volmar's face.

"Hildegard! You must be feeling better."

"Did you expect to see Jutta instead? Shall I fetch her for you?"

"Don't disturb her prayers, child."

Child! How that word rankled me.

"Do you like the book? I picked it out just for you."

"For me?" I folded my arms in front of myself and glowered. *Not for her?*

"Did you see the picture of Margaret of Antioch slaying the dragon? She looked so fierce and determined that she reminded me of you, little sister."

His words fell on my bitterness like sunlight on snow, melting it clean away. I grinned at him. My favorite part of Saint Margaret's story was when she was trapped inside the dragon's belly and she crossed herself, causing the dragon to explode.

"Volmar, where do visions come from?"

"Holy prophecies are sent by God. Then there are delusions sent from hell, though I pray we will be delivered from such things. Why do you ask?"

"I *see* things," I whispered, praying Jutta wouldn't hear. "Jutta says I must confess." In all honesty, I wondered how long I could stand to carry this burden alone.

"I'm not fit to receive your confession, Hildegard. I'm not yet ordained. Let me fetch the prior."

"No," I begged him. "Please. You're the only one I trust."

I wished the floor would open up and swallow me.

"Tell me if you must, but remember I'm only a novice and a scribe."

"Are you my friend?" I dared to ask him.

"Absolutely."

"Then promise not to tell a soul. Even Jutta."

My lips to the screen, I whispered of my vision of the maiden at the center of the wheel of creation, all of life springing from her. God, on the outside of the wheel, contained her just as she contained Christ in her body.

Volmar was silent a long while. I was about to creep away in humiliation when he finally spoke.

"A powerful vision indeed for one so young. Are you sure you don't want to tell Prior Cuno?"

"Don't tell him, Volmar. You *promised*."

"So I did and I'll keep my word. But why can't you talk to Jutta about this?"

"She'll think I'm mad—or wicked. Do *you*?"

"No, Hildegard. Let me find you some more books. Maybe if your mind's fully occupied, you won't be so troubled by these things."

I thanked him before quietly closing the shutters. Then I sank to the floor, my heart rattling sickly. Volmar possessed a heart full of kindness. He did everything in his power to help me, yet even he regarded my visions as trouble.

That Christmas Day we shared a rare feast of carp, quail, and apple cake. Bright-cheeked, Jutta spoke of the brand-new sewing needles her mother had sent her along with a letter filled with news of home. My magistra told me of every single thing that had transpired in Sponheim in her absence, yet she never once mentioned her brother.

"Did anything come from *my* mother?" I asked in a small voice.

Jutta shook her head. "Sorry, child. No."

My tears splashed down on my half-eaten piece of carp. Mechthild—that was how I thought of her now—had truly washed her hands of me. I even wondered if Rorich still kept me in his heart.

"Come, child." Jutta cupped my chin and raised it, smiling into my eyes. "This is no day for weeping. Tomorrow I want you to write the First Psalm in Latin. Do you think you can do that?"

Swiping at my eyes, I nodded. Mechthild had never learned to write even her own name.

That night after Compline, the golden orb came floating, bearing inside it that loving face I had beheld my first morning in the courtyard. The motherly face in the orb was different from the maiden I had glimpsed, but she was every bit as shining, as full of Living Light that flowed outward, wrapping around me until I quivered, hugging my knees to my chest. *Mother.* I wasn't pining for the woman who had birthed me and then forsaken me; I was crying out to God. I turned to

God and called her Mother, my true Mother who would cherish me as Mechthild never had.

She began to speak: *I am the supreme fiery force who kindled every living spark. I flame above the beauty of the fields. I shine in the waters. I burn in the sun, moon, and stars. With the airy wind, I quicken all things. For the air is alive in the greening and blooming. The waters flow as if alive.*

4

VOLMAR WAS MY SHINING sun, my guardian angel, offering me
the most precious gift of all, the outside world. He fed my undying
hunger with the books that I gradually learned to read on my own
without Jutta's help. He also brought me tender young plants dug
up from the forest floor, wet earth still clinging to their roots. In the
spring of the year, he gifted me with seedlings of medicinal herbs.
Woodruff that bloomed sweetly in a cloud of delicate white flowers.
Lady's mantle that gathered raindrops resembling liquid diamonds in
her pleated leaves. Chamomile with its golden flowers that soothed the
stomach. Motherwort that banished nightmares. Valerian that stank
like something rotten yet had the power to quieten Jutta's nerves when
she was too overwrought to sleep.

Each plant I watered with care, shifting its pot by the hour to make
the most of the sparse sunlight angling down into the anchorage courtyard. I prayed over the herbs, my voice ringing so fervently that Jutta
accused me of loving those common weeds more than God. But I kept
murmuring my psalms to the plants. If I couldn't escape to the forest, I
would plant this wild meadow inside our very enclosure, tend it as best
I could. Such a miracle of greening unfolded before my eyes, seedlings
shooting into full-fledged plants, moist and luscious, full of growing
power that seemed to conquer everything empty and stale. Soon the
plants outgrew their small pots, and I begged Volmar for more earth
and bigger vessels, the largest he could squeeze through our hatch.

How I adored the rich loamy smell of soil on my hands. How Jutta despaired of me, grubbing in the dirt like a serf. The courtyard became a lush grove with wild grapevine climbing the walls, feverfew and thyme growing between the cobbles.

Continuing my education, Jutta taught me the Latin prayers of the Divine Office and all one hundred and fifty psalms. I kept confusing *virgo* with *virga* until virgin and branch became one and the same. Almost every day the floating orbs appeared, but I had learned not to speak of them, for they were as unwelcome in the monastery as they had been in my mother's house.

In August, only weeks away from the ninth anniversary of my birth, I made ready for the Feast of the Assumption. Dancing around my garden sanctuary, I prayed to Mary, *viridissima virga,* the greenest branch, who made my plants grow so tall and beautiful. In the floating orbs, I saw the shining maiden at the axis of a great wheel, sitting still and majestic at the center while the wheel spun around her. I smuggled precious crumbs to the courtyard. Holding them in my cupped palms as an offering, I hummed softly until a wild mourning dove flew down to peck the morsels from my hand, her feathers fanning my wrists. Part of me flew with her as she winged away into the forest. Part of me walked beneath those rustling woodland boughs and breathed that pure air, my soul blessed by so many living things.

The first summer of our captivity passed and then the second. Jutta seemed happy, or at least as content as a melancholy girl could hope to be. Her name, uttered with reverence, was on every monk's lips. The glory of Disibodenberg, holy Jutta sat at her screen, otherworldly in her loveliness, and chanted her benedictions to the stream of pilgrims who eased the monotony of our days. Her reputation as a beauty remained undiminished, her new life as a recluse only adding to her mystique.

The magnitude of her sacrifice—interring herself alive to serve God and others through her prayers—seemed to prove that she wielded extraordinary powers and could work wonders on behalf of many, that her blessing and counsel were more potent than all the prayers and Masses offered by the monks. While men who became anchorites were usually priests or monks of many years' standing before they made this final, irrevocable act of renunciation, female anchorites came straight from the world, pitching themselves into holy seclusion without first having had to climb the rungs of hierarchy. And so the pilgrims held us in awe as beings set apart.

Rumors spread that Jutta lived on water and air. So pure and undefiled, she was free of the shame of monthly bleeding. Pilgrims from as far away as Trier walked barefoot over hills and through forests, fording rivers and swamps to seek an audience with their holy woman. Wealthy supplicants heaped endowments on Disibodenberg to win my magistra's good favor while the poor begged for her intercession and mercy, as though a few murmured words from her could protect them from famine and plague. Kneeling outside our screen, matrons and maidens poured out their hearts' sorrows to Jutta as though she could cure their every malady and turn their woe to weal.

But saintliness was no easy yoke to bear. The more Jutta's holy reputation flourished, the harder she struggled to embody it. It hardly mattered if it was Ash Wednesday or Easter Sunday — she ignored the feasts to embrace her fasts until her skin grew as translucent as the inside of a snail's shell. Hunger lent her such a fragile, delicate grace, rarer and more refined than the ruddy glow of good health. But it left her chilled even on the most sweltering days of high summer. Clutching a blanket over her sackcloth, the holy maiden awaited her next lot of pilgrims.

Once a week Prior Cuno sought an audience with Jutta. He whispered to her in a voice so low and strangled that, as hard as I strained my ears, I couldn't catch a word. Once, bringing Jutta a cup of water, I contrived to glimpse the prior's face through the screen. As he gazed at my magistra, he seemed entranced — more like a lover than a monk, reminding me of the way the moon-faced village boys used to gawp at my beautiful sisters.

As I grew older, I would understand that before Jutta's arrival, the monks of Disibodenberg had gone years on end without laying eyes on a living woman, let alone one so lovely. Even at that age, I knew without anyone telling me that Jutta was the most exquisite creature ever to grace this remote abbey: a lady of the high aristocracy who had renounced her fortune and every comfort to join the Benedictines, her crystalline voice soaring with the brothers in song. Even imprisoned in our anchorage, Jutta bloomed like a rare damask rose, her exotic fragrance inflaming every soul inside these monastery walls.

Cuno treated her with reverence, as though convinced that Jutta was indeed a living saint. My magistra's life, I knew, followed the pattern laid out in the hagiographies. None of the celebrated virgin martyrs were born poor or ugly, but were, without exception, noble maidens of legendary beauty who had forsaken their wealth and privilege to follow God. As far as I could gather from reading the stories, no lowborn woman such as Walburga could hope to become a saint, even if she was twice as pious as Jutta von Sponheim. I pondered whether beauty, too, was a necessary ingredient. Didn't Cuno preach that one's outer features mirrored the inner soul, that a plain face and awkward figure betokened a coarse nature? All the more reason for me, a child born without the least gift of prettiness, to skulk deeper into the shadows. *You will never be a saint, never be anything the least bit special.* In deepest humility, I would have to resign myself to be Jutta's handmaiden, a servant to her greater glory. Jutta was the shining pinnacle, the alabaster statue upon the pedestal.

When Countess von Sponheim visited and spoke to Jutta through the screen, my magistra shrank inside her veil, as if tales of worldly life now galled her. She no longer asked about family, old friends, or life at court, but only how her mare fared in her absence. Sometimes her voice caught when speaking of the horse she had loved so much.

After her mother retired to the guest lodgings, Jutta swept me up, hugging me tight. "On warm summer days, Silvermoon used to doze off with her head in my arms. I taught her to curtsey like a lady. She gave me kisses and took sweetmeats from my lips so delicately. She was always so good and brave on the hunt. Once, when we were cantering around a tight corner, I lost my balance and would have come off, only she slowed down so I could right myself again. She's such a big, powerful creature, Hildegard, but so gentle. She looked after me."

"Did your mother have any news of *my* mother?" I asked, but the answer, as always, was no.

Days and weeks, months and seasons dragged past in dull procession, but I received no visitors, not a single letter from my mother. At first I counted off a litany of spiteful excuses for Mechthild to ease the pain of that gaping silence. *She can't write. She's ignorant and unschooled.* But Mother could have asked her chaplain to write a letter, even a short one, a few sentences to tell me that she loved me and kept me in her thoughts. Was even this too much trouble for her?

I knew it was a sin to hate, to refuse to forgive, but the raw and hurting place inside me grew and grew until I feared it would swallow my heart. Just when I thought I would never hear another word from any of them at Bermersheim, those cold strangers whose blood I shared, who had abandoned me to these two dusty cells, a letter came from Rorich.

Ripping open the seal, I devoured his words as though they were bread. My brother's essence filled the lonely rooms, his laughter and gibes, his smell of dusty summer leaves and healthy sweat. Two years had gone by since I'd last seen him. Now I was ten and he was twelve, only two years older than I was, and yet he no longer sounded like the boy I had known. Now he sounded older than Volmar and Jutta.

Hildegard, you must hate me for not writing earlier. Mother would not allow it. She said we must leave you in peace while you grew used to your life in seclusion. Any distractions from us would only make it harder for you and make you yearn in vain for what you could no longer have.

Sister, now it is my turn to say good-bye to my freedom, for I, too, must go to the Church. Mother is sending me to study with the prelates of Mainz. The youngest son must become a priest—even you knew that. Everyone, says Mother, must face their lot.

As for Mother herself, her health has been poor ever since she sent you away, but she has at last succeeded in finding Clementia a husband, although I confess I don't like him and, if I were her, I would rather be a nun than marry a man who smelled like a goat.

Remember, Hildegard, when we used to dream of running away and becoming outlaws? Can you keep those happy days alive in your memory? Keep me in your prayers.

I remain your loving brother.

I will remember, Rorich. Running through the tunnel of memory into that light-filled forest, I raced with him once more, beating down nettles with hazel sticks.

One baking September afternoon, I busied myself in the courtyard, moving my wilting plants into the shade and offering them water, fussing over them and telling them stories as though they were tiny children who depended on me, body and soul.

"Now drink your water! Soak it up! You have to grow up big and strong," I admonished my potted Saint-John's-wort, "because I might not always be here to look after you. One day," I whispered, "my brother will come for me."

Jutta had accused me of the sin of stubbornness and now I allowed my contrary streak to carry me along in its sweeping torrent. Surely Rorich wouldn't let them force him into the priesthood. He *would* escape, my brother who was always so courageous and strong-willed.

"He'll come cantering through the forest on a snow-white stallion," I confided to my saxifrage plant, "and he'll take me far away from here."

I refused to let my childhood dreams die, even though each month in the anchorage took me further and further away from the barefoot seven-year-old who had once raced at her brother's side. I was growing taller, bursting the seams of my habit, my sleeves riding up to my elbows. Prior Cuno had promised to procure cloth for me to stitch a new one, but he lectured that it would do me no harm to learn some patience in the meantime.

"Don't fret, my little one," I crooned to the heartsease, pinching off its wilted blooms. "When I leave, you won't die. Volmar will plant you in the garden. It will be much better for you there." I strode over to the greater Solomon's seal, rising majestic in its tub. "Imagine sinking your roots into the earth instead of a pot. Think how much you'll grow!"

With a glance toward the anchorage door where all seemed peaceful, Jutta being occupied with her pilgrims, I kicked up my bare feet and pranced around the courtyard pretending I was on horseback, galloping away from Disibodenberg. My fists closed around imaginary reins, I careened in circles. Offering my face to the sun, I let it scorch me, let it soak into me, its warmth sinking into my muscle and bone, so that it would shine forever inside me, even on the darkest days of midwinter.

The courtyard door banged open. I jumped out of my skin to see Jutta collapse on the cobbles. Despite the heat, she shivered violently, her face white, her eyes frozen as though she had beheld the maw of hell. Her hands clutched a sweeping skein of coarse silvery hair. Lifting it to her lips, she sobbed and choked, then doubled over as though someone had gutted her with a fish knife.

"What is it?" I ran to her.

Jutta moaned and wept, making no sense, until I tried to lead her back inside out of the sun. Then she snatched her hand free and shrieked out three words.

"*Send him away.*"

The horror in her voice drove a spike of terror through me. *Be strong.* I pictured Margaret of Antioch, steadfast and brave, even when imprisoned in the dragon's belly. Creeping into the shadowy anchorage, I shrank to think what I might find awaiting me at the screen. Perhaps the monks had mistakenly let in some madman, or a murderer, or an awful beggar bearing blooming pustules of the plague. My bones knocked together. But then the figure lurking beyond the wooden slats hailed me in his warmest voice.

"Is that you, little Hildegard? God's teeth, you aren't so little anymore. A few more summers and you'll be taller than my sister."

The last time I'd laid eyes on Meginhard von Sponheim, he'd been a strapping lad of seventeen, horsing around with Rorich. Now he was a man—a handsome one—with a beard to match his fine head of curly brown hair. His smile was as blinding as the late summer sun.

"I've brought gifts," he said. "An ell of linen and fine embroidery thread. Isn't that how you ladies spend your days, praying and stitching?"

I blushed to have someone as noble as Meginhard von Sponheim calling me a lady. But my thoughts roved back to the courtyard where his sister sobbed and shrank.

"Jutta wants you to go away."

Sorrow seemed to tear at his face. "I brought sad tidings, that is true. My sister's old nag broke its leg and I had no choice but to slit its throat. It was the most merciful thing I could do. I didn't expect a religious woman would take the death of a beast so tragically."

I remembered how Jutta had pined for Silvermoon, her mare. That hank of silvery hair in her hands—it could only be horsehair.

"You brought her the dead horse's *tail?*"

"A keepsake. I meant no harm, child. Can you fetch her back to the screen for me? I'd hate to just leave her in tears after coming all this way."

His face was as beautiful as a man's could be, and Cuno preached that a fair face mirrored an even finer soul. Then why did Jutta dread him so much?

"She wishes you to go away. She *is* a recluse. Even the *abbot* doesn't disturb her when she wants to be alone."

Meginhard laughed, grinning as though he wanted to reach through the screen and pinch my cheek.

"My sister has made you her creature, I see. Her faithful little lap-dog."

The mocking tone that came through under the cloak of his charm left me cold. Instead of smiling back, I stared at him, the muscles of my face hardening.

"The bells are ringing for Vespers. The hour of visiting is over."

"But I must say goodbye to her." He laughed, as though I'd only been jesting. "I'm her brother, her only living sibling. There's a chain that binds us."

His words made my skin creep. I imagined an invisible chain stretching from him to Jutta's slender throat, fettering her in a stranglehold. For nearly two years, I had awakened to Jutta's nightmares, her voice shrieking out his name in the dark. I'd been privy to the way Jutta beat herself over and over. To the pains she took to hide her wounds from the monks. My stomach twisted at the memory of how Meginhard had once held me in his lap, his hands strumming through my hair as he bellowed out his tales of heathen gods just to make his sister cry. What had he done to make Jutta so afraid of him? What kind of brother brought his sister her dead mare's tail?

Behind him, the church filled with monks come to sing Vespers.

"Volmar!" I shouted.

But it was Abbot Adilhum who stalked toward the screen and glowered at me through the slats. "It's hardly seemly for an oblate to cater-waul."

My abbot's scrutiny made me quail. Then he turned his attention to Meginhard. If any other visitor had presumed to linger this late, causing such a stir just as the brothers assembled for the Holy Office, Adilhum would have booted the offender out of the gates. But Meginhard stood his ground, the smile never leaving his face.

"The cloistered life certainly hasn't robbed that child of her spirit—or her big mouth," he told the abbot.

Adilhum rested a fond hand on Meginhard's shoulder. Heir to the Sponheim dynasty, Jutta's brother was the abbey's greatest benefactor. Judging from the amount of gold he'd given our abbot, Meginhard might as well write his name on the monastery's title deed.

"Come, my son," said Adilhum. "Join us for Vespers."

When the two men had turned their backs, Volmar appeared at the screen.

"Why did you call me?" he asked.

"Meginhard made Jutta cry. She hates the sight of him. Can you make him go away?"

Volmar's eyes locked on to mine. "If she's crying, go to her at once. I'll make sure she's not disturbed again."

I wondered how he, a mere novice, could hope to stand up against the abbot and Meginhard.

"*Go*," Volmar urged, before melting back to join the others.

In the courtyard, Jutta lay stunned, a gash on her forehead. It looked as though she'd bashed her head into that unforgiving wall. Blood dripped down her face like tears. Her eyes were so still and unblinking that my heart stopped—was she dead? But when I touched her, she sobbed. I tried to hug her, but she shoved me away and crossed her fists over her breast.

Volmar kept his word. That evening, while Meginhard and Adilhum supped on roasted swan in the abbot's private parlor, a violent ague gripped Meginhard's bowels. The spasms left him squatting on the privy the entire night. The next morning, he was in too much agony to sit astride his horse and he was obliged to be carried away in a litter.

When Volmar told me this, I leaned toward the screen in excitement, as though the lives of the saints were unfolding before our eyes.

"God *smote* him!" I cried, thinking of how Saint Barbara's tyrant father chopped off her head, only to have God strike him down with lightning.

Volmar shook his head sadly. "It was my doing. I committed a grave sin, Hildegard. Do you know the properties of senna?"

"It loosens the bowels!"

"Indeed. I slipped a huge dose of the tincture into Meginhard's wine."

After Meginhard took his leave, Jutta sought an audience with Abbot Adilhum. Her head bowed in humility, she told the abbot that, after much reflection and prayer, she believed it was God's will that she renounce contact with secular men, including her own brother.

With Adilhum, Jutta was soft-spoken and poised, her veil drawn over her face to conceal the gash on her forehead. But after the abbot departed and Volmar came to the screen, she wept like a broken child.

Banished to the other room, I huddled behind the curtain in the doorway and eavesdropped, shedding tears of my own to hear Jutta so anguished. I couldn't help but listen to Volmar's murmurs, pitched with such sorrow and care. Volmar, the soul of compassion. I placed my every hope in him, for he alone had the power to comfort Jutta when she wanted to beat herself.

Jutta was just like the maiden in one of Walburga's tales. A wizard had cast his spell upon her and she lay in a dark, enchanted sleep, surrounded by a ring of fire. Only the chosen one, the true hero, could step through the flame. Volmar was the one soul Jutta let in as close as any human being could approach her. Peeking around the curtain, I saw his face at the screen. His innocent, hopeless love for Jutta bloomed before my eyes and I could not look away.

Volmar gave me precise instructions on the medicine I must administer to my ailing magistra. Steeped valerian root, its vile taste and smell disguised with forest honey, made the rigid mask of Jutta's face relax. She stopped crying, surrendered to the wave of drowsiness, and let me tuck her into bed. Within moments, she sank into sleep, her face peaceful, no longer looking haunted.

"Hildegard." Volmar tapped on the screen.

Even as I whispered to him in secrecy, my magistra was there, her spirit between us. When I looked into Volmar's eyes, I saw poor tortured Jutta.

"You must try to understand," he said. "She can't help what she does to herself." His voice was more tender than I thought a boy's could be. "A great wrong has been done to her. You must always remember that and be as gentle to her as you can, little sister."

"Her brother did something." I both longed and dreaded to know what had happened.

"May he sear in hell for the pain he caused that pure soul" was all Volmar would say on the matter. Whatever Jutta confided to him, he kept locked inside his heart.

What would it be like to have so faithful a friend, I wondered. *What would I have to do to make anyone love me half as much as Volmar loved Jutta?*

One night after Compline, as I was about to crawl into bed, Jutta pulled me close and cuddled me as though I were her doll.

"Hildegard," she whispered. "Have you ever carried a secret so shameful you thought you would die from it? Something too awful to tell your confessor?"

Thinking of my visions that both dazzled and frightened me, I nodded. Jutta's arms tightened around my waist.

"I've only told Volmar. But now I must tell you because . . . because you must understand why I took you with me."

Between ragged bursts of weeping, she revealed what she thought to be her gravest sin. She was no virgin. Her brother had stolen away her chastity against her will.

"He's my mother's darling golden boy." She spat out the words as if they were an anathema. "Whatever he does, Mother can see no wrong in him. When . . . when I tried to tell her what he did, she thought I was making up slanderous stories. Or that I was insane. Even you must have heard those rumors—they couldn't find me a husband because I'm madder than a cuckoo."

I just huddled there, limp and silent in Jutta's lap, as her pain cinched me, winding round and round my body like the spiked chains that penitents wear.

"She wouldn't believe me, even when I showed her the blood—"

Jutta clapped her hand over her mouth before going on.

"She tried to place the blame on a boy at court, someone I'd once flirted with. She tried to force him to marry me, but I knew he would despise me. I swore I'd kill myself if they wouldn't let me go to the monastery. But I'm soiled! Meginhard could betray my secret anytime he likes. I have nightmares about Adilhum casting me out as a whore."

"Cuno will protect you." I remembered the lovesick devotion I'd seen on our prior's face. "Besides, it's not your sin. It's your brother's." I squeezed her hands.

How I wished Volmar was here. He would be able to offer Jutta so much more comfort than I could with my clumsy stammerings.

"God will punish Meginhard," I told my sobbing magistra. "God will strike him with lightning and burn him in eternal fire."

"Now you understand why I brought you here at such a young age," Jutta choked out. "Before any man could do to you what Meginhard did to me."

I wished I didn't know. Jutta had saddled me with such an unwelcome knowledge. That night her nightmares became my own. In the deep trough of my dreams, Meginhard clawed his way through the screen, intent on punishing us both for our defiance. He hounded Jutta, then me, through our two small suffocating rooms.

Before, the tales of the virgin martyrs had just been stories. But Jutta's passion brought them to bloody life. Ursula and Barbara, Catherine and Agatha had been raped and defiled. Before Jutta's revelation, I had no idea what those words even meant. Barbara's father had locked her in a tower, and just like the saint, Jutta and I had landed in this prison because our families had wanted to be rid of the shame of us. My own mother had cast me out because of my visions. Jutta had chosen this confinement to heal her invisible wound that never stopped bleeding. Hidden from the world, we could at least find solace in the fact that God had vindicated each and every one of the virgin martyrs. Awakened them from the dead. Clothed them in pure gold. Raised them to the throne of heaven.

Just after the Feast of All Souls, which marked our second anniversary in the anchorage, Volmar gifted us with a white lily bulb in a pot of earth.

"I planted it myself," he said. "It will grow and blossom in time for Easter."

Cradling the pot, I gazed at the black soil and imagined the bulb opening, the plant bursting forth like a trumpet on Easter morning. The lily, pure and sweet. Jutta's favorite flower.

5

❧

AT FIFTEEN, I'D GROWN into a gawky thing, dwarfing Jutta, who seemed baffled that I, her handmaiden, stood taller than she did. Perhaps when she first took me into her care, she imagined I would remain a child forever, pliant and docile.

Now I was an ordained nun, having made my permanent vows of poverty, renunciation, obedience, and stability to Disibodenberg Monastery—as if I, an anchorite, had any other choice. No family members had come for my ordination, nor had the new Archbishop of Mainz, Adalbert, appeared, for he was held prisoner for daring to oppose Emperor Heinrich, a man so drunk on his own vainglory that he would have taken the pope captive to get his way. Instead, Archbishop Otto of Bamberg had made the long journey from distant Bavaria to perform the rite outside our anchorage screen while I prostrated myself on the cold stone floor and swore my obedience to God and to Jutta. The man had made such a monumental journey not for my sake, but because he was in thrall to Jutta and her holy reputation. Her disciple, I remained in her shadow, my entire existence relegated to submission and humility.

As far as my education was concerned, Jutta regarded me as finished. Though my grasp of Latin grammar was only elementary, I could read and write it as well as my magistra. I could recite each psalm from memory. The Rule of the Order of Saint Benedict and the lives of the saints had been drilled into me. Yet still I thirsted for a real education, the kind that my brother Rorich was receiving under the patronage of the prelates of Mainz. How I fevered to study the seven liberal arts: the trivium of grammar, logic, and rhetoric, and the quadrivium of arithmetic, geometry, astronomy, and music. The closest I could come to scaling such heights was to devour every book Volmar brought me from the library and to compose my own chants and antiphons on Jutta's ten-stringed psaltery.

My herbs flourished. I sowed and harvested in accordance to the phases of the moon and the feasts of the saints. After hanging my plants up to dry, I ground them with a mortar and pestle to make the philters and tinctures I passed through the hatch to Brother Otto, who administered them to pilgrims who came to be healed.

Watering my plants, I dreamt of the forest, so filled with greening. In my visions, I strode beneath rustling boughs loud with birds. The pictures streamed inside my head, one after the other, as unstoppable as blood, until one morning I awakened from a dream of a radiant cloud pregnant with a million stars. Drawing back my blanket, I discovered a red stain on my thighs, the curse of Eve. Even in this prison of shadows where Jutta dwindled and consumed herself, I witnessed the miracle of my own unfolding flesh, my girl hands turning to young woman hands as I repotted the chaste tree Volmar had given me. From my flat chest, swathed in shapeless wool, breasts emerged like new buds.

Every month the moon waxed to fullness, unleashing the flow that made me unclean. Jutta's never came — she had grown too thin for her woman's flesh to betray her in that way. Indeed, she ate and drank so sparingly that she hardly needed the privy pot. Her joints creaked and cracked as she hauled her frame, more bone than flesh, around our two tiny rooms.

Mirrors were forbidden, so I contrived to hold a pan of water in the sunlight, seeking to capture my reflection, but I only saw a pale, rippling phantom. Still I felt myself flourish. My body ripened, breasts and hips filling out, and I prayed I might grow into something as stately as a silver birch. According to Walburga's ballads, this burgeoning womanhood was the zenith of a girl's existence. *This time should be special and tender, even for me.* I thought I should at least have the liberty to walk in the full sunlight of the monks' cloistered garden rather than make do with the narrow shaft of daylight that was all our anchorage courtyard contained.

Mutiny raged inside me. I plotted how I might nab Jutta's shears from their locked casket and hurl them over our wall into the Nahe River so that my magistra could never again hack off my hair. I secretly wished she would pray herself into a stupor while I hid my growing tresses beneath my veil until they cascaded, gleaming and waving, down to my waist. Sometimes, when Jutta was having one of her spells, I seized the hair she had sliced off me the first day. Fingering that braid's softness, I tried to imagine its weight on my head.

How I longed to take one of my earthen garden pots and smash it through the wooden screen, forcing open a way to freedom. I'd bolt out of the gates into the forest, never to return. But before quitting this place, I'd seek Volmar, grab his wrists, make him look me full in the face so he could witness my transformation, that I was no longer a child but a woman. When I peeped at him through the slatted wood, I saw that he, too, had changed — now a young man and an ordained monk and priest. Yet whenever he spoke Jutta's name, his eyes glittered with love and sorrow.

Autumn drew in, heaping leaves of garnet and gold in our courtyard as my plants shriveled to stalks. Cupping each brilliant leaf in my palm, I traced every vein and curve. This was my devotion, my contemplation, during those short days when twilight stole in early and October fog muffled the church bells.

Around this time my chest seized up with the premonition that something was about to happen. At the pit of my stomach, I feared that Meginhard would return. After Jutta had banished him, he had established a brand-new Benedictine abbey in the shadow of his castle at Sponheim. For all we knew, he might have taken holy orders just to have an excuse to force an audience with his sister.

One afternoon Volmar announced an unexpected visitor at our screen. Blessedly, it wasn't Meginhard, but a woman of middle years who looked half-feral, as though she had been living in the wildwood with the lynx and deer.

"This is Trutwib," Volmar said. "The hermit."

I gaped hungry-eyed through the screen. A female hermit, living free, not enclosed but wandering wherever the spirit willed her? And what a creature she was with her graying hair, unveiled and unruly, looking as if a comb had not touched it in months. Her hands, as brown as acorns, were grained with dirt. She smelled of leaf mold and rich earth, of pine needles wet with rain. How did she survive, a woman alone outside the protection of monastery walls?

"Where is the holy Jutta?" the hermit demanded, her eyes wide and frank. "I've traveled many days to seek her."

Trutwib's broad vowels revealed her to be of peasant stock.

"My magistra is praying in the courtyard."

Jutta was huddled bare-kneed on the cold stone with rain pelting down on her. Her sufferings would bring salvation to others—this was what she swore. If Volmar's calling was to be a scribe and scholar, Jutta seemed to think that hers was to inflict as much pain upon herself as she could bear. *This is what God has called me to do, Hildegard. I am a living sacrifice.*

"The holy woman must not be disturbed," Volmar informed our guest.

"I'm a holy woman, too," Trutwib countered, hands on her hips. "Though I was never mad enough to let anyone brick me in a cell. I'll wait until she appears."

"What makes you a holy woman?" I asked.

Volmar had told me plenty about male hermits who, inspired by John the Baptist and the Desert Fathers of ages past, lived in the wilderness, some of them attracting hordes of disciples despite their professed desire to be left alone. He'd explained that the first nunneries were founded when enough female hermits gathered in the same place and they needed to provide asylum and shelter for themselves. But no one had told me that an ordinary peasant woman, no more exalted than Walburga, could declare herself holy, abandon her family and her overlord, and simply choose to live in the woods like a vagabond. Perhaps she was a heretic, one of the Cathari that Jutta had spoken of—men and women who called themselves the Perfecti, the pure and perfected ones who rejected the Church and all earthly possessions to wander around preaching, men and women alike. Or maybe Trutwib's low birth and lack of dowry, coupled with her willfulness and pride, prevented her from entering a religious house, even as a lay sister.

"I call myself holy," Trutwib said, "because God has granted me the gift of prophecy. I see visions, my girl." Her eyes burned into mine.

Every part of me prickled. Trutwib's visions were sacred, then? Who had told her so, what priest? Or had the hermit simply decided for herself? I decided that Trutwib must be one of the sarabaites that the first chapter of the Rule of Saint Benedict warned about—those stubborn souls who refused to submit to the authority of any religious order, who shunned the guidance of prior and abbot to elect only themselves as the best judge of what was holy and good.

"You may wait in the refectory," Volmar told her. He sounded awkward, as though unsure of how to address a woman of such low rank who seemed to exhibit every intention of courting heresy.

"No, I'll stay right here. Fetch me a stool, boy," she said. "I'll rest my bones until the holy Jutta is ready to see me."

"Where do you sleep?" I asked, when Volmar, now muttering to himself, went off to hunt for a stool. "What do you eat?"

"I sleep on a bed of branches, far cleaner than any bed of straw, dear girl. I am never bitten by fleas nor troubled by lice. I eat whatever God sends my way. I set snares for rabbits—"

"You eat the flesh of four-footed animals?" I asked, both scandalized and thrilled.

With no abbot or magistra standing over her, Trutwib was free to do whatever she pleased.

"Look at my cloak," Trutwib said, holding it up to the screen.

"It's made of rabbit pelts sewn together with sinews. Nothing goes to waste. Besides, I'm no refined lady like your mistress with pilgrims to heap gifts upon me."

"How do you know your visions don't come from the devil?" I asked, my eyes darting to Volmar as he lumbered through the church door with a three-legged stool.

Trutwib's glowing green eyes looked at me, looked *into* me. The hermit smiled. "I just know." She turned to Volmar. "Thank you, boy. Now fetch me a mug of beer, if you please."

I giggled before I could stop myself, watching Volmar, exasperated beyond reason, struggle not to snap at her impudence.

"We do not take refreshment in the church," he huffed. "If you wish to eat and drink, you must go to the refectory." He looked so pained that I winked at him.

"And you, my girl," Trutwib said, continuing to inspect me after Volmar had left. "How did the holy Jutta come to choose you as her companion?"

"I was only eight when she brought me here. She had no other takers. My mother wanted to be rid of me." The words spewed from my mouth with a bitterness that made me cringe.

"You're an honest one," Trutwib said. "Without illusions. This is good, my girl. Keep your clear head. It will be your salvation in years to come."

"Were you really going to drink beer in the *church?*"

"Who doesn't? The nave of the church belongs to the people. If you had any experience of life outside these walls, you would know that. Besides," she said, beaming at me, "beer is most wholesome and pleasing to God."

Smiling back at Trutwib through the screen, I longed to follow her out into the forest, adopt her as my new magistra. But just then Trutwib lifted her eyes and looked into the space behind me.

"There she is at last, the holy anchorite," said the hermit.

I turned and tried to see Jutta as Trutwib did—a woman of twenty-one, but as scrawny as an undeveloped child. My magistra had no breasts or hips, yet she was beautiful, her eyes as blue as larkspur, her cheeks stung pink from the cold.

"Who is this?" Jutta asked me, making a great show of ignoring the peasant woman who presumed to address her so directly.

Our guest spoke before I could. "I am Trutwib the Prophet. I have come to reveal your future."

Jutta lifted her chin in disdain, an aristocrat looking down at a tramp. "A prophet, you say? Only the pope himself may bestow such a title."

Trutwib didn't blink. "I know your destiny, my lady. Will you hear it or not?"

Jutta knit her hands together. She seemed as flustered as Volmar had been, not knowing how to contend with this person.

"Hildegard, leave us," she said.

Drooping in my disappointment at not being able to hear what the prophet had to say, I trudged out of the room, pulling the curtain in the doorway behind me. In the outer chamber, I pricked my ears to their murmurings. At first I only made out a few words here and there, but as Trutwib went on speaking, her voice picked up volume and power until I heard her prediction ring out, her words that changed everything.

"The one who lives under your wing, my lady, shall grow and grow until she outshines you. You will die, forgotten and obscure, and she shall blaze like the sun."

There being no brazier in the outer room, I was doubled over from cold when Jutta finally allowed me back in the main room where the shutters were now bolted to block the screen. Trutwib, I wagered, was long gone, her broad peasant feet taking her into the thick of the woods. I hoped the monks had found some beer for her, though it was more likely that Trutwib had to content herself with our sour apple wine.

"Come stand before me," Jutta said, her voice imperious. "Take off your veil so I can see you."

Trembling, I obeyed. Jutta's eyes were so hard and cold that I couldn't bear to meet them.

"That *woman* says you see visions. Is that true?"

Dumbstruck, I froze, tears flooding my eyes. Trutwib had only to look at me to divine my secret shame and then she had pulled the scales from Jutta's eyes. My magistra glared at me as Mother once had, as though I had betrayed her out of spite. No longer could I be Jutta's pet, the living doll she hugged for comfort when her anguish and loneliness overpowered her. No longer could I be her trusted handmaiden. Trutwib's revelation had turned me into my magistra's rival. First cast out of my childhood home and now out of Jutta's confidence, my heart raced in panic. I truly had nowhere left to hide.

Her bony fingers dug into my arms. "Tell me what you see."

As I stared at her, I saw the skull beneath her skin. The stench of her breath, rank from fasting, struck my face, forcing me to recoil. I could only sputter and stammer about things far too strange to understand. The Lady at the axis of the wheel of creation, the greenest branch sprouting from her and flowering. The sapphire man emerging from her bosom, his hands outstretched. Adam lay before him, naked and asleep, and from Adam's side, the blue Christ conjured a white cloud pregnant with a million stars and that brilliant cloud's name was Eve, shining and innocent till the serpent rose to throttle her in his great black fist.

"Nonsense," Jutta spat. "Those aren't visions, just wicked and heretical fancies. I must inform the abbot. Once he knows the truth, he'll cast you out."

I couldn't say anything more for the pounding of my heart. Could Jutta truly convince the monks to banish me? If my long-cherished dream came true and I could leave this place, where would I go? Mechthild, I was certain, wouldn't take me back. I could no longer flee to Rorich, who was owned by the Church as much as I was. What happened to the tithed souls the Church no longer wanted?

A throbbing ignited in my head, a poker-sharp pain behind my left eye that left me queasy. As Jutta continued to berate me, I saw her mouth open and close, but I could no longer hear her voice. *God has struck me deaf and mute for my presumption, my unholy vision. The Church has used me up and now she will spit me out.*

Somehow I groped my way to my pallet. Lying as corpse-still as I'd done when they first laid me in this tomb seven years ago, I waited for something to happen. For Abbot Adilhum to appear at the screen, drag a confession out of me, and then lay on a penance that would make hell seem merciful.

Instead, a cloud descended and from that billowing mist emerged a pale blue woman, crowned in majesty. *My name is Ecclesia, the true and hidden Church.* In her great arms, she cradled a company of consecrated virgins. They weren't veiled, weren't starving or frightened. They sported neither hair shirts nor scourges but were dressed like royal women, robed in crimson damask, crowned in gold, their unshorn hair flowing free. Faces alight with joy, they lifted their hands in prayer. The most beautiful girl with long black tresses smiled at me as though I were her dearest friend in all the world. *Have courage and endure. One day I shall come to you.*

As the apparition vanished, I sat bolt upright, my face burning, as though Jutta had caught me in some shameful act. My magistra regarded me with eyes as glittering and cold as frost.

Awaiting my audience with the abbot, I hovered between dread and mad hope. *Let them toss me out.* I had prayed for this moment for so long. Oh, to be free of this place, free of the fog of Jutta's pain, that poisonous vapor I was forced to breathe every living moment. I imagined myself staggering out of the monastery gates, an outcast left to find my own way in the forest. I'd set off like a lost pilgrim until Trutwib heard my cries and took me under her protection. Trutwib was a seeress—she would know how to find me. She would teach me how a free and masterless woman could embrace God. *Let the abbot come.* I would hurl my most heinous sins at Adilhum to force his hand. *I never desired this life. I hate this place. I hate Jutta. I hate you.*

The meeting never transpired. After another week dragged by, I understood that Jutta had thought better of the idea. Why should my magistra draw attention to my visions? Why should she take my fancies, as she called them, the least bit seriously? Perhaps she feared that if she divulged my secret to Adilhum, I might be tempted to reveal hers—that the holy Jutta was in fact no virgin.

The only thing Jutta said to me that week was one stark sentence.

"Trutwib is no prophet but a fool."

What could Jutta do with me, then? The sullen truth dawned that there was no way she could be rid of me, for like my magistra herself, I had made my vows before God. When she knelt at the screen to chant the Holy Office, she left no room for me but blocked my view into the church, my only glimpse of the outside world. Crouched behind her, I murmured my psalms in a whisper too choked to disturb her.

I turned my face to the wall, my head swimming, my entire body gone numb. My last chance of escape had turned to dust. *I will grow old and wither and die here.* This was my living death. I was but a ghost. I had become nothing.

To further escape my presence, Jutta sank even deeper into her sufferings, haunted as ever by Meginhard, whose crime remained etched on her body, racking her. When she awakened screaming from her night terrors, she beat me away if I dared to comfort her. By day, she fasted, scourged herself, moved through the anchorage rooms on her bare knees until they bled and festered, as if this could finally purge her of her brother's stain. If she couldn't make him vanish from this earth, she would make herself disappear, starving herself until her skin went gray and her teeth were stained brown, till her shorn hair began to fall off her scalp and down grew upon her face. Until her eyes, as huge as medallions, were her only beauty that remained.

Stirring inside my breast, the whisper grew into a roar until I was forced to admit that I mourned the Jutta I had loved. Once, like Eve, she had been as innocent as that white cloud full of stars, but then the serpent's poison sank into her, sickening and corrupting her. Now I could only watch, powerless to plead or help, as she grew more and more distant, shrinking deep inside herself to a place where even Volmar could no longer reach her.

"If only I knew what to do," Volmar whispered from his side of the screen.

Over and over again, he called Jutta's name until his voice grew as hoarse as an old man's. A few feet away, she knelt, her eyes open but unseeing, her soul flung into some other world.

"She used to trust me." He sounded so heartbroken that I longed to reach through the screen and clasp his hands.

"She despises me," I told him. "She'd get rid of me if she could and, by God, I wouldn't mind."

"Don't be disrespectful. She's still your magistra." Volmar sighed. "At least we know she'll remain safe and undisturbed. Her brother"—he merely mouthed the words lest Jutta hear them and fly into a panic—"has gone on a pilgrimage to the Holy Lands seeking penance."

I roiled with hatred for Meginhard. How easy for him to play the penitent, jaunting off to Jerusalem with the sun on his face and a fine horse to carry him, while I remained trapped in this hell with the fruit of his mortal sin, this shattered woman who would never be right again. My old love for Jutta brimmed, bringing tears to my eyes.

"It's melancholy," I said. "I told you from the beginning. One day it will kill her."

"She's so much more than a melancholic." Volmar's undying adoration illumined his face. "Jutta's a saint. Cuno appointed me to write her Vita, but how can I if she no longer speaks to me?"

Jutta would deny herself every last comfort, even Volmar's chaste, unselfish devotion. *If only he would cherish me that way.*

"Ask *me*." I grew bold. "I'll tell you anything you need to know."

Cuno appeared at the screen daily, not speaking but only kneeling to gaze at Jutta as she prayed, her face hidden in her veil. Like Volmar,

his love for her remained steadfast. It was as though the sainted anchorite were some tragic maiden locked in a tower. Though Cuno could
never touch her, he guarded the ground beneath her citadel, pledg-
ing himself as her champion, determined to protect her till her dying
day.

You foolish man, I wanted to scream. *If only you knew.* Now that my
magistra had withdrawn from the screen, the men who adored her
couldn't smell her rancid breath or see how her once-white teeth had
rotted to black stumps. Only I was privy to that.

As Jutta wasted away, the miasma of her unspoken resentment filled
the room until I thought I would gag on it. My magistra had never
forgiven me for Trutwib's prophecy. *The one who lives under your wing
shall grow and grow until she outshines you. You will die, forgotten and
obscure, and she shall blaze like the sun.* I wished Jutta would listen as I
struggled to persuade her that I, too, thought Trutwib was mistaken. *I
am no saint. I am full of sin. I will never be your equal.*

But as lacking in holiness as I knew I was, I was still everything
Jutta longed to be and was not, a true virgin gifted — or cursed — with
visions that came as pure gifts in their gleaming orbs, without my having to pummel or starve myself to summon them. In Jutta's mind, I
had done nothing to earn God's favor. Little could I dispute my magistra — I hadn't chosen any of this. But even as Jutta tried to freeze me
out, she appeared unable to ignore my absences when I knelt unmov-
ing, in thrall to the things I saw that she would never see. If these visions indeed came from God, why had God chosen me over Jutta? If
I could, I'd give it all away, lay every last gift at her feet, only to have
peace again.

Jutta ignored her pilgrims. In vain they loitered beyond the screen
while their holy woman huddled barefoot in the courtyard, clad only
in her hair shirt, regardless if it rained or snowed or pelted down hail-
stones. And so it fell upon me to receive our visitors. Over the months,
I grew accustomed to sitting beside the screen during the hour of visi-

tation and listening as the matrons and widows poured out their torments, telling me such secrets that blistered my ears. They revealed the unspeakable illnesses their husbands brought home from foreign battlefields. They poured out the sorrows they could tell to no priest. Of the cancers that ate away at their very breasts, of their struggle to love their own children, those infants who died like flies, one after the other, from croup and small pox, grippe and flux.

A fifteen-year-old bricked inside my anchorage, I knew little of the outer world in which these women struggled to survive. Their laments were my education. As my vocation demanded, I offered them my prayers, but I also told them what herbs might ease their afflictions. For those with cancers, I bade them go to the hospice and ask Brother Otto to give them yarrow, which helped prevent the growth of tumors, and violet salve, which healed existing tumors. To those maidens and matrons who believed themselves under attack from a man's love spell, I prescribed mandrake root. For those who simply wished to curb their husband's insatiable lust, I suggested marjoram and cowbane.

"Tell Brother Otto you need them to cure your headache."

One warm June day, a young priest appeared at the screen. He was tall and beautiful, and his brown eyes were shot with flecks of gold like brook agates. Upon seeing me, his face lit up with such love and pain that I could only gape at him stupidly, my palms dripping sweat.

"Hildegard," he said. "Don't you know me anymore?"

"Rorich?" Tears clouded my vision of his beloved face.

I threw myself at the screen, coming as close as I could to embracing him.

"I thought I'd never see you again!" I pulled back so I could gaze into his eyes. "Have you come to take me away?"

Hope beat so madly inside me that I didn't care if Jutta overheard and came charging in from the courtyard to upbraid me.

"Get me out of here, I beg you." My fingers poked through the screen to touch his. For seven long years I had dreamt of the moment when Rorich would rescue me.

His face crumpled. "Hildegard, you know I can't undo your vows."

"*Vows?*" I spat the word back at him. "I was just a child!"

He rested his brow against the screen. "Do you think your abbot will knock down those bricks even if I beg him on my knees? I had to grovel to the prelates just to get permission to visit you. I am bound by obedience just as you are."

Desolation swept through me and then a boiling rage.

"Those are fine words when you can walk out of those gates whenever it pleases you. Why did you even show your face here if you can't help me?"

"Mother is dead."

My brother's face turned ashen.

Mechthild. I sank to my stool. How many times had I tried to convince myself that she wasn't really my mother, that chilly, toothless harpy who had pressed me down into the grave dust beside Jutta seven years ago? Why did the news of her passing make me shrivel up and sob?

"The prelates allowed me to go to Bermersheim during her final weeks," Rorich said. "She died of cancer of the stomach."

I winced, my hands knit over my belly.

"Her agonies seemed endless. She struggled to form the simplest of words, yet we could tell she was trying to say something. The last word she managed to say, over and over again, was your name. She died regretting what she did to you."

I covered my face.

"She loved you. Truly. She thought to save you from a fate that might even be worse. Our sisters weren't lucky in marriage. Clementia has taken a vow of celibacy in order to leave her husband."

At least no one bricked her in. But my brother's grief forced me to acknowledge that I wasn't the only one to suffer. What must my sister have endured in her marriage to take such a drastic measure? The sad stories of my women pilgrims came back to me. Thick-headed as an ass, I had allowed my self-pity to blinker me from the fates of others. At least I could honestly say that I had never endured a man's violence.

"If Clementia seeks shelter, she may find it here, with Jutta's permission, of course." My words came choked and wooden.

"She has found refuge in a women's cloister in Mainz," my brother said. "Her health is frail. I don't know if she would survive the journey here. Keep her in your prayers."

I nodded, my throat swollen up.

"Father, Drutwin, and Hugo have returned from the Holy Lands. Father went to Mother's deathbed, but she didn't recognize him." The tears glistened on my brother's face. "She only wanted you."

Speechless, I remembered the times she had been tender, taking me in her lap and stroking my hair.

"Father is a broken man," Rorich went on. "Crippled in body and soul. I can only imagine what he witnessed—and committed—in the wars. Hugo is now acting as lord of Bermersheim. He's thirty, but he looks sixty and still needs to find a wife. Drutwin has joined me in Mainz. He wishes to take holy orders to cleanse himself of the blood he shed."

All those murdered Saracens and Jews. How sheltered my life was here. I hung my head while listening to my brother's litany of loss.

"You must have heard of the diseases brought back from the Crusades. Bermersheim has its first lepers. Before she died, Mother donated the monies for a lepers' squint to be built in the village church so that the poor souls can look in and follow Mass even though they may never step inside the church again."

"Rorich." Again I tried to touch his fingers through the screen. "Are you happy in Mainz?"

He was silent, his face in shadow. "The prelates seem to favor me. In a year or two, if I continue to enjoy their good graces, they might make me canon."

This, I knew, was the most fortunate outcome he could hope for, considering that his master, the Archbishop of Mainz, remained the emperor's prisoner.

"Sister," he said, "if and when I become canon, I'll return for you. I swear I'll do everything in my power to take you back with me then. Your abbot might listen to a canon."

I looked at my brother through my tears. So much was out of our hands.

"Give my love to Clementia and the rest," I managed.

"I know you aren't allowed to keep any personal possessions," he whispered, taking something from the pouch at his waist. "But Mother wanted you to have this."

After a glance around to make sure no one was watching, he slipped something shining through the screen into my palm. Mother's ring of jasper and silver. Mechthild had possessed no rubies as the Countess of Sponheim did, no garnets such as Jutta had worn before she renounced the world. The jasper ring was the finest adornment my mother had owned, more precious than any trinket my father had thought to give her. The ring had been her own mother's gift to her. Mother could have bequeathed it to any of my six beautiful sisters. Instead she had given it to me.

"Forgive her." My brother's eyes were imploring. "Pray for her soul."

Holding my mother's ring to my lips, I nodded, the tears streaming down my face.

Before taking his leave, Rorich presented me with an ell of wool, an offering from Father and Drutwin. The fleece had come from our sheep at Bermersheim. The women in our village had carded, combed, and spun the wool before our best weaver had woven it on her loom and dyed it pale green. Fingering the fabric, I imagined the women of Bermersheim singing their spinning songs, distaff in one hand, drop spindle in the other. I could picture them at work, but try as I might, I could not summon Father, Hugo, or Drutwin's faces, those men who were strangers to me, riding off to the Holy Lands while Mother still carried me in her womb.

With Jutta's and Cuno's permission, I cut the cloth to make vestments for Rorich.

"May your handiwork bring glory to Disibodenberg," Abbot Adilhum said, no doubt hoping that my brother would indeed rise to canon and inspire the wealthy merchants of Mainz to make donations to the humble monastery where his sister dwelled.

While I stitched, I tried to remember Clementia, how gracefully she had danced at the court of Sponheim, once upon a time, outshining even Jutta. My magistra, had she deigned to speak, would have ordered me to embroider the vestments with angels and saints. Instead, taking threads of dyed silk and wool, I decorated the robes with leaf and flower, agate and nettle, tree and branch, recalling my time in the forest with Rorich, our dreams of running away together and living like bandits.

My love for Rorich trumpeted inside me—all we had shared and might share again if only my abbot might soften. As I lost myself in my work, a vision shimmered before me. Trapped though I was inside the anchorage, the universe unfolded before my eyes, shaped like a great green egg brimming with life, as rich as the virgin forest with the purest streams surging through it. Encircling that wild greening like a necklace of gems were the four winds, the four elements, the sun and the moon, the seven planets, the entire starry firmament. Encircling all this was a ring of flame, the holiness of God, my Mother, blazing everywhere. Our abbot and prior preached that God was above all things, and yet my vision told me that God was *in* all things, alive inside every stone and leaf.

A white cloud, filled with light, opened and a voice began to sing. *I am the breeze that nurtures everything green and growing, that urges the blossoms to flourish, the fruits to ripen. I am the dew that makes the grasses laugh with the joy of life.*

Joy. I was transported, a child again, barefoot and laughing, lazing with Rorich on the mossy stream bank while the trees arched above us, mighty and protecting. One day my brother would keep his promise. He would come for me and take me back into that greening world of sunlight and leaf.

6

AT SIXTEEN, I WAS in the full flower of my young womanhood, such as it was, and scribbling a furtive letter to Rorich.

> My abbot has told us that Adalbert, Archbishop of Mainz by the grace of God, shall soon be released from his imprisonment and restored to his rightful office. And that you, my brother, shall become canon.

My wooden stylus scratched the words on a wax tablet before I committed them to the precious parchment I would have to beg off of Cuno.

> Don't forget your promise, I beg you. Life has become unbearable here. Jutta is a walking corpse who stinks of the grave. Before long, I shall die of my own despair.

My stylus hovered over the tablet. If I penned such an outrageous letter, Cuno would surely show it to Adilhum, who would not only refuse to allow it to leave the monastery gates but also inflict a severe penance on me.

"What are you writing?" Jutta's bony fingers stabbed a needle through the linen altar cloth she was struggling to embroider. Hunger and imprisonment in these dark rooms continued to exact their toll—her eyesight was fading. Her stitches, loopy and uneven, resembled the efforts of a five-year-old.

"I'm copying out the Vita of Saint Ambrose from the book Volmar lent us," I lied, showing her the tablet that I knew she could no longer read. "Is there anything I may copy for you, magistra?" I pitched my voice as sweetly as I could to hide the insolence that beat so hard inside my chest.

"For that I have Volmar," she replied, cool and aloof, holding his devotion to her over my head.

My eyes stung and my skin burned. If only I could keep my thoughts chaste, I might have some peace. But I couldn't chase Volmar out of my heart, my only true friend in this hell. In truth, my secret yearnings would have him become much more than a friend. The dreams I had of Volmar left me quivering like plucked psaltery strings.

Volmar was acting as Jutta's private secretary, for Prior Cuno deemed it fitting for a woman of Jutta's stature to have a dedicated scribe. Volmar appeared each morning between Prime and Terce to write the letters she dictated and to attend to her every wish. Did she require fresh straw for her bed, mulled wine to ease her cough, new strings for her psaltery? Could the lay brothers launder her blankets and linens?

During her audience with him, Jutta sat well back from the screen, hiding shadowed in her veil, so he couldn't see her wasted face or smell the stink of her slow starvation.

That particular March morning I arose from my stool, my wax tablet in hand, prepared to leave the room to give Jutta and Volmar their privacy. My magistra, however, called me back.

"Stay and listen, Hildegard. This concerns you."

Like a scolded child, I returned to my stool and lowered my head while she conversed with Volmar, who couldn't mask his love for her if he tried.

"I must write a letter to my mother," she informed him. Beneath her brusque words, her speech revealed a vulnerability, a loneliness aching to be soothed.

Volmar sat with his wax tablet to take down the message that he would later transcribe to parchment, forming each letter with grace and beauty, perfecting Jutta's grammar until the Latin was flawless. Of course, Jutta's mother couldn't read German, let alone Latin. When the letter arrived, the countess's chaplain would read it to her and then write down the countess's reply.

Ignoring Jutta's dictation, I tried to catch Volmar's eye through the screen, but his head was bent over his tablet. Reaching under my veil, I fingered a tendril of hair growing past my nape. With Jutta's eyesight fading, I had taken outrageous liberties. When she handed me her shears every quarter, I only pretended to cut off my hair. Hidden beneath my veil, it grew and grew. What would Volmar make of my flaxen curls? I wondered if he had ever laid eyes on a girl's uncovered hair. Did his thoughts also stray to the impure? Did he dream, as I did, of carnal love? I closed my eyes as a warm flush enveloped my body.

On my tablet I wrote, *Like billowing clouds, like the never-ending rush of the stream, longing can never be stilled.*

"The sad conclusion I must draw," Jutta dictated, "is that Hildegard is an unworthy companion for this life. Her spirit is too coarse, too full of stubbornness and sin."

My heart stopped. Did she mean to be rid of me after all? The wax tablet fell from my hands and hit the floor with a clatter that made my magistra cringe.

"My sister in Christ," Volmar interjected. "Surely you can't mean that. Hildegard has been your steadfast friend."

My eyes moistened to hear his kindness.

Ignoring him, Jutta soldiered on with her letter. "But Christian mercy forbids me to cast her out of this, her only home."

Picking my tablet off the floor, I wrote in a shaking hand. *Rorich, save me before I rot here.*

"After much prayer," Jutta continued, "God has revealed to me that it would be most pleasing to his eyes if I could receive new and more fitting handmaidens. Let them be young oblates with tender hearts who respect what a gift it is to join me in this holy seclusion."

The inside of my mouth went dry. So dragging me down into this living grave wasn't enough. Now that I had grown into a woman with my own mind, she would demand that yet more young lives be sacrificed to her madness. She would force me to stand by and watch as she broke those children just as she had broken me. And I had no doubt that the oblates would come. Their parents, eager to earn the favor of the court of Sponheim, would offer their girls to Jutta as they might have shunted them off into unwanted marriages. This had nothing to do with God and everything to do with the vanities of the world.

Closing my ears to my magistra's reprimands, I staggered out into our courtyard. Reeling between my potted seedlings, I prayed to the Spirit pulsing all around me, in every grain of soil, in the wind that swept the mare's tail clouds. *Please stop her.*

Later that day I committed my gravest sin to date. Tearing a page from the *Life of Saint Ambrose,* one of the four great Latin Doctors of the Church, I worked with my knife, scraping off each letter till every last trace of ink flaked away, leaving the parchment as bare as Adam beneath the Tree of Life. Dipping my quill into the ink I had mixed for myself from pulverized oak gall and gum arabic, I wrote my pleading letter to Rorich. What would happen when Volmar — or Cuno — discovered the missing page? My fear of never reaching Rorich was greater.

After Prime the next morning, I pushed my scrolled missive through the screen into Volmar's hand.

"Make sure it's delivered, I beg you." I didn't hide my tears from him.

Jutta, stirring beneath her veil on the far end of the room, asked me what I was doing.

"She only asked for another book to read," Volmar told her.

His eyes, as wide as heaven, locked on to mine as he hid my letter in his sleeve.

. . .

The clouds opened, lashing down March rain that flooded our courtyard and threatened to wash my fragile seedlings from their pots. My head fuzzy from the Lenten fast, I bent over the monks' cowls I was sewing. The paths and tracks of the forest would turn to deepest mud. Rain would swell the rivers, the Nahe and the Glan, until they burst their banks. Even if Volmar had succeeded in passing my letter on to a messenger without attracting Cuno or Adilhum's attention, would it ever reach my brother? And supposing Rorich received my message—could he truly presume to come here and demand my release even if he was elected a canon of Mainz Cathedral?

Pentecost brought summer's full tide of light and heat. My surviving seedlings began to grow, tender and fragile as their leaves struggled upward to embrace the sun. I played the psaltery for Jutta, whose fingers had become too stiff and sore to pluck the strings. In the baking heat, she shivered, her skin goose-pimpling as though she were in the grip of frostbite. She shrouded herself in her veil as if to block out the entire world, even Volmar when he came after Prime, his tablet in hand.

While my magistra turned her back on his wounded face, I tiptoed to the screen to deliver her message. "She only wishes to speak to you once a week. She says this daily hour of business has taken too much time from her prayers."

My heart in my throat, I watched his eyes brim red. Neither Volmar nor I had imagined the day would come when Jutta would spurn him, her most trusted confidant. A true ascetic, Jutta would deny herself every conceivable solace, even Volmar's blameless love.

"The Rule of Saint Benedict forbids special friendships," she told me later, as though for my personal admonishment since she knew how I pined for Volmar just as he longed for her. "Even if such attachments are as pure as David's love for Jonathan, they come between us and God."

No, I wanted to argue, *other people's love brings us closer to God, for how can God be found if not through love?* It even said so in the First Epistle of John: *He who does not love, does not know God, for God is love.* If it hadn't been for Volmar's kindness, I would have lost all faith during my first year in the anchorage. Only his friendship gave me the courage to endure this life that Jutta deemed so holy.

My magistra summoned Cuno for some whispered conversation, presumably on the subject of inappropriate affections. Cuno must have relayed her message to the abbot, for the following week Adilhum sent Volmar to Worms Cathedral, supposedly to copy manuscripts for our library. With my only friend gone, my heart splintered to pieces. My life became a scorched wasteland, devoid of hope.

Part of my soul traveled with him, for I knew that Volmar was sick with melancholy. The woman he had loved so patiently had banished him from his own abbey, punishing him for his very empathy. Eight years of constant care he had lavished on Jutta, yet she had turned on him, haughty and contemptuous. No one could touch her anymore.

In Volmar's absence, Cuno became Jutta's secretary. When I listened to him read her the letters concerning the two young oblates who would join us in November upon the Feast of All Souls, I prayed that something would happen to save these children from their fate.

Toward the end of August, a message from my brother arrived, his words riddling and oblique.

> Sister, have faith. I will be there when the walls of Jericho come tumbling down. Be prepared. When the hour comes, you must act and not hesitate.

In September, just after the seventeenth anniversary of my birth, Volmar returned from Worms, his satchels bursting with the manuscripts he had copied. When he appeared at the screen after Prime, my friend looked haggard, his eyes dark-rimmed and puffy as though he hadn't slept in weeks. Jutta drew her veil over her face and shuffled out of the room, sending her silent command that I, too, was to shun him and slam the shutters in his face. Instead, I pressed my hand against the screen until he touched his palm to mine. I wasn't Jutta, wasn't his beloved, but his eyes showed how much he had missed me.

Not that day, but later, when my magistra was lost in her tunnel of prayers, he revealed to me his deepest shame.

"Hildegard," he said, his voice a shaken whisper.

I pressed my ear to the screen to hear him properly.

"I've done something so foul that I don't dare confess to Adilhum." His despair cut into me. "Once you told me your secret. About your visions. I kept it safe, Hildegard. I never betrayed you."

"I know," I whispered, catching the glint of his tears through the screen.

"You are the only one," he said. "The only one I can trust."

My throat swelled with my unutterable love for the man.

"I shall carry your secret to my grave," I whispered.

"When I was in Worms, I was led astray." His face twisted away from mine. It seemed his eyes were searching the abbatial church to make sure there were no eavesdroppers.

I waited until he turned to me again.

"I wasn't the only one, Hildegard. The monks there were worldly, hardly seeming to care about their vows. One day I was with two brothers, both of them laughing like village drunkards, and they led me through the twisting streets of that city. The abbot had given us permission to go to the market to buy vellum. We walked past many houses, both rich and poor. Merchants selling every imaginable ware. I was like a child, gaping at the wonders to be seen.

"The press of the crowd was so powerful that I found myself separated from my brothers. Losing my way, I strayed inside the Jewish quarter, which aroused my curiosity, for I've heard that their rabbis are more learned than the greatest scholars in Christendom. All their children, even the girls, are taught to read the Scriptures. They give them cakes shaped in the form of Hebrew letters to teach them that learning is sweet.

"As I was staring at their synagogue, my brothers found me and chided me for getting lost. There was something in their faces I couldn't trust. I sensed trouble ahead, yet still I went with them, for I was but a stranger in that great city. Instead of buying vellum, my brother monks dragged me to a house of ill repute."

Volmar stopped short.

"It's a sin for me to poison your mind. You probably have no idea what such places are," he muttered.

"I've heard of brothels," I whispered, shocking him with my candor. "I'm not wholly ignorant of the world."

After all, hadn't I listened to our pilgrims' lamentations on how their husbands had caught diseases in such places? I prayed that Volmar would be spared such a fate.

"In truth," my friend said, speaking to me as though I were a priest with the power to absolve his sins, "I can't blame the others entirely. I could have resisted, but instead I allowed myself to be tempted. That day I broke my vows."

He shuddered as though an empty chasm had opened inside him where his soul used to be.

"And . . . this is worse, Hildegard, and this is why I only dare tell you. I committed the deed while thinking of *her*."

"Jutta," I murmured, my hand on the screen edging toward his.

"How could I even think of her that way? I'm damned."

"You acted out of love." Every part of me ached with my secret passion for him. "Besides, do you think you are the only one in this monastery who has been beguiled by the flesh?" My heart was pounding so hard that I wondered if he could hear it.

"Sins of thought are one thing," he said. "But I have committed the act."

He seemed as though he might rear away from me in his mortification.

"Your love is the only thing that saved her," I told him fiercely. "She loves you, too, every bit as much as you love her, but she hates herself for it. She might have died by now without your care." I swallowed, the tears running down my face. "There are worse sins than love, Volmar."

He managed a faint smile. "So you don't hate me for what I did, little sister?"

"If I were a man who had the liberty," I said, my cheeks burning fever-hot, "I might have yielded to the same temptation. Tell me," I blundered on before I could lose my nerve, "what was it like?"

His face was awash in deepest vermillion, his eyes transfixed. "I felt as though I were a stag leaping through the forest on the hottest day of summer. I ran on and on with none to stop me until the heat became so exquisite and unbearable that I plunged into a deep fountain. I can't describe the sweetness."

He turned ruefully as I listened with my mouth hanging open, remembering how the stags in our forests bugled in their rut every autumn. Our most fervent chanting, singing, and church-bell ringing couldn't drown out the tumult. I looked into Volmar's eyes.

"Was she pretty?" I asked.

"She had hair like sunlight."

What would happen, I wondered, if I drew back my veil to reveal my own unshorn locks, flaxen pale?

"She was not yet hardened by that life. She laughed and sang to put me at my ease. She was free of shame, Hildegard, and gave every sign of pleasure." Then he stopped himself abruptly. "Now I have corrupted your innocent young mind."

"It's good that I know something of the flesh. Sometimes pilgrims come with their worldly concerns. How can I be of use if I know nothing?"

All I'd heard of the act of carnality had been Jutta's wrenching tales of how her brother had ruined her, body and soul. But Volmar had opened a door for me—desire could be a thing of bliss.

"The Tree of Knowledge," Volmar said sadly. "I've tasted its fruit."

91

"I have something to confess to you," I whispered before he could draw away.

Now I thought I could unveil my secret love for him, offer it to him like a budding rose. When he looked at me with his kind gray eyes, my vision flooded with dancing sparks.

"What is it, little sister?"

Could I tell him? Could I?

Blinking back tears, I began to stammer. "I tore a page out of the *Life of Saint Ambrose* to write that letter to my brother."

Volmar laughed and laughed, breaking the Rule of Saint Benedict.

"Never fear," he said, wiping tears from his eyes. "Your misdeed shall never come to light. Your loyal servant penned a fresh page and sewed it back into the book before anyone could notice it was missing."

Giddy from what I hadn't been able to tell him, I smiled into his eyes to prove my gratitude.

When October gripped us in its fist of shadows, I thought my very soul might dissolve into the rising darkness. A funereal pall clung to everything. By night, the Wild Hunt of Walburga's tales blasted across the skies with the hosts of the dead, drowning out our psalms as we staggered out of bed for Matins. Dawn lagged later and later. At odd moments in the night, my pounding heart awakened me, pain cinching my lungs as I thrashed in a panic, the taste of ash and grave dust in my mouth. Jutta remained serene, counting the days until the new oblates arrived.

Though I prayed that time might stand still, or that an earthquake might destroy our anchorage, or that a flood would hinder the girls' arrival, the end of October was upon us and our monastery was crammed with guests, the most illustrious being Adalbert, the Archbishop of Mainz, newly released from captivity. Lauded as a hero for opposing our despot emperor, he held court among his clerics. My heart burst at the sight of Rorich drawn along in the archbishop's entourage as they swept out of the church after High Mass. Glancing at the screen, my brother's face flashed the message that I alone could decipher. The cryptic promise in his letter burned in my heart: *I will be there when the walls of Jericho come tumbling down. Be prepared. When the hour comes, you must act and not hesitate.*

On the Eve of All Souls, when the girls underwent the ceremony, the monks would knock down the stones blocking our doorway. For a short time that passage would remain open. The walls of Jericho would come crashing down while outside in the courtyard my brother would be waiting. All I needed to do was burst out and hurl myself at Rorich's feet. Jutta, I reckoned, would be happy enough to see the last of me.

My stomach fluttered. My heart raced in anticipation. Light-headed, I couldn't sit still and paced about our prison until I drove Jutta to exasperation. Muttering, she withdrew to the courtyard.

Just as I thought I couldn't be any more agitated, Volmar appeared at the screen, his face aglow in his gratitude to me, his confidante and keeper of his secret. He seemed sadder and wiser after tasting that forbidden fruit, as though his sin had rendered him more forgiving of others. Though I was glad I'd been able to give him some peace, I blushed and flustered even to look at him, for my unspoken desire still flamed inside my breast. How could he not see it? My throat burned to confess my love, yet as always I was silenced, stymied. But what if I succeeded in fleeing this hell? Could I really leave Volmar behind without revealing my true feelings for him?

I opened my mouth, my confession on the tip of my tongue, but he spoke before I could.

"Hildegard, here are the new oblates."

A girl who looked about eleven or twelve approached the screen. Not such a terribly young age. Not as young as I had been. Old enough to choose for herself, please God. Girls only a year or two older were given in marriage. But did she really know what lay in store for her? I felt like a traitor even to speak to this child whose living entombment offered my only chance of escape.

"Brother Volmar says you are as learned as Saint Catherine herself," she blurted out. "He said you'll teach me Latin and scribing and music and astronomy. I want to learn about the planets."

"Your name, child?" I longed to screech out a warning, order her to run away while she still had a chance.

"Adelheid." She spoke in the long, flat vowels of those who lived in the northern reaches of Saxony. Mother of God, the girl was so far from home. "I can already write my name and the Pater Noster," she went on. "But I would learn so much more from you!"

Her hair was mousy and her skin was sallow, but she was bursting with intelligence. Her face shone with the hunger for knowledge that I knew so well. I wanted to crumble in a heap as she gazed at me with such hope. After my exodus, I hoped Volmar would be as kind to her as he had been to me, lending her every book she requested. Then I wondered if Jutta, with her clouded vision, was still capable of teaching a child much of anything.

"And this is the other oblate, Adelheid's sister, Guda," Volmar said. He appeared troubled, his face creasing.

Looking through the screen, I saw no other girl until I followed Volmar's lowered gaze to a child who appeared no older than five, so tiny she could barely peep over the bottom of the screen. With her golden ringlets, she was as pretty as the wooden doll she clutched as she craned her neck to stare at me, her eyes so frightened that I lost all composure.

"She's too young." I made no attempt to hide my outrage. "Blood of Christ, what was their mother thinking?"

"Hildegard, you speak out of turn." Jutta had crept up on me, her fingers closing like pincers on my arm as she attempted to yank me from the screen, but I planted my feet, as obstinate as a cardinal's mule.

"Our mother's dead," Adelheid said quietly.

"Then who decided to offer you to Disibodenberg?" My voice was scathing.

"Our aunt." Adelheid's face was as red as clay.

"Am I wanted?" A tall woman stepped into view.

Though she didn't appear to be much older than my seventeen years, her dignity of bearing rendered her queenly. Her woolen gown was embroidered with silk and golden thread, and her veil was of whitest linen. A circlet of fine white brass crowned her brow. The pearls at her throat matched the translucence of her fair skin.

"Kinswoman," Jutta said from the depths of her veil, her voice almost obsequious. "Hildegard, show some deference. This is the Margravine Richardis von Stade."

As a margravine, she outranked even Jutta's mother, the countess. Stade, her home, was a port on the Elbe River, close by the North Sea, where, not so long ago, Viking ships sailed in to trade and plunder. This woman with her ice-blue eyes looked bold enough to take on those Norse barbarians.

"Lady margravine, I beg you to reconsider," I said. "The anchorage is no place for a small child."

Jutta drew breath as though she were about to spit fire at me. "Hildegard, that's enough."

"Magistra, let her speak." The margravine's cool blue eyes rested on mine. "Truly, it pleases me to know that Sister Hildegard has greater concerns for my little niece than the size of her dowry. Unlike your abbot, I must say. Lest you think me heartless, let me tell you that an even harsher fate might befall these girls outside your walls."

Adelheid looked from me to her aunt, then hugged her little sister's shoulders.

"When I was scarcely older than Adelheid," the margravine said, "I was married off to a man thrice my age. Of the six babes I have borne him, only two sons still live. Meanwhile the girls' mother, my sister, is dead. Their father thought to offer Adelheid in marriage, only the intended bridegroom refused her, thinking her not beautiful enough, and set his sights on Guda instead. I am their godmother, as well as their aunt. Do you think I would allow this?" The pain on her face was stark.

Adelheid spoke up, fierce and fervent. "That man is *hateful!* I don't want to die having his brats. I want to learn Latin so I can read the books in your library. Brother Volmar told me that your library is full of treasures!"

"He speaks the truth," I conceded, touched that my friend had taken such pains to make Adelheid welcome. "But why an anchorage, my lady? Would not a nunnery be more suitable?"

"Sister Hildegard, what stronghold could be safer than this?" the margravine asked, as though bemused by my ignorance of the world. "Jutta's reputation for holiness is unparalleled. Even the girls' father and my own husband must bow before your magistra's might."

At that, Jutta shouldered past me to welcome her oblates. "Only virgins may know the heights of heavenly bliss, my children."

Evidently the margravine and Adelheid had made up their minds and no words of mine could dissuade them. Indeed, it was no secret that men stooped to arranging marriages for girls as young as Guda, although presumably the consummation of such a match would not take place until the child was of age.

Trying to look at it through the margravine's eyes, I could understand how, for some, the anchorage might appear to be a refuge. There were parents who liked to deposit their daughters within cloistered walls, sheltered from the ravages of war and the machinations of dynastic marriages. Some were not above whisking their daughters back into secular life when they thought it prudent and could arrange a more advantageous betrothal. I imagined that even our abbot could be persuaded to release Adelheid and Guda with the right sort of bribery, though he would be sure to hold fast to their dowries.

The whole matter galled me.

Hours later, when the veil of darkness descended, I knelt behind Jutta and stared through the screen at the church alight in funeral tapers. My sweating hands were clenched in a mockery of prayer while the awfulness I had spent nine years struggling to forget swam before me. The abbot and archbishop, the monks and priests, my brother Rorich among them, chanted "*Veni creator*" while the Margravine von

Stade led Adelheid and Guda toward the bed of grave dust and naked branches. Clad only in their scratchy hair shirts, the girls shivered and quaked, their bare feet treading the cold stone floor.

Little Guda gazed up at her aunt as once I had gazed at my mother, as though trusting that her kinswoman would sweep her up in her arms and take her home. But the margravine stood firm until the child did as she was bid.

Two girls buried forever with a skull-faced madwoman. As the bile forced its way up my throat, I silently mouthed Rorich's name. Once, twice, I caught him glancing at the screen. If it was too late to save these children, I could at least save myself.

Jutta drew back her veil to smile at me with her black stumps, as though she divined exactly what I conspired and she expected no better of me. Again and again, I had proved myself to be the most wretched sinner, utterly unfit for this vocation. My visions were aberrations that rendered me a heretic. Let the Church spit me out as unworthy. Cowering behind my brother, I would creep away from this place.

A white cloud burst before my eyes, its light leaving me faint. A pale blue woman towered above me, so mighty that her crowned head reached into heaven. Ecclesia, the Mother Church, she whom I'd seen before, her arms embracing a company of maidens, their long, unveiled hair flowing free. Not a single sad anchorite among them, they rejoiced, the sun gleaming on their faces, gold and jewels adorning their brows. Consecrated virgins to whom God's service was perfect freedom, unbridled bliss. My fists against my temples, I tried to force away the shimmering vision.

The first hammering blow struck our blocked-up doorway.

Jutta did nothing to stop me from lurching forward as close to the shuddering stone as I dared. Fragments of mortar and chipped brick hit my face until finally the pick struck all the way through, allowing in a draft of cold air scented with frankincense. The drone of chanting filled my head with an unbearable buzz that vibrated down my bones.

Chisels and picks kept hacking away as though the monks were miners searching for the motherlode, a vein of gold. First the opening was only big enough for my hand, then it widened into a passage broad enough for an infant to pass through. I caught glimpses of torchlight, those many assembled bodies, and the oblates in their hair shirts, their faces ghostly with smeared ash. Adelheid dared to dip her head and peek through the aperture, her eyes, stark with fear, meeting mine as though I had the power to soothe away her terror.

With the monks working steadily, the opening grew to a size big enough for Guda to squeeze through, but they would have to keep on laboring until it was large enough to admit a grown man. I remembered how, during my own induction rite, the old Archbishop of Mainz, now dead, had entered the anchorage to admonish Jutta and me to obey God before he left us there, giving word to the monks to brick up the passage.

My moment would come soon and be all too fleeting. Rorich had begged me to *act*. Before the archbishop stepped in, I must shoot forth. I searched the throng for my brother's face, but everything was a blur of smoking torches and cloudy incense. Please God, let Rorich stand where I could see him. If I just flew out in a blind panic, Adilhum or Cuno could force me back inside.

Brick and stone crumbled to the ground until at last the doorway was free. *Now, now, now.* But I could see Rorich nowhere. Had he lost his nerve? What consequence would he face if he went through with this, what dire penance? I edged forward. Even if I failed, this was my only chance.

Shaking as though palsied, I took my first step, placing one foot in the rubble. But then the archbishop himself was blocking my escape. The holy water he flicked ran down my face like tears. *Be bold. Squeeze past him. Quick.* Another faltering step, this one over the rubble, my sandaled foot in the courtyard. Friendless except for Volmar, I was of no importance to the brothers of Disibodenberg. They could discard me as easily as they would a moth-eaten rag.

In the courtyard I whirled round, seeking Rorich. Stumbling on, I spotted my brother's face at last. His lips silently mouthed my name.

A small hand clutched mine. I looked down to see Guda gazing up at me, scared and imploring, begging to be comforted.

"Magistra," she lisped.

I shook my head. "Jutta is your magistra, not I."

Rorich jerked his head, urging me to come quickly to his side.

Adelheid took my other hand and smiled bravely. "Our godmother told us we could trust you."

Far from seeing me as a Judas attempting to escape, these girls thought that I had emerged from the broken doorway to welcome them into their new and eternal home. Adelheid squeezed my hand while Guda clung to my skirts as though I were her new mother. The little girl broke my heart, the way she hugged my legs as though she'd never let me go.

Nine years ago I had made my solemn promise before the old archbishop to love God and love my neighbors. Now the enormity of my vow overshadowed me. I didn't care for poverty or renunciation. Obedience rankled me most of all. But it was the commandment to *love* that held me in its grip. The plight of these girls loomed greater than my own misery, even my own freedom. Someone must guide them, protect them, mother them, save them from despair and the specter of Jutta's long and languorous dance with her true bridegroom, who was not Christ but Death.

The tears spilling from my eyes blinded me to my brother's imploring face. I was a sinner through and through. But even I couldn't bear to abandon these young souls to Jutta. This was the moment my true vocation began.

I shall never forget the look Jutta threw me when I staggered back into the anchorage with my arms around those frightened children who were meant to be *her* oblates, *her* protégées. Though her eyes were dimmed, they raked me over, sharp and accusing, as I held the girls instead of letting them lie like corpses on the floor while the archbishop spoke his blessings over them. My heart in my throat, I crooned to Guda to still her sobbing as the monks blocked up the doorway again, brick by brick. Smoothing the ashes from the girls' hair, I whispered stories about the halcyon bird laying her eggs and the mother bear tenderly licking her unformed cubs into shape before I finally eased the shivering children to sleep in the new pallets prepared for them.

Afterward, my Bridegroom came to me in a vision, sapphire blue, his wounded palms outstretched. *In me, the weak are made strong and mock the mighty.* Gazing straight into the sun, I cried out to him, the most beautiful youth, whose Light eclipsed me.

7

JUTTA SOON TURNED away from her oblates, as I knew she would, sinking back into her sepulcher of deprivation.

The reality of the children in our anchorage, their sheer physical presence and noise, little Guda's inability to stay awake through the endless night office of Matins, their inevitable tantrums and defiance drove Jutta to despair. She couldn't fathom that, even in this tomb, Guda was still a little girl who needed to play. The child was forever scooping the rushes off the floor and bundling them into dolls that she hid up her sleeves until I finally found where Jutta had hidden the baby Jesus doll she had once tried to give to me.

Jutta with her skeleton hands and corpse breath—the girls called her Lady Death behind her back. At first Guda and Adelheid were amazed at how our magistra could survive on so little sustenance, but near the end of their first week of captivity, Jutta's ravaging hunger left her so greedy that she stole the food off the oblates' trenchers, leaving me no choice but to surrender my own portion to the children.

The entire care of those girls fell upon me, the one with heretical visions. Even my hopeless infatuation with Volmar was swept aside as I struggled to infuse the children with some spark of purpose, some tiny light of happiness.

My first task was to educate the oblates. Wax tablet in hand, I did my utmost to delight them with the miracle of my scratches in the wax transforming letter by letter into the psalms we sang for the Divine Office. But Guda writhed in boredom before bolting away to the courtyard. Even Adelheid seemed listless, the fierce fire of her hunger for learning dwindling from the lack of air in this suffocating place.

"You want to learn more than the psalms," I said, thinking that if I proved I understood Adelheid, she might grow to trust me. "I'll ask Volmar to send us the bestiary. It has the most wondrous illuminations. Even Guda will love it."

Adelheid regarded me contemptuously, as though I had insulted her intelligence.

"What use is a bestiary?" she asked. "The only creatures we'll see here are spiders and mice."

The girl's resentment filled the room like black smoke.

"You said you wanted to learn about the stars," I said, desperate to coax a smile from her. "Why, I've heard about a Moorish instrument called the astrolabe—"

The roar and crash echoing from the courtyard made my heart leap out of my chest. Next came Jutta's outrage as the racket jolted her from her prayers.

"Demon spawn! The child is possessed."

Dropping the tablet, I raced to the courtyard. Little Guda was tearing around, smashing every herb pot she was strong enough to lift. Howling in her fury, she'd kicked off her sandals. I winced to see her bare feet stomping on the jagged shards.

"Darling, stop. You'll hurt yourself." Falling to my knees in the spilled dirt and broken pottery, I took hold of her arms.

Wriggling loose, the little girl clawed my cheeks and spat in my eyes.

"You're an ugly witch! I hate you!"

Jutta smiled like a lizard while administering Guda's penance.

The child was to stand out barefoot in the late November cold until our magistra deigned to let her back inside. I awaited her with a blanket and a pan of burning embers to hold under her stiff blue feet.

"It's all right," I whispered as I chafed the little girl's skin to coax back the flow of life-giving blood. "This time of year, the plants were sleeping. We'll sow new seeds in the spring. Together we'll watch them grow."

Guda screwed up her face and hurled herself at the screen, pummeling the closed wooden shutters as she bawled for her aunt, who had departed for faraway Stade weeks ago. When I tried to soothe her, she roared, not letting me touch her. What a powerful pair of lungs she had—if she would only allow me to teach her to sing. At last Adelheid caught hold of her. Guda buried her face in her sister's skirt and sobbed as though she'd never stop.

Watching the little girl break down in the terrors of our prison, I relived my own shattering. I'd sacrificed myself for these girls in vain. Adelheid threw me a stony look, as though she now hated me as much as Guda did and blamed me for all their misery.

That winter an ague spread through the monastery, with more than a dozen monks languishing in the infirmary. Before long, I, too, succumbed. In my dizziness, my soul floated over my body to gaze down dispassionately at that wretch below, that seventeen-year-old drained of every hope. Even my memories of Rorich brought no solace, for I had strayed beyond his reach, my one chance of freedom dashed to pieces. I was like a dead branch severed from the living tree, no more sap left inside me.

As I lay drenched in cold sweat, I heard Jutta order the oblates to stay away from me lest they, too, catch the sickness. Except the children refused to obey her. Instead of shunning me, Adelheid and Guda hovered by my bed.

"I'm sorry I killed your herbs." Guda's eyes were solemn and huge.

"Brother Volmar promised us seeds and new pots of earth," Adelheid said. "We'll plant them again for you, we promise. Now drink this."

She gave me an herbal brew steeped in warm honeyed wine while her little sister offered me a hunk of soft bread, still warm from the oven. The girls fed me a bowl of turtle broth.

As I shivered and tried to speak, my vision shifted. Before my eyes, Adelheid grew into a serene young woman, brimming with quiet power. Her once mousy hair shone in the sun, streaming long and free, and she was crowned in gold. In her arms, she held a book. *See me, Hildegard. I am Sapientia. God's Wisdom.* A ray of light from her heart touched mine.

Guda had grown into a beauty with her golden curls and emerald eyes, crowned like Adelheid. She offered me a cup overflowing with blood-red wine, her eyes brimming in joyful welcome. *Know me, Hildegard. I am Ecclesia, the true and hidden Church.*

From between these two women, a third appeared, an utter stranger, and so beautiful. Crowned like the others, her long black hair swept to her waist. Her silk gown was as red as the Virgin's beating heart, and her smile gleamed in tenderness as she stretched out her arms. *Hildegard, seek me. My name is Caritas, Divine Love.*

Before me this trinity of women blazed, the sacred shimmering through them. My fever was broken by the vision of these three divine maidens dancing around a flowing fountain of pure grace. Three women who formed the face of God.

We formed a pact, my girls and I, the three of us united against Jutta's tyranny. When our magistra railed at them, they clung to me. The resignation on Jutta's face almost made me pity her, for Trutwib's prophecy was unfolding before her dimming eyes. Despite her every effort, Jutta had not succeeded in crushing me under her heel—Adelheid and Guda's presence only made her slipping grasp of authority more evident. When she ordered me to cut the girls' hair, I only pretended, the blades slicing empty air. Into Jutta's cupped palms, I offered my own severed locks and let the children's hair grow. Jutta had no need to cut her own hair, for her fasting had left her as bald as Methuselah.

Our magistra turned a bitter face to me, her traitor. She who believed herself an eternal maiden, still the girl of fourteen with pearls of rain glinting in her auburn hair, was growing into a feeble crone before her time, her bones as brittle as glass. What seemed to pain her most was how Adelheid and Guda took to calling me "Mother," the title they should have reserved for her.

Adelheid soon mastered her letters and sums. Her appetite for knowledge seemed as ravenous as my own as she pounced on the books Volmar brought us. When she turned fourteen, the two of us were poring over the newly copied manuscript of Constantine the African's *Book of Medicine,* full of the secrets of the Arabs, the most advanced physicians. We studied the mysteries of the four bodily humors and the way that blood coursed through the human body in a delta of pulsing streams.

More adept with her needle than the stylus, Guda could sew and embroider with astonishing delicacy. As her skills waxed, her altar cloths and banners became so exquisite that our abbot gifted them to cathedral canons in Worms, Mainz, and Trier. Most of all, Guda loved to sing. By the time her first bloods came, her voice had grown so sweeping and magnificent that she outshone our magistra. Since Guda's voice was a pure instrument of God, it would have been a sacrilege not to let it develop to its fullest beauty. So I composed canticles for her. Her voice turned my compositions into shimmering revelations.

Years passed. My visions blazed, the visitations that made the girls withdraw to a corner while Jutta simmered in envy that the Bridegroom should appear to me and not her, his face as gentle and soothing as Volmar's when he came bearing the books that were my consolation for all I had renounced. As I sought to mother the oblates, my own youth ebbed. A girl no longer, I was a woman growing ever older, ignored and unseen, a bush left to blossom down a dank ravine with no one to even notice that the flowering had ever occurred.

Adilhum died, and then the brothers elected Cuno as our new abbot. His rule was more austere than Adilhum's, more in keeping with the Benedictine ideal. Not for him the feasts of stuffed pheasant and wild swan to woo wealthy patrons. Cuno's fasts could rival Jutta's.

After rising to the rank of abbot, he summoned me to compose music for the entire monastery. This was Volmar's doing — my friend had praised my talents to highest heaven. Although Cuno had never particularly liked me, he went along with Volmar's suggestion, perhaps in hope that my songs might coax his beloved Jutta to sing again, she who had remained silent for so long, as though her vocal cords had dried to dust.

As my young sisters and I joined our voices in the Holy Office, singing the songs I had composed, I gazed through the screen to see Cuno's face soften in adoration, as though he had somehow convinced himself that Guda's voice, so soaring and angelic, was Jutta's.

Caritas habundat in omnia, we sang.

> *Divine love abounds in all things,*
> *From the depths to the heights,*
> *Above the highest stars.*

I could lose myself in ecstasy, our voices weaving in a circle of prayer, rising like incense to touch heaven, so far away from this abyss.

My girls grew into women, ordained nuns to whom the world outside our prison was a lost dream. The margravine visited every summer. Meanwhile, her husband died, leaving her with three sons and her only daughter to survive infancy.

Rorich traveled to Disibodenberg when he could, but an awkwardness had come between us ever since that night those many years ago when he had offered to help me escape only to have me turn away. As

the years passed, he had become increasingly important in the archbishop's court, climbing the rungs of influence that might even lead,
God willing, to his own election as bishop one day. *If I had, indeed,
thrown myself at his mercy that night, would Rorich have risen to these
heights*, I wondered, *or would the infamy of our deed have dragged him
down?* I tried to be happy for him, to treasure what few moments were
left for us to share.

In the year 1136, I was thirty-eight. Jutta was forty-four and had no
teeth left in her gums. *Ora et labora*, prayer and work, ruled our days
in a rhythm as fixed as the seasons. Volmar brought us herbs of the forest and field that Adelheid, now thirty-two, helped me grind and mix
to prepare ointments and tinctures for the monastery infirmary. Adelheid and I devoured our texts of science and learning, while Guda,
now twenty-six, embroidered and sang with a voice that made the
monks fall rapt inside its beauty.

Our magistra had abandoned every employment apart from praying and fasting. More grimly determined than ever, Jutta made a spectacle of her pain to admonish the rest of us for the pleasures we took in
our work and studies, our circle of friendship. We were blinded by our
vanity and mortal pride, she chided. Did we not understand that this
earthly life was intended to be nothing more than a vale of tears? We
would do better, she warned, to mortify our bodies so that our souls
might earn their passage to paradise. When Jutta slept, it was not in
her bed but on her knees on splintered planks.

I thought our life would drag on like this for eternity, the three of us
bumbling around our sainted magistra while we struggled to live the
most useful lives we could in the confines of that cage. But even stasis
cannot last forever.

That November a package arrived through our hatch. It seemed
a plain enough gift, wrapped in rough sacking, perhaps an offering
from some grateful pilgrim whose prayers had been answered. Guda
pounced on the bundle, her face glowing in delight at this diversion

from our dreary routine. She tore open the sacking to find a deerskin pouch.

"It's for you, magistra," she called to Jutta, who swayed on her knees. "From the court of Sponheim."

The pouch bore Jutta's family's coat of arms.

"Don't disturb her," I whispered.

Her eyes squeezed shut, Jutta seemed determined to ignore us. It was as though we, her chosen companions, were flies—minor nuisances that distracted her from her holy duties.

The mere sight of the arms of Sponheim made the old panic beat in my throat. Jutta's mother, the countess, had died four winters ago. The only one who could have sent this was Meginhard. Though he had taken a wife, God had cursed his seed and left him without an heir. Banished from our abbey, Meginhard hadn't sent his sister as much as a letter in more than two decades. My eyes filled at the memory of fifteen-year-old Jutta bashing her head against the stone wall and screaming that she was polluted. Did he think to torment her again after twenty-nine years?

"What could it be?" Adelheid asked, grabbing the pouch before I could stop her. Though wise as far as book learning was concerned, she was possessed of a curiosity as fatal as Eve's.

"*No,*" I said.

Too late. Adelheid untied the pouch's string, spilling its contents, which hit our table with an awful clang. While Guda and I looked on, frozen and speechless, Adelheid bent to examine the triple rows of interlocking brass links more than a yard long. Exclaiming at how cleverly it was made, she grasped the thing, then shrieked. On each link was a sharp, inward-pointing barb, designed to pierce the skin.

"Hildegard, what is it?" Adelheid lifted her bleeding hand to her mouth.

"A penitent's chain." My heart was like lead.

Twenty-nine years ago, Meginhard von Sponheim had smiled at me through the screen, his serpent eyes glittering, venom dripping from his every word. *I'm her brother, after all. Her only living sibling. There's a chain that binds us.*

"Get rid of it," I hissed. Wrapping my hand in the sacking it had come in, I was about to stuff the damned thing back into its pouch and fling it back through the hatch. I'd beg Volmar to pitch it into the Nahe.

But Jutta stood before us, her dimmed eyes open wide, as though she had just awoken from a twenty-nine-year sleep.

"What is it?" she asked. "What has arrived from the court of Sponheim?"

My lips trembled. My tongue turned to wood. Reaching out, she took the chain from me. I thought that once its teeth bit into her skin, she would scream and drop the thing like the poisonous snake it was. I braced myself for her tears, her terror, but she remained utterly still, not flinching or making a noise until she finally spoke.

"Sisters, go to the courtyard and take your exercise. Leave me."

Later, after the three of us had stepped in from the November chill with wind-chapped faces, I scoured the anchorage. But I found no trace of the chain or the pouch and sacking it had come in.

"Maybe she got rid of the thing," Adelheid murmured, as though in hope that such a torturous device was too much for even Jutta to suffer.

But the knowing pierced me like the barbs on that cold chain. While we were in the courtyard, Jutta had stripped to the skin and wrapped that evil thing round and round her wasted body before concealing it under her hair shirt. I thought of Satan coiling his serpentine body around the Tree of Life, despoiling it, turning its nourishing fruit to poison. Meginhard had meted his final humiliation upon Jutta. Her debasement was now complete.

What a grip her brother held her in. After three decades within the impregnable fortress of the anchorage, Jutta still wasn't free of him.

From that day on, she remained as still as the grave, as though she had taken a vow of silence. She didn't scold us, even when Adelheid and Guda chattered and laughed during the hours of enforced stillness. She just knelt on her splintered boards, leaving us to tiptoe around her while her lips moved in an inaudible stream of prayer, her eyes frozen on the invisible.

Each morning after Prime, Abbot Cuno appeared at our screen, his fifty-year-old face alight with a young man's love. Whispering behind their hands, my sisters called him Jutta's suitor. But Jutta turned her back on him, as though her sins and inner turmoil had strayed even beyond his powers of absolution.

In that sepulchral gloom, my sisters and I endured our days as best we could. Guda would not stop talking about the margravine's upcoming visit—their godmother had promised to make a rare winter journey and visit us at Christmas. She was bringing along her youngest child and only daughter, a girl of thirteen, to meet Guda and Adelheid for the first time.

Adelheid diverted herself by tearing through one book after another, eager to cram every scrap of knowledge into her brain. In bleak November she was particularly fond of reading herbals and bestiaries, then sharing the illuminations of plants and animals with Guda, who embroidered pomegranate and cedar, lily and dove, lion and hind on silk vestments and altar cloths.

The hunger on my sisters' faces ran me through like a blade. How they needed to see real trees, real birds and beasts, real meadows full of wildflowers again, or they might go mad. How could anyone go on living like this, year after year, decade after decade, without cracking apart, as Jutta was cracking before our eyes?

The three of us were unwilling witnesses as Jutta broke, piece by piece. It was as though she had taken upon herself our despair and failings until this burden crushed her.

In the past, she'd had plenty of spells of weakness and illness that I had nursed her through. But she'd never been as bad as this. Not only did she refuse to eat, she also refused to sip water, even though we begged her down on our knees. She wouldn't budge from her planks, even to make use of the chamber pot. Our magistra's skin went as dry as old bark and came off in scaly flakes. She was disintegrating, dust to dust.

Adelheid lost her patience and tried to shove a spoonful of broth between Jutta's lips, but Jutta remained as rigid as a marble effigy while the liquid dribbled down her chin to stain her hair shirt.

"Leave her be," I said, for I knew from sad experience that we'd have to wait until Jutta grew so weak that she toppled over. Only then would I be able to gather her in my arms and carry her to her bed. When her frailty overpowered her, she would weep in my embrace and finally allow me to spoon turtle soup into her mouth.

I prayed she would give in and let us help her. But Jutta hovered for days in a realm between life and death, without even closing her eyes to sleep.

"It's impossible," I told Volmar. "How can she do this? She defies every human need."

Volmar's hair was beginning to thin around his tonsure, yet his eyes were as gentle as those I'd first learned to love and trust thirty years ago. My heart still swelled with my undeclared love for him, though the fiery heat of my youthful passion had mellowed into a warm glow. Through my many sorrows, Volmar had been there for me, his compassion the shining lamp that lit my way. In the secular world, we might have married. We might have had a son or daughter almost as old as Guda.

"Cuno's right," he said. "Jutta's truly a saint. She has transcended this earthly existence while still living here among us."

Just as I went on quietly loving him, he continued to adore his Jutta. Let him believe in his holy anchorite. Who was I to spoil his illusion?

Since Jutta rejected our proffered cups of water and broth, since the blankets we wrapped around her just slithered off her bony frame, we could only gather around and pray while she knelt there, her whole being shuttered to us. Meanwhile, Abbot Cuno led the monks in a vigil for our holy woman. The still center of this storm, Jutta remained on her knees, propped up by an unearthly might, for seventeen days and nights.

On the first of December, I awakened for Matins to find that our magistra had finally collapsed. Her breathing was shallow. Tears trickled from her eyes. She huddled on her side, curling into herself like a child in the womb.

Flat on her bed, Jutta stared with spectral eyes, her skeletal hands lifted in prayer.

"Behold," she said in a reedy old woman's voice, as though she had aged one hundred years since emerging from her seventeen-day trance. "My bridegroom has come to end my travails. He shall take me home at last."

A needle of ice stabbed at my heart. Of course, it was not Christ she spoke of. How fervently my magistra had wooed Death, her true mystic husband, these thirty years. How languorously she had drawn out their courtship, leading him on, then holding him off, delaying their coupling until this rapturous moment on the brink of consummation. We, her handmaidens, circled round Jutta, born to be a countess, then ruined by her brother and locked away. Haughty as ever, she commanded us to lay her on a mat of coarsest goat hair strewn with ashes, for she would suffer till her last breath.

How she craved pain, how it thrilled her, weeping tears of blood. Our Savior died for the sins of the world—that was the true meaning of passion. Jutta mortified her flesh for her own self-indulgence. How she basked in this attention, how she played the saint, she who had never really grown up, she who was never anything more than a vain and broken young girl. Turning her face away from the bowl of broth I offered, she would take no food but the viaticum of communion bread and wine offered to the dying.

Coyly, she took my hand, her bony grip already death-cold.

"Please," she said, assaulting me with her ghastly breath, "when my soul departs, don't let them uncover my body."

I lowered my head without giving my word, for I knew Jutta had only said this to beg the opposite. She longed to be exposed, longed for everyone to witness how she had tortured herself with her brother's chain.

"Have them bury me in a place where I might be trodden upon by each passerby."

Not knowing how long Jutta could draw this out, I sent the others to bed while I held vigil. The most traitorous prayer welled up inside me: *God, let her die so that we might live.*

What an awful wretch I was. I had spent thirty years locked away with this woman, my mentor, my sister, my magistra, my spiritual mother, only to look on with a heart of granite when her chest juddered and sank, the last air bursting from her lips with bubbles of spittle. Her eyes rolled back. It wasn't until the stink of her emptied bowels filled the room that panic seized me.

In a frenzy, I awakened the others. Together we raised the alarm, Guda and I banging on the church screen while Adelheid beat on the revolving hatch. Before long, the monks came running. I sank to my knees, my heart beating hard enough to bruise as the hammers and picks pummeled the bricked-up doorway.

"And the walls of Jericho came tumbling down," I whispered to Guda, who knelt to take my hands. "When the moment of freedom comes," I told her, cupping her cheek with my palm, "we must act and not hesitate. Step over the threshold before they can stop you."

At last there was a path through the rubble, gray dawn shining through that aperture. Like a grieving widower, Cuno stumbled in to claim his beloved's corpse.

"The holy anchoress," he murmured, his eyes spilling tears.

Leaving him to mourn, I turned to my sisters. Adelheid took my one hand, and Guda the other. Squaring her shoulders, Adelheid led us out into the cobbled yard crowded with monks, their heads bowed in reverence at Jutta's passing. Not letting go of my sisters' hands, I gasped, arching my face to the winter dawn. The pale sun painted the clouds pink and yellow, more beautiful than even Guda's embroidery. Fresh air bathed our faces. So much sky above us.

"Are we in heaven?" Guda asked, laughing, then weeping.

I staggered on my weak prisoner's legs, but I had to be strong. A little farther and we might reach the gates, go out into the forest. Did we dare? In the dead of winter — what was I thinking? Without food or shelter, we would perish within days.

Egon, who had become prior when Cuno became abbot, planted himself in our path. "Sisters, where are you going?"

"To the mortuary," I told him, thinking fast. "Surely our lord abbot would agree it's only proper that a woman washes our sainted Jutta's body." I turned to my companions. "Sisters, let us gather what we need to lay her in her final resting place."

I barely had a chance to accustom myself to the freedom of the open air before the morgue's gloom enclosed me. Wishing to spare my sisters the spectacle of what I was about to behold, I worked alone.

After hacking away the soiled hair shirt, I gagged to see the rusting chain wound three times around Jutta's torso. Spikes cinched her waist and ribs. They crushed her withered breasts. They bit deep into her festering, oozing flesh. This was Jutta's last admonishment to me, her undeserving protégée. She had wanted me to see how her pain proved her holiness. She had expected me to reveal this to Cuno himself.

Gulping back my bile, I washed and bandaged her seeping flesh.

Gray and shrunken, Jutta von Sponheim lay on the mortuary slab, clad in the gown she had first arrived in as a fourteen-year-old girl. It hung loose on her skeletal frame. Her hands crossed over her bony breast in prayer and her bald head was veiled in Damascus silk. At her side lay her severed braid of soft auburn hair.

My work completed, I called in the monks. Silent and dry-eyed, I stood by while Cuno sobbed into his hands. Volmar's spine threatened to snap under the weight of his distress. The men who had loved Jutta crowded round, touching her sleeve, her cold hands, the hem of her gown, as they never would have dared while she lived. I listened to them convincing each other how they could see the holiness rising from her. Their adoration covered my dead magistra in silver and gold.

Blinded by his tears, Cuno nearly trod on me. But then his eyes snapped open, as if horrified to find me still standing there. I confess I needed to breathe deeply and gather my strength to face my abbot, face these milling monks that I had only ever viewed from the other side of a screen. After thirty years of seclusion, I found this strange and new. My eyes sought Volmar's. My hands burned to touch his, to offer him consolation. Only I understood how he had loved Jutta, and how she had loved him, as much as she was capable of loving any human being.

Abbot Cuno loomed before me, his disapproval written on his face. Unlike Jutta, I was no saint, no martyr, no ascetic, but a mature woman of little beauty and middling breeding. And yet I was his last link to his great love.

"Did our holy woman tell you where she wished to be buried?" he asked, not looking me in the eye but past my left shoulder.

I spoke the truth. "She wanted to be laid in a place where people would tread over her."

"Such humility," Cuno said, his face flushed and lost. "She humbles us all."

My head bowed, I kept my own thoughts private. Even after death, Jutta wanted to make a display of herself and be buried where her self-abnegation would attract the most attention.

"We could bury her beneath the floor in the chapter house," Brother Otto suggested. "That way she'll be with us in spirit every morning during chapter meeting."

"But do we want pilgrims traipsing into our chapter house at all hours?" Prior Egon asked, eager to trounce his brothers with the authority our abbot had vested in him.

"We could house her relics in the church," Brother Udo suggested. "At the Lady Altar, perhaps."

"Relics," Egon said, latching on to the word as if it were a golden coin—Jutta's relics were sure to draw pilgrims with their fat purses. He turned to Brother Otto. "Before we lay her in her coffin, could you not amputate a finger bone or two?"

"How dare you!" Cuno placed himself between his prior and his saint. "You shall not despoil her corpse."

"But it is *customary*," Egon began to argue.

Then even he shut his trap when he saw Cuno reverently lift Jutta's severed braid to his lips.

"Her hair shall be placed in the reliquary," our abbot said with finality. "That shall suffice."

Their backs to me, the men continued their discussion, leaving me to vanish back into my invisible existence. Instead I planted myself before Cuno so that he had no choice but to acknowledge me.

"Let those of us who were Jutta's disciples"—I picked my words judiciously—"attend her funeral. I have composed songs in honor of our holy woman."

I strove to sound as docile as they would have me be, when, in fact, I wanted to spit and scream at the thought of being bricked inside that anchorage again. What was the use of our isolation and suffering? What purpose could it possibly serve?

"Lord abbot, leave the doorway open, I beg you. Give my sisters and I leave to accompany our beloved magistra to her final resting place."

"Very well," he said. "The doorway shall remain open until after her burial."

So he planned to brick us back up after Jutta was laid to rest. I swallowed, arranging my face to mask my true emotions. If I was to win this game, I would have to play it with cunning.

Prior Egon had to stick his nose in. "But the funeral might not be for weeks."

I stifled a smile as my heart raced in hope.

"We must send for the archbishop," Egon went on, "not to mention our saint's relatives. In the meantime, are we to have females wandering around the monastery, gabbing about like market wives?"

"My lord abbot," I said, my head bowed to the floor so the men could not glimpse my rage. "I give you my word that my sisters and I shall not disturb the holy brothers."

"You may go," Cuno said, as though dismissing a servant.

"Reverend father, wait just one moment," Volmar said, before I could depart. "There is one other matter of business. Hildegard, you and your sisters must elect a new magistra."

My head brimmed with a thousand thoughts as I stepped into the glittering sunlight, my sandals scraping the crust of snow in the courtyard. How like Jutta to choose to die in December, which made any notion of escape daunting. I was thirty-eight, older than my mother had been the last time I'd seen her, well past my prime. If I reneged on my vows and attempted to live once more in the secular world, I'd be unlikely to find a husband, not that I wanted one. My thoughts turned to Trutwib, proud and alone, how she'd survived in the woods. *Did she still live*, I wondered, *and how did she survive the winters?* I doubted I could survive such a rustic life. My only choice would be, as before, to throw myself at my brother's mercy, beg him to let me live out my dotage in some nunnery in Mainz, where I would sew his vestments and learn to keep my mouth shut.

Reaching the courtyard where I had left Adelheid and Guda, I saw no trace of them. Sandals slapping the snow, I ran into the anchorage, my voice echoing through the abandoned cells that reeked of hopelessness and death. Had my sisters absconded while I was washing Jutta's corpse? My heart raced, caught in a place between terror and elation. What if my girls had indeed broken free? Those brave souls.

No doubt Cuno would hold me responsible and assign some unspeakable penance.

Unused to such freedom of exercise, I was soon winded, staggering through the warren of monastery buildings and courtyards in search of my sisters, part of me praying that I wouldn't find them, that they were already miles away, never to see this place again. But in the cloister garden I found Guda, her fingers tracing the figure of a siren carved onto one of the pillars as a warning to the monks to shun the temptation of women.

"Hildegard." She spun to face me. "I can't find Adelheid."

Bolder than Guda and I, Adelheid must have taken to the road. Fiercely intelligent, she had studied many a map. She would find her way, following the Nahe to the nearest hamlet where she might seek shelter. Of the three of us, she had the best chance, so practical and courageous was she. Then, as I held Adelheid's face in my heart, another possibility occurred to me.

A novice monk came down the cloister walk, took one look at us, and stopped dead in his tracks.

"Brother, can you take us to the library?" I asked him.

The boy seemed flustered. I doubted that he had stood face to face with a woman, much less been addressed by one, since he'd arrived in this place. Though I was old enough to be his mother, Guda was lovely enough to make him blush. Stammering and blinking, he reeled off the directions to the library before backing away, beating his retreat without giving me a chance to thank him.

"He might be shy, but he's not bad looking," Guda whispered with a smothered giggle.

Turning a corner, we mounted a stairway. I felt as weak as a convalescent, my muscles wasted from the confines of my prison. How could I even contemplate life outside this place if I could barely manage to climb a single flight of stairs?

At last we reached the door to the sanctum that housed the many books that had kept me from going mad. Guda opened the door and stepped through, tugging me behind her as she flew to the glassed window that looked over the abbey walls to the winding Nahe River below. Tears moved down my face at my first glimpse of the outside world in three decades. How my eyes feasted on the forested hills stretching as far as I could see. The emperor himself wouldn't have been able to pry me from that window, but finally Guda did.

"Hildegard, there's Adelheid."

Our sister sat with Herodotus's *Histories* open before her. Oblivious to everything else, she was in the transports of ecstasy, her mind wholly engaged.

Brother Matthias, the librarian, appeared content to let her read to her heart's desire while he contemplated the miracle of the woman at his table.

When the bells rang for None, we dragged ourselves back over the shattered threshold of our anchorage to observe the Divine Office, the three of us kneeling behind the screen as though nothing had changed. But as we sang the psalms, Guda's voice rang out with an exuberance that reminded me of a reeling lark.

Adelheid elbowed her. "Careful," she whispered. "We're meant to be mourning."

Afterward, as we shared our sparse meal, I told my sisters of my discussion with Cuno.

"So after Jutta's buried, they'll just brick us up again?" Adelheid's voice shook.

When I saw the fury on her face, I feared she would indeed run away, but this time the picture of her exodus was far from romantic. How easily she could freeze or starve in that winter forest.

"I'll find a way, I promise you," I told them.

"You're powerless," Adelheid said. "Cuno will do what he likes."

"We must elect a new magistra," said Guda, as though anxious to keep us from quarreling.

I looked at Adelheid, her face alight with brilliance going to waste.

"I would vote for you, sister. At a real nunnery, you might have become a great abbess."

"No, Hildegard," she said. "You are our magistra. Who else is there?"

Guda took my hand and kissed it. I quaked to see the trust in her eyes—she seemed to truly believe I had the power to end our captivity.

8

ON JUTTA'S FUNERAL day, my hammering heart awakened me long before Lauds. This was to be our last day of freedom before they bricked up the anchorage once more.

Guda and Adelheid's faces revealed that they, too, had hardly slept. From Compline to Matins, the three of us had held vigil, stitching by candlelight, at work on the secret plot I had hatched. This was to be the gamble of our lives. In preparation for this day, our one and only chance, I had implored Cuno to let us open Guda's dowry chest, filled with damask, brocade, and golden wire.

"My lord abbot, allow my sisters and me to sew a banner to honor Jutta, our magistra who is now a saint in heaven."

Outside our broken doorway, the courtyard brimmed with dignitaries. As our many visitors squeezed into the church for High Mass, I searched the crowd for Meginhard. Would he show himself? Part of me, I confess, longed to see Jutta's tormentor brought low in shame, a wasted stick of a sinner. Let him cower under the glares that Volmar, Cuno, and I would hurl at him, we who knew his crime. Let him take that spiked penitent's chain he had given his sister and wind it around his own neck to strangle himself. But the hypocrite kept out of sight, pleading ill health and hiding in his castle, though he had sent Cuno the gold to pay for Jutta's burial.

Peering through the screen, I located my brother in the archbishop's train. During his last visit, Rorich had revealed how Adalbert had come increasingly to rely upon him, making my brother one of his most trusted men. I prayed that this would work to my advantage, though I'd neither the opportunity nor the courage to confide to Rorich what I would do this day. For now, I remained hidden behind our screen, not daring to set foot outside. No, my sisters and I must appear as meek as mice until we made our move. Only an hour or two remained.

The Margravine von Stade approached the screen, her arm entwined around her only daughter, a girl with black hair rippling to her waist. Now widowed, the lady was richer than ever and her own mistress with no husband or master. The wrinkles around her eyes and mouth betrayed her age of forty-one, but her ice-blue eyes were as piercing as I remembered them.

"Sister Hildegard, please accept my condolences." She sounded restrained, no doubt owing to the somber occasion. How was she to know that her Christmas visit would coincide with Jutta's funeral? She had set sail down the Elbe and the Rhine before the news of Jutta's passing could reach her. "Your magistra was fortunate to have so loyal a disciple."

"Lady, I am unworthy of your praise." I bowed my head lest she read in my eyes how disloyal I truly was.

"This is my daughter, Richardis." She drew the girl at her side closer to the screen.

In her younger days, the margravine had been a beauty, but this thirteen-year-old was a jewel. She stood slim and straight, and her dark blue eyes had depths in them, like the starry sapphires encircling her white throat. No cloistered life for her, I reckoned. Her beauty and title, coupled with her family's riches, would make her the most desirable bride in Saxony.

"It was good of you to come so far to meet your kinswomen," I said to the girl.

She only stared at me and said nothing.

As if to cover her daughter's discourtesy, the margravine spoke in a rapid, breathless voice. "Her brother, my second son, Hartwig, is the newly elected Archbishop of Bremen."

"What an honor," I murmured.

Her son couldn't be much older than twenty, which left me to wonder what role the margravine's money and influence had played in his appointment. At that, I withdrew from the screen so that Guda and Adelheid could greet their godmother. Though my sisters offered their warmest greetings to their beautiful young cousin, Richardis remained silent, her eyes downcast. The girl was either painfully shy or dreadfully rude.

"Sister Hildegard!" The margravine called me back to the screen.

The lady's eyes couldn't quite meet mine, but her daughter gawked at me shamelessly, in harsh examination, as if to uncover what sort of person I was. Could she tell that I was less grieved at Jutta's passing than terrified about my sisters' future? Could she sense that my stomach filled with ice when I thought what my sisters and I must do in the next hours? That child had the eyes of an inquisitor. What a strange young person. With her youth, beauty, and good fortune, she should have been sanguine and light of heart.

"There is a private matter I must discuss with you," the margravine told me.

"Tomorrow, noble lady." I bent my head in apology. "We must make ready for our magistra's last rites."

When my sisters and I emerged from our prison to join the procession of mourners, the margravine and her daughter gaped, their hands cupped to their mouths. Cuno froze, as if God had turned him into a statue. Prior Egon's face purpled, his neck thickening like a mastiff's. Archbishop Adalbert's eyes flamed with astonishment. When my brother's gaze met mine, it was as though he were staring at another woman, for I had become a brand-new person.

This was our gamble, our way of engraving ourselves forever in the assembly's memory, so that we could never be forgotten, never again be consigned to dust and a quiet, slow death. Even if we lost the battle, this moment would live forever. The legend of our deed would endure.

My sisters and I had shed our black Benedictine habits and donned the jewel-colored damask from Guda's dowry trunk. As well as sewing the banner in Jutta's honor, thus keeping our promise to Cuno, we had wrought gowns for ourselves grand enough to grace the margravine's court. We were brides of Christ—why should we not adorn ourselves for our Bridegroom? Like the maidens of Saint Ursula, we processed unveiled, our hair flowing long and free, crowned in circlets of woven gold wire that Guda had fashioned into the shapes of lambs and doves. I will never forget how lovely Guda looked with her golden hair and emerald gown, or how Adelheid shone with her wise brown eyes and her gown of deepest garnet. Even I was majestic, clad in amethyst, my flaxen hair falling nearly to my waist. *We are daughters of the King.* I smiled at Volmar's transfixed face.

My vision of the consecrated virgins rejoicing in the arms of Ecclesia was made real, my two companions radiant, their faces glowing in the December chill. The revelation of their beauty left the monks reeling, unable to utter a word of censure. Looking at the men's awestruck faces, I sensed they saw their dead Jutta restored. They beheld the vision of that lovely maiden who had come to their lonely abbey three decades ago. Jutta's resurrection blazed before their eyes.

The assembly hardly seemed to breathe as my sisters and I gathered around Jutta's coffin, lined with lead so none could smell her corruption and decay. While Adelheid and Guda joined hands, I held aloft the banner that we had sewn and embroidered with roses and lilies, doves and hinds, apples and pomegranates, rivers and trees. Our breath turned to mist in the cold air.

To mark our magistra's death, we three sang the songs of life that I had composed during our endless captivity. At the pounding center of my heart, I held my image of the Lady at the axis of the wheel of creation, the Virgin and matrix from whose body our salvation proceeded. *I bore you from the womb before the morning star.* Everything she touched greened and bloomed, even in this corpse-cold end of the year. The verdant branch that awakened all life, she unveiled my eyes to the eternal paradise that had never fallen.

This was our song for Jutta's passing.

> *O viridissima virga ave*
> *Hail, greenest branch,*
> *brought forth on the breeze of prayers.*
>
> *You flourish among your fronds,*
> *hail, hail to you,*
> *The warmth of the sun keeps you moist*
> *like the scent of balsam.*
>
> *A beautiful flower flourished in you*
> *and gave odor to all scents*
> *that were barren.*
>
> *You are the reason the heavens bestowed dew upon the turf,*
> *and the whole earth was made joyful*
> *because its flesh*
> *brought forth grain,*
> *and because the birds of heaven*
> *made their nests on it.*
>
> *Then there grew food for us mortals*
> *and great rejoicing at the banquet.*
> *O sweet Virgin,*
> *no joy is lacking in you.*
>
> *Eve rejected all these things.*
> *Now again be praised to the highest.*

With my entire soul I embraced the living, nourishing power that Jutta had scorned.

As the last note of our song died down, the enchantment ebbed. Suddenly I was standing in the cold, dressed only in thin silk and linen, my jaw clenched to keep from shivering. Guda looked pale and uncertain, while Adelheid's face was unreadable. What we had done—making a mockery of the Rule of Saint Benedict and humiliating our abbot in front of the Archbishop of Mainz—could never be undone. We would have to face the consequences, whatever they might be.

Regaining his composure, Cuno led our procession into the church, where he sang his beloved's Requiem Mass, his voice stretched high and thin in grief. The monks bore Jutta's coffin to the chapter house where they laid her to eternal rest beneath a carved stone slab.

Seizing my only chance, I stood before Cuno, my head unbowed, and spoke my will before the Archbishop of Mainz. Before my brother, Canon of Mainz Cathedral. Before the Margravine von Stade, aunt and godmother to my sister nuns and the abbey's greatest living patron, her donations exceeding even those of Meginhard von Sponheim.

I spoke *my* will, but I had the temerity to say that it was God's will.

"It is God's will that my sisters and I keep our liberty," I said, a shivering woman trying to speak out in a firm, unshakeable voice. "This night we will return to our cell to sleep, but you shall never brick us in again, my lord abbot. We are freeborn women. Our door must remain open. From this day forward, our rooms shall be a nunnery but no anchorage."

Cuno bridled, but what easy retort could he find with the archbishop standing to his right and my brother, the archbishop's trusted friend, to his left?

In that chasm of silence, only the margravine dared to move. Rushing forward, she cried out, embracing Guda and Adelheid for the first time in twenty-one years. My eyes brimmed to watch them, to listen to

Guda's gulping sobs as she clung to her godmother. The margravine turned, holding out her hand to Richardis, inviting her to partake in this passionate family reunion, but the girl held back, her body rigid, as though she had turned into a post. Her eyes, moist and bewildered, locked on to mine, as if demanding to know who I was and why I had done this thing.

Still holding fast to her goddaughters' hands, the margravine faced Cuno. Ferocious determination illumined her face, as though she were Margaret of Antioch, seizing the cross to slay the dragon.

"Hildegard speaks the truth," the Margravine von Stade told our abbot. "Only a tyrant would lock away freeborn women against their will. The old magistra may have been an anchorite, but the new magistra has chosen a gentler path."

Before Cuno could interject, she swooped in to kiss the archbishop's ring.

"Your eminence!" she cried to Adalbert. "In gratitude for your mercy to my kinswomen, I shall offer Disibodenberg the most generous endowment it has ever known—but only if the nuns keep their liberty."

Every part of me sang out in gratitude. I thought I would fall to my knees before her and weep.

However, it was not Cuno's way to allow a woman, even one as wealthy as the Margravine von Stade, to have the last word.

My abbot summoned me to his private chamber where Adalbert and Rorich waited, their faces drawn. Properly clothed in veil and habit, I appeared before them as a penitent. What I had committed this day was the biggest breach of propriety the monastery had ever known. Cuno had every right to saddle me with the most excruciating penance. My brother also seemed perturbed. How I had shamed him, my scandalous scene compromising him before the archbishop.

"We have spent some time discussing your transgressions." The look Cuno gave me was devastating. I was everything his beloved

Jutta had not been — a weaver of strife, a sower of mischief. Without my sainted magistra to hold me in check, there was no telling what I might wreak. How was he to tolerate such insubordination?

Still I did not crumple before him. "If my presence here displeases you, my lord abbot, I am prepared to take my leave."

A pain spread through my chest as I turned to Rorich, a silent entreaty written on my face. *Please. You offered to deliver me once before.*

Rorich's eyes slid away from mine. "Hildegard, I can't take you with me. Bischofsheim Abbey is under quarantine from an outbreak of pestilence. Our sister Clementia nearly died. Far better that you stay here, where the air and water are so pure."

Picking his words apart, I gathered that he was lying to me, my own brother. He feared me. If he brought me to Mainz, I might provide even more occasion for embarrassment. If he indulged me, he risked being cast out of Adalbert's chosen circle. Rorich had ascended to such heights that he was now terrified of falling from the archbishop's grace.

"However," Cuno said, his voice sounding like ice cracking beneath boots, "we have taken into consideration the thirty years you have spent here as Jutta's chosen disciple. You're a woman past your prime with few if any prospects of beginning anew elsewhere."

My abbot would waste no effort in putting me in my place. I felt myself dwindle under the blizzard of his derision.

"We must bear in mind that Hildegard has an important office to fill," my brother said, trying to catch my eye but I thought that if I looked at him I would dissolve into tears. "Her sisters have elected her as their new magistra."

Finally Adalbert spoke, his every word weighted with an authority that made me tremble.

"It seems only right to allow Hildegard, a woman in her middle years, to remain at Disibodenberg, the only home she has. Today she has demonstrated that she is not of the same making as the holy Jutta. Hildegard lacks the will and discipline to lead the life of an anchorite. We must be clement, Cuno. Not all are called to such an austere path

128

of grace. Let us not condemn our sister for her weakness, but allow her to live out her dotage as a nun, rather than an anchorite, free to come and go from her rooms, provided that she never again make such a flamboyant mockery of the Benedictine Rule as she did today."

My face on fire, I knelt before Adalbert and kissed his ring. This man had been the emperor's prisoner, held without trial for three long years. Perhaps he pitied me and understood only too well my longing for liberation. Yet I still didn't know whether I had won my battle or if I had been subdued forevermore.

"If we are to grant you free passage in the abbey," said Cuno, "you must forbid your nuns from traipsing about where they could lead the holy brothers into temptation."

Against my better judgment, I lifted my face to his and opened my unholy mouth. "Surely on *my* account, you needn't worry. I am far too old and plain to lead any man astray." My words rang out as scathingly as his had.

"So it is agreed!" my brother said, speaking quickly before Cuno and I could lock horns and become embroiled in a dispute. "Hildegard shall obey the Rule under her abbot's authority and guidance."

It was as though I were still a child of eight, powerless and voiceless, made to stand silent while the men decided my fate. My brother had joined the ranks of those to whom I had to scrape and grovel.

"With your permission," I choked. "I will take my leave."

"You are dismissed," Cuno said coldly.

I fled the room, my vision blurring with the tears I didn't want them to see, least of all Rorich, my dearest sibling who now acted as my master. Staggering down the dim stairway, I burst out into the cloister walk and then smothered a yelp. A cowled figure blocked my way.

"Hildegard." Volmar stepped out of the shadows so that I could see his face. "There's still some time left before Compline. Ever since you were a little girl, you've told me how you've longed to see the forest again."

My heart burst with impossible hope.

"Come quickly," he coaxed, "while the gates are still open."

As we hurried off, he spoke in a low and confiding voice. "Sister, you were magnificent today. That song you sang was the most exquisite thing I've ever heard."

The man I had loved since I was a girl took my arm, guiding me out of the abbey gates. Such freedom! I trembled from crown to toe with joy, laughing in my delight. First we strolled through the orchard. In the red setting sun of that winter evening, I beheld the frost-rimed apple trees from which Volmar had cut the Barbara Branch for Jutta and me thirty years ago, the twig that had burst into blossom on Christmas Day. My life, once a withered stick, would flower now, too. With tears in my eyes, I cupped the bark to feel the hum of life, the sap inside the wood, just waiting to surge into greening at the first hint of spring.

Volmar led me to the edge of the forest where I laid my cheek against the smooth trunks of beech and the rough bark of oak.

"Your dream has come true," he said. "I will send the lay brothers to build you a proper door that opens and closes."

I turned to him, clasping his hand between my own. At a loss for words, I arched my face to the tracery of branches glittering with ice and snow. In the endless blue dome above, the first stars of evening shone like a promise. Though I was past my prime, I felt brand-new. Yet beneath my rapture gaped an abyss of loss. Rorich had abandoned me, just like Mother had those many years ago. Apart from Volmar, the margravine, and my sister nuns, I was friendless and forsaken.

"Come," Volmar said gently, his hand still enclosed in mine. "Before they lock us out."

"You have an ally for life in the margravine," Volmar said as we walked back through the cloister garden. "She has assured your victory this day. Cuno wouldn't dare go back on his word. Her daughter's dowry will make him one of the richest abbots in the bishopric."

I turned to him in confusion. "What do you mean?"

"Did the lady herself not speak to you?" Volmar squeezed my elbow. "Her daughter is to be your new postulant."

• • •

In the guesthouse, the margravine sat before the roaring hearth with Adelheid and Guda while young Richardis hovered in the shadows. When I entered, the margravine snapped to her feet.

"Magistra, we must speak," she told me with such authority that I could imagine her commanding an army.

Guda and Adelheid withdrew at once, and Richardis prepared to creep away as well, but her mother called her back.

"Don't be silly, my dear. Your new magistra wishes to make your acquaintance."

"Madam," I said, my face smarting from the fire's unaccustomed heat. "I had no idea your daughter wished to take the veil."

I cast my eyes toward the girl herself, but her long, loose hair obscured her face. Her mother went on speaking with brisk confidence.

"Magistra, what you have done this day was truly God's will. Know that I have assured your continued liberty, for I have told Cuno that my daughter shall join the sisters, but *only* if the nuns are granted the run of the abbey and are no longer confined to the anchorage like rabbits inside a hutch."

She spoke so fast that my head spun. Had this been an impetuous decision or had she been planning this? Who could commit her daughter to a monastery on a mere whim? Perhaps this was what she had wanted to discuss with me earlier this morning when I had abruptly ended our audience. If that was the case, had she been willing to commit her daughter to this house even before I had made my desperate bid to end our captivity? She had, after all, consigned her goddaughters to the anchorage. What game did this woman play?

"My lady," I said, when I managed to get a word in. "I am in your debt, but I must hear from Richardis herself."

"Oh, I have pondered her future for quite a long while," the mother blustered on, not giving her daughter a chance to speak. "After much prayer, I have concluded that there is no better place for her than in your care, Hildegard."

I imagined that the margravine had become adept at using flattery to twist others to her will. Ignoring the mother, I turned to the girl.

"What do you say to this, Richardis?"

The girl's eyes gleamed red. She was fighting tears, leaving me to conclude that this was her mother's doing, that the girl herself wanted none of it.

"It's all right," I whispered, and then I addressed her mother once more. "Margravine, exalted lady, I am grateful for your patronage, but please understand that I can't take Richardis unless she's willing. The archbishop would tell you the same. It's canon law."

Her repartee came razor sharp. "After today you presume to lecture me on canon law? I think not, magistra." Her brittle smile put me in my place. "Your abbot has already agreed. He would be deeply perturbed, I think, if you presumed to turn my daughter away, especially seeing how I have intervened on your behalf."

Her veiled threat left me cold.

"You have bribed Cuno with the girl's dowry," I said, "but you can't bribe me. It must be her choice."

Richardis's mouth hung open, as though she were dumbfounded that a mere nun would dare stand up to her mother. Indeed, I was terrified of the consequences, for now that I had refused to bow to the margravine's scheming, she would surely abandon me to my fate. My sisters and I would lose our freedom, lose all we had fought for. I had failed, alienating my only powerful well-wisher. But even so, I would not play prison keeper to an unwilling girl.

Before the margravine could blast me to hell in her next tirade, I took her daughter's hands. Her pulse beat like the heart of a sparrow caught in a snare.

"Richardis, speak your mind."

The girl only stared at me until the tears brimmed from her sapphire eyes. Snatching her hands from mine, she covered her face.

"Why won't you speak?" I pleaded.

"I have asked the same question for the past two years," her mother said. The arrogance vanished from her voice. She sounded melancholy, as though she bore an impossible burden. "She has not spoken a word since she turned eleven."

"Your daughter is a mute," I said, finally understanding.

The lady's face drained of color. "She wasn't born with this affliction. She can hear perfectly well, and until she stopped speaking, she was a girl like any other. At first I thought it was a sin born of willful pride, but now she's thirteen and won't make a sound, even if you prick her with a needle."

I winced. The girl crouched by the hearth, her back to us.

"Mind you, she isn't stupid." Her mother paced back and forth, her hands knit together. "Her brother Hartwig taught her to read and write the psalms in Latin."

I was at a loss, for this conundrum rendered me as speechless as Richardis herself.

"But now I know," the margravine said. "This was no sin of hers but a sign from God." Her voice cracked. "She belongs to God, not to the world."

My heart hardened when I remembered how my own mother had banished me to the anchorage at the age of eight because of the embarrassment over my visions. I thought how poor, ruined Jutta had been left to rot inside our enclosure until her madness and self-hatred consumed her. Perhaps the margravine hoped the shock of abandonment in this monastery would bring back the girl's voice.

"You mean that her affliction has spoiled her chances of gainful marriage," I said. "You fear she shall bring shame on your family. So you'll put her in a monastery far from your home."

Richardis stared, as though astounded by my audacity. I braced myself for her mother's outrage, but the lady only looked at me in sadness.

"Tell me, Hildegard, what would you do if she was your daughter? Keep her at court so everyone could ridicule her? Lock her away? Wed her to a man who will take her for her beauty and fortune, even though she can't say yes to him? Or offer her to God? At least here she will have dignity."

To my mortification, the margravine sank to her knees before me.

"She's my only daughter. I'm not washing my hands of her. I have your abbot's permission to stay in the guesthouse for as long as necessary, to see that she's settled and content. Here she shall live with her kinswomen."

My heart in my throat, I knelt on the floor beside her, took her arms, and drew her to her feet.

"Of course Richardis is welcome here," I said. "She may live with us as a postulant. But she cannot make any vows while she remains voiceless."

"By God's grace, she might regain her voice at Disibodenberg. Cuno said that the relics of holy Jutta might cure her."

I smiled grimly, imagining my abbot making just such a claim to convince the lady to entrust the girl and her wealth to him.

"But to hear the story from my nieces, Jutta wasn't quite the saint of your abbot's imaginings, was she?" The margravine turned to me with shining eyes. "I put more faith in your prayers and goodwill, Hildegard."

Flustered, I bowed my head. "I am no miracle worker, my lady."

Before I could say anything more, the margravine tenderly joined my hand to her daughter's. "Do you see, Richardis? Sister Hildegard cares only for your happiness."

"At least make a sign if you want to stay with us," I begged her.

The girl regarded me for a long moment, as though testing my patience. At long last she nodded, squeezing my fingers.

PART II

The Greenest Branch

O noblest greening, who have your roots in the sun.

—Hildegard von Bingen

9

SUDDENLY WE WERE free, my sisters and I. In place of the bricked-up passageway stood an oak door that bolted only from the inside. With Volmar as our guide, we learned to find our way around the abbey and its grounds, not only in the church, library, and scriptorium, but in the kitchen gardens, medicinal gardens, pastures, and fields. After my hours of work and prayer, I burst out of the gates and made for the forest, that living Eden where I felt myself renewed, greening like a willow in spring. Though I was thirty-eight, a second youth came upon me, the many sad years I had accumulated in that anchorage-hell melting away.

But I also served, spending hours in the hospice and infirmary helping old Brother Otto, who passed his wisdom on to me. It was one thing to study books of medicine, quite another to work with patients under the guidance of a master physician who had devoted his life to the healing arts. My head sang with the new knowledge. I was giddy, the whole world opening to me.

Likewise, my sisters found far more useful employment than they had in the confines of our enclosure. Guda tended the altars, arranging them with the cloths and banners she had sewn, and she sweetened the rushes on the church floor with dried lavender and rosemary. Adelheid spent her days in the scriptorium, copying texts in her excellent hand. She only regretted never having learned the alphabets of the Greeks and Arabs. As much as I coveted scholarly books, I myself would not have been able to bear spending all the daylight hours inside stone walls—I couldn't allow a single day to pass without the sun and wind on my face, something growing and alive touching my hands.

Then there was the matter of our new postulant, that voiceless girl living in our midst.

The first gift I gave Richardis was her own wax tablet and stylus, so she would always have means to communicate. Other than that, instead of trying to mold her as her mother had perhaps tried too hard to do, I let her be. After all, she was neither oblate nor novice, and I questioned whether she had a religious calling. Neither did I deem it necessary to saddle her with too many restrictions. The mute girl, by her very nature, obeyed the most important rule, which was silence during the hours of contemplation. Yet I confess it was unnerving to see her standing there, as soundless as stone, while Guda, Adelheid, and I sang the Divine Office. Richardis refused to even move her lips in the shape of the words. So I taught her to play the psaltery, which seemed to soothe her. She could spend hours plucking those strings, inventing her own melodies.

I expected Richardis to find friendship and affinity with Guda, who was closest to her in age, but Guda never seemed at ease around this strange girl with her otherworldly beauty. Yet she made a long-suffering attempt to employ Richardis with embroidery—a thing for which the girl only seemed to bear contempt. Perhaps it reminded her too much of the accomplishments her mother had expected her to master back home in Stade. With Adelheid cocooned in the scriptorium, Richardis took to following me on my daily rounds. That voiceless girl became my shadow.

When the white of winter melted into spring's verdant tide, Richardis was at my heels as I stole out of the gates into that realm of shoots and blossoms. In the forest I gathered fresh herbs for the hospice and infirmary.

How much more peaceful Richardis seemed out here, beyond those walls where her mother met with Cuno daily to discuss her spiritual progress. Since the girl was unmarried and had made no religious vows, she walked unveiled, her black hair snaking in a thick braid down her back. Out of the corner of my eye, I watched her slyly kick off her sandals so that she could tread barefoot in the moist April loam where violets and white wood anemone bloomed.

How stifling her life at home in Stade must have been, how her mother must have paraded the lovely girl around court to be appraised by potential bridegrooms, how that girl's very existence had been warped to serve her mother's ambition, that margravine whose second son was an archbishop. But Richardis had refused to dance to her mother's tune, retreating inside her bulwark of silence instead.

"Your mother named you after herself," I mused aloud. "But the name doesn't suit you, does it?"

The girl shook her head.

"What would you name yourself, I wonder, if you could choose?" I thought I might tempt her to communicate, to scrawl something on her tablet, but her face closed like a shutter.

Not pressing her with further inquiry, I gave Richardis my basket to carry while I stooped to dig up a primrose, roots and all.

"The primrose takes its power from the sun. And so it cures melancholy."

The girl stared at the plant with its buttery yellow flowers that I held in my outstretched palm.

"When melancholy arises in people, it makes them agitated and sad, so they rail against God. Demons of the air notice this and surround the poor soul, turning him toward insanity."

I thought of Jutta, of the thirty years of misery we had shared, how I had been an unwilling witness to her self-annihilation.

"The person should place the primrose near her heart. The demons of the air will flee before the plant's power and cease their torment."

Out here, surrounded by burgeoning life, Richardis's silence became companionable. She seemed to love the forest as much as I did, her fingertips skimming a filmy sweep of forget-me-nots. Raising her eyebrows in inquiry, she pointed to the tiny blue flowers.

I shook my head. "For all their beauty, they are not useful as medicine. If someone should chance to eat them, it would cause more harm than good."

The girl nodded, ducking beneath branches and gazing around with starry eyes, her hair crowned in a diadem of spider silk. Something inside her reminded me so much of the rebellion that had simmered within me when I was her age. This was why I chose to confide my secret that I had previously only dared confess to Volmar.

"My whole life long, I have borne an affliction not unlike yours." My voice was as hushed as the wind in the tender new beech leaves as I described the visions that had haunted me since earliest childhood. "Jeweled trees came floating down inside golden orbs. My mother didn't know if I was blessed or mad. That's why she packed me off to the monastery."

Richardis seemed to hang on my every word.

"Yet the curious thing is that since you arrived and we began to live a freer life, the visions ceased. Isn't that extraordinary? What do you think, Richardis? Have I been cured of the visions? Or has my life itself become the vision?"

I swung my arms wide in my longing to embrace this entire forest that rang with cuckoos and the rushing waters of the Nahe.

"God is not just in heaven, but in every living thing. You see it, too, don't you?"

Reverence overwhelmed me as I knelt to cradle a sweet violet, so pulsing with holiness that I was almost afraid to sever the plant from its roots.

Only when we were walking back toward the monastery did I dare ask the question that had plagued me since I first learned of her muteness.

"Tell me, what made you stop speaking?"

Her eyes hardened. How zealously that girl guarded her secrets. Still, I hazarded a guess. She was eleven when it happened, a common enough age for betrothal ceremonies.

"Your mother is very forceful, is she not? Did she attempt to betroth you to someone you didn't like?"

The look she gave me then, at once wounded and murderous, seemed to prove my hunch had been accurate.

"Richardis," I said, reaching out to her, but she reeled away from me.

Grabbing her wax tablet, she worked the stylus, her face set in trancelike concentration. Breathless, I waited to see what she would reveal. When at last she thrust the tablet into my hands, I found myself staring at a caricature of a veiled woman, her face rendered comical for being so overly inquisitive. The young are given to insolence. I could only conclude that she meant to mock me, yet I was enchanted. Since the age of eight, mirrors had been forbidden to me, but this voiceless girl had revealed my image with grace and skill.

"Is that what I look like?" I asked, grinning until she returned my smile and nodded.

"God has given you this gift. Now we must find you some parchment, ink, and pigments."

The girl flushed, as though suddenly shy. My basket in her hand, she sprinted across the grass, her steps becoming more measured only when she slapped her sandals back on her feet and entered the abbey gates.

"You need to find a task that will give you meaning and purpose," I told Richardis the following morning. We sat in the scriptorium, among the many scribes and illuminators submerged in their own silent worlds that mirrored hers.

Volmar showed her how to grind pigments to make paints. He lent her herbals and bestiaries so she could copy the pictures, first on wax before committing them to precious parchment and illuminating them in color. By early June, Adelheid had Richardis illustrating a newly copied psalter. The margravine looked on while her daughter ground malachite to a powder so she could adorn the margin with brilliant green leaves. Though the margravine hovered over her for hours, it was as if she weren't there. Nothing could shatter the girl's concentration or disturb her serenity as she painted ivy, fern, and oak leaf.

Finally her mother departed home to Stade, but not before bidding me to send for her at once if her daughter needed her.

As summer blazed on, I ventured deeper and deeper into the forest's emerald hush. From time to time, Richardis tagged along.

Just before the midsummer feast of John the Baptist, we were winding our way through a shadowy glade when she seized my hand and pointed. We stood face to face with a young hind. For a moment that seemed to last forever, the creature held us with her liquid brown eyes. Then she wheeled and leapt away, sailing clear over the underbrush, leaving us to marvel at the power of her springing limbs. As the wind whispered through the oak leaves, Richardis bent over her tablet, the stylus swift in her hand before she passed the tablet to me. She had written a verse from the Eighteenth Psalm.

HE MAKES MY FEET LIKE HIND'S FEET AND
SETS ME UPON HIGH PLACES.

Looking at the light shining in her eyes as she gazed off in the direction the hind had fled, I thought how this girl was a mystery to me. I wondered if I would ever know who she truly was.

Abundant with fish, the Nahe and Glan flowed on either side of the abbey promontory. Richardis insisted on accompanying me as my self-appointed scribe when I ventured forth to catalogue each creature that lived in those rivers, from the trout to the beaver to the pike that was as fierce as any boar. This was for the infirmary's use, so we would have a record of which river inhabitants were wholesome for the sick to eat.

Standing on the shore or wading through the shallows, I observed the creatures for an entire year, during which they revealed their natures to me. Some loved the day while others preferred the night. Pike and perch adored the shining sun and lived in the light-filled waters. Sturgeon came to life beneath the splendor of the moon and stars. The crawfish loved both night and day in equal measure, walking forward with the sun on its face and backward following the moon. Some fish poured out all their roe and milt at once, weakening and debilitating themselves. Others kept a greater interval between their effusions, which preserved their vitality.

"The fish that feed on clean foods and that dwell in the clear waters of the upper or middle depths are the healthiest to eat," I dictated to Richardis, who inscribed my words on her tablet. "But the bottom-feeders, or the carp that dwell in stagnant marshes, should never be eaten by the sick."

Despite, or perhaps because of, her affliction, the girl seemed infused with a breathtaking innocence. She was a margravine's daughter, who might have worn gold brocade and danced in the arms of some princeling. Instead, here she was, hunkered barefoot on the riverbank, peering through the water at those darting silver shapes. Grabbing her tablet, she began sketching.

"Those will inspire some fine illuminations," I told her.

The girl ducked her head, as though my praise both pleased and embarrassed her.

"Stade is very close to the sea. You must have laid eyes on all manner of marine creatures that I can scarcely imagine." I spoke breezily, in hope that the sun on the waters and her love for the wild life around her might coax her to speak.

She scribbled at the bottom of her tablet.

ONCE I SAW A WHALE-FISH. IT WAS BIGGER THAN A CASTLE.

Beside this, she had etched a leviathan spouting a huge plume of spray. Then she wrote:

I HAVE SEEN DOLPHINS THAT CAN LEAP OVER TALL-MASTED
SHIPS AND SEALS THAT TURN INTO MERMAIDS
BENEATH THE LIGHT OF THE MOON.

Before I could frame a suitable response, she cracked a grin, as though laughing in silence.

I laughed along, sharing her joke before asking her, as gently as I could, "Do you miss home?"

The girl pulled a face and flipped her braid over her shoulder. Fleet as a hind, she launched herself into cartwheels down the riverbank. Kicking her legs heavenward, every part of her seemed to revel in the freedom previously forbidden her—her mother, no doubt, would have thrown a fit to see her marriageable daughter indulging in such infantile play. Her joy was so infectious that I could only think that God had liberated me in order to give this girl sanctuary.

Richardis became my steadfast companion. Although she made no vows and remained as mute as she was the day her mother delivered her to us, she matured into a stately young woman of seventeen, an accomplished psaltery player and illuminator. In the scriptorium, she worked with Adelheid and Volmar, embellishing their manuscripts with her trumpeting angels and fruited vines. She grew even more beautiful, a fact not lost on her mother, who visited each summer and seemed crestfallen that such an exquisite girl remained unmarriageable.

As for my other sisters, Adelheid seemed well-contented with her scribing. Only Guda seemed unhappy. Of the three of us, she seemed to like Richardis least, perhaps because that girl's arrival had displaced Guda from her position as youngest and loveliest. Now even golden-haired Guda was thirty. In the secular world, she would have had a great brood of children by that age. As she grew older, Guda appeared to regret her vocation more and more. Her deepest misgiving, I thought, was that she would never experience the joy of motherhood. This loss only seemed to deepen her resentment of Richardis. She muttered that the girl's supposed muteness was something she had freely chosen in order to spite her mother — had Richardis deigned to utter even the simplest of words, her mother would have whisked her away and married her off with every honor. In Guda's view, her cousin was a spoiled, over-indulged child who frittered away her youth, beauty, and fertility by painting pictures and tramping through the forest with me. My worst fear was that Guda would grow into a bitter old woman.

I myself was happier than I ever dreamt I could be. Studying God's wild creation, the river and forest teaching me more than any book, my days passed in bliss. Cuno had no love for me and yet he was prepared to suffer me, he who had loved Jutta with his entire soul, who lifted her up to the shining pinnacle of womanhood. Since I was only six years younger than my dead magistra, perhaps he didn't expect me to outlive her by much.

It could have ended there, with my spending the remaining days left to me at Disibodenberg, enjoying the fruits of friendship and study, taking over the hospice duties from Brother Otto as he aged. *Ora et labora*, work and prayer, devotion to God and service to others, set the rhythm of my days.

One balmy May afternoon in 1141, I set to work on a new lapidary with Richardis as my scribe. We sat in what had once been the anchorage courtyard, its formerly high blank walls now lowered to reveal sweeping views of the Nahe and the forested hills beyond.

In my open palm, I held Richardis's sapphire necklace. How it glittered in the midday sun.

"Sapphire," I dictated, "is hot, more fiery indeed than airy or watery. It symbolizes both divine love and wisdom, Caritas and Sapientia, for Caritas and Sapientia are one — God's love cannot be separated from God's wisdom."

As I spoke, the noontide heat began to oppress me. A band of pain encircled my head, but I strove to ignore it.

"If the devil should incite a man to love a woman so that he goes mad with desire, and should this annoy the woman, she should pour a bit of wine over the sapphire three times and each time say: *I pour this wine over you; just as God drew off your splendor, wayward angel, so may you draw away from me this man's lust.*"

Needle-sharp pain pierced my temples, forcing me to cry out. Richardis's necklace tumbled to the ground as I lurched forward, pitching myself from my chair. My innards churned in nausea, then everything dimmed into nothingness. Only the pain was real, that blade that would not stop stabbing.

Richardis gripped my shoulders, cradled my cheek. She managed to lift me off the floor and guide me to my bed before darting to fetch help. Meanwhile, my head hammered in such agony that I feared my skull would explode.

Brother Otto laid a poultice on my forehead. The good physician offered me herbs steeped in honeyed wine, but nothing would ease my torment. My throat burned like hellfire and I couldn't swallow a single mouthful of water or broth. My womb convulsed, robbing me of my bodily powers until I no longer knew myself.

Was God punishing me for my very happiness, for daring to embrace life instead of suffering without end as Jutta had done? Did God truly desire nothing less than martyrs roiling in wretchedness? At the age of forty-two years and seven months, I felt as though I were about to die.

Imprisoned in the infirmary as I had once been imprisoned in the anchorage, I thought it could get no worse. Then the visions returned, wrenching me from my stupor. The Light seared me, turning my bones to putty, burning away my eyelids so all I could do was gape at that overpowering brilliance. And from that luminosity came the voice that shook me to my core. *It is time. Time to do what you were born to do.*

The Light dazzled every cell in my body as I thrashed in its grip. I fevered and panted while Brother Otto and my sisters gathered round, powerless to end my ordeal. Adelheid and Guda held each other while Richardis clung to my hand, her face only inches from mine as she wept noiselessly. Cuno watched from the doorway, as though in solemn expectation of my demise. Volmar, weeping as openly as my sisters, hovered at the foot of my bed. He moved his mouth to speak, but I was deaf to everything except the roaring within.

No longer could I idle away my days puttering about the forest and hospice. God had given me the visions for a purpose and yet I had hidden them away like rags soiled with menstrual blood. My task was to awaken. The command now reverberated within the chamber of my heart. *See and speak. Hear and write. Be God's mouthpiece.*

Shrinking inside myself, I considered the many books in our library penned by scholars whose erudition put me to shame, those great men who had mastered rhetoric, who could debate theology and philosophy in Latin, Greek, Hebrew, and Aramaic. The vastness of their knowledge left me cowering, for what was I but a weak, ignorant woman? My Latin grammar was no better than a young boy's — how dare I presume to write anything? But the vision seized me and would not let me go. *O fragile human, ash of ashes. Speak and write what you see and hear.*

Heaven opened, fire descending like Pentecostal flame. Fiery light permeated my brain and inflamed my heart, blinding and illuminating me at once. I thought I would burn up in its radiance, but then it warmed me as the sun warms all she touches. *Now I know.*

Meaning filled me. For more than three decades I had studied the holy texts, but now I understood them. Flames stoked my heart and mind, revealing the secret riches in the sacred writings: the psalms, the Gospels, and the other catholic volumes of the Old and New Testaments. The voice sang out like a trumpet. *I am the Living Light that illuminates the darkness.*

Dawn broke through the infirmary window. Echoing through the walls came the voices of the choir brothers singing Lauds. Though Cuno had vanished, my sisters, Brother Otto, and Volmar kept their vigil by my bed. As the first ray of sun touched my face, my voice returned.

"Volmar, please receive my confession."

Brother Otto and my sisters tiptoed from the room, leaving me alone with my oldest friend. His hand enclosing mine was warm, his strength infusing me.

"The visions have returned," I told him. "I'm not dying, but my old life is over. God has commanded me to do this thing, to speak and write what I see and hear. Only I don't know how. God should have chosen *you*." I smiled at him through my tears. "Not someone as ignorant as I am."

I feared he might react with alarm, as he had done when I first told him about my visions as a child, or that he would think these apparitions the sign of a troubled mind. Instead, he gazed at me in reverence.

"You were chosen for a reason," he said. "I'll help you however I can."

"Say not a word to Cuno. He'll have me burned for heresy." I spoke only half in jest.

At the very least, my abbot would think it presumptuous that I, the erring and unworthy nun, was trying to outshine holy Jutta whose relics graced our abbatial church, whose bones lay under the chapter house floor. Even after her death, her holy reputation was a beacon that drew a steady stream of pilgrims.

Before Volmar could say another word, Richardis stepped from the shadowy alcove where she had been eavesdropping. Her eyes brimmed as she bent to kiss me. Then, with a nod to Volmar, she handed me the tablet and stylus I had given her four years ago. Both she and Volmar seemed to hold their breath until I pressed the stylus into the wax. Trembling and faint-headed, I wrote and wrote until I emptied myself. Only then did the pain ebb. In its place came a humming energy, green fire surging through my veins. Throwing off the blankets, I planted my feet on the floor and stretched my arms. Both dazed and ecstatic, I turned to smile at my two dearest friends.

After I had washed and dressed, Richardis accompanied me to the church where Guda and Adelheid sang Terce along with the brothers. My sisters' faces lit up in joy and relief as I joined them in song, our voices soaring in harmony. After the Holy Office had ended, my sisters enclosed me in a tight embrace. Cuno stared before drawing away.

If my miraculous recovery flummoxed our abbot, it was not his way to encourage me to wallow in excess attention. In truth, I was grateful that he chose to ignore me in those first fragile days of my awakening.

Until that morning when I arose like Lazarus from my infirmary bed, I had lived under my abbot's thumb. From the age of eight, my every act had been under scrutiny, governed by the monks' rules and restrictions. Apart from my flamboyant bid for freedom on the day of Jutta's funeral, my life had been harnessed to one aim — submission. If I was no longer dead to the world in the tomb of the anchorage, Cuno still expected me to be silent, obedient, invisible. But the voice inside shattered the chains. It welled up in an unstoppable gush of words, a song that could never be stilled.

Every moment I was not in prayer, I was writing feverishly, covering tablet after tablet with revelations of divine love and the nature of the universe, of the macrocosm and the microcosm, of how the rift between the created world and the fallen world might be healed. Adelheid and Guda left me to my business — I wanted it that way lest I bring Cuno's wrath upon them as well as myself. But Richardis stuck to me like a burr, just as Volmar did. He who had once been Jutta's appointed secretary now offered himself as mine, behind Cuno's back. While Volmar transcribed my words to parchment, correcting and polishing my Latin, Richardis gathered pigments, quills, and brushes.

With colors as brilliant as the wildflowers that spangled the forest, the girl illuminated my every vision.

In the chamber of my heart, I discovered a door flung wide open, the enclosure of the mysteries now unlocked.

"Such splendor I see," I told Volmar and Richardis.

The vision unfolded as the three of us huddled in an overgrown corner of the medicinal garden where rosebushes grew tall to conceal us, enfolding us in their paradisial perfume.

"I see a mighty, towering woman." My voice rose like a melody over the drone of bees. "Around her, there glimmers a brightness as white as snow, as translucent as crystal."

Volmar's stylus scratched his wax tablet while Richardis bent over her own tablet, making a preliminary sketch.

"Like the dawn, she shimmers, shining forth as high as the secret places of heaven. In the heart of her embrace, I see the most beautiful maiden with long dark hair. Her red gown flows to her feet."

Richardis glanced up, a strand of her own hair caught in her mouth while I looked on with double vision, seeing Volmar and Richardis in the garden, and then the woman and girl in my revelation.

"Around the maiden I see a great throng of men and women, brighter than the sun, each adorned in gold and jewels."

The glory half-blinded me.

"The voice speaks. It says, 'Behold Ecclesia, the true Church and uncorrupted Bride.' She is the towering woman. The maiden in her arms is Caritas, Divine Love. The virgin clothed in the red of life."

Before me I saw the face of my God, my Mother, as awesome as lightning striking the earth, yet as gentle in her goodness as the sun's rays. She was incomprehensible to humans because of the dread radiance of her divinity and the brightness that blazed in her. For she was with all, and in all, and of a beauty so great that none could comprehend how sweetly she bore with us mortals and how she spared us with her inscrutable mercy.

As I opened my mouth to pour my vision into words, Cuno and Egon burst into our sheltering bower.

"What is this?" my abbot demanded, his eyes bulging in disbelief. "A monk, a nun, and a girl convene in secret? What are you writing?"

Hoping to shield Volmar and Richardis from any blame, I thrust myself forward.

"Abbot," I said, my head drooping lest he accuse me of any breech of humility. I anchored my eyes on his hairy toes peeping from his sandals. "I am but a weak and ignorant woman. I presume nothing. It is not my own thoughts I write but wisdom revealed to me by God. For God is so mighty that he might choose one as lowly as I am for his vessel."

"Out of everyone in this abbey, God chose *you* to be his mouthpiece?" My abbot's voice swelled in scorn. "If this is true, why did you not tell me? I think you hid your deeds because you knew them to be wicked. Your mind is deranged, beguiled by demons of the air."

"Reverend father," Volmar interjected. "I swear to you that I have detected nothing heretical in Hildegard's visions."

"Visions, no less!" Egon exchanged a look with Cuno, whose face went as dark as Judgment Day.

As Cuno snatched the tablet from Volmar's grasp, my dear brother whitened in dread.

"This demands discipline," our abbot said. "We have granted you every freedom, Hildegard, and you reward us by making us your fools, wasting Brother Volmar's time with your delusions. I'll wager you've wasted our parchment as well."

"Her visions are holy!" a voice cried out. A young voice. A breaking voice.

Even Egon was stunned as we turned to the trembling girl with her crimson face. Tears in her eyes, she placed herself between Cuno and me.

"Her visions are *beautiful*. Why would you punish her for something so good?"

I could see only her slender back, her arms rigid at her sides, her hands balled into fists as though to hold on to her courage. My knees buckled to behold the marvel—that mute girl had regained her voice in order to defend me.

Cuno stared at her, his face incredulous. "The girl speaks? Have you heard her speak before, Brother Volmar?"

Our abbot looked past Richardis and me, as though he trusted only a man to answer his question.

"My lord abbot, I have never heard Richardis speak until just now," Volmar said. "According to her mother, she's been mute since the age of eleven. Surely this is a miracle."

"Yes, I can speak," Richardis said, full of mettle. She sounded nearly as unshakeable as her mother. "It's all because of Hildegard. You can't say her visions are sinful now, can you, abbot?"

My heart was so full. It was as though my inner calling to speak and write of my visions had also unlocked Richardis's voice. In the May garden, the girl glimmered like a chalice overflowing with grace. Even the harsh set of Cuno's face softened before her. The most curious thing was that she spoke not with the long Saxon vowels of her homeland, but just like Volmar and I did, as though she were our daughter, born and bred in this Rhineland.

"We must write to your mother at once," Cuno said.

"Write to her, abbot," said the girl. "Tell her that Hildegard has given me back my voice."

"Or the relics of holy Jutta," Cuno said, glancing over the tablet he had confiscated, covered in my words that Volmar had recorded. "I must take this away for further study. Brother Volmar, if you have written any more of Hildegard's supposed visions, I must examine them as well."

Before our abbot could depart, Prior Egon clutched his belly and brayed. "If God can speak through Balaam's ass in the Book of Numbers," he chortled, so full of his own importance that I had to clamp my lips shut lest my temper flare and ruin everything, "then perhaps he can even speak through Sister Hildegard."

Cuno pursed his mouth and went on his way, with Egon at his heels like an eager dog.

As soon as they were out of earshot, I threw my arms around Richardis. "Oh, my dear blessed girl, it *is* a miracle. Never stop speaking, no matter what they might do."

The May sunlight illumined her lovely young face as she smiled at me and then at Volmar, who looked at her fondly, as though she were his daughter.

"It would be worth any penance," he told her, "just to hear you speak, my child."

As it conspired, Cuno decided to leave us in peace, at least for the time being. It might have gone no further. This could have been the end of my story: Hildegard, the eccentric nun in her dotage, tolerated as a curiosity by her long-suffering brethren, who, out of Christian charity, allowed her to write. No longer in secret, I embarked upon my first book, *Scivias,* or *Know the Ways,* revealing my visions concerning creation and redemption, and how humans might be brought back into harmony with the divine plan, that great cosmic wheel ever whirling. As the book unfolded before me, I saw my own salvation — this, my offering to God, would redeem my entire existence, healing the wound of my long imprisonment.

And thus the word went out, traveling far and wide on the tongues of passing pilgrims. Before long, I received a letter from Rorich in Mainz.

Sister, are the rumors true? Everywhere I've heard it said that Hildegard of Disibodenberg fancies herself a seeress, and that you even claim to cure the mute. What do your abbot and confessor say? I pray you won't be led astray by the False One.

My brother, who had thought me long cured of my childhood affliction of the far-seeing, seemed concerned that my divine awakening would only damage his own reputation. Grabbing my penknife, I scraped every last trace of ink from his letter before passing the bare parchment to Richardis so that she might put it to good use for her illuminations.

Richardis transfixed us all. How she enthralled the brothers, this lovely and noble virgin, her speech miraculously restored in a living embodiment of holiness. She was the most dazzling person to enter this abbey since Jutta in the days of her youth and beauty. Of course, Cuno wasted no time in sending word to her mother, appealing to her for further donations in gratitude of the glorious wonder that he attributed to the sainted Jutta's intercession.

We expected the margravine to swoop down on the abbey any day, though in truth, I was not eager to see her, as I blamed her overarching ambition for her daughter's affliction. I hoped and prayed that the mother's journey from Stade would be slow, granting the girl a few more weeks in which to savor her brand-new voice before her mother dragged her back home to find a bridegroom.

My deepest joy was hearing Richardis sing the Divine Office. Her unschooled voice was surprisingly rich, setting a lovely counterpoint to Guda's ethereal vibrato. Though the two did not always get along, their voices wove together in angelic harmony. Candlelight glinting off her long black hair, Richardis closed her eyes, as though in ecstasy, as she sang the words I had composed.

> *O tu suavissima virga*
> *O sweetest branch*
> *growing from Jesse's stalk,*
> *how great a power is this*
> *that divinity looked upon*
> *this fairest daughter*
> *as an eagle directs*
> *his gaze to the sun.*

. . .

Watching Richardis sing with my sisters brought back the vision I'd had so many years ago, when Adelheid and Guda were children, before Richardis had even been born. I recalled how in my illness I had witnessed three maidens glowing with divinity. Adelheid appeared in the guise of Sapientia, Divine Wisdom, while Guda shone in majesty as Ecclesia, the true and inner Church. Then, from between them, emerged the most splendid figure, glowing in innocence and joy — the black-haired girl, whom I knew now to be Richardis, blazing in my vision before she was even conceived in her mother's womb. *My name is Caritas, Divine Love.*

My memory dissolved in sadness, for I knew I would soon be losing her. But if she lacked a true religious vocation, there was little point in her staying here. I kept thinking back to how that once sullen and silent girl had opened her heart to me, infecting me with the fire of youth as she cartwheeled down the riverbank. She had been a comet blazing her trail through my constrained existence. At seventeen she was as ripe for marriage as a plump peach about to fall from the tree of its own accord. Even her youth would end all too soon.

One August evening as we sang Vespers, the margravine tiptoed into the church unannounced. From the corner of my eye, I watched her weep in awe. Secretly I feared how her daughter would receive her, if she still harbored resentment. But when the service ended, Richardis launched herself into her mother's arms and covered her in kisses. The bond between mother and daughter was so tangled and fierce that I could only pray they had reconciled.

"I can sing! I can speak!" my young friend cried out. "Hildegard cured me."

"You have God to thank, not me," I said before leaving her and her mother to their reunion.

The following day the margravine met me in the cloister garden. She appeared as magnificent as the Queen of Sheba in her silk gown with a necklace of Baltic amber encircling her throat. But when I looked at her more closely, I noticed the worry lines etched around her eyes and mouth. I had expected her to be elated, leaping over the stars that her daughter could speak again.

"Cuno tells me you are writing a book of your visions," she said, speaking as though it were a scandal.

Perhaps the margravine feared I'd be condemned for heresy, thus compromising her daughter's good name. What manner of woman had the temerity to write a book and hope not to disgrace herself? Still, it seemed rather moot since Richardis would soon be leaving us.

"My lady," I said, "we don't choose our path, but we are called. Sometimes God's calling appears unfathomable."

"Indeed," she said archly. "My daughter certainly seems to have discovered a calling in illuminating your visions."

"I'm most grateful for her devotion to this work." I spoke as peaceably as I could, having little desire to turn Richardis's mother against me.

"I wonder, magistra, why you could not have chosen another illuminator. Why my daughter?"

My skin prickled beneath her scrutiny. "My lady, I didn't ask her to do this. She offered, and illuminating seemed to bring her such delight." I smiled, hoping to ease my way past her anger. "But now I imagine her life will be quite different. When are the two of you returning to Stade?"

The color rose in the margravine's cheeks. "Sometimes I think you are not a nun but a witch."

I froze. "What can you mean?"

Within me, annoyance battled confusion. Four years ago this woman had thrust her mute daughter upon me and though I had been at a loss in the beginning, the girl had learned to trust me and opened herself in friendship. Now, through the grace of God, Richardis had regained her voice. Why couldn't her mother be grateful?

"You and your music," she said. "You and your visions that she turns into pictures. My daughter has fallen under your spell and chosen you."

I shook my head, stung.

"My lady, in your absence I may have acted as a mother to her, but once she leaves these walls and returns to court, she will be your daughter again, through and through. And some lucky man's bride."

I imagined Richardis in a gown of crimson, surrounded by countesses and courtiers, hawks and hounds. I pictured her dancing in the arms of her future husband, of them drinking from the same goblet, the loving cup, rimmed with gold.

"What? And break her heart?" Tears slid down the margravine's face. "If I forced her away, she would hate me forever."

"What are you saying?" My throat grew tight as I watched the lady weep. I longed to take her hand, but everything in her stance warned me to keep my distance.

"Richardis says she wants to stay with you."

A buzz like a thousand bees arose inside me. I could not comprehend any of this.

"Richardis wishes to take the veil," the margravine said at last, each word coming out of her mouth like a thorn.

This lady had placed her daughter in my care, as though leaving a diamond within a vault, to be removed at any time she wanted. Except Richardis had proved that she was no dumb stone, however precious, but a young woman who could speak her own will.

The cloister garden shimmered in the late summer heat. The roses, the sunlight, the gushing fountain, and the margravine's clenched white face blurred together. Richardis, that unbound soul, truly wished to commit herself to Disibodenberg, as I had done against my will as a frightened child? That beautiful young woman had set her heart on remaining here, on helping me finish the book that might condemn me? I pressed my fingers to my temples to clear my thoughts.

"She's no longer my daughter," the margravine said. "But your protégée."

"And for all you know, I might be a heretic," I said, reading her unspoken fears. "You dread what might happen to Richardis if she joins her fate to mine." I sighed. "My lady, she hasn't spoken a word about her vocation to me. Let me talk to her."

With a heavy heart, I sought out Richardis. *Did she truly wish to embrace the religious life*, I wondered, *or was she merely eluding and confounding her mother?* Surely it was my duty to prevent her from rashly making vows she would spend a lifetime regretting.

I found her in our courtyard where she stood with her back to me, not yet aware of my presence, gazing out over the forests and hills. On a clear day such as this, I could make out the faint shape of Sponheim Castle, Jutta's birthplace, on the far horizon. Richardis seemed lost in her contemplation of that rolling landscape, a tide of green that had reached its zenith and would slowly dwindle back as autumn approached. Loathe to disturb her reverie, I was about to creep away like a coward, when my footsteps betrayed me. The girl spun around. Rushing toward me, she took my hands. She must have been preparing shell gold pigment, in the scriptorium, for her fingers brushed mine with particles of pure gold.

"Hildegard! I mean, magistra. Did Mother speak to you? Did she reveal to you my deepest desire?"

The girl's face was flushed and expectant. The look she gave me, filled with such affection, left me weak. The dear, dear girl, so beautiful and spirited. So full of life, like a silver birch still growing, its branches stretching toward the sun, its leaves brushing heaven. Something fierce beat inside my heart. For one blinding moment, I couldn't imagine my life without this girl and that terrified me.

"You must think long and hard about your vocation," I told her. "This is no easy path. Besides, I fear you would disappoint your mother very much. Return with her to Stade, Richardis. You're her only daughter. If she loses you, it might break her heart."

"You think me unworthy of the calling? Have I displeased you?" Richardis went pale.

"Listen to me, child," I said, fighting the tremor in my voice. "If God has truly called you, none may stand in your way. It's your choice and yours alone. It mustn't be forced or hurried. But *think*, my dear! Among the vows you must make are stability and fidelity to this abbey. Is this truly what you want, to live within these walls for the rest of your earthly life?" I squeezed her shoulders. "In your place, I would choose freedom."

The girl smiled at me through her tears. "If you think the courtly life is a free one, Hildegard, you're ignorant of it."

She clasped her hands, glittering with gold dust, over her heart.

"The years I've spent here with you and Volmar and the sisters have been the happiest I've ever known! You yourself just said that if a religious life is *truly* my desire, then none may turn me away."

"That's correct," I conceded. "But think of your poor mother."

The girl spoke in a clear, decisive voice. "When she had no use for me, she cast me off and left me with you. But now she wants to drag me back into her world and use me as her pawn."

How I hated standing on that battleground between mother and daughter. Not knowing what else to say, I stepped past her and gazed out on the Nahe, emerald green beneath the trees. In my silence, she took her place beside me, resting her hand on mine as I gripped the stone wall. She gazed shyly into my eyes.

"*You* are the one who truly cared for me, through good times and bad. You and Volmar and Adelheid. But *you* were there at the beginning when the rest of them didn't know what to do with me. From the very first, you loved me for what I was."

Not even Volmar had ever spoken to me with such fondness. My face was as hot as a brick within a kiln and my heart beat so hard that I thought she must hear it. The dear child. Was it right that she should cleave to me? What if God had sent her to me for a purpose, that my visions should be the channel for her unfolding as well as my own? Could it be that her destiny was inextricably linked with mine, this girl whom I had seen in a vision those many years ago, when I was as young as she was now? Deep inside

159

me, pulsing light welled up in a fountain, cascading in brilliant white flame.

Regaining my self-possession, I began to admonish her on the waiting period she must undergo before entering her novitiate. She cut me short with a whoop. Dancing around the courtyard, she nearly knocked over our potted herbs before throwing her arms around me, covering me in gold.

The following year, upon July twentieth, the Feast Day of Margaret of Antioch, the abbatial church was transformed into a garden out of the Song of Solomon, the altars laden with roses of every color, their perfume mingling with the swirling incense. But that splendor faded into the background as the loveliest of brides led the procession up the nave toward the sanctuary, where Cuno and Archbishop Adalbert of Mainz awaited.

Walking behind her, bearing a lighted candle, I could not see Richardis's face, only her cascade of black hair, loose and unbound to mark her maidenhood. Her gown of crimson damask swept the floor before my feet. Her joy seemed to illuminate the church like a thousand suns while the monks sang and her mother wept.

Wax from the dripping candle seared my fingers as she prostrated herself before the high altar during the Litany of the Saints, her body forming the shape of the cross. Under the archbishop's gaze, I set the candle on the altar. Adalbert looked strained and ill. His men were arrayed around the chancel, my brother among them. My eyes slipped past him, for we hadn't spoken since his last leave-taking, when he'd announced he had no choice but to abandon me to my fate at Disibodenberg. The scourge of Rorich's betrayal still stung. Yet I could feel his eyes on me, as though he had something urgent to communicate. Was this a glimpse of the old Rorich, the one I had adored? I turned toward Richardis, who arose, her eyes radiant as she placed her hands in mine.

"Magistra," she said. "I offer myself to God through obedience."

Obedience. The vow I had wrestled with all my days. Yet in her I saw no doubt, only surrender to the call. This woman of eighteen was more innocent than I had been as an eight-year-old. A shiver went up my back when I remembered how my mother had pushed me face-first into that bed of grave dirt.

Adelheid brought the wreath of white roses and lilies, which I placed on Richardis's head as a sign of her consecrated virginity. Before the assembly, the archbishop praised Richardis, lauding her as a torch shining in the darkness, and prayed that her chastity and perfect submission might work toward redeeming the sin of Eve and womankind. With the agility of youth, Richardis plunged to her knees before him. More slowly, I knelt to her right while Adelheid knelt to her left.

"My daughter," the archbishop said. "You have left the world and turned to God. What then do you ask?"

"The mercy of God." Richardis's breath touched my cheek as she held me with her sapphire eyes. "And the holy companionship of Hildegard and my sisters."

After the monks had sung *Veni creator,* the archbishop admonished her.

"Do you, daughter, then desire to persevere in your sacred resolution?"

Tears of rapture shone like diamonds upon her face as she uttered the words of an ecstatic bride. "I do! I do!"

Adelheid removed the garland from Richardis's head while I held out the black veil of the Benedictines, which she kissed as passionately as though it were her Bridegroom. She closed her eyes in reverence as I draped the veil over her beautiful hair. When I removed the veil, she knelt again before the archbishop, allowing him to cut off those flowing black tresses that swept down to her waist. Unable to watch, I turned away, only to see the margravine's face glazed with tears. Along with her grief and loss, I sensed a burning pride in all her daughter might become, her illuminations the glory of Disibodenberg. My eyes locking on to hers, I made my silent promise to safeguard her daughter's happiness.

Richardis and I then withdrew into the sacristy where I unlaced her bridal gown, its crimson tumbling to the floor in a silken swoosh. Standing before me in her shift, she looked utterly transformed, her girlish giddiness given way to dignity and devotion. Humbled, I thought to myself that her vocation was true, that she embraced the vows with her entire being. She would be saintly, everything Cuno could ever wish a nun to be.

Richardis held out her arms to receive the black tunic.

When we had returned to the church, she knelt before me as I fitted the scapular over her and then belted it over her tunic with the cincture. Biting my lip, I arranged the wimple to hide her ravaged hair and covered the wimple in the white veil of a novice. My heart caught in my throat as I handed her the lighted candle, the symbol of the light blazing inside her.

After the ceremony, highborn well-wishers thronged around Richardis, her mother, and her brother Hartwig, Archbishop of Bremen, their many voices rising in a din. How Richardis glowed, one arm linked with Hartwig's as she smiled at him, the brother who had been her childhood hero, as Rorich had once been mine.

Turning away from the festivities, I walked alone in the cloister garden, my thoughts clouded, wondering if one day Richardis would find this life too stifling. She would never see her North Sea again.

The sound of footsteps caught me by surprise. I swung around to find that Rorich had followed me.

Mumbling a formal greeting, I made a reverence to him, as though he were any other visiting cathedral canon and not my brother. There was a broken place inside me where my love for him used to dwell.

"Sister," he said, "you bring honor to your abbey in gaining so promising a novice."

The emptiness of his words grated on me.

"Indeed, I fear the abbey, and not Richardis, has the better end of the bargain," I said. "Her dowry is even greater than the holy Jutta's."

Only then did I observe how unwell my brother looked. Rorich had dwindled, his cheek bones protruding, his eyes shadowed, his hair thin and gray. There was something dead and dull in his eyes. What had he suffered, my brother, who had once raced through the forest, beating down a path for me to follow?

"You must take better care of the tabernacle of your soul," I told him. "Does the archbishop never feed you? Drink beer. That will put some color in your face."

"Hildegard," he said, ignoring my advice, "there is so much talk of you in Mainz that the archbishop wonders if you seek to steal away Jutta's flame."

With a sigh, I raised my face to the clouds chasing each other across the blue vault of heaven.

"I cannot touch Jutta's saintliness. I seek nothing but to follow God's command to write of my visions."

"But is it truly God's glory you serve?" my brother asked, a pale sweat blooming on his brow. "Or your own?"

A wave of white-hot anger shook me. How dare he speak to me this way? He who had every benefit of an education in the seven liberal arts, who ate at the archbishop's table and lived in his palace. How dare he forbid me my humble writing, my one hope to offer some gift to God that would outlive my short existence?

"What glory do you think I could hope to find in Disibodenberg?" I asked him, unable to disguise my rage.

"Hildegard." He reached for my hand, but I backed away out of his reach. "I've done my best to defend your reputation. But if you keep making a spectacle of yourself, I won't be able to protect you."

"Protect me from *what?*"

"If you don't take care, the talk of you will wend its way to Rome."

A laugh burst from my lips, as ugly and jarring as if I had broken wind. "You would have me believe that the men in Rome will trouble themselves over one lowly nun?"

"It's because you write," he said, an edge of desperation creeping into his voice. "Everyone knows that certain women are gifted with prophecy and foresight—even the ancients knew this. But they do not write books! Once you put your visions to parchment along with your name, some in the Church might find wickedness in them. Or even dispute that your visions come from God."

"Are you saying my visions come from Satan?" I stared at him in such contempt that he held his hand over his eyes.

"I don't. Others might. Hildegard, let this Brother Volmar pretend he is the author of your book. That would attract less attention."

"And let him risk his reputation so that I might keep mine safe? A fine reward for his friendship."

Rorich clasped my arm, his fingers burning through my sleeve. "All those years ago, when I tried to help you and you chose to stay. You never told me why. It was for the oblates, wasn't it? You put their welfare above your own."

I nodded, wondering why he should speak of this now.

"I could never have made such a sacrifice," he said, still gripping my arm as though I might give him strength. "Of the two of us, you're the better one, my sister. The most loving and courageous. I'm just one of Adalbert's underlings, but you are as brilliant as the evening star. Just be careful, I beg you. Tall trees are the first to go down in the storm."

Tears pricked at the back of my eyes to hear the tenderness behind his words. In the last moment before the bells rang for Sext, I wrapped my arms around my brother.

Rorich spoke the truth. By this time, I had become something of a local legend, as Jutta had been before me. Cuno, of course, chafed under the attention I drew to our abbey. What if it proved he harbored a heretic? But if he was tempted to silence me, he was also tempted by the pilgrims' coins and by the new novices, drawn by my budding fame. My dead sister Roswithia's daughter Hiltrud and a young girl named Verena enriched Disibodenberg with their dowries and so forced Cuno's hand. Although Abbot Cuno and Abbot Adilhum before him had never intended this to be a double monastery, Cuno reluctantly gave permission for two new rooms to be added to our nunnery.

10

THREE YEARS PASSED, during which time Richardis, Verena, and Hiltrud made their final vows as ordained nuns. Two further novices, Sibillia and Margarethe, came to join us. Meanwhile, *Scivias* grew into a great stack of pages.

The outermost room of our cramped nunnery with its large window had become our private scriptorium, the panes of horn now replaced with glass to allow the fullest flood of light. Outside the open door, the courtyard hummed with bees greedy for the nectar of those flowering herbs, their perfume holier to me than frankincense.

Adelheid sat at her desk, copying a text of Aristotle, while I sat with Richardis and Volmar. In the next room, its door open to let in the light and air, Verena and Hiltrud embroidered while Guda taught the new novices to play the psaltery, using the melodies I had composed for them. Their music provided the counterpoint to our studies. With the young women to guide and nurture, Guda had finally found her happiness, doting on those girls as though they were her daughters.

As I described my visions, Volmar made notations on his wax tablet while Richardis, now twenty-one, sketched on hers. To my joy, she didn't appear to regret her vows, but seemed to rejoice in this life. That I would be blessed with so dear a companion! Though my youth had been harsh, these later years had brought me gladness and true friendship. Indeed, everything in my little world seemed right and good, everything flowing, as the purest waters flow from their source high in the Alps before joining the springs and brooks that feed the mighty Rhine. *For every thing there is a season.* And this was the late blossoming of my life when I unfolded like an autumn crocus.

We were absorbed in our tasks when Guda raised her voice in alarm. Volmar, twisting on his stool to look into the other room, went a shade paler. Before my friend could utter a word of warning, Prior Egon swaggered into our sanctuary. Egon, not Cuno. Our abbot, it transpired, was too great a coward and so he let his prior be his messenger.

Without preamble, Egon snatched my *Scivias* manuscript and clutched it to his chest with the malice of a glutton stealing our daily bread.

"What are you doing?" My heart caught in my throat—those precious pieces of parchment were the revelations given to me by God.

"The pope's envoy has graced us with a visit. Eugenius has heard of your writings and so he has sent his delegation to question you."

As the shock descended upon us, the only noise was Richardis's stylus falling to the stone floor.

"To what purpose?" Volmar demanded, his mild face distorted in outrage.

But I already knew. Three years ago Rorich had tried to warn me. *Tall trees are the first to go down in the storm.* My vision grew dark, as though the moon had eclipsed the sun.

"To examine Hildegard for heresy." Egon's every word rang like a nail being driven into a coffin lid.

How long, I wondered, *had the prior been biding his time, waiting to fling those words into my face?* And why now? Why had they allowed me to write for four years before making their move? How much deliberation and discussion had gone into this? The Archbishop of Mainz had to be behind it—it would have been his duty to alert Rome. Rorich had promised to defend me for as long as he was able, but he was only one man.

"Prepare yourself, Hildegard. They will interrogate you in the chapter house tomorrow."

Smug as a gargoyle, Egon stalked away with the unfinished *Scivias*, the fruit of four years' labor, in his greasy fingers.

"It's over," I whispered as Richardis reached for my hand. My awakening, my flowering, my unfolding had been in vain. It was as if Egon had bricked me into the anchorage once more and the daylight would never again touch my face.

I'd been a fool to think I could write and be left in peace! This was no private endeavor of mine, it couldn't be. Everything written on theology was the Church's business and must be dissected and discussed, for any whiff of unorthodoxy undermined the whole institution. The fate of heretics was something I understood only too well, both from my reading and from Cuno's blistering sermons on the subject. How easily my brethren could excommunicate me, cast me out, leave me with nothing. The very clothes on my back belonged to Disibodenberg.

Even that mighty philosopher, the castrated monk Pierre Abélard, once the glory of the cathedral school in Paris, had been declared guilty of heresy, not once, but twice, at the Council of Soissons and finally at the Council of Sens, only five years ago, when he had been condemned unheard and commanded to write no more. The Church had burned his books. Only a year later he died, the fight and fire gone out of him. If they could silence so great a scholar, surely they would make short work of a woman such as I.

I turned to my sisters. "You shouldn't have to suffer on my account. If they put me away, you shall vote in a new magistra. Your life shall go on."

"*You* are our magistra," Adelheid said, looking to Guda, who wept quietly, her arms around the novices.

"I will send for my mother," Richardis said. "She would never allow you to be treated this way."

"Child," I said, "even your mother cannot stand in the way of the pope."

The bells rang for Vespers, but instead of leaving to join his brethren for the Divine Office, Volmar remained with us, in the depths of what had once been our prison—and might soon be again if Egon got his way.

"Hildegard, you must act, and quickly," Volmar said. "Your very life depends on it."

"What can I do?" I closed my eyes.

Volmar refused to let me give in to despair. "Who is the most powerful man in the Church?"

"The pope, who has sent his inquisitors after me!"

"Even the pope relies on the wisdom of his counselors. Who is Eugenius's mentor? At whose feet did he learn?"

"Bernard of Clairvaux," I said. "The Cistercian."

Even I knew that Eugenius had been Bernard's postulant and that his path to the papacy owed much to his friendship with that great man.

"You must write to him." Volmar found an empty sheet of parchment hidden at the bottom of the desk.

"Tomorrow," I said, fearing that my friend risked too much on my behalf. "If you don't show yourself at Vespers, Cuno will punish you."

"I'll take any penance," Volmar said. "We must begin."

Even as my heart brimmed in gratitude, the futility weighed on me. "Bernard was the very man who denounced Abélard. Why would he help me?"

Throughout Christendom, Bernard of Clairvaux was famed for his asceticism, which might have put even Jutta to shame. He had worked to establish the Cistercian order since he found our Benedictine Rule too lax, our abbots too enticed by luxury.

"Abélard," said Volmar, "was an arrogant man whose philosophies would explain away the great mysteries of faith. Yet even so, had he shown the proper humility, he might not have been condemned. You are but an unknown nun in an obscure abbey, Hildegard. I think the holy Bernard will look kindly upon your visions of the Divine Lady."

At last I understood Volmar's reasoning. Bernard of Clairvaux preached that the Bride in the Song of Songs was none other than Mary, whom he proclaimed the great intercessor for human redemption. He, who had received true visions of the Mother of God, might indeed give his blessing to my writings on the Lady at the axis of the wheel of creation.

"We must capture Bernard's attention quickly." Volmar was already scoring lines on the parchment. "He's a busy man. Eugenius has commanded him to preach a second Crusade."

Darkness was falling. Guda directed the novices to light every candle and lamp so that we could work long past sunset. Searching my soul, I summoned the words that Volmar put to parchment. My friend's verdict on Abélard rang like an admonition. To survive this, I must appeal to Bernard with deepest humility.

> *O Bernard, venerable father, I am greatly disturbed by visions that have appeared to me through divine revelation. Wretched in my womanly condition, I have from earliest childhood seen great marvels that my tongue has no power to express, but which God has taught me that I may believe. Gentle father, in your kindness respond to me, your unworthy handmaiden, who has never lived one hour free of fear.*
>
> *I seek consolation from you that you might reveal to me whether I should speak about such things openly or keep my silence. And so I beseech your aid, through the sublimity of the Father, who sent the Word with sweet fruitfulness into the womb of the Virgin, from which he soaked up flesh, just as honey is surrounded by honeycomb.*
>
> *Once there was a king sitting upon his throne. It pleased him to raise a small feather from the ground, and he commanded it to fly. And so the feather flew, not because of anything in itself but because the wind bore it along. Thus I am but a feather on the breath of God.*

I stood in the chapter house, the only woman in that ocean of men. Cuno positioned me directly upon the stone in the floor marking

Jutta's grave, as though this could invoke the intercession of my holy magistra, who would have never caused her brethren such bother.

The papal prelates assembled in their ranks as if they were foot soldiers awaiting the command to charge. But the Archbishop of Mainz had not come, owing to his poor health, and thus my brother was not present to speak in my defense. That morning I felt not as if I were a feather on the breath of God, but a dead autumn leaf hurled along in the tempest.

"How do you know your visions come from God?" one of my inquisitors asked me.

The pages of *Scivias* rested in his lap. Watching his fingers sift through the pages, I shook.

"How do you know you are not deceived by Satan?" he continued, his voice rising in impatience as I gaped at him, my clenched hands dripping sweat.

When I finally brought myself to speak, my voice was choked and small. "The Living Light I have seen could only come from God."

My arguments were simple, like the stammerings of a child. What made my claims any different from those of the Cathari, who would also declare that their beliefs had been revealed to them by God? These men would denounce and disparage me forevermore. How could I have presumed to put pen to parchment, they must have wondered, poor creature that I was, formed from a rib, a sinful daughter of Eve?

Another prelate spoke. "You must have known that you courted heresy with these unauthorized writings. Calling yourself a prophetess!"

I cast my eyes down to the stone covering Jutta's corpse. "My lords, I serve the Church with all my heart."

But as I said this, my soul banished those dour-faced clerics, replacing them with a vision of the majestic woman crowned in gold who cradled the rejoicing and unveiled virgins in her arms. Ecclesia, the true inner Church, forever uncorrupted.

"Eugenius himself must examine your writings," the prelate hold-ing *Scivias* told me.

My forehead throbbed. So it wasn't to end here, this day? My trial could last for months, even years, until the pope and prelates reached their verdict.

Scivias, which had arisen from the depths of my being, a gift of the Light, begun in secret with Volmar and Richardis as my only confi-dants, would now be dissected by the Holy Father himself. Had I guessed this in the beginning, I would never have dared write a word.

Volmar had spoken the truth—only Bernard of Clairvaux could save me now.

Many months I waited, my despair as deep as winter's snow. In that purgatory, forbidden to write, I could only await news of my fate. Cuno and Egon went out of their way to ignore me, as though I were already condemned and banished.

When Bernard of Clairvaux's response to my letter finally arrived, he offered me the blandest of good wishes, for he had much weightier matters requiring his intervention than the plight of one irksome nun. The Second Crusade had begun and none other than his own queen, Eleanor of Aquitaine, rode forth for the Holy Lands.

I have made some effort to respond to your letter, Hildegard, beloved daughter of Christ, although the press of business forces me to re-spond more briefly than I would like.

We rejoice in the grace of God that is in you, and we most urgently beseech you to respond to your gift with humility and devotion. But, on the other hand, when the learning and the anointing (which re-veals such things to you) are within, what advice could we possibly give?

Volmar and my sisters, upon reading the letter, tried their best to lift my spirits.

"It's a great blessing that such an esteemed man replied to your letter," Adelheid told me. "He holds you in his prayers."

"His letter finds no wickedness in your visions," Richardis pointed out. "Does he not say you are gifted with God's grace?"

My trusted friends were not the only ones to have read Bernard's letter. Cuno, I discovered, had scrutinized every word before allowing it to pass into my possession. When I entered the church to sing Vespers, my abbot looked me in the eye for the first time in half a year, his tight-lipped smile betraying his confidence that Bernard was far too occupied to interfere on my behalf. Cuno had won. It was only a matter of waiting for the Synod of Trier, one year away, to hear the final outcome. Meanwhile, I might as well wall myself in again, so little had I to live for.

Such darkness I was plunged into that even prayer seemed empty. My soul withered to a husk. It was as though God, who had once bathed me in Light, had abandoned me.

That night, when I lay in bed with my face turned to the wall, I broke like an egg. Weeping seized me like a fit of falling sickness. This was my end. Cuno had silenced me forever. Such was my penance for aspiring to be anything more than a drudge, cringing before his will.

As the silent sobs racked my body, footfalls as soft as fluttering moth wings crossed the floor. Freezing, not daring to breathe, I willed my sister to return to her bed. Instead a weight settled on the edge of my mattress. Hands pulled the blanket off my head before turning me around to face her whose fingers smoothed away my tears. By the light of the dormitory candle, kept burning all night long in accordance to the Rule, I saw Richardis.

"Don't you dare give up hope," she whispered.

Laying her soft body beside mine, her unbound hair spilling over my pillow, she embraced me, containing my grief like a vessel.

"Do you think God gave you your visions in vain?" she asked, her lips against my ear. "Have you so little faith? What do you *see?*"

I saw her, shining like a torch, her face only inches from mine. Her arms wrapped around me. Her lips were in my hair.

"We mustn't," I whispered, pushing her away.

As much as I longed to surrender to the solace she offered, I dreaded doing anything that might bring shame on her.

"We aren't doing anything wrong." In perfect innocence, Richardis pressed her cheek to mine.

"But the Rule—"

"Does the Rule tell me to ignore my sister's pain? If I was in despair, surely you would come to comfort me, just as I have come to you."

Her words rendered me mute. In the secular world, two sisters of flesh and blood, or even two fond friends, might hold each other without reproach. A voice inside told me this could be no sin, this tenderness, so freely offered. As she drew me into her arms once more, I forgot myself, went out of myself, leaving my cares in that glad night where all things ceased. She remained with me, murmuring her words of consolation until just before Matins when she slipped back to her own bed.

O shining gem, o noble Lady who has no blemish, you are a companion of angels. How does God move in our lives if not through love?

In my darkest hour, when I was certain my ruin was at hand, Richardis sustained me. She was the pillar of strength that allowed me to go on, her devotion the proof that I was not forsaken, that the Light still shone even through a night that seemed endless. If I was condemned, if my story was to end then and there, at least I had known this before I died. At least I had known what it was to be cherished.

How different this was from that girlish infatuation I had once harbored for Volmar, my ardor overshadowed by the cold knowledge that he would adore only one woman—Jutta. My unspoken passion for him was destined never to be requited but to mellow into the chaste friendship that had endured until this day. But Richardis revealed what it was to love and have that love returned, measure for measure. Even though I was twice her age, she held up a mirror. In her gaze, I was beautiful.

What Richardis and I shared was something ineffable, as though God had brought us together for a purpose. Together we grew into nobler souls than we would have been apart. She was so precious to me, this girl who had found her voice just as I began to write of my visions.

I was not ignorant of Eros by any stretch. Three decades ago, when Volmar had whispered to me of his brothel visit, his shame had mingled with his wonder at the ecstasy he had discovered, the force that moves the stag to bugle in the rut. My women pilgrims had described for me the rush of warmth in their wombs and breasts, that vehement heat bursting into rapture. The greater their delight, the more beautiful the children they conceived. I had read many texts, including Constantine the African's *De Coitu*, that outlined the many ways in which men and women coupled, and also how certain men and certain women desired their own sex—this was why the Benedictine Rule insisted that we sleep fully clothed in separate beds and in communal dormitories where a candle burned the entire night through. I knew all this, yet my love for Richardis seemed to emerge from a different place, a secret chamber only we could enter, as pure as Felicitas's love for Perpetua when she followed her beloved mistress through the fiery gates of martyrdom.

Richardis's virginity was a shining vessel, forever inviolate, and I'd written my own vows of perpetual virginity in blood. Yet such visions of her filled my dreams, transfixing me with such light. I could only think that God had delivered these revelations, that God wanted to show this to me. What united Richardis and me was not Eros, but Caritas, that blinding glimpse of divine love.

"What do you see, Hildegard?" Richardis asked, as though yearning for my visions to return.

And so they did, even in that mire of unending fear and enforced silence when I was denied ink and parchment. I saw the womb of the Virgin of Virgins, a matrix of honeycomb, its sweetness nourishing my sisters and me. Not allowed to work on *Scivias*, I composed music instead, more than ever before, for even Cuno could not dare deny me the Holy Office. This was the purest form of prayer, my voice weaving with my sisters' as our songs rose to the very vault of heaven.

> *Ave, generosa*
> *Hail, nobly born,*
> *Glorious, and virginal girl!*
> *The beloved of chastity,*
> *The substance of sanctity,*
> *Pleasing to God.*
> *You are the white lily*
> *That, before any other creature,*
> *God looked upon.*

Rorich's letters from Mainz were my only connection to that outside world where my fate would be decided. His messages arrived crumpled, betraying Cuno's prying fingers. Though I cursed my abbot's interference, I soon became more worried about my brother's predicament than my own. Rorich was in danger. Archbishop Adalbert, his master for three decades, was dead, and the newly elected Archbishop Heinrich found himself and his entire household under siege.

My sister, more than ever I beg your prayers, for if we do not receive God's protection, Heinrich and those of us whom he shields might be dead by the time this letter reaches you. No doubt you have heard how Bernard of Clairvaux preached the Second Crusade with such fervor that entire villages emptied as every able-bodied man pledged to defend the holy shrines in Palestine. For all Bernard's good intentions, unspeakable barbarities have come to pass in our own native land. The cursed monk Raoul has found his way to Mainz, where he incited our citizens to wage slaughter against the Jews who have dwelled within our city since the time of the Romans. Heinrich, abhorring every injustice, now shelters the Jews within his palace and has sent urgent word for Bernard himself to come and put an end to these riots before the mob murders us along with those we protect.

Powerless as I was, the only thing I could do was pray that Bernard would arrive before the horde outside the archbishop's palace bashed down the gates or set fire to the place. Would this tide of evil ever end? Had Bernard only known what bloodlust would erupt from his preaching of the Second Crusade, the unlettered masses using his call to arms as their excuse to murder the Jews who lived in our midst.

I found no peace until my brother's next letter arrived.

Bernard reached Mainz just in time. Standing courageous before the throng, the sainted man denounced the monk Raoul as a murderer and a liar, and thus the wretch has fled like the coward he is. Sister, pray for us as we prepare for the Synod of Trier this November when Bernard and Pope Eugenius will convene, along with the prelates and bishops.

My brother was no fool—he knew that Cuno read his letters. Though Rorich did not say it outright, I read his intention to appear at the Synod of Trier along with the new archbishop to plead my case.

In a matter of months, I would finally learn my fate. My mortal end seemed to glimmer on the horizon, like a ship drawing ever nearer. Feverish, I wrote song after song, prayers of light and love to banish my dread of what loomed before me.

O noblissima viriditas
O noblest greening,
You who have your roots in the sun,
And who shine in bright serenity on the wheel,
Whom no earthly excellence contains.
You glow red like the dawn
And you burn like the sun's fire.
You are held all around
By the embraces of the divine mysteries.

My sisters and I raised our voices in song. Would our prayers be heard?

Late one February afternoon, a frantic knock sounded on our nunnery door. Volmar burst in, pulling another man behind him.

The sight of Rorich, his face red and chapped from his long winter ride, made me cry out. Before I could say anything, Volmar spoke in a low, urgent voice.

"Quiet, please. Cuno doesn't know he's here. The synod has ended. Rorich came to deliver the news before the official messenger."

My brother, who was no longer young, had traveled at the greatest speed all the way from Trier. Guda ran to fetch him wine while I guided him to the chair nearest the brazier. Kneeling at his feet, I tugged off his riding gloves and chafed his cold hands in mine.

Rorich must have been riding hard, for he was completely out of breath, only able to utter a few words at a time. "Sister, I must tell you . . . Eugenius read from *Scivias* . . . before the prelates."

My breathing was as shallow as my brother's. I trembled at the very thought of the pope reading those words I had written — God's words that I had midwifed. Richardis knelt beside me and held my arm. She looked so determined, as though she would be my shield and armor no matter what happened.

"I saw their faces . . . their scorn . . . several denounced you."

Richardis's grip on my arm tightened, her pulse beating with mine.

"Then Bernard spoke."

Bernard of Clairvaux, the holiest man in Christendom. I bowed my head.

"He praised your visions . . . the others were silenced."

My heart banged like a drum.

"Eugenius declared you God's sibyl."

The room was spinning so fast that I forgot to breathe. Dumbfounded, I gaped at my brother.

"Hildegard," he said. "You are vindicated."

My sisters' voices arose in a happy clamor. Richardis pulled me to my feet and hugged me, but still I swayed, for I could scarcely believe this miracle. Instead of condemning me, the pope had become my champion.

"In a week or two, Eugenius's letter will arrive." Rorich had recovered his breath. "But I wanted to tell you sooner. To put an end to your worry."

"Bernard and the Holy Father believe in my visions." Overwhelmed in my wonderment, I searched my brother's eyes. "Does that mean you do, too?"

He kissed my brow. "I believe that God has chosen you. Who else could be so fearless?"

Before I could throw my arms around him, he opened the leather cylinder he carried and pulled out the scrolled manuscript of *Scivias*. I cradled those pages against my heart as warmth flooded my chest.

"Not only do you have the Holy Father's blessing," said my brother, "but he commands you to finish this work for the glory of God."

"We shall begin tomorrow after Prime!" Richardis's eyes shone like the day star.

My sisters gathered me in a tight embrace. I reached for Volmar's hand.

"God be praised," he said, my oldest friend. "Cuno can't touch you now."

My joy seemed bottomless.

Fourteen days later, the pope's letter arrived like a flaming spear breaching Cuno's fortress walls. My abbot's perfect plan was foiled. Suddenly I, Hildegard, his most nettlesome charge, was famous, declared a prophet by Eugenius himself. Pilgrims came pouring in, peasants and aristocrats, from every part of Burgundy, Lorraine, and Flanders, and all the German lands.

11

APPLE AND PEAR trees encircled us in their clouds of blossoms. The forest rang with the cuckoo crying its herald as Richardis and I strode across that waving tapestry of wildflowers and lush new grass. Soon we would return to the monastery, but for now we breathed in the greening, that verdant tide that left me reeling in reverence and gratitude.

"Here you hide in the orchard!" a voice rang out.

We turned to see the prior huffing his way toward us, his face ruddy with the unaccustomed effort of hiking down the steep slope.

"An unwashed mob has arrived, demanding an audience with you," Egon said, clearly in a temper. "The lay brothers despair over how they are going to feed so many!"

Our trickle of pilgrims had swelled into a crowd. The prior seemed vexed that this common rabble streaming into our abbey would only be a strain on our guesthouse and larders, and offer very little in the way of donations. Egon and Cuno seemed to have little clue what they were to do with me now that I had received the pope's benediction.

When Richardis and I entered the monastery gates, the brothers scattered to open a path for us.

Over two dozen pilgrims awaited me, most of them simple, unlettered folk.

"There she is, the holy sibyl!" A ragged widow fell to her knees before me. "Mother Hildegard, can you reveal to me the fate of my dead husband's soul?"

An injured stone mason begged me to bless his withered arm. A visitor from Aquitaine addressed me in his own language, of which I did not understand a word, until one of the brother scribes came to translate.

"He says, 'I have heard of your reputation, which is spreading in my country, and I have walked barefoot for months just to hear your voice, sainted lady.'"

Another young man approached me. "Most holy lady, since you are a seeress gifted with divine vision, could you please tell me how I may uncover a horde of Roman treasure buried near the city of Worms?"

I veiled my smile. "The true treasure, my son, is to be found within your soul, not buried in the earth. Nonetheless, you may pray to God who will help you according to his will and your need."

A cleric regarded me with tormented eyes. "Hildegard, I suffer such despair. I am crushed and broken, and I fear for my soul, fodder for the devil that I am."

I offered him my counsel and prayers. Other pilgrims were so ill that I ushered them into the hospice and worked with Brother Otto to find the right remedies.

When I finally emerged from the hospice, it was past Compline. Bone-weary though I was, I tingled from crown to foot. Such a presence filled me, something unutterable working through me.

In the moonlit cloisters, Richardis waited with yet another visitor — Rorich, his smile as wide as the starry sky.

"Hildegard," he said, hugging me close. "I've come to take you to Mainz. The archbishop requests your presence."

Overpowering joy welled up in my heart. With the archbishop's summons, Cuno could do nothing to forbid my journey.

"What will happen in Mainz?" I asked him, my heart racing.

"Heinrich will finally meet the woman whose visions have so moved him." My brother took my hands. "Once he's befriended you, you'll be protected. No one will dare trouble you again."

When I shared my happy news with my sisters, they gathered round, as overjoyed as when Rorich first delivered the news that the pope had declared me a prophet.

"Hildegard, you must take one of us with you!" Hiltrud, my niece, said. "It would be unseemly for you to travel without another nun."

The younger nuns and novices exchanged glances, as though anticipating who would be chosen.

But like a pin pricking a soap bubble, Guda's voice punctured their excitement. "No doubt, the magistra will ask Sister Richardis."

There was something cool in Guda's voice, as though she disapproved of the way I favored her young cousin.

"I have no wish to raise myself above the others," Richardis said, her face bright red. "Perhaps you wish to go with the magistra, Guda."

With a stab, I saw the price my friend paid for our bond, laying herself open to her cousin's ridicule.

"But, of course, Richardis must go," Adelheid said, speaking before I could. "She's the magistra's scribe and illuminator."

"Indeed," I said. "If I am to speak to the archbishop about *Scivias*, it would be most practical to have Sister Richardis on hand, for she has helped me with this work since its inception. In truth, I wish I could take each one of you, but I doubt Cuno would allow that."

My duty as magistra was to smooth ruffled tempers and keep the peace. I must not appear to put Richardis before the rest, and yet I could hardly disguise my love for her, shining like a lamp within my breast, or my dependence upon her, for she had been as crucial to the writing of *Scivias* as Volmar himself. Without her encouragement, her belief in me, I might not have written a single page.

She was my inspiring angel made flesh, confidante to my soul. While the Rule of Saint Benedict forbade special friendships, the fact remained that our close and cloistered life fostered intimacy of the heart. Guda herself adored the novices for the energy and liveliness they brought to our strictly ordered existence. Hiltrud and Verena were devoted friends. Only Adelheid remained at a distance from us, but only because she loved her solitude and books as passionately as a famished man loves bread.

Two days later, Rorich, Richardis, and I boarded the barge at first light.

Forty-one years I had waited for this passage away from Disiboden-berg. Though I was forty-nine years old, I could barely refrain from dancing like a child when the oarsmen pushed away from the landing. I could not quell my ecstasy. The entire abbey had come to see us off. When I first arrived with Jutta as an eight-year-old child, there had been eighty monks, but now I counted fewer than sixty. As the brothers aged and died, their numbers dwindled, and precious few novices came to replenish their ranks. The youngest faces were those of Sibillia and Margarethe, who waved so hard that I thought they would wrench their arms from their sockets. Standing between my sisters and his brothers, Volmar smiled at me with such faith and goodwill. How I wished he could come with us.

"God keep you, Abbess Hildegard!" one of my simple pilgrims cried out, honoring me with a title above my station.

The look Cuno threw me then was enough to burn me to cinders—abbess indeed!—but soon the Nahe's current swept us away and instead of my abbot's glowering face, I saw the forest, that great pulsing emerald heart. As Disibodenberg was lost from view, my soul soared free. It was as though I'd dragged a great leaden weight with me for four decades and had suddenly cast it off.

The Nahe unfurled, its silky surface belying the powerful current that pushed us ever onward, farther and farther away from Cuno's imprisoning walls. Richardis's face was as rapt as mine must have been as she gazed out at the dense tangle of trees. She pointed to a crane rising from the green to soar on angel-wide wings. My heart quickened, for I had learned the lore of birds and the secret portents they revealed.

"A door long bolted shall now be opened," I told her.

Something unreadable flitted across my friend's face.

"I know very well that the door is opening for you," she murmured, keeping her voice out of my brother's earshot. "But what of the rest of us? Sometimes I fear you will leave us behind as you march toward your glory."

Her words struck me like a lance.

"Do you think I'm chasing my own selfish glory?" For a moment I panicked at the thought of losing her love, of being left alone to face whatever the future would bring. "Wherever I go, I want you by my side."

She blinked, her eyes bright with tears.

"And our other sisters, too, of course," I added hastily, longing for the dream to be true, that our entire nunnery might sail forth together, free and joyous, never to suffer Cuno's rule again. "One day, while we are still in this earthly realm, we shall be liberated."

"How?" she asked, shaking her head as though I mocked her with an impossible dream. "For now we travel forth, but you know as well as I that we must return."

If my hopes were like the crane rising high in the air, Richardis's anxieties brought them crashing down to earth. This journey was but a temporary reprieve. Even with the pope's approval, it could still go wrong for me. Like all mortal men, pontiffs die. The next one might not view me so kindly. Why had God given me these visions if my sisters and I were destined to live out the rest of our days in that cramped nunnery as the underlings of Disibodenberg?

Before my thoughts could become mired in melancholy, Rorich joined us, the beloved companion of my childhood, now a stooped man with thinning gray hair and a timeworn face.

"It may be a shock for you both to enter a city after a life of seclusion," he told us.

Better a shock than a slow living death, I thought.

"I remember the city of Bremen from my girlhood," Richardis said, her sapphire eyes transported to a place that I would never see.

Though she was half my age, she had more experience of the world than I did, for I had never even laid eyes on a large town. Maybe Rorich was right and it would be too much for me. I was like a benighted prisoner, held captive so long in the land of the dead that I might turn to dust if I dared set foot again in the land of the living. Even to hear my brother describe the wonders of Mainz filled me with amazement.

"The city itself is walled, like an abbey, but covers a much larger enclosure with gates that are locked at night. All manner of people, rich and poor, Christian and Jew, live there, and the Romans themselves built their fort in that place, for once it marked the northernmost frontier of the empire. You will see every aspect of secular life on display, from the merchants in their furs to crippled beggars on the cathedral steps. But Heinrich will make you both welcome. This archbishop is the greatest man I've ever served."

My brother's face softened with what looked like genuine love when he spoke of his master. He sang out his praises for that great man. Of course, I knew already that Mainz, with its cathedral modeled after Saint Peter's in Rome, had its own Holy See and that the Archbishop of Mainz was the substitute for the pope in the lands north of the Alps. The archbishop was also one of the archchancellors for the Holy Roman Empire and one of the seven prince electors whose task it was to select the emperor.

As Rorich described for us the glories we would soon see, impenetrable forest gave way to fields, farmsteads, and hamlets with churches as tiny as hermit cells. Ragged children scampered to the riverbanks to wave and shout at the sight of me with my magistra's crook.

"Hildegard of Disibodenberg!" they cried. "The holy sibyl!"

Their mothers lifted infants and cried out my name until I raised my arms in blessing.

"Even these poor souls have heard of you," Rorich said, unable to hide his amazement.

We floated past teeming villages where girls chased escaping goats and geese, their flashing bare legs reminding me of how Richardis once cavorted in the forest before she made her irrevocable vows.

When the Nahe flowed into the Rhine, that mighty highway, I gripped Richardis's hand in awe, for I'd never thought to behold such majesty. At the place where the two rivers met, a crag arose, hazy in the evening mist. There loomed a mysterious chapel ringed by a grove of apple trees blossoming in pink and white.

"How beautiful it is," I said. "Is that a shelter for pilgrims? Will we spend the night there?" I imagined glimpsing the stars through those flowering branches.

My brother laughed. "No, that place is in ruins." He went on to explain with his easy knowledge of the sights and places that had been forbidden to me. "That's Rupertsberg. Once it was a hermitage, founded by a pious widow, the holy Bertha, in memory of her son, Rupert, who died very young. He made a pilgrimage to Rome when he was only fifteen."

"Who owns that land?" I asked, surprised that such a commanding site could be left derelict.

"The archbishop, of course," my brother said. "He owns most of the lands around here. We will spend the night at one of his estates just a short distance down the Rhine."

Soon my view of Rupertsberg was swept aside as I gaped at the many ships, boats, and barges jostling for position in the Rhine's broad sweep. Richardis pointed out the castles, towns, and toll towers that she had seen before, having journeyed up the Rhine with her mother en route to Disibodenberg when she was thirteen.

Suddenly she took my arm, her eyes sweeping over me. "Hildegard, are you ill? You look faint."

"No." I beamed. "I've just risen from my grave."

After four decades, I had at last rejoined the great world.

On the third day, when we reached Mainz, a cacophony assailed my senses. The stink of sewage and fish guts arose from the quay, and once inside the city walls, I marveled at the many bodies crowding the streets. The throng's voices rang out in a babel of German dialects and foreign tongues. From the markets came the smell of roasting meats and the flash of trinkets gleaming in the sun. A waft of attar of roses filled my nose as we passed a perfumer's shop. Then we turned a corner to be assailed by the smell of swine rooting among refuse-filled ditches. Dirty-faced waifs begged for alms. We walked past the Jewish quarter, where my brother pointed out the synagogue and bathhouse. Farther down the streets, he tried to shield us from the sight of sharp-eyed women whose red hoods marked them as prostitutes.

The city itself was the ring enclosing the jewels—Saint Martin's Cathedral with its triple spires and the archbishop's palace.

As my brother guided us through the guarded palace gates, I thought what an honor it was just to set foot in this sanctum. A tightness seized my chest. What if I did or said the wrong thing, offending the archbishop who had been so gracious to invite me here? How easily I could disgrace myself and Rorich, not to mention Richardis and my other sisters.

Before us loomed the Great Hall, built of the same red and yellow sandstone as the cathedral. Its windows of white-green glass glittered in the last light of day. At one end of the Great Hall was a chamber block, three stories high, and behind that I caught sight of the roof of the archbishop's brand-new chapel, dedicated to Saint Gottfried, and yet another wing containing the archbishop's private chambers and library. It seemed impossible that Rome or Constantinople contained any structures more exquisite.

"Come along." Rorich led us to the porch, facing west, and into that Great Hall, more than one hundred and twenty feet long. The tile floor was cushioned in rushes strewn with herbs that released their sweetness with our every footfall. Richardis and I marveled at the six white pillars stretching toward the lofty timber ceiling. The sunset cast its glow through the high windows.

Torches set in the walls illuminated the hall, as did countless candles hanging from chandeliers. Down the center was a long row of trestles and benches. Closest to the warmth of the great blazing hearth was the archbishop's table, set upon a dais. Above his throne, now empty, hung a silken banner bearing his coat of arms — two silver six-spoked wheels connected by a cross against a crimson background. Servants bustled around, laying out goblets and jugs, knives and spoons and salt cellars, as though preparing a feast fine enough for the pope. To think that my brother had been a part of this household for more than three decades.

"I feel like a beggar." I wrung my hands, gritty from our journey. "I should join the poor at the almoner's gate."

My brother, looking utterly at ease in this palace, smiled. "Here comes a servant to show you and Sister Richardis to your room."

"Is this heaven?" I asked Richardis as soon as we were alone in our guest chamber high beneath the eaves.

"Not even my mother's castle was this fine."

I felt lost, as out of my element as a fish upon dry land. Luckily Richardis, no stranger to courtly life, took charge, opening our traveling trunk to pull out fresh linen shifts and clean habits and wimples. We must appear spotless before the archbishop. But before she could close the shutters to give us the privacy to wash and change, I wandered to the window, which looked out on the archbishop's private wing. To my delight, I saw a labyrinth below, made of hedges that appeared inky black in the twilight. Though I had read of such things, I had never thought to see one with my own eyes. A pale-clad figure wandered those spiraling paths with an air of deepest contemplation.

"Do you think that's the archbishop himself?" Richardis asked, joining me at the window. She looked almost impish.

Too nervous to reply, I drenched half the floor as I washed myself. Richardis, already in her clean shift, handed me a towel and stood behind me to work the comb through my hair.

"Don't act so petrified." Her breath was warm against my nape. "After all, he's only a man." She spoke with such calm authority that she reminded me of her mother.

"Only one of the most powerful men in the Holy Roman Empire," I said.

When we entered that Great Hall, nothing could have prepared me for the sight of Heinrich, Archbishop of Mainz, rising to welcome us to his table.

Adalbert, his predecessor, had been an older man, wide of girth and heavy of jowls, but Heinrich in his simple linen tunic hardly looked older than Richardis. As beautiful as the Angel Gabriel, his hair was golden and his eyes a warm brown, his smile kindly. His skin seemed to glow from within. This man exuded such saintly purity that I was convinced he was as fair on the inside as he was on the outside. Little wonder Rorich was in awe of him.

My reverence was real as I bowed to kiss his ring. This was the man who had sheltered the Jews of Mainz from the murdering mob, the man who championed my writings, speaking in my defense alongside Bernard of Clairvaux until the pope himself was convinced.

Heinrich honored me by bowing in return. "Hildegard of Disibodenberg, I rejoice to meet you at last."

Although the good man tried his best to put me at my ease, I was tongue-tied as I took my seat. It being Wednesday night, meat was forbidden, but such an array of fish was laid out that Richardis exclaimed she hadn't seen its like since leaving her home near the North Sea. Plaice, there was, and baked cod, roach and bream, pike and turbot, sole and salmon from the Atlantic, scallops served in their shells, and eel, as tender as spring chicken, cooked in a green sauce. There were cheeses and many fine breads with sweet butter. The richest wine filled our goblets. Heinrich himself ate and drank sparingly, but urged us to sample each dish, as though this fabulous hospitality was for our sole benefit because he preferred simpler fare. Yet I could hardly eat a morsel. Rorich was right—my four decades in Disibodenberg had rendered me incapable of functioning outside its prison. I was as clueless as a peasant would be about how to conduct myself at the archbishop's feast. Richardis and Rorich came to my rescue, conversing with the canons and prelates, the many glittering members of Heinrich's household.

Blessedly, the archbishop seemed to mistake my discomfiture for true humility — a virtue that he embodied to his core.

"Many think me too young for the honor of this post," he confessed. "Indeed, I was as surprised as anyone when they elected me. Would you pray for me, Hildegard, that I might be worthy to carry on Saint Boniface's legacy?" he asked, speaking of the English-born apostle to Germany who had been the first archbishop of Mainz.

"You have all my prayers, your eminence." I summoned the courage to lift my eyes to his beautiful face.

"What I have read of your work impressed me greatly."

Under the warmth of his praise, I blushed like a novice.

"My sister also composes the most sublime music for the Holy Office," Rorich said, speaking to cover my silence.

"How I would love to hear it during your visit," Heinrich told me, his smile like the sun in June.

"Your eminence," Richardis said, "if it would please you, my magistra and I shall sing for you this very evening."

I shot her such a look. How could I be expected to sing for this hall packed with dignitaries when I could barely string together a coherent sentence? But it was too late to refuse now that Richardis had spoken. My face must have been as white as death for she found my hand under the table and squeezed until at last I lifted my eyes from the untouched food on my trencher and told the archbishop that nothing would give me greater pleasure than singing for him.

A servant brought us a psaltery, and then Richardis and I took our place before the assembly of nearly fifty men.

Her eyes locked with mine, Richardis plucked the strings. It was she, my dearest friend and soul's companion, who chose the song, my canticle *O viridissima virga*. The greenest branch. Composed while I was still captive in the anchorage, this song embodied my deepest longing for freedom and union with the natural world. This was the song that

Guda, Adelheid, and I had sung for Jutta's funeral in our desperate bid for liberty, the three of us daring to appear unveiled to arrest the attention of Heinrich's predecessor, the old Archbishop Adalbert. And this was the song I had sung when Richardis and I had met for the first time, when she was still a mute young girl. I remembered that look of astonishment she had given me, as though I were some miracle worker the way I had transformed myself and her cousins from drab anchorites into dazzling, silk-clad brides of Christ.

And so I began to sing in a voice far stronger than the one I used for speaking. In truth, I was not as gifted in song as Guda, or our departed Jutta, or Richardis herself, but my voice was the instrument God had given to me and now I raised it heavenward, closing my eyes as I surrendered to the flow of melody and words, Richardis joining me in harmony. The archbishop and his retinue faded away as I stood within that sphere of pulsing light.

My vision blazed before me, so beautiful I could taste it. My sisters and I, consecrated virgins, sailed down the Rhine in a mighty ship, as merry and free as the maidens of holy Ursula. Silks we wore and our long sweeping hair was unveiled and crowned in gold and jewels. No shackles or walls contained us. Rejoicing, we journeyed toward our own blessed paradise, an island of women. The Living Light flashed like the sun on the Rhine.

When our song ended, I felt faint. Taking Richardis's hand, I bowed deeply to the archbishop. Did these men cheer us or was this a dream? Would I awaken in Disibodenberg to face Egon as he moaned about the next lot of pilgrims emptying the larders?

The archbishop spoke, his every word riveting my gaze to his. "Hildegard, beloved in Christ, your brother did not exaggerate your gifts."

I saw that my song had moved the man to tears.

"In return for your heavenly music, it would give me great joy to bestow a gift on you," this young man said, Heinrich, Archbishop of Mainz.

Richardis's words came back to me: *Don't look so petrified. After all, he's only a man.* Heinrich was so utterly different from the archbishop before him, and the next archbishop might be entirely dissimilar from Heinrich. What a difference one man could make. I wondered if I, just one woman, might make a difference, too.

What did Heinrich think I would ask of him? Doubtless, he would have granted me one of the precious illuminated Gospels from his library or some holy relic to bring back to Disibodenberg as a tribute for my abbot and brother monks. Perhaps it would have been most appropriate to demur and say that the archbishop's prayers and blessing for *Scivias* would be gift enough for one as humble as I.

Instead, something inside me—was it God or my own vanity? —compelled me to speak up in a mighty voice, shocking everyone in that hall.

"Your eminence," I said, "though I am but a weak and ignorant woman, God has graced me with revelations of such holiness and commanded me to speak and write of these visions that I might be of use in the world. But how can my sister nuns and I be of any use if we are banished to the wilderness?

"In the name of the Living Light, I beg you to grant me the freehold of Rupertsberg on the Rhine, so that I might build a new abbey for my sisters and the glory of God."

Heinrich's handsome face froze. My brother looked as though he wanted to dive beneath the banquet table and bury himself in the rushes. The other men looked from one to the other, as though they had never fathomed such audacity coming from a backwater nun. I was afraid to even look at Richardis for fear that even she thought I had lost my mind.

Yet what purpose could my visions serve if I was to live out my days under Cuno's thumb? In God's name, we had to leave Disibodenberg and found our own community. My dream of my sisters sailing forth like Ursula's virgins shimmered. A cold cord snared me when I remembered how Ursula's story had ended. Head drooping, I was prepared to skulk away in shame when the archbishop came to take my hands.

"Sister Hildegard, what you ask is no small thing. You must speak with your abbot to arrange the particulars. But I gladly grant you the freehold of Rupertsberg so that you might build your own abbey, dedicated to Saint Rupert, the holy pilgrim whose hermitage now lies neglected."

Richardis, being young, could not resist crying out in delight. She smiled at me as though I had returned from Jerusalem bearing wood from the True Cross.

"An abbey of our own making!" I murmured to Richardis as we lay in the guest bed with the curtains drawn to enclose our whispers.

This room, intended to accommodate visiting noblewomen who would have shared the broad bed with their daughters or maids, was like another world. What luxury it was to lie nestled on this feather mattress instead of our hard, narrow pallets.

"Imagine!" I said. "We can design the church. Every pillar. Oh, it will be paradise on earth."

Already I could picture our new home on that bend where the Nahe joined the Rhine, in the center of trade and commerce, of vineyards, towns, and great estates. No longer would we be hidden away like lepers.

"Heinrich has given us the land," Richardis said, "but how will we pay for the building of the abbey?"

"Our dowries, of course."

My sisters were gifted with trunks of silk and jewels, gold and silver. Why should that wealth not pave our way to liberty?

Richardis laughed nervously, as though I had told a filthy joke. "You think Cuno will let us leave with our dowries?"

"Why should Cuno have for his own selfish profit what is ours?"

Our abbot himself complained that there were fewer and fewer novice monks. While our nunnery flourished, his monastery declined. So he would use us, the nuns he loved to belittle, as his golden nest egg. *No longer.* I had the archbishop on my side.

"I will write to my mother and ask for her help," Richardis said as she nestled in the pillows. "Oh, I wish the other sisters could have seen you tonight. Especially Guda! Think of the look on her face when you made your request to the archbishop!"

I could only imagine what Guda would say when I announced we were leaving Disibodenberg to build a new abbey. Though she didn't love the cramped confines of our nunnery, she also feared change the way others dreaded the plague.

"Did you plan this from the beginning?" Richardis asked. "First you are so shy and meek, then you knock the man off guard and he's too shocked to refuse you."

Though her voice was full of sleepy affection, she made me sound so calculated. My pulse beat fast as I asked myself if I should swallow my ambition, but then the vision caught hold of me again.

The following morning, I sat with the archbishop in his library and discussed *Scivias* with him, along with Bernard of Clairvaux's writings concerning the Holy Mother. All awkwardness between Heinrich and me melted away. I could not disguise my regard for the man as I basked in the sunlight of his benevolence. Rorich looked on, his face pink with relief at how well the visit had gone despite my outrageous presumption the evening before.

When my brother escorted Richardis and me back to the barge, he seemed to walk on air. "Never forget how fortunate you are, sister! It's a rare nun who receives such patronage. Heinrich is loyal and honest. He'll look after you."

My heart overflowed as we sailed past Rupertsberg once more.

"This is ours!"

Taking Richardis's hands, I led her in a dance around the swaying barge. I felt young again, energy tingling in my veins, as though I were that child racing through the forest with my brother. Except now I was a woman grown and, instead of being a mere passenger on life's chariot, I had taken hold of the reins and was driving it ever forward, blazing my own path.

"It will be magnificent! We shall build an abbey big enough to house fifty nuns! Families of the nobility will rejoice to send their daughters when they see how beautiful our house is."

"You grow ever bolder," Richardis said.

I shot her a glance, bracing myself for her disapproval, then relaxed to see the admiration in her eyes.

What a life we would lead when my dream was made real! My soul rose on crane's wings to the very heights. Was this how men felt when they seized their power and caused great changes to come about? I felt as though I were a knight, fully armed and astride a galloping destrier. *Nothing can stop me now.*

"The ingratitude!" Cuno's rage crackled like lightning. "We have looked after you since you were a child. Now you wish to leave, taking with you the fame and fortune you have gained under *our* patronage. And you spoke not a word to me first but went over my head to the archbishop."

I had expected resistance, expected him to lay me low and come up with a thousand reasons why I was too weak and unworthy to lead my daughters to their new home and to live without what he called his guidance and protection. But I'd no idea to what depths he would stoop.

Trembling in his fury, he raised his hand, which made me flinch, for I was convinced he would strike me. Instead, he gestured to every monk, nun, and novice assembled in the chapter house, inviting them to join him in dressing me down. His mob of monks glared at me as though I were a sow with three heads.

"Why would this foolish woman want to leave our house where she has lacked nothing to set up camp in a muddy field?"

"My lord abbot," I managed. "God has shown me in a vision that I *must* build a new community at Rupertsberg."

"God, or your own vainglory?" Breaking the Rule, my abbot roared in laughter, as though determined to grind me to dust beneath his feet. "Do not deceive yourself that this is God's will."

"She is deceived by the devil," Egon proclaimed. "As we suspected from the beginning."

"How can you say that when the pope himself declared Sister Hildegard a prophet?" Volmar demanded. Behind his anger, I sensed his terror of what Cuno would do to punish me.

"The Holy Father has granted her permission to write of her visions," Cuno said, his voice curt and dismissive, "not to abandon all obedience and humility. He certainly hasn't given her leave to remove her nuns and their dowries to some ruined hermitage."

"What woman has ever founded a monastery?" Egon seemed eager to ape Cuno's contempt of me. "It's unheard of."

"The hermitage of Rupertsberg itself was built by the holy Bertha of Bingen," Richardis said, looking shaken but defiant. "To honor her son, the sainted Rupert. And I have read that in England in the age of Saint Aidan, Hilda of Whitby founded a double monastery where she was abbess over both monks and nuns."

I threw her such a look of gratitude before I faced Cuno once more. "My lord abbot, Heinrich, Archbishop of Mainz, has already given me permission and the freehold of Rupertsberg."

How dare Cuno stand in the way of what the archbishop had ordained? But Heinrich was far away and Cuno looked angry enough to spit.

"You double-crossed the archbishop. Like Eve, you hoodwinked him into bending to your will."

"Like Eve, she is beguiled by the devil," said Egon, who appeared to relish mentioning the False One whenever he could.

I looked at Richardis, who stood stricken. Then Guda stepped forward.

"Magistra," Guda said, the girl I had nurtured from the age of five. Though she addressed me, she bowed her head in deference to the men. "Pray heed our abbot's counsel. How can we abandon our home? Our sisters and novices are daughters of the nobility. Surely we can't expect wellborn girls to live in tents like camp followers while you build the new monastery, even supposing you can raise the monies. Magistra, would you condemn us to penury?"

I shook my head at her, my eyes blurring at the shock of her betrayal. Had she completely forgotten the horrors of our anchorage, the prison we would still be living in had I not taken a stand? Maybe, like Jutta, Guda had come to love her prison. Or perhaps this place had broken her to the degree that she couldn't imagine any other life.

"It was a mistake to allow you to travel to Mainz." Cuno spoke with finality. "For it has swollen you with unholy pride. Hildegard, hear your penance—you are not to set foot outside the abbey gates for the rest of your mortal life."

12

~

MY ABBOT NEEDED neither chains nor rack to torture me, neither poison nor fire to lay me in my grave. When he scourged me with the worst possible penance — eternal captivity within his walls after my tantalizing taste of freedom — it was as though he had heaped boulders upon my chest, crushing my lungs, shattering my every rib. My eyes clouded over till I could no longer see. My flesh was laid waste, my stomach seething till I could neither eat nor drink. Overwhelmed by intense pains, I collapsed on my bed and there I remained as though fettered. They could not even manage to move me to the infirmary.

"The magistra must have drunk unclean water on her journey," Brother Otto said, as he fretted by my bedside. Though the gentle old physician labored tirelessly, I fevered, trapped in a torpor. Everything in my world had turned to ash.

Against the abbot's wishes, Volmar visited me daily. "Hildegard, I never thought I would see you like this. You were always so fierce and fiery."

In my weakened state, every barrier between us as monk and nun, man and woman, broke down. He held my hand and stroked my brow as tenderly as Richardis did. And what a price Volmar paid for his loyalty to me, coming to offer me his comfort in defiance of Cuno, who punished him by ordering him to lie prone in the chapter house doorway so that all his brethren might tread on him. Yet even the most humiliating penance couldn't tear Volmar from my side.

Richardis and Volmar knew the true reason for my malady—Cuno had at last broken my spirit. Perhaps the time had come to admit defeat. Not many reached the age of forty-nine years. Maybe this was meant to be the end of my story.

"I have written to my mother and your brother," Richardis whispered. "Even the archbishop. I told them everything."

How good she was, and yet I wondered if her efforts weren't in vain. Her mother was in faraway Stade. Even if the margravine made the long journey here, I might be dead by the time she arrived. As for Rorich, would he intervene or would he silently regret bringing me to Mainz in the first place? The archbishop was a busy man with mountains of correspondence. Most likely, Richardis's letter would fall into the hands of some lesser clerk rather than the archbishop's own. Even if the message reached him, I could hardly expect Heinrich to sail up the Nahe just to rescue me. Disibodenberg was so remote and cut off from the rest of the world, allowing Cuno to play the despot with none to stand in his way.

"You should be the new magistra after me," I told Richardis. "Adelheid is wise and scholarly, but she prefers books to people. Guda is motherly with the novices, but she lacks courage and conviction. You possess both love and wisdom. Your true name is not Richardis but Caritas." My vision of the Lady of Divine Love glimmered before me, that black-haired maiden, clothed in crimson, crowned in gold. "You would make the best abbess. Perhaps you might see Rupertsberg built, even if I don't."

"Don't talk like that," she pleaded. Her soul, so full of inner beauty, glowed like a lamp even in this hell. She would never age, a voice inside me whispered, but keep her youth for eternity like the angel she was.

"When I am gone, Cuno will relax his rule," I told her. "It is me he fights, me he despises. It shall be easier for the rest of you when I depart this place."

Before Richardis could say a word, Guda's voice rang out. "Magistra, the church is packed with pilgrims begging for an audience with you."

"You can see for yourself how ill she is," Richardis said, an edge to her voice as she spoke to her cousin. She held a protective arm over my chest so that I couldn't have risen even if I'd had the strength.

Ignoring her, Guda pressed on. "Magistra, do you at least have a message I can deliver to them?"

"Yes," I said. "A mighty voice has forbidden me to speak or write anything more of my visions while we are imprisoned in this place."

"I'm to tell this to your pilgrims who have walked for weeks just to hear your voice?" Guda demanded.

Richardis sighed. "*I* will tell them!"

I listened to her footfalls as she marched to the screen looking into the church, once my only window into the outside world. Then I heard her tell the pilgrims what I had told her, word for word. Their outcry arose in a deafening din. Such a journey they had made only to find their sibyl had withdrawn into a cocoon of silence. No one within the walls of Disibodenberg could remain in ignorance of their dismay.

"The gossip will spread like fire," Guda said. "Because of you, they'll call our abbot a tyrant."

"The truth must be spoken."

"If the pilgrims stop coming, the entire abbey will be poorer."

"Cuno complains how much they eat, yet he'll miss their donations." I stifled a smile.

"You did this out of malice! Are we all to suffer for your ambition, magistra?"

Her words lashed me like a scorpion's tail.

"Guda." I reached through the dark fog to find her hand. "Do you remember when you were a girl of five and so furious with me? You blamed me for your misery over being confined here and then you threw such a tantrum that you smashed all my herb pots."

What I would have given to coax any sign of warmth from her. But Guda's hand stiffened in mine and she snatched it away.

The fever raging through me made me lose track of the days until rough hands wrenched me from my stupor. Through the haze that cauled my eyes, I saw Cuno, he who had never physically touched me or any living woman, who had only dared to touch Jutta when she was dead. Now he took my arms in a bruising grip and tried to heave me from my bed.

"You make a mockery of us all. You *will* speak to your pilgrims."

"My lord abbot, please! You're hurting her." Richardis attempted to pull him off me, but he shoved her away.

Yet as hard as Cuno struggled to manhandle me, he could not move me from my bed. My body turned to lead. A force greater than his weighed me down.

A blur in the background, Egon harped yet again about the devil. "Only infernal powers could make her so stiff. An incubus lies upon her—this is why she can't be moved."

Unable to keep any nourishment in my belly without heaving it back up, I must have resembled our departed Jutta. Richardis's tears burned my face. She held me so tightly, as though to keep me in this world. But everything was fading fast, as if I were being sucked into a tunnel of mist. I hardly felt Volmar's touch as he anointed me with oils in the rites of the dying, hardly felt the Host on my tongue as he offered me the viaticum. My sisters' voices were ghostly and muffled as my soul wafted its way up that passage where darkness and light swirled in an endless vortex.

Then, O miracle, the dimness faded from my eyes to reveal Walburga's face—she whom I knew to be long dead. My old nurse hugged me to her breast. Over my fevered body she chanted the charms she used to croon over me in earliest childhood when I lay ill. Jutta appeared, her wasted body restored to its youth and beauty, and she gave me the kiss of peace. "*Lux aeterna,*" she murmured. My long-dead mother came forward to embrace me, tenderly rubbing my hair. Tears in her eyes, Mother gently pushed me away from her, propelling me back down that tunnel, out of this realm of spirit and back into the world of flesh and blood. *Awaken!*

My unclouded eyes opened to see Richardis and Volmar. My sisters gathered round, crying as they chanted their prayers. Even Guda wept. I recoiled at the sight of Cuno looming over my bed until I detected the fear and uncertainty coming off him like a foul odor. The pilgrims, I would come to learn, were casting aspersions his way, saying that his harshness had silenced me and rendered me mortally ill. What would happen when such talk reached the archbishop? My suffering exposed Cuno's cruelty in a blinding light.

Behind him cowered Egon. The prior, who had taken every opportunity to slander me and call my visions diabolical, found his throat swollen in a horrendous goiter, as though God had punished him for everyone to see. Both Cuno and Egon seemed to quake before the specter of my body that gave the appearance of the very pall of death.

"Cuno." I grasped my abbot's hand.

His face blazed red, as if he were affronted that I would dare touch him. He stiffened as if my hand were a serpent coiling around his, yet he dared not pull away.

At least a dozen monks were crowded round, forming an outer circle. Their eyes shone in sadness, these men who had been my quiet allies, those gentle brothers of the library and scriptorium, the herb garden and hospice. The nuns' dormitory was so packed that it resembled a chapter house meeting in miniature — one with a very ill woman at its center.

"You who are a father in your office," I said to Cuno, "I pray that now you may be a father to me in deed. Have mercy on me."

"My mercy you have," he said woodenly. "And my forgiveness," he added, as though to remind everyone that I, not he, was the erring one.

"Will you allow me to depart in peace?" I asked him.

"Go in peace, dearest daughter in Christ," he said.

Behind his pious words beat his loud hope that he would soon be rid of me, that he would bury me in the cold earth, brush the grave dirt off his hands.

"Do you promise before God to release me?" I asked him, still clinging to his hand. "Release me and my sisters from this confinement you have held us in?"

His nostrils flared as he understood how I had tricked him. But he held on to his composure lest he disgrace himself on the deathbed of some nun who would soon be forgotten.

"I am no prison keeper," he said, puffing out his chest. "After you leave us for your true and eternal home, the sisters are free to join the nuns of Schönau if they so desire, for Disibodenberg was never meant to be a double monastery but merely to provide an anchorage for the sainted Jutta, now in heaven, may she pray for us all."

At last he had spoken his true will—to be rid of us women while still holding on to our dowries, no doubt.

"And if through God's grace, I were to regain my health," I said, my fingers pressing his, which went clammy in my grip, "do you swear before God that my sisters and I may leave for Rupertsberg?"

The look he gave me then was so murderous that there was no telling what he might have done had we been alone in that room. But with all those eyes on him, he had no choice but to feign magnanimity. He arranged his face in an attitude of deep regret.

"I fear that it is too late for you, Hildegard, to place your hope in miracles. You must submit to God's true will. But should you ever recover your full strength, then you are free to go to Rupertsberg." He spoke as though he were a gracious man pacifying the ravings of a hysterical woman. I could almost hear his inner turmoil as he tried to convince himself that this was a matter of no consequence, that I would never again rise from my bed.

Seven days passed and still I did not die. Indeed, I rallied, sitting up in bed to take the turtle broth and milk-soaked bread Richardis offered me. Verdant power, like the sun gleaming through beech leaves, shot through my veins. Something was stirring, something was coming—my senses were honed and alert.

On the ninth day, a mud-spattered woman burst into our nunnery, bringing with her the smell of horses and sweat. Richardis leapt from my bedside, her face lifting in joy.

"Mother!" she cried, throwing her arms around our guest. "I knew you would come."

After kissing her daughter, the Margravine von Stade seized my hand. Steel shone in her eyes. Here was a woman as firm and upright as a spear.

"I met with the Archbishop of Mainz." Wasting no words, she handed me a scrolled letter. "Here's his decree written in his own hand. Cuno is to release you and all the nuns without delay and obstruct you no longer. I have horses on loan for the journey."

I could only gape at her in awe.

"Everything is arranged," she said. "I have endowed Rupertsberg. The stone masons and carpenters are already there, waiting to begin work under your direction."

"But, Aunt, our magistra is still very weak," Guda said, her face white with shock. "It will do her no good to leave Disibodenberg for some makeshift shelter."

Richardis cradled my cheek. "Speak the truth, Hildegard. Are you well enough to make the journey?"

"God has delivered our miracle." My heart opened wide. "Now God shall grant me strength. Daughters, bring me food and drink. We have much work to do."

The novices hugged each other, exclaiming what an adventure it would be, sleeping beneath the stars on that beautiful hill covered in apple trees. How romantic this sounded to my young women who only knew the stranglehold of our existence within Cuno's walls.

Ecstatic power thrummed through my veins as I packed the *Scivias* manuscript along with the other texts, both religious and scientific, that Adelheid had copied for us—the beginnings of our new library. I would come to remember this time as one of the happiest in my life, Guda's nay-saying silenced in the breathless haste of packing, the sisters speaking dreamily of the new life awaiting us.

Nothing could stop us now that we had the archbishop's letter and the margravine on our side, her face blazing with ambition for her daughter, her nieces, and for me. What we set out to accomplish—founding our own community of women, consecrated virgins wedded to my vision—was something that hadn't been done in living memory. This would create a lasting legacy to honor us all—especially the margravine, our benefactor.

Every monk, nun, and novice assembled in the chapter house. Unfurling the archbishop's letter, I read it for everyone to hear—there was no mistaking the finality of his message. Cuno swayed as though he were a tree about to be felled.

"You are a fortunate woman, Hildegard," my abbot said, his face drained. "Fortunate in your alliances. Even your deathly illness has waxed and waned to suit your own designs."

Prior Egon looked as though he longed to elaborate on the abbot's opinion of me, but his goiter-swollen throat rendered his speech hoarse and grotesque.

"My lord abbot," Brother Otto said, "I can assure you that our sister's fever and paralysis were genuine enough. We must thank God for her recovery."

I smiled at the old infirmarer before addressing Cuno. "You speak of my designs, but God's designs are at work here. God has spared me that I might be released from my captivity and lead my daughters to our true home."

"You speak as though I were your jailer," he said loftily, "when I have only held your spiritual welfare at heart. Nonetheless, if you truly wish to pursue this folly, you are free to go." He spoke as though he could not wait to see the last of me.

Before I could say anything, he continued, "With the following stipulations. Rupertsberg, if you succeed in seeing it to its completion and consecration, is to be a daughter house of Disibodenberg and you shall remain subject to me, your abbot—not an abbess in your own right, but still a magistra. As your abbot, I alone have the power to appoint your provost from the monks of Disibodenberg."

"In that case, my lord abbot, I beg that you choose me." Volmar stepped forward, his hands folded in entreaty. "Nothing would give me greater joy than joining my sisters in their new home."

Cuno lifted his eyebrows. "It surprises me that you, Brother Volmar, one of our finest men of letters, wish to abandon your studies in order to serve women." He spoke as though Volmar's friendship with us nuns had rendered him a eunuch. "But if that's your desire, you may leave this house and all its comforts."

At that our abbot waved a dismissive arm, as though to adjourn the meeting without further discussion. I did not budge.

"My lord abbot," I said, "there is still the matter of our dowries."

His face clenched in ice-cold fury. "Your audacity knows no bounds, woman. You shall not get a single coin from our coffers. But then you have so many *alliances*," he said. "Perhaps the margravine and her friends shall pave the way for you."

There was no time to haggle over money. We needed to set forth now, while it was still summer, before autumn storms held us hostage or Cuno conjured up some new excuse to bind us to his monastery.

The first of August marked our exodus. Before Lauds, the margravine's servants saddled the horses. Why should we ride and not travel by water, we cloistered women who hadn't straddled as much as a mule in years, I asked the margravine. She insisted that we ride in procession.

"You and your nuns shall fare forth like victors," she said, this noblewoman who was so adept at winning the worldly game. "Like knights who have just won an impossible battle. The villagers and farmers you pass on your way shall run out to see you."

The pale palfrey they led out for me seemed as tall as a steeple.

Before I could open my mouth to protest, the margravine's groom hoisted me into the saddle. He eased my feet into the stirrups, then turned aside so the margravine could discreetly wrap my skirts around my legs to cushion them from the stirrup leather.

"She's steady and quiet to ride," the margravine said. "My groom shall ride alongside you and keep hold of her lead rein. You only have to sit in the saddle and trust her to carry you. But in your new life, I think you must learn to ride. It's expected of a great abbess."

Before I could reply, the powerful animal shifted her weight beneath me, making me gasp. Volmar handed me the crook that marked my office. I'd never seen his eyes shine like that, so full of hope. He spoke to me in a quiet, confiding voice, the way he used to whisper to me through the anchorage screen when we were young.

"Believe me, I'm as eager to be gone as you are. Cuno used to be a good man, back in the days when our holy Jutta still lived, but his jealousy of you has made him petty and small-minded."

"I couldn't make this journey without you," I told him. This was how I had always dreamt it would be—Volmar and I escaping Cuno. We would grow old together, steadfast companions who had weathered every storm.

"In truth, my brethren will also be relieved," Volmar said, "that you and Cuno no longer share the same roof. For I fear that if another battle broke out between the two of you, only one would be left alive." He cracked a smile. "And I think it wouldn't be Cuno."

He patted the mare's shoulder before going to mount his own borrowed horse with an easy grace that astonished me. The margravine handed him the crucifix he would carry on our journey.

Looking as triumphant as her mother, Richardis sat astride her chestnut mare as if she had been born to ride. She bore the fluttering silk banner we had sewn of Saint Bertha and Saint Rupert of Bingen, whose refuge would be our home.

I twisted in the saddle to smile at all my daughters, their faces so joyful and expectant, save Guda who looked as though she had swallowed a hedgehog. I feared she might leap off her horse and hurl herself back inside our abandoned rooms. But her novices chattered in excitement. She would make this journey for their sake if not for mine.

"Daughters, rejoice," I said. "We're setting off on pilgrimage to our true home."

While Cuno looked on, his face like a mask, his monks behind him, we rode off into the rustling green forest. Swallowing my panic at feeling so helpless and small on the huge mare, I caressed her silky withers. Then I took a deep breath and raised my voice in song, leading the others in a canticle of praise. The soul is symphonic. Such is the sweetness of music that it banishes human weakness and fear, and draws us back to our original state of grace, reuniting us with heaven. All creation seemed to share our joy, the sky a pure and cloudless arc above our heads, the rising sun filling the leaves with gold.

Hours and miles went by as I jolted in the saddle, my every muscle aching, but my soul was jubilant. I felt like Miriam leading my people out of slavery and into the Promised Land. As we passed through farmstead and hamlet, peasants darted out to hail us.

"Bless us, holy seeress! Bless our crops and our children."

While I chanted my benedictions, mothers pressed their babies into my cradling arms. Young girls braided flowers into my mare's mane and forelock. People offered us barley bread and ale, and brought water for our horses.

At last, when we rode around a bend, our horses weary and my hips cramping, Mount Saint Rupert came into view, eclipsing everything. As the setting sun cast its radiance on the chapel, my spirit trilled like a blackbird. A questing pilgrim, I had at last reached the Holy Land—not some distant desert landscape full of battlefields and carnage, but this green hill, as gently curving as a woman's breast. I had last seen Rupertsberg in April, when the many apple trees were in their full froth of blossom. Now ripening fruit hung heavy on the branches. Never will I forget the looks my daughters and I gave one another as we ascended that slope. A flock of sheep, blindingly white against the dusky twilit green, darted from our path.

An old soldier and his wife lived there as stewards. Shouting their hearty welcome, they led us to a torchlit table set up outside the chapel. When the margravine's groom helped me down from the saddle, my knees buckled and I nearly sprawled upon that lush earth, but Richardis caught me. Her eyes flashed with a rapture that matched mine.

"We are home," she whispered.

"When we build the abbey," I told her, spinning in a circle, "we must preserve as many of these apple trees as possible."

Her arm linked with mine, she led me to the table set with bowls of steaming pottage, rustic bread, and cups of apple wine as sweet and potent as the rising moon.

After Compline in the chapel, we retired to the pavilion set up for us, and there we slumbered beneath the apple trees like daughters of paradise.

PART III

Music of Heaven

There is Music of Heaven in all things and we have forgotten how to hear it until we sing.

—Hildegard von Bingen

13

⁓

MARCH RAIN LASHED down on the tent roof. Rivulets of water dripped through the seam where the peaked roof met the sloping walls of felted goat hair. Rainwater seeped from beneath the walls to puddle on the beaten-earth floor.

Dawn was nigh—there was just enough light to see without candle or lamp. Shivering, I pushed off the clammy bedclothes and reached for my sandals, yet even the damp couldn't dim my happiness, radiating from my heart to warm me to my fingertips and toes. I had escaped Disibodenberg. My vision was made manifest. It was alive. Never had I felt more assured, more like myself, than I did here, sleeping in a tent under the open sky, a prisoner no longer.

Our first winter had been an ordeal. During those dark, bitter months, we had quit the tent to sleep in an old cow byre, which was as warm and dry as it was odorous. Indeed, Guda, the novices, and the younger nuns slept there still. But a few days ago, I had resumed sleeping in the tent, since the weather was milder now that the constellation of Aries sailed above us in the heavens, bringing the promise of Easter and spring, and an end to our Lenten austerities.

On the other two camp beds, Richardis and Adelheid slept, their heads burrowed beneath the blankets. Like me, they had returned to the tent, leaky and cold though it was, to escape Guda's bickering. I was not looking forward to today's chapter meeting.

Slipping out of the tent, I trod the planks that formed pathways across our muddy building site. Rain drenched my cloak as I passed the makeshift shelters where the workmen slept, only a hundred yards or so away from my nuns—a great scandal as far as Guda was concerned. As mistress of the novices, she had insisted that an inner bolt be made for the byre door. She refused to use the pit latrines unless three other sisters were standing guard. Now that the romance of our move to Rupertsberg was wearing thin, Guda's resentment spread like contagion. Even my niece Hiltrud sometimes spoke longingly of the comforts of Disibodenberg.

So muddled were my thoughts that I tripped over my skirts and nearly pitched face-first into the mire. As I picked myself up, the doubts set in, crowding my head like a murder of crows. What an upheaval I had put my daughters through. What if I had failed them, proving both Guda and Cuno right, that I had been a fool to ever leave our old monastery?

Cuno still exerted his control over us, hanging on to our dowries with an iron grip. The margravine's endowment had gone to pay for the workmen and building materials. Meanwhile, our supplies ran dangerously low. For now, I could mollify my daughters by reminding them that it was Lent, but what would we do after the time of fasting was over? Our tenants would pay their tithes, but last autumn's harvest had been miserable and this year's harvest was still a long way off. Did Cuno think he could starve us into submission?

Meanwhile, the villagers relied on us for charity, sending their hungry children and old women to us daily. The ruined gateway to Saint Bertha's hermitage had become our provisional almoner's gate. The poor shared the same rough oaten bread and pottage as the rest of us.

Following the path of planks, I stepped inside the old chapel that would do for us until the new church was completed. Its interior was so frigid that it made the outside seem warm, but at least the roof didn't leak. I tugged on the bell ropes, ringing in the Office of Lauds. From the workmen's tents arose a rumble of cursing at the racket I made.

When at last I let go of the bell ropes, I discovered that the rough fiber had burned my palms. Rubbing my smarting hands, I awaited the others.

Before I could even turn, her footsteps came as swift as a hind's. Richardis bore her lamp that we would use to light the candles. How young she looked at this early hour, her face still sleepy, her veil dampened from the rain. And yet every last trace of girlishness had gone out of her. I ached to see how thin and pale she had grown.

Since our move to Rupertsberg, she was more and more given to silences, though nothing like her former muteness. She sang the Daily Office without fail, yet she could go days without uttering a word more than was necessary. Her deep silences seemed to provide a refuge for her, as though they raised her up to a serene mountaintop, a world away from Guda's strife-weaving. Too much arguing drained my beloved friend, while her wordless concentration over her artwork restored her. She had spells where she appeared to sink inside a dream, as though incubating her illuminations. Rapt in her secret world, she'd let her silence build to the bursting point and then she would grind her pigments. Hues as rich as jewels would explode onto the parchment. Under her brushstrokes, the illuminated visions of *Scivias* became hers as much as they were mine. But we were nearly out of parchment and pigments. Unless we received funds soon, work on the book would grind to a halt.

Sometimes her voicelessness dismayed me, for it almost made her appear aloof, as though she were harboring as many criticisms of me as Guda was but could not bring herself to say them aloud. When she handed me the lamp, I set it down and took her hands.

"Cara," I said, calling her by my secret endearment. "Tell me the truth. Have I made a terrible mistake, uprooting us and moving here?"

She didn't answer at once but stopped to reflect. As I waited, a chasm of emptiness opened inside me. At moments like this, I thought that, despite our bond, she held part of herself back, a secret self that remained veiled and obscured, unknown to me.

"A true love," she said at last, "sees past the beginnings of things. It sees them through to the end. Anything less is mere vanity."

As she stared into my eyes, I saw the fire in hers. Every part of me melted. She smiled, touching my hand. Together we lit the candles.

In the candlelit chapel, I could lose myself in the elation of our sung devotions, but in the chapter meeting, held in the open air, there was no ignoring Guda. Her once beautiful face appeared haggard, her eyes dull and shadowed by dark circles, as though she had aged a decade since we left Disibodenberg. My heart ached to remember that golden-haired girl who had come into my care at the age of five. Guda with her angel's voice, her singing that could move even Cuno to weep.

As I addressed my daughters, I strove to embody a nurturing mother who could soothe away their anger and fears, and coax them to look to the glory that would be our reward if only we persevered in bringing our new community to fruition. *A true love sees things through to their end.*

"My daughters in Christ, Provost Volmar, the heavens have cleared." I lifted my hand toward the widening gap in the clouds.

"The sun shines upon us. Soon the warmth of spring and summer shall lighten our days. The workmen have given me their word that our new dormitory shall be completed by summer's end. I am at work on a new composition that shall embrace all of you — a musical morality play, the *Play of Virtues.* We shall perform this for the archbishop when our new abbey is finished and consecrated."

I smiled at each one of them.

"Everyone shall have a part, even you, Volmar. The Virtues, embodied by you, my daughters, work together to rescue Anima, the soul, from the devil's grasp. I have written the lead role for Sister Guda, since God has blessed her with the most heavenly voice."

Surely Guda would soften to hear this tribute. How I prayed that the soul of our community could be delivered from the dissention that threatened to tear us apart. But the faces I saw before me remained glum.

"That's all very well, magistra, but we can't eat music," my own niece Hiltrud said. "Meanwhile, we sleep in a byre like animals!"

At this, I made myself smile sweetly. "But sister, our Bridegroom himself was born in a byre. If it was good enough for him, surely we can make do for a few more months."

Richardis met my eyes before ducking her head lest the others see her smile. My niece flushed red and looked in confusion to Guda, who had no doubt put those words in her mouth.

Then Guda herself took the floor, her words as unsubtle as a hammer bashing my skull. "Hildegard, you have led us into the wilderness and now we starve and live in deprivation, as I feared from the beginning."

I bade myself to remain calm. More than ever before, I needed to sound strong and assured.

"Sister Guda, pray, do not exaggerate. The beggars at our gate know what true starvation is. Without our charity, they would not have survived the winter. We have enough to sustain our bodies, though it isn't the richest fare. We didn't choose this life in order to wallow in worldly luxury."

Guda's eyes brimmed. She was not just angry, she was despairing. Her look of hurt reminded me, yet again, that neither she nor I had freely chosen this life. Our families had cast us into the anchorage as children.

"The workmen stuff themselves while we go hungry!" Sibillia, the youngest novice, said.

"The builders need more rations than we do because their labors are more arduous," I told her. "Hewing stone and cutting wood are more toilsome than sewing and praying."

"But it's been raining and they've been doing *nothing!*" Guda spat. "They sit in their tents like great lazy lumps, and they drink and curse and leer at us." She spoke with such vehemence, as though a stonecutter's glance could set fire to her habit and kill her in the conflagration.

"My mother didn't send me into holy orders so I could be ogled by some filthy carpenter," the novice Margarethe cried.

"No doubt the magistra will now remind us that our Bridegroom was a carpenter," Guda said in cold spite.

As I wrestled down my temper, their voices rose in a cacophony.

"Volmar, could you please speak to the builders?" I asked, pitching my voice above the pandemonium. "Please remind them that they are not to pester the sisters or cause any unpleasantness."

"Of course," he said. "I will speak to them directly after the meeting."

Volmar looked as beaten down as I was.

"Magistra, you promised you would convince Cuno to release our dowries," Adelheid said. Quiet, thoughtful Adelheid who usually took my side. She, too, was looking gaunt. "You said you would write to the archbishop."

"Indeed I have." Pain shot through my temples. "I have written to Archbishop Heinrich and to Cuno, but I lack the power to force their hands. We must pray that God will guide Cuno to do what is right."

"We're losing what little support we have," Guda said, her eyes glittering and sly, as though she were a lean, hungry she-wolf leading her pack to circle me. "Margarethe and Sibillia's parents have elected to withdraw their donations."

I shook my head at Guda and wondered how she had come to be privy to this when the parents must speak directly to me, the magistra, concerning their donations to Rupertsberg.

"They have richly endowed Disibodenberg," Guda went on, "only to have you move their girls to this muddy hilltop where we live like wretches."

"Sister Guda," I began, but she cut me off.

The she-wolf went straight for my throat.

"How much longer must we suffer for your folly? If your pride, magistra, prevents you from returning to Disibodenberg, perhaps we might join the sisters at Schönau Abbey."

Everything in Guda's stance told me that she was prepared to leave, taking the novices with her, in a rebellion as radical as my own when

I had led our community away from Cuno. Guda was threatening us with schism.

I wanted to shriek in her face, remind her that I was the one who had saved her from Jutta's ghastly punishments those many years ago. Instead, I pressed my hands together and looked at all my daughters, from the tearful novices to sullen Hiltrud and Verena to bewildered Adelheid. Even Richardis appeared perturbed. Although she did not speak against me, she did not defend me from the others' outrage. Had Richardis done so, Guda would have undoubtedly accused her of being my favorite. Guda would have reminded everyone present that my special regard for Richardis broke the Rule of Saint Benedict. Richardis kept her silence, her eyes on the muddy ground.

"May I remind Sister Guda and everyone that you have sworn an oath of stability to this community." My heart was as heavy as the sandstone blocks the masons cut to build the dormitory that would remain empty if Guda had her way. "But those who undermine our holy sisterhood with ill will are free to go."

With my crook, I pointed to the path snaking down the steep slope.

"Those who are unhappy may go where you will and leave the rest of us in peace to build our new home on this sacred hill of Rupertsberg."

Guda sagged. In calling her bluff, I had stolen away her power. How easy it was to tear things down, how difficult to build something up from the ground. Guda could grumble, but could she lead? Would the novices dare to follow her into some uncertain future?

The nuns looked from one to the other. It appeared they had nothing more to say.

"Is there any more business?" I asked, preparing to adjourn the meeting.

Volmar stepped forward, his eyes rimmed red. From the folds of his habit, he drew out a scroll. "Magistra, dearest Mother of Rupertsberg, Cuno has ordered me to return to Disibodenberg. He says he requires my services as secretary and scribe."

His words, spoken with such regret, knocked the breath from my lungs. This was Cuno's final insult. He would let us come this far, watch us flounder and go hungry without our dowries, and then deliver his death blow. Without Volmar, our provost, there could be no new abbey. Without a priest, there would be no Mass, no sacraments.

I didn't dare look at Guda for fear of seeing the vindication in her eyes. I, Hildegard, had failed, and now we would be forced to return to Disibodenberg.

"Hildegard, my dear sisters, I'm so sorry. This is not of my choosing," Volmar said. The good man wept.

"When do you leave?" I asked. My mind raced as I thought how I might unravel this snare Cuno had woven.

"Tomorrow," he said. "Forgive me."

"I shall go with you," I said.

Turning to my sisters, I spoke in such a loud voice that the builders turned their heads.

"Tomorrow I shall return to Disibodenberg to ask Cuno to release our dowries and restore Volmar as our provost. I will go to Mainz on my knees if I have to and speak to the archbishop. But the building of Rupertsberg shall go on."

At last I faced Guda and prayed that she could love and trust me once again.

"Daughters, I give you my word that I won't return empty-handed."

Volmar and I made ready to ride at dawn on borrowed horses. Decency demanded that I travel with a female companion, but this time Richardis refused.

"Forgive me," she said. "But think how the others see us."

My heart dropped like a stone. By *the others*, she meant Guda.

"It saddens me," I said, "that one with a spirit as noble as yours should be swayed by such pettiness."

"Hildegard, don't you understand? There's already enough enmity between the sisters. I don't think we can endure any more. At least *I* can't. If they goad me one more time for being your favorite . . ."

"Then it is I who must beg your forgiveness," I said, beside myself to see how she had suffered.

Only when her eyes met mine did I notice how glassy they were. I touched her brow, which burned in fever.

"Cara, you're ill! Why did you not say anything?"

In a panic, I took her to our makeshift infirmary where I brewed infusions and laid damp cloths on her forehead. She had always been so robust, this young woman who had nursed me through illness and paralysis. But our hardship had ground her down to nearly nothing. With purple smudges beneath her eyes and every spark of color drained from her cheeks, the girl looked as hard done to as the beggars at our gate.

"I'll call off the journey," I swore. "I can't leave you like this."

Weak though she was, her hand pressed mine. "You *must* go. For all of us. You must see this through, Hildegard."

When I asked Hiltrud to accompany me, my niece seemed too shocked to say no. At daybreak the following morning, I watched her exchange wide-eyed glances with Verena as we set off down the muddy track.

Once I had been frightened to perch atop a horse, but now I sat deep in the saddle and squeezed my legs to urge the bay mare forward in a ground-covering trot. I had been riding more and more on my trips back and forth to Bingen to order supplies from the tradesmen.

"You must prepare yourself," Volmar told me, riding at my side. "Disibodenberg has gone into decline since we left. Brother Otto has died, bless his eternal soul, and the new physician is a poor substitute. Cuno's failing is that he appoints men not according to their ability but because of their loyalty to him."

"What about Egon and his goiter?" I asked. Surely Cuno thought it reflected poorly on him to have a disfigured prior as his second-in-command.

"Egon has given up his office," Volmar said. "I understand the new prior is named Helengerus."

As we hastened toward the place I had wanted to leave behind forever, I plotted what I would say to Cuno. Never in my life had I been so grimly determined.

We reached Disibodenberg at dusk, just before they locked the gates. When we trotted into the courtyard, our horses' hooves clattering on the paving stones, a mob encircled us. Such foul looks they threw me, as though I were a bird of gloom. How their eyes raked us over, as though they rejoiced to see how scrawny and sorry we had become, these men who were fat off my daughters' dowries. They looked hostile enough to drive us out to sleep in the forest like outlaws. The whites of my niece's eyes shone in dread, her mouth frozen in a silent cry. Little wonder that Richardis had refused this mission.

"Brothers!" Volmar shouted in his attempt to pacify them. "I have come at Cuno's behest. Hildegard and Hiltrud are my guests. Kindly let us pass."

Cuno emerged from the throng. "Volmar, I expected you to arrive alone." He didn't even deign to glance in my direction.

"Abbot," I said, towering above him on my horse. "I will speak to you now, if you please. Unless you are afraid of a poor weak figure of a woman."

Cuno stalked off, leaving us to follow in his wake. After twelve hours in the saddle, I staggered like a cripple, using my magistra's staff as a cane, which seemed to provide the brothers with untold amusement. Cuno would have his revenge by letting me appear as foolish as possible, a woman misled by her sinful pride, her humiliation laid bare.

As I limped through cloisters and corridors, my empty stomach howling for sustenance, the walls of Disibodenberg reared up, a prison once more. The very air seemed noxious, as though the monks, angry and bitter as never before, exhaled poisonous smoke.

In his private parlor, my abbot sat as though enthroned, with a cup of wine in hand and his most trusted men clustered around him like courtiers. Instead of inviting Volmar, Hiltrud, and I to sit, he let us kneel before him on the cold stone floor, as though we were penitents. Filthy from our long ride, the smell of horses rose off our garments, causing the men to wrinkle their noses.

"Hildegard said she would never darken our threshold again," Cuno told his men. "Yet here she is."

"I have come at God's admonition," I said, "to ask you, once again, to release our dowries."

"*God's* admonition?" Cuno appeared bemused. "I fear there is nothing godly in your impudence. Those monies rightfully belong to this house. A pity you acted so rashly, causing your nuns to starve on account of your ignorance."

His words evoked a picture of Richardis in her sickbed. An icy terror gripped me that I would ride home to find her dead. For her very sake, I forced away those thoughts and locked eyes with Cuno before staring at each monk in turn. Rising to my feet, I spoke, my words slow and deliberate.

"My lord abbot, my brothers in Christ, hear the words of the true vision I have received."

From my lips emerged not my own voice but another, as terrible as thunder. An unearthly power filled me as I spoke in prophecy as God's sibyl.

"The Serene Light says: Cuno, you should act as a loving father to my daughters and cast off your greed. Their dowries have nothing to do with you. But if it is your will to persevere in the gnashing of your teeth, then woe betide you."

My entire body shook, possessed of a might far greater than my own. When I slammed my staff on the tile floor, everyone jumped. Cuno spilled wine on his robes.

"If any among you say 'We intend to diminish their holdings,' then I Who Am says you are the worst despoiler. If you attempt to steal from my daughters their Brother Volmar, the shepherd who applies their spiritual medicine, then again I say that you are like the sons of Belial. God's justice shall destroy you."

Their faces as white as the moon, the brothers looked from one to the other. Once more that foul smell, worse than our stink of sweat and horses, filled the room. No one could deny that this abbey had become a stagnant place, full of woe, since my sisters and I left. Who was to say that this was not God's wrath at work?

Cuno himself looked jaundiced, his teeth blackening in decay. He slumped in his chair, an aging man of failing health. But a man who would die fighting before he gave in to me. He opened his mouth, as though to denounce me, then seemed to think better of it, looking instead to the young man beside him, who eyed me gingerly, as though I were a viper that required careful handling.

"Sister Hildegard, reverend magistra," the young man said. This could only be Helengerus, the new prior. "We shall meditate on your words. You must be hungry and weary from your journey. Please let us offer you food and drink."

In the guesthouse, I watched my niece devour six bowls of thin Lenten pottage before that haunted grip of hunger vanished from her face. My heart sank to think that even this poor fare was probably the best she'd had in half a year.

The following morning brought no progress, only Helengerus wringing his hands to tell me that Cuno had yet to make a decision regarding our dowries. Immediately I asked for our horses to be saddled, for there was no point in lingering.

Then one of the young brothers I remembered from the scriptorium appeared. His eyes were oozing white pus.

"Hildegard, dear lady, have pity," he said.

So I accompanied the boy to the infirmary, where I instructed the surly new infirmarer on how to prepare a compress of pounded field mint tied in a cloth.

"This will draw out the discharge. Make a fresh compress three times a day until his eyes are clear and free of infection."

"This has become a house of pain," the boy whispered. "I think my eyes have clouded because it's so miserable to see."

In the courtyard, I crowed in delight to see Volmar waiting with our horses.

"My friend! You're coming with us?"

"I told Cuno I believe the truth of your prophecy," he said, helping me into the saddle, "and I dared not go against God's will. If Cuno insists on my return, he'll have to appeal to the archbishop. Besides, do you think I would let you two ride alone?"

"You can't bear it here anymore," Hiltrud said, her voice overflowing with her fondness for him. "Nobody can. If they could, they'd all leave."

How much more spirit the girl had with food in her belly and distance from Guda and her carping.

"Will we ride home now?" she asked me.

I warmed to hear her call Rupertsberg her home.

"Not empty-handed," I told her.

The next days were a blur of hard riding and hunger.

"This is where I was born," I told my companions, pointing to the castle on the hill skirted by vineyards, nestled in the fields and forests where I had once run wild with Rorich. My heart raced to see Bermersheim again after forty-two years of exile. How I wished Richardis could have been here, how I longed to share this homecoming with her, to offer her my girlhood memories in a jeweled casket. In the mirror of her understanding, my pain and loss might be transformed into something precious.

No doubt Bermersheim was humble compared to her family's palace in Stade, but how abundant this land was. My eyes devoured the rich sweep of newly sown fields, the budding green grapevines, the orchards about to burst into blossom. The pastures were bursting with new lambs and calves, the woodland with game and swine.

Hugo, the only one of my three brothers not to enter the Church, was heir to this place, and he was very old, a widower with no living children. Hope beat inside me that this, my family birthright, might be Rupertsberg's deliverance.

The servants, unfamiliar faces all, greeted me as if I had returned from the dead. That seemed not so far off the mark as, after the day's hard ride, I limped to the solar where my brother received me. During my childhood, he had been away in the Holy Lands, only returning after I had become an anchorite. Though we were born of the same womb, this was the first time we stood face-to-face.

As we exchanged our formal greetings, I thought to myself how ancient he looked, like one of the patriarchs of the Old Testament. Twenty years my senior, Hugo was old enough to be my father and I was already half a century old. His sparse hair was as white as hoarfrost, his face and hands marked by scars he had reaped in the First Crusade. But his gaze was shrewd and his mind dagger sharp.

"Hildegard, welcome," he said. "I thought you might come. Rorich writes that you're in trouble."

"Yes," I said, for what point was there in denying the truth? "My daughters go hungry because my abbot won't loosen his grip on our dowries. See how thin Hiltrud, our niece, has grown." I put my arm around the girl who gaped at her uncle as though he were a relic from the time of the Romans. He was probably the oldest man she had ever seen.

"So you've come to implore me to leave this estate to you." He regarded me wryly, for I was the supplicant and he the judge. "For the glory of God, no doubt. You'll tell me to think of my immortal soul and hint that my donation will ease my passage into the heavenly kingdom."

"Brother, clearly you are far too astute to be swayed by such talk," I said. "I know we have nephews in plenty who are clamoring for your lands. Perhaps you're well-weary of hearing the arguments over who most deserves Bermersheim."

"You're certainly no less ambitious than any of our nephews." The aged knight probed my eyes as if recognizing the fellow warrior in me, his sister. "God should have made you a man. You'd have been a boon on the battlefield. But I fear your ruthless striving ill suits a nun."

My face burned as I clasped his scarred hands. "I'm fighting for Rupertsberg's very existence. Would you not fight till your death if Bermersheim was under siege?"

"I'd fight to my last, but with no joy. By the time I was your age, Hiltrud," he said, turning to our niece, "I'd seen enough death and gore to last a lifetime. In truth, I envied you, Hildegard, safe within cloistered walls and innocent of slaughter."

"Brother, I'm so sorry to hear how you suffered." My eyes traced the jagged scar running down his cheek. "I shall pray that you find peace."

"Pray for your own peace," he said. "You do yourself no favor by waging war with your abbot."

His words pierced me where my armor was weakest.

"I only want to feed my daughters," I said, remembering Richardis's thin face. "Our nephews are welcome to your castle and your gold, but I beg you to lend me your flocks and herds so we might at least avert starvation. And horses, if you could spare them. I think I will need to travel to Mainz and plead before the archbishop."

Futility and despair weighed on me, for I feared Hugo would see me as a grasping, greedy woman. As I fought back tears, he sat with me in silence for what seemed an age.

"If I give you what you ask for, will you bury me in your churchyard?" he asked. "And keep my soul forever in your prayers?"

Something in his voice was broken. When I looked into his eyes, I saw that he was closer to the next world than this one and that, despite his gibes, he genuinely feared for his salvation. The blood he had shed still tormented him, as though it were an indelible stain on his soul.

"Yes, brother, of course. Even if you don't grant us a single hen, you're forever in my prayers." While Hiltrud and Volmar looked on, I held the old man like a child, rocking him back and forth.

To my unending gratitude, Hugo endowed Rupertsberg with his entire estate and its tithes, its tenants and crops, its flocks and fields, its forests and fish, its wool and flax. Thanks to him, Volmar, Hiltrud, and I rode home with full bellies and fresh horses. Behind us, servants herded the cattle and sheep and drove wagons laden with wheat and wine. After a two-day journey, we returned to Rupertsberg in triumph, reaching the gates at sunset. How the builders and stonecutters stared to see us bringing home the train of livestock. Though it was still Lent and we were forbidden meat, there would be milk and fresh cheese in plenty and enough wheat to provide bread until this year's harvest rolled in.

As we rode up the twilit hill, Richardis awaited us, bearing a lantern that illumined her wondering face. How I rejoiced to see her restored to health. Adelheid and Verena stood with her, gathered in her circle of light.

"My daughters, I told you God would provide," I said, elated but too stiff to leap down from my saddle until Richardis helped me, her arms around my waist. I had grown so thin that even she, so recently ill, could lift me in her arms.

"You did exactly as you promised," she murmured, her cheek soft against mine.

Underlying the warmth of her welcome, I sensed a somberness, something she feared to tell me. She squeezed my hands and looked at Adelheid and Verena. The three of them glanced at one another, as though searching for words.

Slowly it dawned on me.

"Where's Guda?" I asked. "Where are Sibillia and Margarethe?"

"While you were gone, they left for Schönau Abbey," Richardis told me. "I'm sorry, Hildegard. I begged them to wait until your return, but you *did* give them leave to go."

With the edge of her veil, she brushed away the tears that clouded my eyes. The sense of betrayal knocked me sideways. After everything I had done to secure our future, Guda had fled behind my back like a coward, taking the novices with her.

"Perhaps it's for the best," said Adelheid. "They will no longer sow discord. We who remain are your true core."

My loss was like an unstaunched wound. I had thought that if I tried hard enough, if I brought home the right treasure, provided the right comforts, I could win back Guda's love, that girl who had been like a daughter to me, that five-year-old child I had once cradled in my arms. She hadn't even bothered to say goodbye.

This was supposed to be my victory, yet I sobbed in Richardis's arms like a broken thing. Volmar laid a consoling hand on my shoulder.

"Hildegard, *we* have stayed," Verena said, "because we believe in you."

"Onward," Hiltrud whispered.

Not many days afterward, when I was still reeling from Guda's abandonment, a withered old man came to call. If it weren't for the servants bearing his coat of arms, I would never have guessed his identity. Once he had been tall and straight, shining and beautiful with his lion's mane of curls. Now he drooped and dragged as Richardis showed him into the tent where Volmar and I were writing yet another letter to the archbishop.

"Hildegard," she said. "Count Meginhard von Sponheim requests an audience with you."

Volmar bristled, his face washed an angry red, his eyes shrinking to hard points.

"You dare show your face here?" he demanded, casting down his stylus to glare in undisguised hatred at the man who had destroyed Jutta, Volmar's eternal beloved.

My stomach seized up in both dread and fury to see Meginhard, the author of my misery, this hypocrite whose rape of his own sister had cast her—and me—into living death while he had gone on living his life of opulence, as though he were spotless. It took all my self-discipline not to spit in his face.

"What do you seek here, Meginhard?" I asked. If Volmar's rage was boiling hot, mine was as frosty as a winter wasteland.

His face was so sallow that he reminded me of an old dried-out cheese. His youth and beauty now faded, the mortal sin that had been corroding inside him for more than four decades lay exposed, as shameful as excrement.

Ignoring Volmar, who looked mad enough to floor him, Meginhard spoke directly to me. "Hildegard, I have committed grave misdeeds, may God forgive me. In holy Jutta's name, I wish to do good."

From behind him, his servants stepped forward bearing a chest of gold so heavy that they staggered from its weight. Dumbfounded, I stared at Meginhard, who blinked hard, a tic in his eye.

"Magistra, please accept my offering."

Volmar looked as though he wanted to hurl the man's guilty bribe into the Rhine. But I confess my first thought was one of temptation. Even if we never saw our dowries again, this was a handsome endowment and one we needed. It was certainly true that Meginhard had a debt to pay. Would it be a sin to accept his money? Was his gold as tainted as his soul? The burden of these questions and Rupertsberg's uncertain future hung on my shoulders like a leaden cloak. God had punished Meginhard by rendering his seed sterile. Meginhard had no heir. He had no one. His life was a loveless desert.

"Little Hildegard," he said, with a grimace that was probably meant to be a smile. "Let me do this one good thing. We grow old."

Not awaiting my answer, he hobbled away, abandoning his chest of gold.

. . .

As summer waxed, so did the fortunes of Rupertsberg. Heinrich, Archbishop of Mainz, bequeathed to us a mill at the Binger Loch and also a toll tower on its island in the Rhine, both of which would generate a steady, lasting income. Prior Helengerus sent us a written charter in which he agreed to return part of our dowries and promised that Disibodenberg would not revoke Volmar against our will. This wasn't to say that Cuno had given in to me, but rather that he had allowed his prior to arrange the sort of compromise that made him appear munificent.

14

~✦~

THE SUMMER OF 1151 seemed to be the shining pinnacle of my existence when all my dreams came true. In September, I would turn fifty-three, and instead of bowing to the inevitable decline of advancing age, I seemed to flourish like the orchards encircling our monastery. Such good fortune abounded that I confess I succumbed to the sin of pride.

Despite our every obstacle, my daughters and I had established a self-sufficient monastery with its own mill, its herds and flocks, its stables and crops, its fishpond and vineyards. Our every workshop boasted running water, and our newly finished dormitory could accommodate fifty nuns. Before the first snows came, we would have latrines with working sewers and a bathhouse with a steam bath. Like guests drawn to the banquet table, daughters of the nobility entered our house, enriching us with their dowries. We gained more than a dozen new postulants.

Our new home was no hermitage but a landmark, crowning the hill where the Nahe joined the Rhine. Ships from far and wide sailed past our ramparts. How could people fail to marvel at how Rupertsberg had sprung up in the space of a few years? A great monastery founded by women—not by an emperor, bishop, or prince—was unprecedented in the German lands, a miracle. Pilgrims flocked to us, many of them unschooled souls who could not read a word of my

writings, but who had heard of my visions and the restorative powers of the medicine we practiced in our hospice. In defiance of Cuno,
who said I was only a magistra and subject to him, nearly everyone
addressed me as abbess, from my own daughters to the writers of the
letters that flooded in as Rupertsberg's reputation spread through the
land.

Blessing begat blessing. That summer I completed *Scivias*, the fruit
of a decade's work. We sent copies to my great patrons Pope Eugenius,
Bernard of Clairvaux, and Heinrich, Archbishop of Mainz. Everything in my world seemed perfect and complete. We only needed to
finish construction on our new church, and then, the following spring,
the archbishop would come to consecrate Rupertsberg, our hard-won
paradise.

Upon a glorious August morning, I read through my correspondence.
Since Volmar was busy with other matters, Richardis sat with me in
his stead, taking dictation in her flowing hand. My soul seemed as ex-
pansive as the sun streaming through the open window. Thus, I could
regard the unflattering letter with good humor.

"Cara, listen," I said, before reading aloud the pointed epistle from
a certain Magistra Tengswich, superior of the sisters at Andernach, a
Benedictine house about fifty miles north.

> *We have heard about certain strange and irregular practices that you*
> *countenance. They say that on feast days your virgins stand in church*
> *with unbound hair when singing the psalms and that they clad them-*
> *selves in white with silken veils so long that they sweep the floor. It is*
> *even rumored that they wear crowns of gold filigree, into which are in-*
> *serted crosses with a figure of the Lamb in front, and that they adorn*
> *their fingers with golden rings. And this despite the express prohibi-*
> *tion of Saint Paul, who writes in the First Book of Timothy: "Let*
> *women comport themselves with modesty, not with plaited hair, or*
> *gold, or pearls, and costly attire."*

O worthy bride of Christ, such unheard-of practices far exceed the capacity of our weak understanding, and strike us with no little wonder. Although we feeble little women rejoice in your fame and success, we still wish you to inform us on some points relative to this matter.

I had to laugh at the barbs rendered all the sharper by their ironic guise of humility.

"A sharp-witted woman, this Tengswich," I said. "A pity her intelligence isn't put to better use than attacking us, her sister Benedictines. What shall we write back to her?"

I expected Richardis to share my mirth, but my friend appeared preoccupied, her eyes rooted on her writing desk.

"She is right," she said quietly. "About Saint Paul's admonition."

"That pertains to married women, not virgins. Why should consecrated women, in the shelter of their own cloister, hide away their beauty as though it were something shameful?"

My mind raced ahead, seeking out the right words for my reply to Tengswich. "Cara, please write this for me." I closed my eyes as the words flew from my tongue. "These words," I dictated, "do not come from a human being but from the Living Light: *O woman, what a splendid being you are! For you have set your fountain in the sun and have conquered the world.*"

Writing down my dictation, Richardis flushed, as though I had chosen those words specifically for her and, in a way, I had, for there she sat in the full stream of sunlight, which illuminated her beauty. Though she was twenty-seven, she didn't look a day over nineteen. This was our gift, the secret jewel of sworn maidenhood, freed from the burden of constant pregnancies. When my mother was only a few years older than Richardis, she had lost nearly all her teeth to childbearing.

Our mortal lives were so brief, I reflected. We did not live for ourselves alone. Every abbess sought a protégée. Even Jutta, in her own tortured way, had tried her best to pour her learning into me.

My dream was that Richardis would take the abbess's staff when I departed this world. My visions, my writings, my music, this abbey, my entire legacy, would become hers, she who was my soul's companion. I smiled at her fondly only to see that her hands were trembling, spilling ink onto the parchment.

"Is something wrong?" I asked.

"Hildegard, I ask your leave to return to my homeland in Saxony. The sisters of Bassum Abbey have elected me as their superior."

"My dear, is this a jest? How could they elect you having never laid eyes on you?"

"Such things are not unheard of," she said. "I've served you for many years. Now I may serve others."

I realized she was dead earnest.

"This is your mother's doing," I said. "Bassum is in your brother's archdiocese, is it not? Your brother is archbishop and she would have you be an abbess. An exalted rank to match the exalted position of your family. Another gem in your mother's crown."

"How dare you mock her?" My friend turned on me in genuine anger. "You would be nothing without her! This abbey would not exist. You would still be at Disibodenberg under Cuno's heel."

"Why?" I asked her. "Why would you want to leave after everything we've endured together?" My heart raced through my memories of her muteness and then the miracle of her speech, of how she had raised me from the deepest abyss when I thought I would be damned for heresy. "Cara, I built this house for *you*."

My voice tore at this admission. Of course, I had built Rupertsberg for all my daughters and the glory of God. Yet at the still center, at the axis of the wheel around which everything revolved, was Richardis, my vision of Caritas made flesh. My Anima, my soul.

Her eyes filled with tears, as mine did, but she folded her arms and turned her back to me, her stubbornness reminding me of how she had erected a wall of silence to thwart her mother. It stabbed my heart to see her throwing that same defiance at me.

"Did you think I would always be the pale moon reflecting your sun?" she asked me.

"This is your mother's will, not your own!" To my horror, I found myself shouting at her. Softening my voice, I added, "Don't let her meddling tear us apart."

She set her jaw. "How can you be so sure it isn't my will?"

"You can't leave. I need you here." I gulped for breath, still not believing any of this. "My dear girl, let's speak no more of this. Write to your mother and tell her you refuse."

"I'm not a girl anymore. And my mother grows old. She would have me in Bassum, close to home. After all she has done for you, how can you deny her this?"

"Your mother bought the office for you." My voice grew cold and quiet. "This is simony, a sin against God. I forbid it."

She laughed, as though in shock. "Didn't you once promise me that you would never hold an unwilling girl as your prisoner? Now you act like Cuno, the one you fled. Guda was right. Ambition has swollen your head and made you hateful."

"Guda?" Annoyance and bewilderment swirled around me in an unholy dance. "What does Guda have to do with any of this?"

Richardis's face went as red as blood.

"She wrote to Mother. She said she worried that our friendship was impure."

At first I could not believe it. Then a white-hot rage gripped me. I could have smashed the precious window glass.

"You know that's a lie. I love you as Paul loved Timothy."

She wept, her face looking pale and exhausted. "Hildegard, you have been kind. You were a friend to me when my own mother despaired of me. But the time has come for you to let me go. I've helped you finish *Scivias*. There are other illuminators among the new postulants to replace me."

I kept shaking my head. "No, no, no. You can't."

Hurt blazed in her eyes. "You think you can stand in my way? The archbishop will release me, even if you don't." Walking away from

236

me, she had reached the door when she turned to me again. Her head was bowed, her voice leaden. "Adelheid is leaving, too. She has been elected abbess of Gandersheim."

The summer of our triumph bore the bitter fruit of loss. My heart turned upside down, a cup emptied of its life-sustaining fluid. For fifteen years I had shared my life with this young woman, my confidante through every victory and humiliation. Then, like a bolt of lightning striking down from a clear summer sky, came this. The girl who had come to me as a mute and then opened my heart was prepared to shake the dust from her sandals and walk away. The shock left me floored—I simply couldn't grasp how my dearest friend could so abruptly announce her wish to leave.

Had the warning signs been there all along, I asked myself, evidence of a cooling in her regard for me, which I had been too blind to see? Perhaps she resented my rule over her as superior, or perhaps she even had ambitions of her own that her mother was only too happy to help her fulfill. Maybe she had become weary of living in my shadow. Or had Richardis, at the age of twenty-seven, finally outgrown me? That thought made me sag and feel impossibly old.

To think her mother would act so rashly behind my back. I tried to calm myself long enough to piece together the sober facts. At some point after leaving Rupertsberg, Guda had written a dire letter, full of lies and exaggerations, to the margravine, her aunt. The margravine, taking the message to heart, had then decided to withdraw from Rupertsberg her two remaining kinswomen—Richardis, her daughter, and Adelheid, her niece. The abbeys she had selected for them were the most elite in Saxony. But having never set foot in those houses, Richardis and Adelheid could not expect to be elected abbesses without strings being pulled and gold changing hands. I could not fathom a more blatant case of simony. Bassum was a Benedictine house of high esteem, established nearly three centuries ago. Gandersheim, Adelheid's destination, was a convent for vowesses rather than nuns—secular noblewomen who made simple vows of chastity and who lived under an abbess's spiritual guidance while still holding on to their wealth and possessions.

Tengswich of Andernach, among her other allegations, accused me of snobbery in soliciting novices of the aristocracy, whose dowries would secure Rupertsberg's financial underpinnings that had hitherto been so precarious. I wondered what the good Mistress Tengswich would make of the ladies of Gandersheim.

My thoughts whirled back to the black heart of my anguish. *Why* was Richardis leaving me? Surely it was not in blind service to her mother's ambition. I remembered how her face had gone dark as she divulged Guda's insinuations. Had Richardis been persuaded to believe that my love for her was something monstrous?

There seemed little point in standing in Adelheid's way if she was determined to leave, and so I granted her permission to sail on the next barge north. On our Rupertsberg landing, she knelt before me and kissed my hands until I raised her to her feet.

"A good tree is known by its good fruit," she said, tears glittering in her eyes as she spoke to me before the assembled nuns. "Mother, never will I forget the years you spent so gently educating me. May our friendship never be cast into oblivion. May God, who is love, make our love strong."

So sincere were her words that I gave her the kiss of peace and every benediction, even though I ached to lose Adelheid after thirty-eight years of friendship and sisterhood.

How much harder it was to allow Richardis to vanish from my life without at least trying to make her see reason. My heart broke to remember how I pleaded with her.

"You are a pure soul climbing your way to perfection," I told her, endeavoring to speak as an abbess rather than a needy older woman who thought she would die if she lost her young friend. "How can you be happy in a faraway place, among strangers your mother has bribed, instead of here where everyone cherishes you?"

As she paced back and forth, I saw how conflicted she was. Though she repeated her mother's arguments, that it was time for her to return to Saxony and be abbess of Bassum, her voice was hollow and deadened. *You love this place as much as I do,* I wanted to cry out. *You have blossomed here.* Underneath that brittle shell, she was still Cara, my beloved friend, if only I could reach through to her.

"Tell me," I begged her, "is this truly what you want? You worked as hard as I to establish this abbey and now you want to abandon your home to dance to your mother's bidding?"

My words could not have been more ill chosen.

"You would have me dance to *your* bidding instead? Don't you see, Hildegard, you are so overpowering that sometimes I fear there will be nothing left of me."

I tried to swallow, but my throat hurt too much. "What did I do to make you despise me?"

Her hands twisted together. "Why must you make this so hard?"

But I had broken through her armor. She began to cry, her raw pain unmasked.

Before I could go to her, Volmar entered the room as though this were a morning like any other with letters to be written and progress to be made on my new book of medicine, *Causae et Curae.* Richardis flew past him out the door. When I prepared to follow, Volmar stood in my path and laid his hand on my arm. My oldest friend stared at me with such disappointment. How much of our conversation he had overheard?

"Hildegard, what are you doing?"

I blinked at him as the tears ran down my face.

"If you truly love her," he said, "you'll let her go with your blessing and prayers, as you did with Adelheid."

In his eyes, I saw the ghost of his love for Jutta, his unselfish devotion to her, how he had resigned himself to her rejection, even as it tore out his heart.

But my will was an unswerving arrow.

"They seek to sully our Richardis by this simony. It's an utter disgrace. We must write to her mother and put a stop to this. The election in Bassum must be annulled."

He shook his head. "I will have no part of this."

Even my gentle Volmar despaired of what I did next.

Scathing letters I wrote to the Margravine von Stade but to no avail. Then my own archbishop, who had been my ally, my shining Angel Gabriel, commanded me to release Richardis. Invoking the voice of God, I lashed out at the man, accusing him of being party to simony. In my last act of desperation, I wrote to Pope Eugenius himself and had barely sent off that missive when, one bleak October morning, a tumult outside our abbey sent me rushing down to our landing, where I saw the barge bearing the Margravine von Stade's coat of arms. Worse still, the monks of Disibodenberg barreled their way toward our gates as though they intended to lay siege.

Under that iron-cold sky, Richardis emerged, her traveling cloak flapping around her slender body. The tall figure of her mother took her arm. Though she was nearly sixty, the margravine was as formidable as ever, half a head taller than I. The look she gave me was so vindictive that I could only conclude that Guda's poisoned words had succeeded in turning her against me.

Yet even now a desperate hope beat inside me that this might be averted if only I could summon the right words. I seized Richardis's hand.

"Cara, don't go."

Her eyes huge and tender, she clasped my fingers. What shattered me to pieces was the look she gave me, as though she longed to say so much, but before she could utter a word, her mother spoke for her.

"Cease your hectoring, magistra. We must be on our way."

The words flew out of my throat before I could stop myself. "You bought the office of archbishop for your son, didn't you? Now you will lay the stain of simony on your daughter!"

The margravine set her mouth in a grim line. "You didn't call it simony when my money went to build this abbey for you. I've given you what you wanted. Now let my daughter go."

Then I uttered the words that made the lady stare at me in pure hate.

"I have authority over her and I forbid this."

Had I truly spoken so covetously, as though she, my soul's light, were a mere possession?

"The archbishops of Bremen and Mainz have authority over *you*, magistra, as do I." A blade twisted in my flesh to see Cuno. "And I command you to release her." Gray and stooped, my abbot had aged immeasurably since I last saw him and still he gloated to see me so undone.

"Stop it," Richardis hissed. "All of you! Listen to yourselves, bickering like children."

She drew back her shoulders and strode toward the barge and her future, leaving Cuno and her mother to scurry in her wake.

My memory flashed with the vision of her cartwheeling down the riverbank, a free-spirited girl who would not let herself be bullied. That young woman was a force of nature, her roving spirit dancing between silence and outbursts of speech, her inner beauty bearing fruit in her illuminations that mirrored the sacred flame inside her. *Cara, Caritas, Carissima.*

Before stepping onto the barge, she turned to give me one last wrenching look, her eyes piercing my soul, as though to tell me she would have indeed stayed had I not been so insufferable. Then the barge set sail, and she was gone.

The dream of our life in Rupertsberg shattered, the soul of our community ripped to shreds. With their drawn faces, the sisters seemed so melancholy, both missing their friend and dreading my temper, for without Cara's love ennobling my soul, I descended to my most ignoble depths, my selfishness laid bare. I was unlovable, detestable. *Ambition has swollen your head and made you hateful.*

To Richardis,

Beloved, listen to me, speaking to you in the spirit: my grief flies up to heaven. My soul is destroying the great confidence I once had in humanity.

Why have you forsaken me? I so loved the nobility of your character, your wisdom, your chastity, your spirit, and indeed every aspect of your being, so that people have asked me, "What are you doing?"

Now let all who have grief like mine mourn with me; all who have held such love in their hearts for a person—as I had for you—only to have that person snatched away, as you were from me.

All the same, may the angels go before you. May the Son of Light protect you. May his Mother watch over you. Be mindful of your desolate Hildegard.

In vain I awaited her reply.

Just past Candlemas, my brother Hugo died in our hospice. Unlike me, he seemed utterly at peace, reconciled with both this world and the next, my warrior brother who had once warned me that my ruthlessness ill suited a nun. I laid him to rest beneath the floor of our new church, his name carved on black marble for eternity.

With its double towers and its tympanum bearing a carving of the Tree of Life, our new church of Saint Rupert and Saint Bertha was completed on the outside, the pink sandstone glowing in the weak winter sunlight. The stone masons and carpenters only needed to finish work on the inside so that it would be ready for our consecration in the spring. But on this Sabbath day all was quiet within, no picking chisels to be heard, only the wind outside moaning like a beaten hound. My eyes swept through the nave with its twelve pillars, its ceiling more than three cubits high, its arched windows mullioned with baluster shafts. Over each arch were the half-finished carvings of saints and angels. A round apse enclosed the chancel. Even with sawdust and masonry rubble littering the floor, the church was magnificent, this sanctuary I had built for my daughters. Why, then, did I feel so hollow, a shadow of the woman I used to be? It was as though I had gained the whole world only to lose the love illuminating my soul.

Keeping my promise to Hugo, I knelt at his tomb and began to pray. A shudder ran down my spine to hear the north door of the church open—the corpse door, through which coffins would be borne to the graveyard after the Funeral Mass.

A slim woman stood in the open doorway. Foggy gray light blurred the edges of her dark cloak as she raised her hands to her mouth to breathe on them, as though warming herself. Then she shut the door behind her, sending an echo through the shadowy nave. Slowly she made her way toward me.

My heart in my mouth, I froze. Richardis stopped in her tracks and stared at me, her hands clasped over her heart, but she didn't speak a word.

"Abbess." My eyes blurred as I made a reverence to her. "You honor us with a visit?"

Just when I had resigned myself to her absence, that void I dragged around with me as if it were a great empty chest, there she was. The sight of her filled me with both impossible hope and the terror that I would lose her again, that she had never been mine at all. One hint of my old arrogance would make her vanish like smoke.

"That title no longer belongs to me," she said. "The sisters of Bassum cared little for me. They loved only my family's fortune."

"I'm sorry." My heart beat in pain. "I behaved so badly toward you. And I regret that your sisters in Bassum didn't rejoice in their blessing to have you among them. Please say you'll forgive me. I fear it was I who drove you from this place. Your home."

How regal she looked. Though she was thinner and paler, her eyes shone brighter than a thousand candles. She stepped forward to take my hands.

"I'm sorry, too. Your letter made me remember everything I'd lost. I've come home to stay among those who love me for who I truly am."

For a long time we only looked at each other, both of us in tears, before shyly, tenderly reaching out to hold each other. As her arms wrapped around me, the church bells tolled. And then I awakened alone in my stone-cold bed to hear the bells ringing in the hour of Matins.

How cruel it had been, the dream that seemed more than a dream. My desolation opened as wide as the maw of hell, forcing me to face the damning truth—Richardis had loved me, truly loved me, the way no other human being could, until my attempt to bind her to me at all costs had driven her away. I, not her mother, was the true cause of her banishment to that cold northern land.

The following morning, Volmar handed me the letter that brought my torment to the surface.

Hartwig, Archbishop of Bremen, brother of the Abbess Richardis, to Hildegard, Mistress of Rupertsberg.

I write to inform you that our sister—my sister in body, but yours in spirit—has gone the way of all flesh, little esteeming the office I bestowed on her. When she made her last confession, she tearfully expressed her longing for your cloister. She then committed herself to her Lord through his Mother and Saint John.

Thus I ask, as earnestly as I can, if I have any right to ask, that you love her as much as she loved you, and if she appeared to have any fault—which indeed was mine, not hers—at least have regard for the tears she shed for you, which many witnessed. And if death had not prevented her, she would have come to you as soon as she was able to get permission. May God, who repays good deeds, reward you fully in this world and in the next for all the good things you did for her, you alone, more even than family and friends; may he repay your benevolence which she rejoiced in before God and me.

She died, my beauty, my love. Died longing for me just as I longed for her. Even her brother admitted how she regretted leaving Rupertsberg. If only I had been kinder, she might never have left at all. My heart stopped. I thought the loss of her would swallow me whole.

Volmar took the letter from me and held my hand. Weeping, I looked at my oldest friend who was also my confessor.

"I wish to be shriven of my sins." My despair sent me plunging down a bottomless abyss.

His grip on my hand was tight and warm. "You once told me yourself, a long time ago, that there are worse sins than love."

He who does not love, does not know God, for God is love. Deus Caritas est. In the shock of my bereavement, the wisdom dawned, slicing through my every delusion. I hadn't sinned because I loved her, but because I had been so grasping and selfish—and this was the undoing of Caritas, true divine love. My love for her was never monstrous, but my attempts to dominate and control her, make her wholly my creature, had turned me into something abominable.

Cara had loved the humble and questing nun I'd once been, when I had only wanted to write of my visions. To know the ways of grace and walk them as best I could. Not the domineering abbess I had become, ruled by the iron fist of my ambition. But if my vanity had overtaken me, Richardis had remained pure, unswayed by the false glamour of worldly glory. God favored her greatly. In her loveliness, she bloomed like a pure white rose in the symphony of her short life. Although I cherished her for her beauty and wisdom, God loved her more. She had been wooed by two very different loves until her Bridegroom, the worthier of the two, had taken home his true bride. *O how tenderly you burn in the King's embraces. How the sun shines through you. Your noble flower shall never wilt.* She would never age. Her beauty would never fade. She was like a star sapphire, shining and eternal.

His hand enclosing mine, Volmar listened to my outpouring of grief and misgiving.

"My sin is my pride," I told him. "And my cursed ambition. How I wish I could be purged of it."

What if Cuno had been right? Perhaps I had been living a lie, not serving God's will, but only my own. Had I been meek enough to remain at Disibodenberg, Richardis and Adelheid would never have left. And Guda—she would have still loved me. Their abandonment was my punishment for pushing myself forward.

"Would you really wish to be purged of your true character?" Volmar's eyes filled with a compassion as wide as the sea. "God made you who you are for a reason. Without your boldness and strength of will, you'd still be in the anchorage. Locked within two rooms."

I gazed at him through my tears.

"You led us to this house," he said. "Now fulfill your true purpose."

"And what is that?" I asked, for I felt as though I had completely lost my way.

"Fulfill the desire of your dear sister's soul," he told me. "Do good works, as she would have wished."

Cara's angel voice whispered in my ear. *A true love sees things through to their end.*

That night I dreamt I was a child, lost in a deep forest, far from home. When I cried out in fear, Cara appeared. She was the wise woman and I the bewildered girl. From the moist spring loam, she plucked a pale gold flower and offered it to me in her outstretched palm.

The primrose takes its power from the sun and so it heals melancholy. Gently she pressed the flower to my pounding heart. *Now open your soul to the Light!*

She rose before me, as tall as a tower, blinding me with her radiance. Her gown was red and she was crowned in gold, a virgin in a vast heavenly chorus singing a canticle of unutterable beauty. It was as though she cast my entire being in an alchemical vessel, firing it to such intense heat that I emerged in a brand-new form, my soul opening like a flower. I awakened with her celestial symphony still ringing in my ears.

Staggering from my bed, I opened my window and gulped the cold, clear air that stung my face and dried my tears. The vault of heaven blazed with stars. The moon cast silver on snow-mantled trees. Below our ramparts, the Rhine flowed, free of ice, while in the forest, a fox barked and owls sang. Even on this February night, life burgeoned. Creation triumphed, brilliant with the divine spark, while the music Cara had given me thrummed inside my soul. Music, the first language of God.

While the rest of Rupertsberg slumbered in the cradle of night, I reached for my tablet and psaltery, and began transcribing the insistent melody. In our first year, back when this was still a muddy building site and we slept in tents, I had begun a musical morality play only to abandon it for more pressing duties as we struggled for our very survival. But with Cara's music echoing inside me, I would finish this symphony of voices as my tribute to her, an everlasting memorial. Already the lyrics were spinning themselves in my mind. Words and images flowed like honeyed wine.

Each of my daughters would sing the role of one of the Virtues seeking to guide Anima, the yearning and erring soul. The drama streamed forth from the might of its own grace, like a waterfall plunging into a woodland pool. Underneath the words, the watery variety of sounds, silences, and terrifying mysteries beat in my pulse, in the ebb and flow of the music. I was not the composer, merely the conduit as this new creation poured out of me, floating like a feather on the breath of God.

Richardis was no longer with me in physical form, yet she remained my companion in spirit, my guiding angel, my vision of Caritas, summoning me to put aside my melancholy and shoulder my duties once more.

My knees trembling beneath my skirts, I stood before my assembled daughters. Grief had eroded my self-assurance, leaving an awed humility in its wake as I looked into their staring faces. Some seemed sullen, others skeptical and guarded, as though they had seen too much of my temper in the months preceding Cara's death. I had behaved outrageously. Had they come to see me as a creature with clay feet?

But something now unfolded inside me, an overpowering sense of tenderness, because losing Cara had taught me how fragile life was, how precious. Even these girls with their youthful skin without shadow of wrinkle could succumb to death at any time, just as I might. Each of these young women was a jewel to be treasured.

What a responsibility I had to be a good mother to them—a kinder and more nurturing one than I had been. My deepest calling was to guide them with love, cherishing each for her gifts, her unique brilliance. There would be no more favorites, no holding one above the others. I must find a place for them all in my vision.

With this in mind, I assigned the seventeen solo parts of *Ordo Virtutum, The Play of Virtues,* which we would sing for the archbishop when he came to consecrate Rupertsberg. I gave each part to the young woman who seemed to most embody that particular quality. Scientia Dei, Divine Knowledge, would have gone to Adelheid, but now it went to Johanna, the twenty-year-old widow who had become our new infirmarer and physician. Sunny Wiebke would sing the role of Spes, Hope, while open-hearted Anna would sing the part of Innocentia. Hiltrud, my invincible niece, would sing Victoria.

"Daughters, remember that virtue means strength," I told them. "You seek to guide Anima on the path of righteousness, only the devil will lead her astray."

We turned to Volmar, the only man in our midst and thus resigned to play the False One.

"My part is the easiest," he said, looking sheepish. "I only need to shout and grunt my lines, for Satan is incapable of song."

The central role of Anima required careful casting. Originally I had intended for Guda to sing it. To make everyone happy, I should give the part to Verena, now our most senior choir nun after myself and one of the most popular among the sisters. Her voice was not as angelic as Richardis's had been, but she was a strong singer and could perform with confidence—perhaps too much confidence. The one who played Anima must appear vulnerable, filled with yearning.

Cara's angel hand pointed my attention to Cordula, only fifteen, our shyest and most awkward postulant, always tripping over her own feet and blushing and stammering if anyone should give her a cross look. Her voice, though still untrained, was of heartbreaking purity. I'd heard her singing to herself while she tended the altars and polished the candlesticks, though she was too bashful to sing louder than a whisper when we gathered for the Divine Office. Yet I sensed that she would gleam like mountain crystal if only I could draw her out and inspire her.

And thus I gave her the part of Anima in full knowledge that my choice would offend Verena, who felt more entitled to the lead role, and deeply embarrass Cordula. The poor girl reminded me of a baby hare, frozen in terror before a mastiff.

"Mother, I'm the least worthy of such distinction," she said, her face burning bright red. "Please choose another!"

"Cordula," I said, "all I ask is that you sing with a pure heart, just this once. If, after today, it still torments you to sing before the others, I'll choose another."

Let me give this girl her voice, I prayed. *Let the silence sing.* All she might become if only she trusted herself, no longer hiding inside her cocoon of shyness but letting the power of her voice unfold.

Finally the rehearsal began in earnest. I sang the part of the Patriarchs and Prophets as they extolled the Virtues. "Who are these beings, who seem like clouds?"

Next, the unhappy souls bemoaned their lot. As my daughters began to sing their parts, surrendering to the heavenly harmonies, their stiffness began to ease. Singing the words revealed the true meanings directly to the soul through bodily vibrations. Music was cosmic, for it embraced the universe, reaching from earth to highest heaven in a pillar of praise.

Her head bent over the score, Cordula sang Anima. Before long, her voice grew in strength and power, as if it couldn't help itself from soaring like a dove flying straight into the sun. Even Verena glanced up, as though in grudging admiration, but Cordula was too immersed in the music to even notice. The Virtues circled around her to offer their counsel. Anima was not content to live out her natural life striving for holiness and grace. She wanted to rush headlong into heavenly bliss, only the Virtues admonished her that her mortal life must first be lived.

"You do not know, or see, or taste the One who has set you here," sang Johanna in the role of Scientia Dei.

"God created the world," Anima sang. "I'm doing him no wrong. I only want to enjoy it!"

"What use is there in toiling so foolishly?" Volmar, as the devil, yelled in what sounded like half a hiss and half a caterwaul. "Look to the world! It will embrace you with honor."

But Volmar was not yet convincing in his role. Cordula only looked at him and burst into helpless laughter. That set Volmar off. His hands on his knees, he giggled and gasped. Soon we were all laughing until the tears streamed down our faces, the first open-throated merriment to fill our house since that fateful day last summer when Richardis announced she was leaving.

"My daughters, how beautiful are your harmonies," I said, when at last we collected ourselves. "There's the music of heaven in all things, but we have forgotten to hear it until we sing."

Only then, when the sisters were smiling at one another, did I reveal my vision for their performance.

"On the night of nights when we sing for the archbishop, you shall appear as no ordinary Benedictine nuns, but as the holy virgins of Saint Ursula. You shall appear in your feast-day garb."

Their eyes flashed, for it was a rare privilege to don their silk gowns and to crown their unveiled hair in circlets of gold.

"You are consecrated virgins," I said, ignoring for the moment that some, like Johanna, were widows. "The strictures of wifely modesty do not apply to a virgin, for she stands in the unsullied purity of paradise, lovely and unwithering, and she always remains in the full vitality of the budding rod. A virgin is not commanded to cover her hair."

My heart beat in my love for my daughters as they gazed back at me. How I longed to unlock the secret gate of paradise and give them a glimpse of Eden before the fall, of what it meant to be a woman and know no shame in it.

In April, when every tree in our apple orchard was in fullest bloom, scenting the air with the perfume of creation, Archbishop Heinrich sailed down the Rhine to consecrate Rupertsberg.

In our outer courtyard, in that soft spring twilight, we performed *Ordo Virtutum* for him and his entourage of dignitaries, my brother among them. My daughters' families were in attendance, as well as local nobility, clergy, and select burghers of Bingen. Our audience crammed themselves on wooden benches while some stood behind the rest in a solid ring. All eyes were on my beautiful daughters, their young faces illumined in the flickering torchlight.

As long as I live, I shall never forget how magnificent Cordula appeared in her white gown, her light brown hair crowned in violets, apple blossom, and sweet woodruff. Heaven on earth it was to watch that shy girl sing Anima, her face transfixed as she gave herself to the role completely. Torn between the path of goodness and the lure of the devil, Anima swirled in the torchlight while the Virtues sought to draw her back into their circle of grace. Watching the unfolding drama, I saw my own soul that had gone astray until at last it returned, like Anima's, into the warm embrace of the sisters who raised their voices in ecstatic harmony.

> *Fugitive Anima, now be strong.*
> *Put on the armor of light!*

Then came my turn to sing, offering up my eternal tribute to Richardis, and as the music carried me on its sweeping tide, I felt her presence, her heart beating with mine.

> *The flower of the field falls before the wind.*
> *The rain scatters its petals.*
> *O Virginity, you abide forever*

In the chorus of heaven.
You are the tender flower that shall never fade.

The applause was deafening. Her face glowing, Cordula dropped in a deep bow before the archbishop, who raised her to her feet and showered her in praise. Though I didn't catch the words that passed between them, I saw the joy in her eyes. All my daughters seemed delighted as they darted out to greet their families. Verena and Hiltrud, Johanna and Wiebke seemed to glide, their feet not touching the earth.

As I made reverence to Heinrich, I braced myself, wondering what he thought of me after that bitter letter I had written to him when he commanded me to release Cara. Did he regret his previous largess, his many kindnesses toward me? When he took my hands, I softened to see how our music had moved him.

"Truly, we have glimpsed into heaven this night," he said, that angel-bright man who had gifted us with this freehold of Rupertsberg. "May you and your daughters flourish here."

My soul leapt. All conflict between us lay in the past, forgiven and buried. The following morning he would give the veil to over a dozen postulants, including Cordula. Under his blessing, our future brimmed with every promise. He gave me a brotherly kiss before going to congratulate Volmar.

As I floated in a cloud of gladness, Rorich appeared, looking as though he could scarcely contain his excitement. But there was something furtive in his manner.

"I've received a message to pass on to you." He slipped me a piece of folded parchment.

I squinted at the wax seal, bearing the royal arms of Friedrich Barbarossa, King of Germany.

"What does Barbarossa want from me?" I asked him.

"He and his army have set up camp in Ingelheim. He would have you come and foretell whether he shall succeed in his bid to become emperor."

Only a year ago, my head would have exploded in pride to learn that no less a man than the monarch requested my counsel. But I shook my head.

"I'm no fortune teller," I told Rorich. "Besides, Heinrich is a prince elector and he distrusts the king as a hotheaded fool."

Rorich lowered his voice to a whisper. "I'm no prophet, but I can predict that Barbarossa will prevail, even if Heinrich opposes him."

I shivered, wondering where my brother's loyalties lay.

"It's no small thing to win a future emperor to your side," he told me. "If war breaks out, as they say it will, your abbey will be protected."

Before I could think what to say, I sensed a presence out of the corner of my eye—a woman waiting her turn to speak with me. When Rorich ended our discussion, leaving me with the troubling letter, she stepped fully into view. I swayed. In that unsteady torchlight, I saw Cara. Cara grown older. Grown to be my age. I had to remind myself that she was not a ghost on earth but a blessed soul in heaven.

Then I blinked to find myself facing the margravine, her face gentler than I ever remembered seeing it. Grief had ripped her apart and put her back together again in a different form, just as it had done with me.

"Hildegard, I heard you were sick with melancholy. How good to see that you're well. My daughter would have been so happy to be here tonight."

As her eyes searched mine, I longed to say so much, but the words wouldn't come, only our shared tears for Cara. How my heart beat for her, beacon of my soul, who had been my earthly companion as I had plunged to the depths and then struggled toward the heights. Her angel presence enveloped me on this night of nights, on this clear green summit crowned in blossoming apple trees, when my vision was made real, manifest and alive.

"May you live long, Hildegard." The margravine drew me into a fierce embrace. "Endure. Your world needs you in it."

15

SOON AFTER THE triumph of Rupertsberg's consecration, our world fell apart. My great patrons, Pope Eugenius and Bernard of Clairvaux passed on. Barbarossa rose to become emperor, as my brother had foreseen, and punished Archbishop Heinrich for opposing him by stripping him of his office and replacing him with Arnold, his slavering sycophant. Heinrich became a Cistercian monk and soon died. Later the emperor's own henchmen murdered Arnold. Then came the papal schism, with Barbarossa raising one antipope after another. He sacked monasteries, burning them to the ground. But not Rupertsberg, for I had done my brother's bidding and prophesied Barbarossa's future, and so the fiery warlord left us in peace and even suffered my furious letters decrying his foul deeds.

Meanwhile, the Church, which should have shone forth with the light of justice, festered in every corruption. Cardinals fought one another like village bullies while bishops amassed fortunes buying and selling religious offices for gold. Village priests, now forbidden to marry, took concubines and begat bastards.

Priests and bishops were meant to fulfill a divine office, serving as intermediaries between the laity and God. But how could people hope to find salvation if those meant to serve them were steeped in vice? Ordinary parishioners abandoned the Church in droves to join the Cathari, who called themselves the True Christians. Instead of attempting to woo back the lost flock, the men who were meant to be shepherds merely burned those poor souls as heretics. Evil begat evil. It seemed as though the apocalypse flamed on the horizon.

No man arose to speak out against such abomination. None dared fill the shoes of the dead Archbishop Heinrich or the sainted Bernard of Clairvaux who had risked their lives to defend the Jews of Mainz. Any man who rebuked either Church or emperor risked making himself a martyr, for both sides relied on the existing corruption as their bedrock. My own brother Rorich was terrified to speak out. Soon after Arnold's murder, he grew ill and died, as though his heart was too broken to live anymore.

What could I do to mend my broken world? God had given me the visions for a reason. More than ever before, I needed to speak and write what I saw and heard, be God's sibyl. If I gave public sermons condemning this iniquity masquerading as religion, people would listen, if only for the novelty of hearing an old nun preach. And thus it fell upon me, woman though I was, to speak out in a mighty voice and castigate the men who had failed in their duty. Only a woman might stand a chance to get away with this. If no one else had the courage or will, then let it be me. Even if I paid for it with my life. Come what may, no matter what I risked or lost, let me be the message bearer, God's harp.

Canon law forbade women to preach, but that did not hinder me. Driven by the inner calling, I hastened across the German lands, traveling to Trier, Metz, Würzburg, Bamberg, and Cologne.

Those years of travel, those long hours in the saddle and on barges, blurred into one moment—the morning in 1170 when I, a woman of seventy-two years, stood on the steps of Cologne Cathedral and lifted my voice to be heard by the assembled prelates. The air blackened with smoke and thickened with the stench of nine Cathari, sentenced to burn to death at the stake. Among them was a woman condemned for preaching the Gospel of Saint John. Yet there I was, a woman preaching. One withered crone before that sea of men. I still remember every word of my sermon, that blistering homily that brought me both fame and the prelates' lifelong enmity.

As the heretics burned on the other side of the cathedral square, their cries filling the air like the wails of the damned, I stared into the faces of bishops and canons, friars and deacons. Behind them, townspeople pressed forward to gawp at me.

Before I could lose courage, my inner sight opened, allowing me to forget myself. The Living Light infused me.

"In a true vision," I said, pitching my voice to pierce through the crowd's chatter, their skepticism and disapproval, "I beheld a Lady so beautiful that no man could comprehend her. In stature she reached from earth to highest heaven."

Their eyes followed my arms as I lifted them toward the cathedral spires.

"Her face shone with indescribable radiance. She was clad in whitest silk. Her mantle was set with emeralds, sapphires, and pearls. Her shoes were made of onyx."

The prelates' faces softened like dough in my hands, as though the transports of my revelation lifted them to a place where they could cast from their minds the tortured screams of the Cathari on the pyre. But this was not my purpose—I preached for the very sake of those poor souls, for if the men I saw before me had fulfilled their godly office, those people might have never been cast out and burned.

"I saw that the Lady's face was besmirched with filth. Her lovely gown was ripped to tatters. Her cloak was ragged and her shoes were soiled."

My audience recoiled.

"The Lady, whose name is Ecclesia, the Mother Church, cried out in a mournful voice." Here something much greater than myself issued from my mouth. The voice came from on high—I was merely the instrument. "The priests who were meant to nurture me, to make my face glow like dawn, my clothes flash like the sun, have instead smeared me in excrement. They have rent my gown, blackened my cloak, soiled my shoes. They have failed me miserably."

The prelates' faces went white, some in shock, others in derision. But the lay people behind them now tried to elbow their way to the front, eager to hear an elderly nun chastise these high-ranking men. The voice coming out of me rose like a falcon, full of an unstoppable power that was not my own.

"This is the way they soil me: they handle the Host, the body and blood of my Bridegroom, while they are defiled by lust, poisoned with fornication and adultery, corrupted by the buying and selling of holy offices. They encompass my Bridegroom's body and blood with filth, like someone putting a precious child in the muck among the swine."

Some of the prelates in front appeared so offended that their bodies twisted, as though they intended to stomp away and not suffer this homily another second, but the press of the crowd trapped them, forcing them to hear me out until the bitter end. The voice issuing forth from me stormed, filling my audience with something that resembled terror.

"Let heaven rain down calamity on these sinful men! Let the abyss tremble. O you priests! You have neglected me, and now the princes of earth and the common folk alike shall rise up against you. They shall take away your property and riches because you have made a mockery of your holy office. They will say: 'Let us drive these adulterers and thieves from the Church.'"

The prelates' faces seemed to freeze in panic as they found themselves cordoned in by that mass of bodies, the lay people who eyed them as if they would indeed rise up to overthrow them. For my message was both apocalyptic and as stark as it could be—the churchmen must reform or be toppled from their seats of power. Some of the men glared at me with blazing, undisguised hatred. How dare I make them look so foolish, subjecting them to public ridicule?

The ominous voice ebbed, replaced by my own. Before the enraged prelates could leap up the cathedral steps and throttle me, I clasped my hands in humility and bowed before my superiors. "O great fathers of the Church, poor little woman that I am, I have seen a great black fire kindled against you. May the unquenchable flame of the Holy Spirit infuse you so that you walk in charity and wisdom."

So ended the sermon that left me staggering and faint. Hiltrud grabbed me around the waist before I could collapse while Volmar shielded us both, drawing us away from the crowd, now rumbling, debating every word they had just heard. My companions drew me into a shadowy side chapel of the cathedral where I could catch my breath.

"You're a brave woman." Volmar spoke gravely, as though he longed to protect me from going too far. "People have been excommunicated for less."

I pressed my brow against his shoulder. Like me, Volmar had grown old, his hair as white and wispy as dandelion fluff. But he was still my rock. Through every upheaval, his friendship had never waned.

"I'm not afraid," I whispered. "What can they do to one old nun?"

Let the Silence Sing

Rupertsberg, 1179

THE HARSHEST WINTER in my long memory held us captive in icy stasis. Huddled in my cloak, I shivered over Maximus's unmarked grave, now further obscured beneath the deep crust of snow. Frigid wind scoured my face as I prayed for the boy, prayed for us all. At this moment the church bells should have been tolling Prime, but they remained mute. A crippling pall hung over Rupertsberg, the choking silence of the crypt, as though our entire community lay dead and buried in that frozen earth.

Over a year had passed since the prelates of Mainz had laid the interdict on us, the heaviest penalty they could have imposed—a collective excommunication, severing me and my nuns, both at Rupertsberg and at our daughter house in Eibingen, from our divine vocation. We were cast down to nothing, forbidden Mass, the Eucharist, every sacrament. The prelates even banned us from singing the Divine Office—we were only allowed to whisper the psalms behind the closed doors of our cells.

Father Gottfried, our provost since Volmar went to his eternal rest six years ago, had been ordered back to Disibodenberg. I had written frantic, beseeching letters to Archbishop Christian of Mainz and to Pope Alexander, who was finally back in Rome after the long schism. But neither man would lift the interdict.

Such punishment, all for one dead boy. I lowered my eyes to the mantle of snow covering Maximus and offered another prayer for the abused young man who had died in my arms. Hiltrud had asked me if it would not be more prudent to surrender the corpse and be received back into the Church. *What if you die without salvation, Mother?* But I would burn in hell before I sacrificed an innocent boy to those hypocrites—surely he had already suffered enough at their hands. Besides, the prelates were only using his burial here as their excuse. Even if we had not given asylum and Christian burial to our supposed apostate, they would have found some other transgression of mine as the justification to punish me for my insubordination. My superiors had won. They had vanquished me.

"Mother, come in from the cold before you catch your death!" Guibert of Gembloux appeared at my side, his young face etched in concern.

It still astonished me that Brother Guibert had elected to stay with us through the scandal of the interdict. As gently as though he were my son of flesh and blood, he took my arm and accompanied me back into the warmth of my parlor where Ancilla tended the fire. She tugged off my cloak and sat me down in my chair. Then Guibert handed me a book I'd never seen before, its vellum pages bound in softest calfskin: *Vita Sanctae Hildegardis.*

"I thought this might cheer you," he said, his dark eyes shining.

"How hard you have worked, my friend," I murmured.

As I leafed through my life story written in his graceful script, a bittersweet chord rose inside me. Now I had come full circle, from my living death in the anchorage to our collective banishment under the interdict. Guibert had sacrificed more than a year of his life to writing the tale of an outcast. The last pages, I observed, remained blank, leaving room for the final details that he could fill in only after my death. So my young friend was committed to abide here until the very end.

"Guibert, you honor me," I told him, undone by his goodness. "Far more than I deserve."

Before he could reply, a knock sounded on the door. Verena staggered in, her face the color of boiled linen.

"My dear, what is it?" I crossed the room to clasp her quivering arms.

"Johanna says you must come to the infirmary at once. It's Sister Cordula."

Cordula lay in her sickbed, her face a grimace of pain until Johanna tipped the draft of sweet oblivion into her mouth, an elixir of poppy seeds and hemlock. Verena held her sister's hand and wept.

"Can anything more be done?" I asked Johanna.

The physician shook her head. "She's dying, Mother."

Cordula had hidden her malady from us for as long as she could, only collapsing when the dolor became too overpowering for even her to ignore. Cancer was gnawing away at her breast. Though we had tried our every remedy from yarrow to mistletoe to violet salve to combat the tumors, nothing had been able to check the devouring disease. We could only pray and offer her opiates to relieve her agonies. Cordula was forty-two, young enough to be my granddaughter. The injustice shattered my heart. My old feud with the prelates had brought this interdict upon us. If anyone should die without the sacraments and risk damnation, it should be me, not Cordula.

"How can we let her die like this?" Verena clasped my hands. "Oh, Mother, what shall we do?"

Our church reminded me of a mausoleum, the air stale from the dearth of incense and song. Though I prayed and prayed to find a way to lead my daughters out of this wasteland, I felt abandoned. Why had God given me this ordeal when I was eighty years old, too broken to fight anymore?

My knees trembled as I moved toward the stone that marked Volmar's grave, he who had blessedly gone to God before any of this had unfolded. We had interred our beloved provost in the church transept, in the floor before Saint Rupert's shrine. Although six years had passed since his death, the loss still rived me. How my soul yearned for his friendship and counsel. What would Volmar have said to see Rupertsberg so disgraced?

"We are ruined," I murmured, as though my confidant still lived. "Poor Cordula! If only I could take this away from her."

Longing for solace, I whispered the words of a hymn I was forbidden to sing. Of all the privations we endured, giving up the Divine Office was hardest for me, even more so than being denied the sacraments. For seventy-two years, sacred song had set the rhythm of my days. Singing the Psalms of David, my voice twining with those of my daughters as our harmonies rose like incense in an offering to heaven, allowed us to glimpse into paradise restored, the fiery life beating at the center of creation. I was a bride of Christ, not because I wore a Benedictine habit or strove to live according to the Rule, but because, eight times daily, I surrendered myself, body and soul, to the ecstatic chorus.

> *Unde, o Salvatrix, que novum lumen*
> *O Salvatrix, redeeming Lady*
> *who bore the new light for humanity,*
> *gather the limbs of your Son*
> *into celestial harmony.*

Among the devotional songs I had written, this was dearest to my heart. Before the Lady Altar, I contemplated the great mystery of how the Virgin had gathered together the limbs of her slain Son, restoring his broken body. And I reflected how, in performing the miracle of the Eucharist to make the body of Christ manifest in this world, the priest took on the role of Mary, the saving mother of our redemption. Would the sacrament ever pass my lips again?

Still whispering my hymn, I crossed the transept and entered the chancel and sanctuary. My heart pounding, I stood before the high altar. Midwinter sun poured through the windows to bathe the immaculately white altar cloth. I quaked as the brilliance dissolved into a vision of pure light. Embraced in its nimbus, I felt like a girl instead of a despairing old woman. The church, the entire outer world fell away. Before me I saw Ecclesia, crowned and resplendent, the true inner Church who would never shun my daughters or turn us away. She smiled with such joyful welcome, as though wondering why I had kept myself from her beauty and grace for so long.

Tears in my eyes, I fell to my knees to behold the radiant man clothed in sapphire blue — Christ, who in dying, destroyed death and shattered hell. Ecclesia stood beside the crucified Christ. With a golden goblet, she received his blood. From heaven descended a flame of ineffable brightness, flooding the chalice with its radiance, just as the sun pierces every living thing with her life-giving rays.

Ecclesia turned her beautiful face to mine. "Hildegard, bride of Christ."

Standing at the high altar, Ecclesia raised her eyes and hands to that overpowering radiance.

"Behold your eternal marriage feast," she sang as she offered me the body and blood of my Bridegroom.

The Light poured down with divine, consecrating power.

My head ringing like a bell, I paced through the medicinal garden, quietly chanting my canticle. No longer would I allow the prelates and their political maneuvering to come between my daughters and their God. *No one can ever destroy the Light or separate us from our source.*

The sun shimmered on the holly bush, its warmth melting off a shroud of snow to reveal the green beneath, the red berries pulsing with life. Lost in my reverence, I collided with Ancilla, who was cutting across the garden with a basket of laundry.

"Mother!" she cried. "I've not seen you smile in so long." Her face, golden in the sunlight, shone as though in hope. "Do you have good news for us?"

If the interdict forbade us from singing in the church, I could find no rule against our singing in the infirmary.

My daughters and I gathered around Cordula's bed while Guibert looked on, his face as anxious as mine must have been. He was tempted, I knew, to disobey the interdict and give Cordula the last sacraments, even if he risked excommunication himself. But first we would sing for our sister. If Mistress Tengswich of Andernach Abbey still lived, no doubt she would have tutted in dismay to see us in our feast-day garb. Verena, Hiltrud, Wiebke, and the rest were arrayed as regal brides, their diadems adorned with the Lamb in the front and the angels at the side. Consecrated virgins, my daughters were the epiphany of Eve in the garden, the vision of womanhood restored to paradise.

Before the fall, Adam and Eve's voices rang out with the sound of every harmony. If they had remained in that state, singing in their joy, evil would have been erased from the world. For the soul is symphonic and music is divine. Angels exulted in constant song whereas Satan lured men and women away from the heavenly chorus. Satan's silence had ruled this abbey for too long.

Cordula stared at us through the haze of poppy syrup. I longed to give her peace and assurance that even the interdict could not sever her from God's love and mercy. Let her hear us sing—sing for *her*—after fourteen months of forced silence. How could it be a sin to offer hope to a dying woman? We were nuns, prayer was our calling, and the highest form of prayer was song. If we were denied the Holy Office, we would at least sing in praise of Saint Ursula, for our sister was named after one of Ursula's eleven thousand virgins—Cordula, the last of their number to be slain.

Sister Waltraud, our precentor, didn't quite have the nerve to lead us in song since it seemed scandalous, as though this one act of rebellion might invoke an even greater retribution from the prelates.

As abbess and instigator, it fell upon me. With age, my voice had grown husky and dry, as dark as smoke. So it was with trepidation that I sang the first bar. The others joined in, hesitant and uncertain. Our voices, so long out of practice, were raw as we struggled to find the pure notes—I feared that we sounded like crows. Poor Cordula would think we were howling demons. Then our voices settled, remembering the cadences, reassembling all that had been fractured. Our voices lifted our song to heaven as we sang in praise of Saint Ursula and her virgins. This was no retelling of Jutta's bruising tale of slaughter, but a hymn of women in love.

> *In visione vere fidei*
> *In a true vision*
> *Ursula fell in love with the Son of God*
> *And renounced the world.*
> *Gazing straight into the sun,*
> *She cried out to the most beautiful youth, saying:*
> *How I yearn to come sit with you, Bridegroom,*
> *At the heavenly wedding feast,*
> *Running to you by strange paths*
> *As clouds stream like sapphire in the purest air.*
>
> *And after Ursula had spoken,*
> *The news spread through all nations.*
> *How naïve the girl is, they cried.*
> *She does not know what she is saying.*

Our song took on body and shape, cresting like a wave then filling with light as it washed over us. We sang how Ursula was soon joined by her eleven thousand maidens. But Satan and his mortal minions scorned them, and soon the fiery burden of martyrdom fell upon them. When they were murdered, their blood cried out to heaven. All of nature joined the angels in a chorus of praise. Ursula and her virgins became pearls strung upon the Word of God and so they choked the ancient serpent. Mere girls crushed Satan.

My daughters' voices, so resonant with beauty, covered my old croaking. We sang as though our harmonies could restore this broken world. As we raised our voices for Cordula, the ecstasy of Caritas, divine love, surged through us all. Let my daughters feel their shackles breaking. No matter what the prelates would decide, our exile ended the instant our song shattered the silence.

O rubor sanguinis
O ruby blood, which flowed from on high,
Touched by divinity,
You are the flower that the serpent's
Wintry breath never wounded.

My heart beat in pure joy when I saw the rapture on Cordula's face, the tears in her eyes, her lips moving silently in the shape of the lyrics she adored.

"Sisters," she whispered. "I see him coming. My Bridegroom has come to take me home."

Something shifted that day. Our canticles broke the dark and crippling enchantment that had befallen Rupertsberg. Stagnant waters now flowed, running pure and clear. The miracle was how our very song transformed our banishment into harmony and belonging.

No interdict could separate us from this whirling cosmos, the wheel of the sacred year, the tide of seasons bringing their procession of holy days. We were still part of it, caught up in that great dance, the round of creation. We offered our songs to the universe, which expanded to receive them.

As my daughters prayed around Cordula's bed, an invisible cord drew me out into the snowy garden, glowing in silvery luminescence under the rising full moon. I lifted my eyes to see two brilliant streaks of light arching across the heavens. What marvel was this — twin comets? Soon the others joined me to watch the unfolding wonder. Verena held Cordula so she could look out the window.

Before our eyes, those two arcs widened into shimmering roads, stretching to the four corners of the earth. At the axis where the two arcs met, a cross blazed, as red as dawn. Fiery light bathed the whole of Rupertsberg. And it was not just my vision, for they saw it, too, my daughters and Guibert, my son, who cried out, their voices ringing in the air.

Afterword

࿔

The supposed apostate buried at Rupertsberg was a man of noble
birth, but nothing else is known about his identity. As a result of her
defiance in refusing to allow the prelates to disinter the man's body
and desecrate his Christian burial, Hildegard and her nuns suffered an
interdict that was lifted only a few months before her death in September of 1179. The appearance of the cross of light blazing in the sky
over Rupertsberg was Hildegard's last vision, seen on her deathbed
and witnessed by her nuns and Guibert of Gembloux, her secretary,
provost, and biographer. In my novel, I moved this reported miracle
forward to coincide with the fictional Sister Cordula's death while the
interdict was still in force.

All major characters and events in this novel are drawn from recorded fact. Sometimes, however, historical accounts reveal discrep-
ancies.

Two diverging versions of Hildegard's early religious life exist. According to Guibert of Gembloux's *Vita Sanctae Hildegardis,*
eight-year-old Hildegard was bricked into the anchorage with fourteen-year-old Jutta von Sponheim and possibly one other young girl.
Guibert describes the anchorage in the bleakest terms, using words
like "mausoleum" and "prison," and writes how these girls died to the
world so they could be buried with Christ. In *Scivias,* Hildegard's first
book, she strongly denounces the practice of offering child oblates to

monastic life. Disibodenberg Abbey is now in ruins and it's impossible to precisely pinpoint where the anchorage was, but the suggested location is two suffocatingly narrow rooms and a narrow courtyard built on to the back of the church. Only the foundations remain.

In 1991, the *Vita Domnae Jutta Inclusae (Life of Mistress Jutta, the Anchorite)* came to light. Probably penned by Volmar, this presents a completely different story, suggesting that Hildegard spent her childhood at Jutta's family estate of Sponheim, only entering the monastery when she was fourteen and Jutta twenty. It's difficult to say which account is more accurate.

According to Guibert, Jutta was a very beautiful and desirable young woman who spurned male attraction on no uncertain terms.

> She put up an unflinching resistance to all the base-minded who told her unseemly stories and who stood in the way of her vow, crying out in imprecation to them: "Get away from me, you detestable purveyors of an oil which shall never anoint my head." (Ps. 140:5)

Did some buried sexual trauma influence Jutta's extreme choice to become not an ordinary nun but an enclosed anchorite and to embrace the fanatical asceticism that eventually brought about her premature death? Before entering the religious life, Jutta longed with all her heart to make a pilgrimage to Jerusalem, but her brother Meginhard forbade her. So instead she renounced the world. Jutta's Vita describes her extensive fasts and how she refused to allow food to pass her lips even when her abbot implored her to eat. The Benedictine Rule itself preaches the moderation that Hildegard herself espoused. Jutta's Vita also provides the detail of Hildegard discovering the penitent's chain wound three times around her dead magistra's starved and wasted body.

Although fervently forthcoming regarding her affection for her lifelong friend Volmar and her deep love for Richardis von Stade, Hildegard is curiously reticent in describing her feelings for Jutta, the woman who was her mentor and spiritual mother. Only after Jutta's death did Hildegard come into her own and begin to write about her visions, which would eventually make her one of the most famous women in Europe. The rest of her colorful life is history.

I've taken some liberties with the time line. It is believed that Richardis von Stade died in 1151, within one year of leaving Rupertsberg Abbey and a year before Rupertsberg's consecration in 1152. It is certainly a possibility that Richardis illuminated Hildegard's visions, though this cannot be proven. We do know that she worked closely with Hildegard during the ten years it took her to complete *Scivias*.

Some traditionalists will point out that Hildegard was deeply conservative in many respects and will argue that she has been unfairly appropriated by feminists and New Age spirituality. Others, such as Kathryn Kerby-Fulton in her essay "Prophet and Reformer: Smoke in the Vineyard," maintain that although Hildegard's sacramental theology was orthodox, her reformist thought was radical, as evidenced in her blazing sermon against ecclesiastical corruption that she delivered in Cologne in 1170. Pope Benedict XVI cited this same sermon in his 2010 address to the Roman Curia concerning recent sex abuse scandals in the Catholic Church. The Lutheran Church in Germany regards Hildegard not only as a reformer, but also as a prophet of the Reformation. Indeed, her theology and philosophy are so complex and multistranded that her work and life continue to inspire very diverse groups of people, from conservative Catholics to feminist theologians, such as Barbara Newman, whose book *Sister of Wisdom: St. Hildegard's Theology of the Feminine* profoundly influenced me during the writing of this book.

The quoted letters are my abridged and paraphrased versions of the authentic letters in Joseph L. Baird's *The Personal Correspondence of Hildegard of Bingen*, and the lyrics of her quoted songs are my own paraphrased versions of those from the liner notes of the following CDs, which I listened to continually while writing this novel.

11,000 Virgins: Chants for the Feast of St. Ursula, Anonymous 4, Harmonia Mundi, USA.

The Dendermonde Codex, Dous Mal/Katelijne Van Laethem, Etcetera.

A Feather on the Breath of God, Gothic Voices, Hyperion.

Canticles of Ecstasy, Sequentia, Deutsche Harmonia Mundi.

Voice of the Blood, Sequentia, Deutsche Harmonia Mundi.

Hildegard's observations on wildlife, herbal medicine, and gemstone healing are gleaned from *Hildegard von Bingen's Physica: The Complete English Translation of Her Classic Work on Health and Healing,* translated from the Latin by Priscilla Throop and published by Healing Arts Press. In contemporary Germany, there are still naturopathic doctors who work with Hildegard's medicine and dietary philosophy.

I wish to dedicate ecstatic canticles of praise to my editor, Adrienne Brodeur; my agent, Wendy Sherman; my copy editor, David Hough; and to the entire team at Houghton Mifflin Harcourt. I received much support from my husband, Jos Van Loo, who read this book in manuscript, and from my writers group: Cath Staincliffe, Pat Hadler, Trudy Hodge, and Kath Pilsbury. The Historical Novel Society and its wonderfully nurturing community of writers and readers is a continuing source of inspiration. My heartfelt gratitude goes out to Karleen Koen, Sharon Kay Penman, Margaret George, Stephanie Cowell, CW Gortner, and Margaret Frazer for their early endorsement and support. My mother, Adelene Sharratt, shared her notes on a course on women mystics taught by Gabriel Ross.